The House of Echoes

Rachel Crowther

BLOODHOUND
— B O O K S —

Print ISBN: 978-1-917449-4-27

To our children and their friends

Prologue

Mab ran. That was all she could do: run and run, letting her legs carry her away from the barn as fast as they could. She wouldn't think about what she'd seen. She just needed to tell them – to tell Con – to come. She ran through the gate and across the field, her heart beating so fast she could hear it in her ears. It hurt to breathe almost as much as it hurt to think, and her legs were so wobbly that she stumbled a few times on the rough grass.

And then there was a dip, maybe a rabbit hole, and her foot caught in it and she fell hard to the ground, grazing her knee. The hem of her new dress was torn and had blood on it, but she couldn't worry about that. She was nearly at the garden, nearly at the house. She picked herself up and ran on, her knee throbbing now, and she could hear herself shrieking, and there was a tiny bit of her hovering in the air, looking down, and thinking how strange it was that everything could change so quickly. One minute the sun was shining and she was noticing how hot it was, and feeling pleased that she was wearing the dress Daddy had bought, and wondering where Nessa was if she wasn't in the den they'd built in the laurel bush, and the next minute...

But she wouldn't think about it. And she didn't need to think about anything now, because there was Con, coming out of the back door. Con with her arms in the air, her hands up to her face, and behind her the kitchen and the hall and the little room they had both been in, such a short while ago, when everything had still been all right.

Part One

Chapter One

March 2024

Mab's first reaction was one of mild surprise, followed by a sort of curiosity that the news hadn't made her feel anything more. That there wasn't a crash of shock and grief, or relief or anger, or any of those other full-blooded emotions you might expect. For a minute or two after Con rang off she stood very still, waiting for those feelings to arrive, and her mind busied itself noticing her surroundings, as if she might have to account for herself later.

When I heard that my father had died I was standing in the kitchen in Littlemore Road, with piles of dirty plates around me and blue sky over the rooftops outside.

Not all the plates were dirty, in fact, and Mab was as responsible as anyone for those that were, but that wasn't the point. The point was that her father was dead – the father she'd only seen once in almost twenty years. Most days, for at least the last ten of those years, she'd hardly remembered he was still alive, but even so she hadn't expected him to die without seeing him again. Without having the chance to think about whether she wanted anything from him: answers, or apologies, or redress of some kind. It was all very odd, said a voice in her head that wasn't quite hers. Very odd and rather vexing.

And then there was the fact that it wasn't her sister, Nessa, who'd told her, or even her aunt Hazel, but Con. *It's Constance*, she'd said, as if she'd imagined Mab might have forgotten who she was. *I'm afraid I'm ringing with bad news.*

Of course Con would have heard before most other people, Mab thought now. She'd been Roy's first wife, and for reasons Mab had never really understood they'd stayed friends after Roy left Con for Mab's mother. Well, maybe you could understand it, because Con was the kind of person you wouldn't want to let go of even if you did divorce them – and perhaps Con had seen that quality in Roy too. There were so many things Mab didn't know about her father. Almost everything, really. Perhaps, she thought, she might understand him better now he was dead, and people could explain him to each other. When he was alive no one had gone in much for explaining him. They'd assumed you knew the worst, and they didn't see why they should tell you anything else.

I'm afraid I'm ringing with bad news, Con's voice said again in her head. *Your father's dead. He had a heart attack this morning.*

This morning wasn't very long ago for the news to have travelled through several people to reach her, but perhaps it had been in New Zealand's morning, not theirs. Even so, Mab was touched that Con had rung her so quickly. She hadn't heard from Con for a very long time, and she wondered, just briefly, how Con had known where she was. How she'd got her mobile number. Had she been in touch with Nessa all this time? That thought gave Mab a funny feeling in her chest. But no – it must have been through Aunt Hazel. That made sense. Hazel hadn't moved; Con would have known how to get hold of her. So had Con asked Hazel to let her break the news to Mab and Nessa, or had Hazel asked her to? Passing on the tidings of Roy's death to his daughters would have given Hazel some satisfaction. Maybe Con had known that, and thought she could do a better job.

I'm afraid I'm ringing with bad news.

Mab still wasn't sure whether it *was* bad news, though. Of course it was bad news for him – for her father – because he'd only been sixty-eight and you expected to live longer than that these days, even if you drank too much and had too many wives. But although Mab had waited several minutes now for the sudden drop in her belly that would signal a proper reaction, the first sign of grief, it hadn't come. Maybe it still would, she told herself. Maybe a few minutes wasn't long enough to know what you felt. She ought at least to feel sorry that they hadn't met again, hadn't even spoken to each other for years. But she'd always known that reconciliation wasn't very likely – at least not the kind of reconciliation she'd have wanted – and her father's death meant the end of those disconcerting flurries of hope, and of scolding herself for letting it take hold, and then things being bad for a few weeks afterwards. Perhaps, she thought, the end of all that made it good news that he was dead – but she knew it wasn't that simple either. Nothing about her father's history, or Mab's, was simple at all.

She put her phone down on the side, then picked it up again and put it in her pocket. It felt like the kind of day when she might easily lose it, and it was easy enough to lose things in this house even on a normal day. Then, because she couldn't think of anything else to do, she filled up the kettle and turned it on, and found a mug and washed it up, and she felt a small surge of pleasure, almost of pride, that she could still do those ordinary things.

Had it all begun that summer they'd stayed at Lowlands with Con, Mab wondered while she waited for the kettle to boil, or did you have to go back further than that? Further, she supposed. To the time she could really only remember as if it was a film she'd watched when she was little. When they'd been a family, her mother and father and her and Nessa, living in a tiny house she knew had been in Buckinghamshire, although all she could remember was the bedroom she'd shared with Nessa and the green space which had been the garden. When her mother had been beautiful and funny and had known the answer to everything Mab could ever think of to ask her.

Her father, who'd always given people his own special names, had come up with more for her mother than for anyone else. He'd called her Willow, or sometimes Wilhelmina, or Rosebay Willow Herb, none of which were very close to her real name, Robin. (He called Mab and Nessa Queen Mab and Lady Vanessa. His names were rarely shortenings, although Mab didn't ever remember him using her full name. The only people who did that were the passport office and the bank. *Madeleine Fothergill*, those letters were addressed to: a person Mab hardly recognised even now, although she supposed she might grow into her one day. Might evolve, like a Pokémon, from Mab to Madeleine.)

Her mother had been beautiful, and then she'd been ill, and then she'd been dead. For most of Mab's life she'd been dead: since just before her ninth birthday. At the time, that was the thing Mab had been most distressed about. She'd wanted her mother to stay alive for just a few more days so that she would have that last birthday with her to remember, even though Robin was in the hospice by then and not even awake very much. Mab had wanted to take a birthday cake and presents and balloons into the hospice, and string banners over her mother's bed. She'd wanted it to be one of her mother's last memories, too. She'd told herself they could manage to let go of each other if her mother could only hang on for long enough to see Mab turning nine.

As it was, her birthday had been the day before the funeral. Nessa had made her a cake, and they'd eaten it together on Mab's bed, which wasn't going to be Mab's bed for much longer because the house was going to be sold and the grown-ups were discussing what would happen to Mab and Nessa. They'd thought they were doing it discreetly enough for the children not to hear, but their father had never been any good at speaking quietly, and the other grown-ups – their aunt Hazel and their grandmother Jenny – couldn't be discreet on their own. She and Nessa had sat on her bed and let crumbs and icing get all over it, because there was no one to tell them not to, and listened to the raised voices downstairs. The cake had been pink and squishy and covered all over with sweets, and she'd eaten so much of it that it had made her sick.

'This is the best birthday cake I've ever had,' Mab had whispered, and she'd meant it – she had no idea how Nessa had managed to make it, in the middle of that dislocated household – but Nessa's eyes had filled with tears.

'This will be your worst birthday,' she'd said. 'I promise you, Mab, you'll never have a worse birthday than this, ever.'

Of all the promises Nessa might have made, Mab thought now, that was one she couldn't possibly keep. Had Nessa known that, and just wanted to find something good to say, something that would cheer Mab up? Or had she believed she would always be able to make things all right for Mab if she tried hard enough? Had it been a solemn vow she was making, on that awful day?

When her phone rang again, Mab knew instantly who it was. Con would have been in touch with Nessa by now, and Nessa would have hurried her off the phone so that she could ring Mab. Not the Nessa who was thirty-two and lived in a flat in

Wanstead and secretly wished Mab would get a sensible job like hers, but the Nessa who was thirteen – one and a half times older than Mab, which made her almost a grown-up; almost a deity in Mab's world – and trying to scrape pink icing off Mab's duvet cover.

And then another thought came into Mab's head: she'd used up all her grief on her mother. The whole store of grief she'd had for both her parents. Sixty-eight was younger than you might hope to die, but her mother had been thirty-six and beautiful, and her father had run away to New Zealand after she died and left Mab and Nessa alone with their sorrow.

Chapter Two

Con's hands were shaking as she put the phone down. She stared at them for a minute, at the trembling that revealed the turmoil inside her. It wasn't because of Roy, she thought. It was because of Mab and Nessa.

Roy was dead, and Con was sad about that, of course she was, but there was nothing for her to regret about it. Roy had lived on the other side of the world for the last nineteen years, and he'd died on the other side of the world, and there was nothing Con could have done about any of it. But Mab and Nessa – that was another story. Mab especially. Hearing her voice on the phone, the voice of an adult who was the same Mab Con had known all that time ago, had been strange and wonderful, and more unsettling than she'd bargained for. Her head was filled with it now, the grown-up Mab summoning the echo of the past but at the same time writing over it, like a video tape whose original contents could never be viewed again. And reminding Con, as if she'd ever forgotten, that there was plenty she could have done differently for Mab and Nessa: for those two little girls who had been in her care, in her house, that summer, and whom she hadn't seen since.

It wasn't that she'd turned her back on them entirely. She had always known what they were doing; how they were. She'd kept in touch, though not regularly, with their aunt Hazel, and with their grandmother Jennifer during the years when Jennifer had still been in touch with herself. Con had made sure she knew that Mab and Nessa were OK, more or less.

But watching from afar wasn't the same thing as looking after them. She'd always told herself that keeping away from them – keeping them away from Lowlands – had been, more than anything, a sacrifice for her. And it had been: a terrible sacrifice. But she was no longer sure whether it had been the right thing to do, or even the equally wrong thing. She was no longer sure how she'd done it, either, except one day at a time, like the rest of life, until the days coalesced into years, and suddenly almost twenty of them had passed. That was the oddest thing about life: whatever you did, time passed. Passed at the same speed, and in the same direction, taking you further and further away from the things you couldn't change, until it felt as if you had no power to change anything at all.

For a few moments, standing in the middle of her house, all Con could think about was how badly she wished that she could turn back the years and see what might have happened if she'd made a different decision all that time ago. Did they blame her? she wondered. What did they remember? Were they at all curious about her? She shook her head, banishing that idea. They probably never thought about her. They'd been very young, and their mother had died that autumn. Why should they remember anything but that?

The grandfather clock in the sitting room began its ten o'clock chime, and Con turned away, at last, from the table in the hall where she still kept the telephone. She hardly used it these days, the landline, but it had rung this morning, bringing her the news of Roy's death, and it had felt more formal, somehow more proper, to use it to call Mab and Nessa. Silly, she told herself – but there was something old-fashioned about a death. The conventions of it. Ursula phoning Con herself, for example. But she and Ursula had always been on civil terms, insofar as they'd been on any terms at all. Ursula had a pragmatic streak that she had always half-admired: she'd treated Con more like Roy's sister than his ex-wife, as if there was no reason for any awkwardness between them. And there wasn't, really. She hadn't supplanted Con: there'd been thirteen years between the end of Con's marriage to Roy and the beginning of Ursula's. There'd been the whole of the Robin era, an entire landscape of heartbreak and tragedy.

It was brighter in the kitchen: small though the house was, daylight didn't penetrate into the hall. Con could see blue sky through the window now. It would be dark in New Zealand, she thought. It had been late afternoon there when Ursula had rung her. She must have chosen the earliest time she felt it was reasonable to wake someone with bad news. Con could see why Roy had stayed with Ursula. They'd all had something to offer, Roy's wives: Con had had money, if not as much as Roy imagined, and Robin had had beauty and sweetness, but Ursula had the kind of competence that made you feel nothing terrible would ever happen – and that if it did, she would cope with it. For a second Con grinned. That was exactly what Ursula was doing now, she thought. She was coping with Roy's death in her own majestic way.

They had talked for longer than was necessary this morning. Ursula had told her things Con didn't need to know, and wouldn't have asked. Had Ursula wanted to speak to someone who'd once known Roy as well as she had? A younger Roy, but no doubt the same one in many respects. A man who was always able to hold several realities in his mind at once. Who had thought himself, Con was sure, indestructible; even immortal. Who'd always assumed there was plenty of time, and that things didn't need to run in the conventional order.

Would he have done anything differently if he'd known he wouldn't make old bones? If it had been cancer that had got him, say, rather than a heart attack, and he'd had a few months to set things straight? Setting things straight had never been Roy's strong suit, but surely he would have thought of his children – of Mab and Nessa, and of Philip? Surely, if he could have done, he would have wanted to do something, to say something to them before he died?

From the kitchen – forgetting the newly boiled kettle – Con wandered restlessly back into the hall and then into the sitting room, halting in front of the French windows she'd put in when she moved here to give her a view away from the big house. She'd worked hard, that first year, on the little bit of garden they looked out on. She'd planted several shrubs – she couldn't remember their names; she'd never really been a gardener – and the climbing roses which covered the whole fence now, and which would start flowering soon. She'd been lucky with those, a chance purchase at the garden centre that first spring.

It had always seemed odd to Con that luck came in so many guises: that even when things went so devastatingly wrong that the centre of your life fell away like a sinkhole, other things, little things, could still turn out well. That you could lose so much, yet still be capable of enjoying the pinpricks of colour that appeared in the garden in the spring.

Con thought about this quite often; about the paradox of it. But thinking about it undid the magic. It was like this: if she turned her mind a certain way, it was possible for her to feel that she'd had a good enough life, after all. She had a home, her son, her health, her work. But when she allowed herself to start believing that story, it turned her against herself. That was the catch. It filled her with a self-loathing so violent, so absolute, that she wanted to rip things apart, to destroy any sign of good luck or of happiness. If it hadn't been for Philip, she was sure she would have done exactly that, long ago.

Chapter Three

'Mab.' Nessa's voice was low, as if she was speaking from the office. Which she would be, of course. Nessa didn't work shifts; she did proper office hours.

'You've heard from Con?' Mab said.

'Yes.'

'Bit of a shock.'

'Yes.'

There was a silence then, neither of them knowing what to say next.

'It was funny speaking to her,' Mab said, after a bit.

'Yes.' Nessa gave a sort of laugh, then said, 'I'm not being very articulate this morning. I feel a bit stymied by all this. I mean – not stymied. That's the wrong word.'

'Not the wrong word,' Mab said. 'Just one of the words.'

'Yes.' Nessa cleared her throat. Mab imagined her colleagues around her, perhaps listening. 'Are you OK, Mab?'

'I wouldn't say that.' It was Mab's turn to laugh; the same half-formed ironic chuckle. 'No, I am. I'm OK. But – could you get away from work, Nessa? Could we – maybe we could meet at lunchtime or something?'

'Yes, let's do that. Let me... Would one thirty work for you? I've got a – I could cancel it, but...'

'No, one thirty's fine. I'm meant to be working this afternoon, but I'll call in and explain. They'll understand.'

'Are you sure? I could move my meeting.'

'There are advantages to working in a bookshop, Nessa,' Mab said. 'The future of the world doesn't depend on me being there.'

There was a tiny hesitation. 'OK. One thirty at Pip's, then?'

'Yes,' said Mab. 'See you then.' She hesitated, bit her lip. 'Nessa?'

But Nessa had gone. Never mind, Mab told herself. She could wait. She was fine, really. The kettle had just boiled, but she remembered now that she'd made a cup of coffee earlier, before Con called. There it was, over by the sink. Like something left behind when the lava hit Herculaneum, she thought, except that the coffee was still warm.

The kitchen was one of the reasons Mab stayed in this house in an inconvenient corner of Lewisham, miles from where any of her friends lived. It was the kind of kitchen you associated with family houses: it had been extended backwards over the scrubby garden and given lots of glass to let in the light. But in the tender care of Mab and the others, it had taken on the look of any other shared kitchen, cluttered with the evidence of five peoples' chaotic catering arrangements, five peoples' hangovers and theses and zero hours contracts.

Even so, whenever Mab was tempted to look for somewhere else to live, she thought about this room. It was more the Socratic ideal of the kitchen, Danny had said when she'd explained this to him, than the kitchen itself. But it occurred to her now that it was the Socratic ideal of Con's kitchen she still had in her mind. A place where there was always something cooking, and someone to talk to, and where meals happened at regular intervals. Where life felt safe, until it suddenly didn't any more.

Con must have been about forty the summer they stayed with her. In every one of Mab's memories, she was wearing the same loose cotton dress: she must have had more than one, but they'd blurred together, their colours merging into a faded cornflower blue. Her hair had been the same rich brown as the oak furniture at Lowlands, prone to an untidiness that Mab had found reassuring. There hadn't been many mirrors in the house, and Con had seemed like the kind of person who wouldn't bother with them much even if they were there. She'd been more interested in looking at other people than herself, Mab thought now, although she recognised that as a new thought, not one she'd have had as a child.

Despite all that happened that summer, Mab had secretly hoped that Con might ask her and Nessa to come and live at Lowlands after their mother died. That somehow, between them, they could get back to the time before everything had gone wrong and find a way forwards from there, with Con in the middle, holding things together. Mab had never said anything, even to Nessa, because – well, because there were lots of reasons Con might not have wanted them, and actually there were lots of things Mab had never said to Nessa. One big thing, really, but there were lots of little things connected to it, and she had to be careful, especially at the beginning, not to find herself saying something that would lead to it. But that hope that Con might take them in had never really gone away, Mab realised now. It had just settled deep in her psyche, the knowledge that there might be – might have been – another path for them. One that didn't involve them being passed between Hazel, who didn't want them, and Granny Jenny, who did, but whose way of bringing them up made Hazel too cross to leave them there for long.

All of that was part of the muddle in her head just now, as Mab looked out of the window at the half-hearted March sunlight and tried to drink her coffee. There was her father, and her mother, and hearing Con's voice this morning. There was death again – and deaths meant endings and beginnings and change and things being stirred up. A sort of cold dread filled her then. Granny Jenny was more or less gone too, and that only left Hazel and Nessa, which didn't feel like enough of a buttress against what life might do to you.

Pip's was a vegetarian place in Rotherhithe where they'd met a couple of times before. It was convenient for them both: only a couple of stops along the Jubilee Line from Nessa's office in Canary Wharf, and fifteen minutes on the overground for Mab.

'We ought to do this more often,' Nessa said, when they were sitting down at a table near the back.

'We do do it sometimes,' Mab said – but that made it sound worse, somehow. 'It's always nice,' she added. She wanted to see Nessa smile. She remembered that as a little girl: desperately wanting Nessa to smile, because she felt better when Nessa was happy.

Nessa had always been her best person. Her anchor. After their mother died, and their father went off to New Zealand, and the outcome of those not-so-discreet discussions about the girls' future had been that Granny Jenny and Aunt Hazel had accepted shared guardianship, it was Nessa who looked after Mab more than anyone else. Especially after Roy decided to stay in New Zealand with Ursula, and what they'd been told was a temporary arrangement became permanent – not that there was ever any permanence, or even any pattern, because their moves between Granny Jenny and Aunt Hazel had never been predictable. Every time they began to feel at all settled, things would change again, schools and everything, and the only thing that always stayed the same was Nessa.

'What do you fancy?' Nessa asked now. 'Are you hungry?'

'I am, actually,' Mab admitted. 'You order, though. We can share. I don't mind what we get.'

'Didn't you like that melted cheese thing last time?'

'Yes,' Mab said, 'but you choose, honestly.'

Nessa frowned at the menu for a moment, and then she looked up at Mab and smiled, and Mab smiled back. But not for long, because the tears came then, a sudden hot gush of them, taking them both by surprise. Nessa moved swiftly round to the bench beside Mab and put her arm around her.

'Poor Mab,' she said. 'Poor baby.'

'I'm sorry,' Mab said, between tears and choking. 'I'm being silly.'

'Of course you're not.' Nessa shook her gently. 'Our father's just died. You're allowed to cry.'

'I don't even feel as if I'm crying for him,' Mab said. 'Isn't that awful? I ought to be sad, but...'

'It's more complicated than that,' Nessa said. 'Of course it is. I've been thinking about Mum all morning. And...'

'Yes,' Mab said, 'me too. And everything else.' She scrubbed at her eyes, and blew her nose on her napkin. 'Con ringing us. That felt so weird.' There was a little quiver, then, about getting close to the things she mustn't say, even now, and another quiver in case Nessa had noticed. But there was so much else to think about, to feel, that surely Nessa wouldn't think of that. Their father's death might bring it all up again, but it might also lay another layer of sediment down over it. Perhaps she could see it like that, Mab thought. Perhaps she could use this death to help bury everything else a bit deeper.

Nessa leaned her head on Mab's shoulder. 'I won't go back to work this afternoon,' she said. 'I'll stay with you.'

'You don't have to,' Mab said. 'I'm OK, really. I don't want you to get into trouble.'

'I won't get into trouble,' Nessa said. 'And even if you're OK, I'm not. We ought to be together today. We could go to Greenwich or something.'

'Let's eat something first, though,' Mab said.

'Definitely.'

'Let's have the melted cheese thing,' Mab said. 'And the cauliflower fritters. But you can order everything else.'

'OK.' Nessa smiled at her. 'And then you can tell me how things are with Danny. I could do with thinking about something else for a bit.'

It was Mab who had inherited their mother's beauty. That wasn't what anyone had expected, except perhaps their mother, and no one could remember now what Robin might have expected for her daughters. It certainly hadn't been part of Mab's idea of what growing up would involve. Mab had grown up beautiful, and Nessa, who had always had the kind of presence and certainty and slight stand-offishness that you associate with beauty, had not. They had the same features, but Nessa's face looked like a novice's copy of the masterwork that was Mab. Or perhaps, since Nessa was older, hers might have been a practice for the real thing. A beta version, to be improved on and perfected.

It was the wrong way round, anyway. Mab had no use for beauty, and although Nessa gave no sign of being dissatisfied with her appearance, you couldn't help feeling – or at least, Mab could never help feeling – that beauty would have suited her. It would have added something; made her invincible. But Nessa was pretty invincible as it was, Mab reminded herself, whenever this subject returned to trouble her. Nessa was well able to fend for herself: that had never been in doubt.

And Mab's beauty hadn't served her well. It had attracted the wrong kind of friends, and the wrong kind of men, and put off the ones Mab might have liked to have. Girls at school had been jealous, and when they found out that Mab wasn't much good at schoolwork or sport they'd made fun of her instead of feeling sorry for her, and they'd got the boys to laugh at her too. Later, when the boys were men and Mab was more beautiful still, the ones who were kind and gentle and funny didn't dare talk to her, and the ones who thought they deserved someone like Mab treated her badly. Nessa had occasionally wondered aloud why Mab made such bad choices, but that suggested Mab had been even a little bit in control of things, which wasn't really true.

Danny was different. Mab *had* chosen Danny. He worked at Books on the Hill with her, and she'd spent months being his friend, asking him questions about the stock control system and his reading tastes and anything else she could think of, before she'd plucked up the courage to ask him if he'd like to go for a drink after work. Just with her, she'd added, so that he couldn't be in any doubt about what she meant. Danny was lovely, and Mab wanted to keep hold of him more than she'd wanted anything for a very long time. She thought Danny wanted that too, but Danny's life had been complicated in a way that was and wasn't the same as Mab's, and between the two of them it was difficult to imagine a simple future.

She didn't know where to start with saying all that to Nessa, though. Especially since Danny was just a prelude, a bit of light relief before they got back to talking about their father.

'Danny's fine,' she said, once Nessa was back on her side of the table and they had ordered their lunch.

Nessa raised her eyebrow in an expectant way. 'Still working at the bookshop with you?'

'Yup.'

Nessa nodded, and Mab thought she was trying hard not to give the impression that she thought one or other of them ought to have a bit more ambition.

'We like it,' Mab said. 'It's not just a bookshop, anyway: there's a café and an events space. It's a sort of community hub, really.' That was what it said on Books on the Hill's website, but it was true. The café was always full, and the events were well attended. Danny organised the events programme, and he was good at it.

'Good.' Nessa smiled. This wasn't a day for contention; they both knew that. 'And he makes you happy?'

'Yes.' Mab wasn't sure that Nessa's idea of making someone happy was quite the same as hers: she'd never felt Nessa's girlfriends did much more than fill a space in her life. It took Mab a moment to remember the name of the current one. Inga. She ran an educational charity, Mab reminded herself.

A thought came back to her then that she'd hardly registered earlier, when she'd thought about how there would only be Nessa and Hazel left soon. They weren't the same at all, Nessa and Hazel: they occupied entirely different places in Mab's mental taxonomy. She loved Nessa more than anyone else in the world, and she almost hated Hazel. But it occurred to her that there were parallels between the two generations of their family. Robin and Hazel had grown up in a hippie commune with Granny Jenny, but while Robin had embraced her bohemian roots – she'd gone to art school, fallen in love with a visiting tutor, worn her beautiful hair long until chemo made it fall out – Hazel had gone in the opposite direction. She'd joined the civil service straight out of university and spent the last twenty-five years working her way up through the Department for Transport.

The difference between Mab and Nessa wasn't as big as that, but from the outside it might seem it. Nessa worked for a financial institution (something to do with currency exchange, Mab thought) and she worked in a bookshop. Nessa had scraped together the money for a deposit on a tiny flat in Wanstead, and Mab lived in a shared house a long walk from the nearest station.

But they'd stuck together, she and Nessa. They'd been loyal to each other, depended on each other – whereas Hazel and Robin had hardly been in touch for years until Robin got so ill. Mab couldn't remember her mother ever saying anything bad about her sister – anything at all, in fact, except that she lived in London and had an important job – but Hazel hadn't had much truck with the notion of not speaking ill of the dead, even to their small children. A part of Hazel, Mab thought, believed that marrying Roy, breaking up a family, was what had given Robin cancer. And perhaps she had a point, except that there was a gene involved too. Hazel knew that, because she'd arranged for all three of them – first her, and later Nessa and Mab – to be tested. But disapproval was one of the few things about Hazel that wasn't rational.

And Nessa wasn't disapproving. She just worried about her, Mab knew. But perhaps there was something else, too: something, apart from sisterly love, that lay behind all Nessa's care and carefulness. The watchful eye she kept on Mab, even now. There was the thing they had never talked about, never once alluded to. The thing Nessa didn't even know that Mab knew.

'I'd love to meet him,' Nessa said.

'Danny?'

Nessa pulled a face, as though Mab was being coy.

'You can,' Mab said. 'Perhaps...' She hesitated. 'Will there be a funeral? I mean – what'll happen, do you think?'

'I expect the funeral will be in New Zealand,' Nessa said.

'Should we go?' Mab asked. 'We ought to go, shouldn't we?'

'Plane tickets to New Zealand would cost a fortune,' Nessa said carefully, 'especially at the last minute. I don't...'

She was thinking that she'd have to pay for both of them, Mab thought. Which was probably true. 'He might have left us some money,' she said. 'Maybe we could use that.'

'If he has, we won't get it in time. Not unless there's some special instruction about the funeral. About getting us there.'

They both knew that their father would never have thought to do that. He hadn't even remembered their birthdays after the first year or two. At Christmas there had occasionally been a present, but it had always been something completely inappropriate. Too babyish, or too grown-up, or just wrong. Tears rose in Mab's eyes again – not tears of sorrow for her father, or indeed for herself, but for the poignancy of the situation. The embarrassment, almost, of realising there was almost no chance that they'd be able to go to their father's funeral: that no one would expect it, even.

'There'll probably be a memorial service in England,' Nessa said. 'We can talk to Con about that.'

If there was a flicker of hesitation when she mentioned Con's name, Mab didn't spot it.

Chapter Four

The irony of their marriage, Con sometimes thought, was that Roy had treated her better – liked her better, perhaps – after they were divorced. Especially in the Ursula years. All that time he'd stayed in touch: there'd been a Christmas card most years, usually something he'd drawn himself. To show her that he was still working, perhaps, or to remind her of the time when her opinion had been the only one that mattered to him, even though she'd protested that she knew nothing about art. *But that's why your reaction is important*, he'd said. *I want it to speak to ordinary people, not those idiots who call themselves experts.*

His work had spoken more to ordinary people in New Zealand, Con knew, than it had to his fellow countrymen, at least since the late 1980s when he'd turned his back on the portrait painting that had brought him such remarkable early fame. Perhaps he'd found serenity in his later years, as well as a measure of success after the decades of obscurity. But no: it was impossible to imagine Roy being serene. Jubilant, resentful, disappointed; filled with a self-doubt he never stopped fighting with belligerent selfishness – all of these were facets of Roy, but there was nothing peaceful about him, ever. Not even in those rare moments when he had a glass of wine in his hand, people around him, and was for an instant still and quiet. Those were generally the moments when he was gathering himself for an explosion.

Perhaps Ursula had had the best of him, though, Con thought, pouring away the stale water from the kettle she'd forgotten about this morning and filling it again. Ursula had certainly had him for the longest. She'd survived him, in every sense of the word. Did she know that Roy had kept writing to Con? That there had been occasional letters as well as the Christmas cards: handwritten letters on thick paper, expensive to post? One every year or two, picking up, always, *in medias res*. Con had been conscious that it would have been better if he'd written to Philip rather than her, and that had made her pleasure in the letters a guilty one, but even so she'd savoured them. Sometimes she'd imagined, reading them, that Roy was just away on a trip; that he'd be back in a month or two. But if there was nothing in the letters to suggest that Roy had left her years ago, there was nothing in them to suggest they'd ever been married, either. Despite their appearance of candour and spontaneity, they hadn't contained any important information about his life. Certainly no concerns about his health. *It came out of the blue*, Ursula had said, about the heart attack. Things coming out of the blue was one of Roy's specialities, although usually, looking back, you could spot the signs; the trail of breadcrumbs leading to the big reveal. But this final, big surprise had been one he had never intended.

The kettle came to the boil and switched itself off, and Con reached mechanically for the teapot. Philip would be home soon; that's what she was preparing for. Perhaps she should have rung him at work, but she'd decided it would be better to wait: to tell him about his father's death face to face. To have tea ready, as usual. But when she heard his key in the door, she jumped like a guilty child. Ridiculous, she told herself. The truth was that Philip had lost his father years ago. He'd lost him when he was four, and again when he was sixteen: there surely wasn't any more that Roy could do to him. But Con knew that wasn't true. She knew that loss could go on causing damage, year after year. And that most of the damage in Philip's life could be traced back, directly or indirectly, to Roy.

Philip at thirty-five looked, sometimes, awfully like his teenage self. He wore a suit these days, and he wasn't quite so skinny, but his hair was just the same, and every time he got new glasses he chose frames that looked exactly like the ones he'd always worn, dark-rimmed and almost round.

His education, as you might expect, had stalled for a while, but he'd got through A-levels in the end, and an Open University degree, and then an accountancy qualification, and he'd got a job with the council which he seemed to have no intention of leaving. Neither did he have any intention, as far as Con knew, of leaving her and finding somewhere to live on his own. Perhaps she ought to suggest it, but she never did. She wasn't sure she could bear him to go. There wasn't much to hold her life together except Philip: except looking after Philip. Sometimes she told herself it was starting to be the other way round, but it wasn't, really. She looked after him, and looking after him gave her a reason to live – and it made her life financially viable, too. She didn't earn enough from her editing to keep even this little house going.

As he came into the kitchen now, she made her face into a smile.

'Good day, darling?' she asked.

'Yes.' He put his briefcase down on the dresser, as he did

every night. And then he stopped, and stood still, looking at her, as if he'd guessed she had something to tell him.

'I'm afraid there's some bad news,' Con said. 'It's your father. He had a heart attack.'

'Is he dead?' Philip asked.

'I'm afraid so.'

Con was seized, then, with guilt and anguish so powerful, so painful, that she felt almost as if she, too, was having a heart attack. She had told Mab and Nessa before her own son, she thought. She had left him all day without knowing.

'I'm so sorry, my darling,' she started to say, but Philip gave a little shake of his head.

'Well, that's all over with, then,' he said.

'What do you mean?' Con was startled.

'Just that he's dead now,' Philip said. 'He won't be coming back.'

Con held her breath for a moment. 'Did you think he would?' she asked.

'When he was alive it was always a possibility,' Philip said. He looked at her, then, as though something had occurred to him. 'Are you upset?' he asked. 'He was your husband.'

'A long time ago,' Con said. 'A very long time ago. But – yes, I am, I suppose. It's always upsetting when someone dies.'

'I'm sorry,' he said. 'I expect you'd have liked to see him again.'

'Maybe,' Con said. 'But to be honest, I was more worried about you. About what you'd feel.'

Philip nodded. 'It doesn't feel like it ought to when your father dies,' he said. 'What I imagine it ought to feel like. He's been gone such a long time.' He hesitated. 'Did *you* think he might come back?'

Con shook her head. 'Not really. Not for a long time.'

'No.' Philip nodded again, as if he was satisfied; as if they were both agreed. 'What should we do?' he asked. 'This evening, I mean? Should we go out for supper? I could take you out, if you like. We could go to the pub in Compton.'

'That's so kind of you, darling.' Con hadn't cried all day – hadn't cried for years – but she felt as if she might now. 'You don't have to do that.'

'I'd like to,' Philip said. 'You've had a shock. It would be a nice treat, wouldn't it?'

'It would,' Con said.

She couldn't tell him that the King's Head in Compton would always be filled with Roy. Roy at his most garrulous and charming, in the days when loving him was so wonderful and so thrilling it almost made her head burst. When he'd just finished her father's portrait in his High Sheriff's garb, and Con couldn't believe he wanted her. When she was twenty-three and he was twenty-seven and already almost famous, and neither of them had any idea that the fame would be so short-lived.

Well, let them go there tonight. Let Roy's son take her there, and let them toast him, the old monster that he was. And let her remember, just once more, their brief heyday.

Chapter Five

July 2005

'It won't be for long,' their father said. He was trying to be calm, but Mab could tell that he wasn't. The look on his face made the tears that were waiting inside her bubble up and spill down her cheeks.

'Why can't we stay here?' she asked, even though she knew it would make him angry if she kept asking questions. 'Why can't Mummy come home?'

'Because the doctors have to make her better.' He managed a smile, and that made Mab feel even worse, because she could see that it was an effort for him, and her father didn't usually make an effort about things like that.

'I thought the operation was going to make her better,' Mab said.

'They're doing some extra treatment to make sure,' Nessa said. She looked at their father, and he nodded.

'And then she'll be properly better?' Mab asked.

'That's the idea.' Her father ruffled her hair.

'But we won't be able to visit her from there, will we? Won't she miss us?'

'Of course she will,' he said. 'But you couldn't visit her

anyway while she's having this treatment. It'll make her feel quite poorly for a while.'

'She'd still want to see us even if she was feeling poorly,' Mab said – but she realised she'd gone too far now. Her father got up from the table and started clearing their plates, and his face looked red and cross. They'd had fish fingers again: Mab thought it might be the only thing he knew how to make. *You're not cut out for parenthood*, she'd heard her aunt Hazel say when she came to visit. That wasn't true, Mab had wanted to tell her, but she wasn't supposed to have heard what Hazel had said. 'But we won't be there for long,' she said now, trying to make amends.

'Just for a bit.' He turned and smiled at her again, and this was a better smile, a proper smile, and Mab smiled too, because she always liked it when her father was pleased with her. 'I knew you'd understand,' he said. 'You're such a grown-up girl now, Mab. You both are.'

'And you have to go away for work,' Mab said, hoping to make him even more pleased.

'Yes, for work,' he said. 'Just a few meetings in London. I can't really put them off, and while your mother's having this treatment...' He turned the tap on then, and the noise of the water made it difficult to hear anything else. They had a dishwasher, but sometimes he forgot that.

'Let's get ready for bed,' Nessa said. 'I'll help Mab, Daddy. And we'll pack our things, too, so we're ready to go in the morning.'

Their father was a famous painter. Some of the portraits he'd painted were in galleries in London, their mother had told them, and in lots of rich people's big houses, but Daddy didn't like to talk about those pictures. He'd moved on since the days when he painted people. That wasn't real art, he said, whenever anyone mentioned it. It was like being a human camera. The annoying thing was that people had liked the portraits better. They didn't understand the new ones because they weren't what they expected, Mummy said, but Daddy said it was because people were ignorant and stupid. It was annoying, Mab knew, because people used to pay a lot of money for the old pictures, and they could have done with more money. Sometimes she heard her parents talking about it. Arguing about it. For a long time money was the only thing she ever heard them arguing about. Her father still made some money from teaching, but he hated teaching and talked a lot about giving it up. If he didn't have to teach, he said, he could produce the work he wanted to, the work he was supposed to do, and then everyone would see. But we have to eat, her mother would say, quietly, and then Mab would creep away because she hated hearing her mother pleading and her father getting angry.

Their parents had met when Mummy had gone to the art school where Daddy was teaching. It was a great love story; Mab had always known that. Their mother had been the most beautiful woman their father had ever seen, and they had fallen madly in love and got married and had Nessa and Mab, and moved to the countryside where Daddy could paint without distractions. Nessa and Mab weren't allowed to be distractions. They weren't allowed to go anywhere near his studio at the end of the garden. It was really a shed, but it was quite a big shed with windows on the side, and there was a blue cable that ran across the garden so he could have light and a kettle and didn't have to come inside for cups of tea. While their mother had been in hospital that summer he had been in the studio almost all the time, and apart from the fish fingers in the evenings Nessa had made their meals and looked after Mab. It was the holidays, so they didn't have to go to school. They had gone for walks and played board games and read books.

'This is a good holiday, don't you think?' Nessa had said, when she had the idea of making paper dolls in long strips, and Mab had agreed with her. But really it had been a horrible holiday, without Mummy. 'Think how nice it'll be when she's better and we're all together again,' Nessa had said then, seeing Mab's face, and she'd promised her sweets next time they walked to the village, which was very nice of her because Mab knew she only had 50p left in her piggy bank and that she was saving up for a present for Mummy to welcome her home.

The thing Mab hadn't known about her parents' great love story was that her father had been married to someone else when it happened. The person he'd been married to was called Constance, and she was also the person they were going to stay with while Mummy was having her treatment and Daddy was having his important meetings in London. Her father hadn't explained it quite like that: he'd just said *my first wife, Constance*. But Nessa had known that he'd still been married to Constance when he met Mummy. That made Mab feel a bit strange. A bit worried about what it would be like, going to stay with her.

'Is she our stepmother?' she'd asked Nessa, when they were in bed.

'Yes,' Nessa had said, and then, 'sort of. Our stepmother in reverse, I suppose.'

That sounded worse than the ordinary kind, Mab thought, because their mother had taken Constance's husband away, but Nessa had said that wasn't necessarily how it had happened – that Daddy and Constance might not have wanted to go on being married anyway – and Mab was hoping that was true. If Constance was angry with him she wouldn't have agreed to have them to stay, Nessa had said, but Mab knew that their father had a way of making people do things for him. He was very charming, everyone knew that, and having a wife in hospital would make people feel sorry for him.

'All right in the back there?' their father asked now, turning his head to smile at them. 'Not feeling sick?'

'No,' Nessa replied.

'Con's looking forward to meeting you,' he said, and Mab hoped that he couldn't tell what she'd been thinking. 'So are the boys.'

The boys were her father's sons, which was another strange thing to get used to. Mab knew that they existed, or at least she sort of did. From time to time their mother would mention them, explaining where Daddy was. 'You know he has two sons from his first marriage?' she'd say. 'Much older than you.' But Mab had never really imagined them as real people.

They *were* older, the boys, but not as much as Mab had thought. Philip was sixteen and Max was nearly fifteen, which was not quite two years older than Nessa. Mab didn't know much about marriage, but she thought it was less likely that Constance hadn't wanted to be married to Daddy any more if she'd had a little boy of two. Also, the times when Mummy explained that he was visiting them hadn't happened very often, and Mab felt a bit sad for them now because they hadn't seen much of their father, because he was too busy being Mab and Nessa's father. And doing his painting, of course, but Max and Philip wouldn't know that. They might think he spent all his time with Mab and Nessa and their mother, and if Mab was them she would hate the new wife and the new children.

'We should have introduced you before,' her father said now. 'But I'm sure you'll like them. Max looks just like I did at his age.' He smiled. 'It's a beautiful place. A beautiful old house with a big garden and lots of countryside to explore. Proper countryside, not like near us.'

'Do they have horses?' Mab asked. She'd been reading pony books this summer, stories about children who roamed the moors on horseback and had adventures.

Her father laughed. 'No,' he said. 'You'll have to explore on your own two feet. But I'm sure you'll have fun. There's a farm next door, so there are cows, at least.'

Mab digested this. She wasn't sure what you could do with cows. 'How long 'til we get there?' she asked.

It was beautiful, Lowlands. Mab loved it as soon as she saw it, and she loved its name too, which sounded just like something from one of the pony books. The big house was called Lowlands and the farm next door was called Lowlands Farm, and there was a smaller house across the fields called Lowlands Cottage. Apart from that there were no houses anywhere near, so it was almost as though it was a whole tiny village where everything had the same name, except the stream which ran through the farm and along the back of the garden, which didn't have a proper name, although people called it the mill stream because it used to have a mill on it. All of this came later though, along with Mab asking where the highlands were, if this was the lowlands, and Con laughing and saying there weren't any highlands, just hills, and they weren't very close, and Mab asking what they were called and Con pointing in different directions and reciting their names – the Mendips and the Quantocks and the Blackdowns.

What came before all that was the car stopping and their father saying, 'Here we are,' and Mab realising that she'd fallen asleep and missed the last bit of the journey, so she hadn't seen where they'd come and it felt almost as if they'd arrived by magic carpet instead of in the old Ford. And then, before they'd got out from the back seat, Con had come out through the front gate to meet them, and she'd had a big smile on her face and Mab had felt such a tremendous flood of relief that she'd started crying, so that everyone had thought she was miserable about being there.

'You must be Mab,' Con had said, bending down to smile at her. 'I'm Con. What a long journey you've had. I've made shepherd's pie for lunch. I hope you like shepherd's pie?'

And somehow Mab had known that Con understood why she was crying, and she'd understood that Mab needed a hug, too, and that first hug had felt so good that Mab had felt guilty because she ought to keep her hugs for her mother, but she hadn't been able to help herself.

'The boys have gone out with some friends,' Con had said, 'so it's just us for a bit while you settle in.' She'd straightened up then, and looked at their father. 'Are you staying for lunch, Roy?'

'For your shepherd's pie, Constanza, I'd cross mountains,' he'd said, and Con had rolled her eyes and smiled at him, and Mab had marvelled at the way grown-ups behaved, sometimes, but she'd been happy about that too – about her father staying for a bit, and about Con not hating him. Even about him having a special name for her, like he did for them, because it made it feel as if they were all part of the same family. Which she supposed they were, sort of.

As they went through the gate and up the path, Con held one of her hands and Nessa held the other, and their father came behind with the bags, and Mab held her breath as the huge front door came into view, with a porch thing on the front that was almost the size of a room, full of boots and umbrellas and sledges and fishing rods, and she'd thought that even if there weren't horses here it was going to be all right.

. . .

37

She and Nessa came out to the car to wave their father off, after lunch and what Con called a meander round the garden, which meant a shortish walk to look at the vegetable patch and the stream and the orchard full of fruit trees and the bee hives and all the other things Con's garden had in it. It had been their father's garden too, once, Mab realised, and her father's house as well, and that made her feel a bit funny again, but not too funny because it didn't seem to bother Con or her father.

Nessa was quiet during lunch and the meander, but on the way back to the house she squeezed Mab's hand and whispered, 'Are you OK?' and Mab nodded, and after that Nessa relaxed, and when they waved their father off she was smiling.

'I hope the meetings go well, Daddy,' she said, and he tousled her hair and then Mab's.

'Be good, my little angels,' he said.

Mab half-wanted to ask how long they would be here, but she didn't. She knew he wouldn't give them a proper answer anyway, and Con was standing behind them and she didn't want Con to think they were ungrateful or that they wanted to leave already. But once their father had driven off, Con put a hand on each of their shoulders and said, 'He'll be back as soon as he can, I'm sure. As soon as Mummy's well enough to see you.'

Chapter Six

Con had put them in a little room near hers, with a view over the garden.

'You can just see the stream,' she said, but you couldn't really, because of all the trees. 'There's a better view in the winter,' she added, when they'd all looked out of the window and realised this. 'There are too many leaves at this time of year.'

'That's OK,' Mab said. 'The leaves are pretty.'

Con smiled. 'It's lovely to have you here,' she said. 'I know it's hard for you, but I hope you'll enjoy yourselves.'

'I'm sure we will,' Nessa said. 'It's a very nice house.'

'And you're very nice too,' Mab said, because she wanted Con to know it wasn't just the house, and then she blushed because it sounded babyish – but Con smiled so much that Mab could see tears in her eyes.

'So are you, Mab,' she said. 'So are you both.'

When Con went downstairs, Nessa unpacked their clothes and their toothbrushes and arranged everything in the chest of drawers and on the little dressing table under the window. She'd forgotten to bring any books or games, but there was a bookcase in the corner of the room which had more books in it than they had at home, and Mab was sure there would be games too, somewhere.

'I didn't think she'd be so nice,' Mab said, as she tested both the beds.

'She feels sorry for us,' Nessa said.

'I suppose so.'

Mab wasn't sure exactly what Nessa was thinking, but she suspected that Nessa didn't like Con as much as she did.

'It's nice of her to have us,' Nessa said, as she shut the last drawer.

'That's what I meant,' Mab said, even though it wasn't. She felt a little twinge of anxiety: it was important to be on Nessa's side, she knew that. It was important that they stuck together.

'I wonder if the boys will be as nice about us coming here,' Nessa said. 'They missed seeing Daddy.'

Mab hadn't thought of that. 'He had to go for his meetings,' she said. 'He couldn't have stayed any longer.'

Nessa smiled: her taking-charge smile. 'Shall we go downstairs?'

When they got to the kitchen, the boys were already there. Con was stirring something on the stove, and they were standing by the back door, talking to her. When they spotted Mab and Nessa, they fell silent.

'Hello!' Con said. 'All settled in?'

Mab nodded, and glanced at Nessa.

'This is Philip, and this is Max,' Con said. 'And this is Mab and Nessa.'

The taller boy came over to shake their hands, as if they were all grown-ups. He must be Philip, Mab thought. He was thin and wore glasses and looked more like Con than their father, even though she was plump and didn't have glasses.

'Hello,' he said. 'I'm sorry your mother's ill.'

'Thank you,' Nessa said, but the words came out very quiet and quavery. Mab was surprised: Nessa wasn't usually afraid of anyone, and Philip was almost like a grown-up, which was less scary than a big boy. It wasn't Philip that Nessa was looking at, though. The other boy was staring at them in a way that definitely wasn't friendly.

'Max?' Philip said.

Max pushed himself off the door frame and took a step towards them. 'Hello,' he said. 'Welcome, I suppose.'

'What do you mean, you suppose?' said his mother. 'Don't be so rude, Max.'

'Sorry.' Max didn't sound at all sorry, but he came and shook their hands in the same way his brother had. 'How was our father?' he asked Con.

'He was fine. He sent his love.'

'Yeah?' Max turned away. 'I'm going to have a shower.'

'We'll eat at six,' Con said, as he made for the door.

'Sure thing,' Max said, over his shoulder. 'Won't be late.'

When he'd gone, Philip gave a little frown and shook his head. 'Don't mind Max,' he said. 'He's like that with everyone. It's his age.'

Mab giggled. She liked Philip too, she decided. He was still standing just in front of them, as though he wasn't sure what to do next.

'Have you seen the garden?' he asked.

'Yes,' said Nessa.

'And the farm?'

'No.'

He nodded. 'I can show you around tomorrow.'

41

'That's kind, Philip,' his mother said.

'I don't mind,' he said. 'I can keep an eye on them.'

'We don't need keeping an eye on,' Nessa said, but Con smiled at her too.

'Philip means making sure you're having fun,' she said. 'We all want you to have fun while you're here. Now, Philip – why don't you go and have a shower too, and the girls can help me lay the table?'

Mab had hoped Max would be more friendly in the morning, but he wasn't.

'He doesn't want us to be here,' Mab had whispered to Nessa after they were both in bed. 'Max doesn't,' she added, although she hardly needed to.

'I don't really blame him,' Nessa had said.

Mab had pondered that while she lay in the dark, waiting to fall asleep. Of course she didn't blame Max either, but she minded it more than Nessa seemed to. Perhaps, she thought, he'd get used to them. Perhaps he'd just ignore them.

But when they came down to breakfast (which was all laid out on the table, plates and bowls and cereal and toast and jam all ready for them to eat) he made a sound which was quite clearly a groan. Philip glared at him, and Max raised his eyebrows and made a show of baring his teeth at them in a horrible kind of smile.

'Morning, small girls,' he said.

Con wasn't there. Mab hoped she hadn't gone out somewhere.

'Mum's gone to get milk from the farm,' Philip said, perhaps seeing Mab looking around for her. 'She'll be back in a minute.'

Max folded a piece of toast in two and pushed back his chair. 'I'm off,' he said.

'You haven't finished eating,' Philip said.

Max stuffed the folded-up piece of toast into his mouth. 'Have now,' he said, with the toast flapping loose over his chin.

'You're really disgusting sometimes,' Philip said.

'Speak for yourself.' Max pulled an even more disgusting face and waggled his fingers at them all – and then he was gone.

Mab thought Philip might apologise for him again, but he didn't. None of them said anything more until the front door slammed and Con came in.

'Good morning,' she said, at the same time as Philip said, 'Max has gone.'

Con stood in the kitchen doorway for a moment, and then she smiled.

'OK,' she said, and then, 'Did you sleep well, you two? What would you like to eat? I could do boiled eggs if you'd like?'

'We just have toast usually,' Nessa said. She was listening out, Mab thought, for something – maybe to try and work out where Max had gone, or to make sure he wasn't coming back.

'It's going to be hot today,' Con said. 'I thought you could take the girls swimming, Philip. Can you both swim?'

'Yes,' Mab said. 'Nessa's got her hundred metres and I've got my fifty.'

'It's quite safe where we go,' Philip said. 'You'll like it.'

The swimming place was in the stream, or rather in a sort of pool off the stream which Philip said had been something to do with the mill once, although there were no buildings left now. It was thrilling to Mab: it felt like something from the pony books, the kind of place the children in them might stop to cool off, after tying their ponies up to a nearby tree. The water was a very dark green, and you could see the reflections of the trees in it, and a bit of blue sky in the middle. It was very cold when they first got in, but once they got used to it it felt warm enough to splash about in happily. Mab had hoped Philip might play a game with them, or perhaps lift them onto his shoulders and throw them off into the water as she'd seen big boys doing at the swimming pool, but he just swam round and round on his own, looking across now and then to check they were OK.

She and Nessa had a nice time, though. They found a place where they could jump in off a rock, and they dived under the surface and had races and played tag. When they finally got out, Philip gave them each a KitKat and an apple and they sat on the grass to get dry while they ate them.

Max was there at lunchtime, but he didn't speak to them. He didn't really speak to anyone, except to say 'yes' and 'no' when his mother asked him questions.

'I'm going to show the girls round the farm this afternoon,' Con said, when they'd all finished eating. 'Do you want to come with us, Max?'

'No,' he said, stretching the word out to make it sound as though it was a stupid thing to have asked.

Con raised her eyebrows, but all she said was, 'Have you got other plans, then? Are you meeting up with Will and Pete?'

'I told you, they've gone away,' Max said. 'I'm going to bother Philip this afternoon.'

'I've got holiday work to do,' Philip said, 'for my A-level courses.'

'Yes, we all know you're starting your A-levels, Philip,' Max said. 'But thanks for reminding us again.'

'I wasn't reminding you,' Philip said. 'I was just saying, I can't play with you this afternoon because I'm going to work. I've made a timetable.'

'I don't want to *play* with you,' Max said. 'I'm not the same age as Ant and Bee here.'

'That's enough,' Con said. 'You can wash the car for me, Max. Earn your pocket money.' She pushed back her chair. 'Philip, could you clear the table? I'm going to take these two out now.'

Chapter Seven

The farm had once belonged to the house, Con told them. The people who lived in Lowlands House used to get most of their food from the farm, as well as rent from the tenant farmer. It had been sold a long time ago, almost a hundred years, but that explained why they were so close together, and why there were still so many ways to get from one to the other. She took them through the garden to a gate that led into a field with a path across it towards the farmyard.

Nessa was glad that Con was taking them out this afternoon. Philip had been nice to them this morning, but being with him felt a bit awkward. He was much older than they were – especially Mab, who was still at primary school – and he wasn't at all interested in them really. He didn't ask them any questions. And Nessa felt too old to be babysat. Then there was Max, who was only two years older than her, but... Actually, she wasn't sure about Max. Max had been absolutely horrible so far, but Nessa thought perhaps he was making a big fuss about them being there on purpose, to annoy his mother and to upset them, but that after a bit he might get used to it and start being a bit nicer. She might be wrong, Nessa thought, but she had an idea that she and Max could maybe be friends, after a bit.

Anyway, it was nicer being with Con. Con liked them, you could tell. There was no reason she should, but she did. Mab really liked Con, too, and that was a relief. Nessa had enough to worry about without Mab being unhappy.

'That's the farmhouse,' Con was saying, 'and there's the old barn, and that's the new milking shed, which they only put up a couple of years ago.'

'Who owns the farm now?' Mab asked.

'Jim and Jean,' Con said. 'The Fidlers. Jim's father bought the farm forty years ago, and now Jim runs it.'

Con showed them the baby calves in a little barn on their own without their mothers, and the big chicken run behind the old stables, and the pond with lots of ducks on it.

'Are the ducks part of the farm?' Mab asked.

'Not really,' Con said. 'They're wild. They come and go, but most of the time they stay here, because it's safe and there's plenty to eat.'

Most of the buildings were made of metal and were rather ugly and functional-looking, but the old barn was more like Nessa's idea of what a farm ought to look like. At one end there were some tractors and farm machinery, and at the other end a tall stack of hay bales that looked as though it might be fun to climb. There were the stables, too, although – to Mab's disappointment – no horses. There hadn't been horses here for years, Con said. The stables were full of feed sacks and old equipment and other things that looked as though they could do with being thrown away, but Mab found a dusty saddle that she was delighted with.

'Can we come here on our own?' she asked. 'Just to see the hens and the ducks and things?'

'We'll ask Jim,' Con said. 'As long as you're sensible, I expect he wouldn't mind. I don't think he'll be at home now, but let's knock on the door and see.'

Jim wasn't at home, and nor was his wife, but a girl who looked about Philip's age opened the door. She had blonde hair, cut in a bob, and she was wearing a pale green crop top and a short denim skirt.

'Oh, Lucy!' Con said. 'I thought you were going away?'

'Not until August,' Lucy said. She smiled at Mab and Nessa. She had an interesting smile, sort of sideways on and slightly pursed up, as though she was trying to think how to say something. But it made Nessa shrink up inside. It reminded her of the older girls at school who smiled at the Year 7s as though they were puppies, and said things like 'so cute!' or 'how can they be so small!' as they walked past. That was worse, in Nessa's view, than the ones who completely ignored them, or laughed at their pristine uniforms and unfashionable backpacks. Nessa had the worst backpack in the year, even if her uniform was second-hand and less pristine than most of the others. Her skirt had belonged to Bonnie Smith, whose name was marked indelibly on the waist band and who was in Year 11 now and part of the ignoring tribe.

'These are my stepdaughters,' Con said now. That word brought Nessa back to the present with a jolt. So Con did think of them as stepdaughters? It certainly sounded better than *my ex-husband's daughters*, which is what Nessa had imagined her saying. She smiled back at Lucy, forcing herself to keep looking at her rather than darting her eyes away.

'I'm Nessa,' she said, 'and this is my sister, Mab.' *Little* sister, she would normally have said, but it was obvious that Mab was younger, and Nessa didn't want Lucy to think of either of them as little.

'Pleased to meet you,' Lucy said. Nessa thought she'd go

back inside then, or at least wait for Con to tell her why they'd come, but instead she said, 'Do you want to see our kittens? They're four weeks old, and they're adorable.'

'Ooh, yes please!' Mab said, before Nessa had a chance to reply. But she caught Lucy's eye and smiled again, and Lucy smiled back, as though it was understood that they were the older ones, indulging Mab's childish delight, and that felt very good.

The farmhouse was completely different to Con's house, even though from the outside it was obvious they'd been built from the same stone. Like two models made from the same Lego kit, Nessa thought, but one of them big and square and grand, and the other L-shaped and rather higgledy-piggledy, with bits of roof and windows where you didn't expect them. Inside, it was even more different, mainly because it seemed to be almost as full of animals as the farm itself. Nessa counted four dogs of different sizes in the kitchen, all of them eager for attention from the visitors, rubbing up against their legs and wagging their tails. Then they went through a dark passageway to a little room where the mother cat and her kittens were curled up on a blanket. Or rather, the mother cat was curled up and the kittens – six or seven of them – were clambering around on top of her.

They were, as Lucy had promised, extremely cute. They were tabbies, their coats making a pattern like a kaleidoscope as they tumbled around together. Their legs were a bit wobbly and they kept falling over and scrambling back up again, but they'd already got the idea of pouncing on each other and kept taking it in turns to make a comic leap towards one of their brothers or sisters, which always ended with a jumble of fur and bright eyes and little pricked ears.

Mab was in raptures. She was down on the floor in seconds, squeaking and cooing at the kittens, trying to scoop them up and cuddle them, then glancing back up at Nessa and the others imploringly.

'Can we have one?' she asked. 'Can we please? We could take it home as a present for Mummy!'

'They won't be ready to leave *their* mummy for another month,' Lucy said. 'But...' She looked at Nessa. Nessa felt a swell of pride: Con was the grown-up, really, but she liked the fact that Lucy could see she was in charge of Mab.

'We'll have to see, Mab,' she said. 'We'll have to ask Dad.'

'Haven't they got homes yet?' Con asked, and Lucy shook her head. Con raised her eyebrows briefly, trying to convey a message, and Lucy nodded.

'I'm not sure,' she said. 'Mum's in charge.'

'I'll *beg* her,' Mab said. 'They're all so so sweet but I love this one the best.'

She held up a kitten that had consented to be cuddled; it peeked out at them through Mab's swaddling arms, then opened its mouth and made a tiny mew.

'It likes me too!' Mab said. 'It wants me to be its owner, don't you, little thing?'

'You can come and play with them again,' Lucy said. 'How long are you staying?'

A frown passed over Mab's face. 'Not very long,' she said. 'Our mummy's in hospital but they're making her better and we're going home soon.'

'That's good,' Lucy said. 'Well, maybe when your mummy's better you can bring her to see the kittens.'

'Could I just take it back to Con's house?' Mab asked. 'Just for today?'

'I'm afraid they need their mother,' Lucy said. 'They're very young still. But you can come back and see them any time.' She grinned. 'Nessa can bring you.'

• • •

Con took them home a different way, through a gate which led out behind the farm and round in a big loop along the side of the stream.

'There are three ways to get to the farm,' she said. 'There's the road as well, but it's better for you to use one of the paths. There isn't much traffic on our lane, but there are tractors sometimes and they go faster than you think.'

'OK,' Nessa said. 'We won't go on the road.'

'Wasn't it kind of Lucy to show you the kittens?' Con said. 'She used to be rather a difficult girl. It's nice to see her growing up more personable.'

Nessa wasn't sure what personable meant, but she nodded. She remembered the way Lucy had smiled at her, specifically at her as though she was the same sort of age, the one she could relate to, and it made her feel warm and happy inside.

'How old is Lucy?' she asked.

'Sixteen,' Con said. 'She's just done GCSEs, like Philip.'

'Are they friends?' Nessa asked, and Con chuckled.

'Not really,' she said. 'They've known each other since they were small, but I think Philip's always been rather scared of Lucy. But don't tell him I told you that.' She looked down at them, folding a grin back into her face. 'She and Max used to do Scouts together, but Max stopped going a couple of years ago. She's at a different school from them. We have separate girls' schools and boys' schools around here, much to Max's disgust.'

Nessa was surprised. She'd have thought Max would be glad not to have girls in his class.

'Can we really go back and see the kittens?' Mab asked.

'I'm sure you can,' Con said. She smiled again; a smile Nessa recognised by now. A Con smile, like opening a door onto a store of good and comforting things. For a moment, just a fleeting moment, Nessa thought how nice it would be to have

Con as your mother, but she was so horrified by that thought that she didn't speak again all the way home.

Chapter Eight

That night, Mab was overcome by homesickness and by worry about their mother.

'I stopped thinking about her today,' she said chokily, when Nessa climbed into her bed. 'When we were swimming, and when we were at the farm seeing the kittens. I almost forgot why we were here until Lucy asked how long we were staying.'

'That's all right,' Nessa said, stroking her hair. 'You can't think about her every minute. It won't make her get better any faster.'

'You don't know that,' Mab said. 'If she thinks we've forgotten about her she'll be so sad she might not get better at all.'

'Of course she'll get better.' Nessa's voice was sharp. 'Daddy said this treatment would make her better. He wouldn't say that if it wasn't true.'

'Maybe he doesn't know,' Mab said, but it felt scary to think that Nessa might be wrong, and their father too. She wriggled deeper into Nessa's arms. 'How long do you think we'll be here? How many days?'

'I don't know.'

'What do you guess?'

Nessa was silent for a moment. 'Daddy's meetings can't last more than a few days,' she said, and then, 'Mummy would be happy if she knew we were having a nice time, Mab. I think we should try and have a nice time. Like a little holiday. Then we can tell her all about it when we see her.'

'Do you think we'll be able to visit her when we get home?' Mab asked. But she knew Nessa didn't know the answer to that question either, so she said, 'I think we will. I think she'll be feeling much better by the weekend.'

'It might take a bit longer than that,' Nessa said. 'I think it's better if we think it'll be longer, then we won't be disappointed.'

There was a knock on the door just then, and Con opened it. 'Are you still awake?' she asked. 'I thought I could hear voices.'

'I'm sorry,' said Mab.

'Why are you sorry?' Con's voice was very gentle; it almost made Mab cry again. 'I just wanted to check you were all right.'

'Mab's a bit sad this evening,' Nessa said. 'She's missing Mummy. And she's worrying about her.'

Con came into the room and sat on the edge of Nessa's bed, a few feet away from them.

'You're being very brave,' she said. 'I'm so sorry you can't be at home just now.'

'It's very nice of you to have us,' Nessa said. 'We're very grateful.'

Con shook her head. 'You don't have to be grateful,' she said. 'You've got quite enough to think about without that.' She sighed. 'You poor little creatures. I wish there was more I could do.'

Nessa sniffed. Mab could tell she was nearly crying too, but she managed to keep her voice steady as she asked, 'Do you know how long Daddy's meetings will go on for?'

Con didn't reply straight away. She reached her hand across the gap between them and rested it on Nessa's shoulder for a minute.

'I know it's hard for you,' she said. 'But it's difficult for Daddy too at the moment. I'm sure you know that. While you're here – it gives him a break from worrying about you as well as Mummy. Can you understand that?' She hesitated. 'He can get on with his meetings, his work, and...'

'Yes, we understand,' Nessa said.

'Good girls,' Con said. 'Brave girls. We'll do our best to give you a nice time here.'

Mab wanted to climb out of bed then and go and give Con a cuddle, or let Con give her one, but she thought that might make Nessa sad, and Nessa was being so kind and looking after her so well when she must feel sad and worried too. But that thought made the tears start up again.

'Ssh,' Nessa said. 'It's all right, Mab.'

'It's OK for her to cry,' Con said. 'It's entirely natural.'

'But everything will be all right, won't it?' Nessa said. 'Mummy will get better, and everything will be all right?'

'I hope so.' Con smiled. 'She's in the best place for the doctors to look after her.'

'Yes,' Nessa said.

Con sat for a few moments longer, and then she stood up. 'I'll take you out tomorrow,' she said. 'We could go to the beach, if you like. It's going to be another lovely sunny day.'

After she'd gone, Mab and Nessa lay in silence for a while, perhaps because they wanted Con to think they'd gone to sleep. There were lots of questions in Mab's head still, and while they were being quiet she thought carefully about which ones she could ask Nessa and which she'd better not. But just when she was about to speak, a sound drifted up from down below.

'Can you hear that?' Mab whispered.

'Yes.'

It was piano music, very slow and gentle. A couple of times it stopped and went back a bit and then started again.

'It's someone playing,' Nessa said. 'Not a CD.'

'Yes.'

'It must be Con. I didn't know she could play the piano.'

'It's beautiful,' Mab whispered. 'Don't you think it's beautiful?'

'Yes.'

After the slow music there was a faster bit, but it wasn't happy fast. It sounded like someone who was upset and worried, and some louder notes kept coming out, as if someone else was trying to reassure the first person. Mab slipped her hand round Nessa's neck, nestling her fingers into Nessa's hair. She wanted to tell Nessa what the music sounded like to her, but it was enough to listen to it together. After the fast bit the music slowed down again, and this time it was the reassuring person who was in charge, and Mab felt herself sigh with relief, then her body relaxing and her mind floating away, as if it was being lulled like a little bird on the surface of the music.

The next thing Mab knew she was waking up and it was the morning. Con had promised to take them to the beach, she remembered, as she followed the sharp line of sunshine that was coming through the gap in the curtains and stretching itself out across the ceiling. She shut her eyes again for a moment and tried very hard to see her mother, lying in her hospital bed. *We're going to the seaside*, she told her. *I hope you don't mind that we're having a holiday while you're having your treatment.*

And probably she made it up, but she could almost persuade herself that her mother had heard her, and had smiled. *I'll pick up some shells for you*, Mab said. Her mother loved shells. When she'd been little, she'd told them once, she used to make necklaces out of them. Perhaps Con could show them how to do that, Mab thought. She could make a necklace and give it to her mother when she came home from the hospital.

Chapter Nine

March 2024

Mab was exhausted when she got home after her afternoon with Nessa. Going to Greenwich had been a classic Nessa idea, she thought: a way of putting her stamp – or at least *a* stamp – on the day. Making it memorable for reasons that weren't all to do with their father's death, so that when they looked back they would remember the river and the beautiful buildings as well as the confusing feelings his death had stirred up. Where, she wondered, had Nessa learned that trick? Perhaps it had started on that day before their mother's funeral, when they'd eaten birthday cake in bed. Perhaps that's what Nessa had been tuning into today, consciously or otherwise.

It hadn't been a bad idea, anyway, but it hadn't been the gentle amble along the river that Mab had imagined. She'd baulked at the Maritime Museum, but they'd visited the Royal Naval College and the Queen's House and the Observatory. It had felt rather like a supercharged school trip.

'I'm sorry if this has been a bit much,' Nessa had said as they parted, and Mab had demurred, of course.

'It's been fun,' she'd said. 'We haven't done anything like this for ages.'

She'd been pleased by Nessa's smile, and by how long she'd held Mab in a tight hug, but as she'd walked away Mab had felt strangely blurry, as though the different parts of her mind weren't quite joined up any more. There was the Mab who lived in Littlemore Road and had a job at Books on the Hill and had got used to not seeing her father, and the Mab who was being catapulted back into the past, or trying to stop that happening. And there were other things too – fragments of memory and emotion, like things falling out of an old scrapbook she hadn't looked at for years. Nessa had kept saying that you had to give these things time, that you couldn't rush the processing of grief, especially not complicated grief like theirs, and she was probably right, but Mab couldn't help feeling that there were things she needed to get to grips with. Things she needed a clear head to consider.

When she opened the front door at Littlemore Road she could hear music and voices coming from the kitchen. To her surprise, her spirits rose. She needed normal people tonight, she thought. The kind of normal that her housemates were.

'Hey,' she said, as she came down the passage to join them.

'Hey.' Three faces turned to acknowledge her. Two of them belonged to Charley and Aster, and another to someone Mab thought might be Charley's new boyfriend. Charley and Aster were doing separate bits of cooking on either side of the oven.

'How are you doing?' Charley asked.

'It's been a bit of a weird day, actually,' Mab said. 'My dad died.'

'Oh, Mab–'

Their reaction was stronger than Mab expected; she lifted her hands, shook her head. 'I hadn't seen him for years,' she said. 'He lived in New Zealand. He kind of ... ran away after my mum died, when I was nine.'

Saying it out loud like that made it sound more dramatic than Mab intended. More of a sob story.

'I'm really sorry,' Aster said. 'That sounds tough.' He looked at the pile of vegetables on his chopping board. 'Do you want some stir fry? I've got enough for two. I was going to take some for lunch tomorrow, but I don't have to.'

'Thanks, Aster.' Mab knew better than to make too much of this offer, because Aster was easily discombobulated by effusiveness, but she was touched. And hungry, she realised. 'That's very kind. I'd love some.'

She felt a bit shaky then, so she sat down on one of the chairs, next to the person who might be Charley's boyfriend, and without any of them saying anything Charley produced a glass and the boyfriend poured Mab some wine, and she lifted it in a token gesture of thanks, or perhaps a toast to her father. It wasn't nice wine, even by Mab's standards, but she was grateful for it. Grateful for people who weren't from her family.

Her housemates did lots of different things, and most of them did at least two. Mab just had the bookshop job, and Yvonne was in the civil service fast stream, which paid enough to cover her rent, but the others had to juggle. Charley was an actor who made most of their money doing online tutoring for rich kids around the world who wanted to come and study in the UK. Aster was doing a PhD in some bit of science Mab didn't understand, and boosted his grant money by doing lab work – which he said mostly meant washing up test tubes and cleaning machinery, but sounded more glamorous than doing the same thing in a bar.

Hamza did the most things of all, which explained why he was almost never at home. His grand plan was to make it big with his band, which rehearsed in someone's garage out in Beckenham, but the rest of the time he was a personal trainer, a boxing tutor and a Deliveroo driver. His parents were both doctors and were sure this was a phase Hamza would grow out of, but Hamza was the oldest person in the house, closer to Nessa's age than hers, so Mab rather doubted that he'd make it to medical school now. Also, she'd heard his band, and it was good. Hamza was her favourite housemate, actually, but that might be partly because the others had fairly straightforward relationships with their parents, especially Aster and Yvonne, and every time they talked about them it made Mab feel like an outlier.

'It's ready,' Aster said. 'Have you got a plate?'

'Mine are the pink ones in the cupboard,' Mab said. She made to get up, but Aster waved a hand at her and got a plate out himself.

The stir fry wasn't bad. Aster ate his portion very fast, but he waited for Mab to finish before collecting both their plates. Aster was the only person in the house who always washed up straight away, which might have been a spillover from his washing up in the lab, but he never said anything about the piles of crockery and pans the others left lying around.

It was only seven o'clock by the time she'd finished eating. Charley and their boyfriend had disappeared upstairs by then, and Mab knew Aster would do the same as soon as he'd put his things away. And who knew whether Yvonne or Hamza would be in this evening. Yvonne was spending more and more time out with her colleagues, or working late.

Mab was used to her own company, and was usually fine with it. But tonight, despite her tiredness, she felt slightly panicky about spending the rest of the evening alone. She didn't feel like watching anything or reading anything: her brain was too full already. A walk, then, said a brisk voice in her head. Over to the park, and then around it. She got her coat, and slipped out of the front door.

Chapter Ten

Mab saw Danny as soon as she turned the corner of the street on her way back from the park. He was sitting on the wall at the front of the house.

'How long have you been there?' she asked. 'Didn't anyone let you in?'

'Aster told me you'd gone for a walk,' he said, 'so I thought I'd wait out here. It's a nice evening.'

'But I might have been hours,' Mab said.

Danny grinned. 'I decided that wasn't likely.'

Mab stopped in front of him.

'How are you doing?' he asked. 'I'm guessing it's been a tough day.'

'I should have called you,' Mab said. 'Do you know...'

'You called the shop,' Danny said, 'so yes, I do know about your dad. I was going to call you this morning, actually, but I wasn't sure...' Mab sat down beside him, and he laced his arm around her shoulders. 'I'm really sorry,' he said. 'It must feel a bit strange.'

'Yeah.' Mab shut her eyes. She and Danny hadn't been together long enough to know how to manage occasions like this, but it felt good to sit with him, and to let him hold her. 'Can you stay tonight?' she asked.

'Sure.'

Tears were trickling down the space between her face and his neck now, a little salty rivulet of pain and bewilderment. Danny didn't move, and Mab was grateful for that, and for the street going on with its evening: people passing on foot and on scooters and in cars; lights flowing past them in the darkness that was never entirely dark in London. After a few minutes she said, 'Oh, Danny...' and he tightened his grip to show that he'd heard, and they went on sitting there until Mab started to notice the dampness of her bottom and the hardness of the wall.

'Are you hungry?' Danny asked, when she moved at last. 'Have you eaten?'

'Aster made me some stir fry,' Mab said. 'But there wasn't very much of it.'

'Takeaway?' Danny suggested.

Mab bit her lip. 'Aster might see. He might be offended.'

'Eat in, then? A pizza? We could share one if you like.'

'Yeah, pizza.' Mab smiled. There was a cheap place near the park; she'd walked past twenty minutes ago and looked in at all the people enjoying an ordinary, cheerful evening. 'Thank you, Danny. How did you know exactly what I needed?'

He shrugged, pleased. He looked so sweet when he was pleased, Mab thought. His face had a way of wrinkling up that made him look like a hamster. As they walked to the pizza place she reminded herself of the other good things about Danny, which was a nicer thing to think about than all the other stuff in her head. He didn't drink, which meant he didn't say things you weren't sure he meant or that he might regret. He liked his job, and he didn't agonise over it and think all the time about giving it up and doing something else, which was somehow reassuring. And he didn't think Mab was mad or high maintenance or needy or any of the other things men had said about her in the past. Sometimes Mab thought he might be too good to be true, and had to remind herself there were things about him that weren't perfect, but she didn't want to do that this evening.

'When did you last see your dad?' he asked, when they'd looked at the menu and plumped for an Americano because Mab felt the need for some meat.

'Years ago. I'd literally seen him once since he moved to New Zealand when I was nine. There was an exhibition of his work in London, and he came over for it even though it was the early stuff that he hated. The portraits. I was still at school – I must have been about fourteen, and we were at a boarding school where our aunt Hazel had got us some kind of special deal. But I came up to London for the weekend – we both did – and we went to the exhibition and stayed at Hazel's house, and we saw a bit of him.'

'What was that like?'

'Strange,' Mab said. 'Very strange. I was so excited about it: I thought it was a new beginning. I thought once he'd seen us again he'd want to stay in touch. And he could do those occasions pretty well, my dad. He was good at being the life and soul. No embarrassment about the years he'd been gone or anything. No over-compensating. He behaved as though this was a regular occurrence, him popping over to visit us. As though it wasn't at all surprising that we were five years older than when he'd last seen us. He seemed pleased that we both came to the private view, even though he was spectacularly rude about it to anyone who'd listen, and then we all went out for dinner, and he suggested we met for lunch the next day. Hazel's face was a picture, I remember, because she'd assumed he'd hardly take any notice of us. She'd imagined we'd be in tears by the end of the evening.'

Mab took a deep breath, and blew it out slowly, up over her

top lip. 'Hazel was right, of course, except that it took a bit longer for us to realise nothing had changed. Because he was too much of a coward to be honest about it.'

'I'm sorry,' Danny said.

'No, it's OK. It's years ago now. Half my life ago.' She shrugged. 'Anyway, that was the last time. Lunch somewhere posh, I remember, and he seemed genuinely sad that he was flying back to New Zealand that night. And perhaps he was. Perhaps he meant it when he said he'd see us next time he was over. I don't know if he ever came to England again, but maybe he didn't. So it wasn't really a broken promise, I suppose.'

'Just a broken moral commitment,' Danny said.

'That was pretty much sealed already,' Mab said. 'Even if he'd turned into a doting father at that point, we'd had the worst years by then. Being orphans, more or less, shuttled between our mad hippie granny and our strait-laced aunt. But we did better than his other children: he left them when they were two and four. Maybe even younger, actually. I don't know the exact chronology.'

She stopped. She'd talked more than she meant to already, but all of that had been fine. It hardly hurt, telling the story, and it was the kind of thing you ought to do on the day your father dies. A catharsis. But she didn't want to get on to Philip and Max. And she'd remembered, just as she got to the end, that Danny's dad was dead too, and his mum was an alcoholic, and he and his brothers had got by almost as much on their own as she and Nessa had. They had a grandmother who was in a wheelchair and constantly in and out of hospital, but who somehow made them all work hard at school and kept them out of any trouble that might threaten the fragile balance of their existence, but that was it. Nessa might think working in a bookshop was a cop-out, but for Danny it was a triumph. And he had his younger brothers to think about, too. One of them was still at school, the other struggling to find a job that might use his hard-won qualifications.

'I'm sorry,' she said. 'I've done nothing but talk.'

Danny lifted his hands, as if to absolve her. 'It's your night for talking,' he said. 'So are you going to New Zealand for the funeral, then? Is that where it'll be?'

'I don't know,' Mab said. 'I expect it will, but...' She bit her lip. 'It's so expensive. I don't have that sort of money.' She looked at Danny, at his pensive expression. 'Do you think I should? Borrow the money from somewhere?'

'What about your sister?' Danny asked. 'Or your aunt?'

'Maybe.' There was one piece of pizza left. Mab looked down at it, and Danny gestured that it was hers. It was cold now, but Mab liked cold pizza.

She and Nessa hadn't returned to the subject of their father's funeral while they'd wandered around Greenwich. Mab knew that had been a deliberate decision on Nessa's part, because it was the kind of thing she would normally have been on top of straight away, making plans and getting Mab on board with them. The vibe had definitely been a bit weird this afternoon, but Mab didn't want to think too much about that, so instead she told herself that it had been nice to spend time with Nessa. They didn't often do things like that. It was surprising, actually, how little they saw of each other, given that they lived in the same city and had always been close. Maybe that was just modern life, everyone being busy and mobile phones deceiving you into thinking you'd seen someone because you'd chatted on text.

When she'd eaten the last bit of pizza, she smiled at Danny, signalling satisfaction over their empty plates.

'How are your brothers?' she asked.

'Is that guilt or deviation?'

'Neither,' Mab said. 'Interest.'

'Liam's fine. Got exams soon, so he needs to keep his head down, but he should be OK. Aaron's got a job interview next week.'

'Where?' Mab asked.

'Teaching assistant. He'd be great at it, but he's not sure it's what he wants.'

'Wish him luck from me,' Mab said. She'd only met Danny's brothers once, on his birthday. Liam looked like a mini version of Danny, except not mini really because he was only an inch smaller, but it was Aaron who had Danny's charm.

'D'you want to talk more?' Danny asked, when the waiter had taken their plates away. 'Or do you want to go?'

'Let's go,' Mab said. 'I think I want to be in bed now. We can talk more then.'

But it only took about two minutes, once they were both under the covers, for Mab to fall fast asleep.

Chapter Eleven

Nessa found it almost impossible to concentrate on her
work the next day. Perhaps she shouldn't be surprised: it
was a major life event, losing a parent, even one you hadn't seen
for years. And yesterday afternoon had reminded her how
responsible she still felt for Mab, even though Mab was an adult
and had all the makings of an independent life, except for
earning quite enough money to live on. Mab seemed happy
enough sharing a house with four other people, and that was
fine at twenty-seven, but it wasn't something you could really go
on doing at thirty-seven or forty-seven. Not in Nessa's view,
anyway.

Nessa had understood early on what a lack of money did to
people. She'd understood the part it had played in her parents'
story, and she worried about what it might start doing to Mab,
quite soon. She was under no illusions that their father would
have left either of them anything, even if he'd had money to
leave. Granny Jenny's money was all going on the care home
she'd been in for five years already, and looked set to stay in for
at least another five, and Hazel – well, Hazel didn't have any
children and she was comfortably off, but she'd made it clear,

when Nessa had tried to talk to her about Mab a couple of years ago, that she wasn't going to support either of them any longer. Mab had a degree, and that was all Hazel had had when she'd started on the civil service career ladder. It was good for young people to learn to fend for themselves, she'd said. Which was probably true, but that only left Nessa to think about Mab's future, and she couldn't dismiss the responsibility as easily as Hazel.

Her computer screen had gone blank now because she hadn't touched the keyboard for several minutes; that jolted her out of her train of thought. She got the spreadsheets she'd been looking at back up, and stared at them blankly for a moment before shifting a column of figures into place with a flick of her mouse. Dammit, what was she doing fretting about Mab's finances? If anything was going to distract her from work it should be the more immediate concern of her father's death and what that might require of her. But for now she was going to banish that, too, and be the diligent employee she knew herself to be.

She'd expected to find some missed calls from Mab when she left work, or at least a text message or two, but there was nothing. Her commute home to Wanstead was straightforward: DLR to Stratford, then Central Line out east. But today it felt strangely arduous, and she felt irritated with Mab, for reasons she couldn't pin down. For not needing her big sister at this moment of crisis? Or for not realising that there were things they needed to talk about?

That was largely her fault, though, Nessa admitted to herself. Their father's funeral was pretty high on the list of things to talk about, and she'd shut down the discussion about it yesterday. She knew exactly why, too. The truth was that she didn't want to go to New Zealand. She'd looked at flights last night, and it wasn't as expensive as she'd thought. She could pay for them both if she needed to. But she didn't want to.

It turned out that she was angrier with her father than she'd ever admitted. She was absolutely furious with him, not just for abandoning them when they'd needed him desperately, but for all the years of blithe neglect since then, and now for dying before she'd had a chance to tell him what she thought. To hold him to account. She was in a boiling rage because Mab had wept for him yesterday, despite his catastrophic failings as a parent, and because so much that had gone wrong with their lives was his fault. How dare he die now? How dare he make the daughters he'd deserted two decades ago feel they ought to spend thousands of pounds flying round the world so that they could stand with his third wife, whom they'd never met, and mourn his passing?

She wouldn't let it happen. She'd tell Mab it was mad, and that their father wouldn't have cared one way or the other. Although that bit, she knew, was untrue. She was certain Roy would have been appalled by the idea of them not being at his funeral. And that, exactly that, was reason enough not to go.

Inga didn't live with her, but she had a set of keys, and Nessa wasn't surprised to find her in the flat when she got home.

'I thought you would like some company tonight,' she said. She had a bottle of wine open, and she poured a glass and gave it to Nessa, tilting her face for a kiss. 'And I've brought food to cook.'

'Thank you.'

Nessa put the wine down while she took off her jacket and hung up her keys. Having a girlfriend who was a nurturer was a new experience. In another life, she thought, Inga would have been a Swedish matron, baking cinnamon buns for her ten blonde children. It was nice to be looked after, but – strange. She wasn't sure yet whether she was getting to like it more or less as time went on. Whether she could absorb enough nurture to make up for the ten children. Which led her to wonder whether Inga wanted a baby: a question they hadn't discussed, and which certainly wasn't one for tonight.

'Are you OK?' Inga asked. 'Have you been OK today?'

'I've found it rather hard to concentrate,' Nessa said.

'I'm not surprised. It was such a shock. I've found it hard to concentrate myself today, and I never even met your father.'

'I hardly knew him either,' Nessa said. 'I last saw him when I was eighteen.'

Inga didn't reply, but Nessa knew what she was thinking. What she thought of absconding fathers. Would she approve of Nessa's anger, though? Sometimes Inga's reactions to things weren't what Nessa expected. Inga had a moral framework that had been carefully constructed through the generations of Lutherans she was descended from, rather than patched together by herself, like Nessa's.

'I've realised I'm very angry with him,' Nessa said, because if she didn't say it it would hang over the whole evening, and no amount of lovingly prepared pasta would banish it. 'I'm absolutely full of rage, and I don't know what to do about it.'

Inga put down the knife she was holding, as if to signal that Nessa had her full attention. 'I would say you should talk about it,' she said. 'I would say, maybe it's time you told me about this wounded childhood of yours.'

Chapter Twelve

When she was about seven, Mab had gone through a phase of being fascinated by people who died in strange ways. One of her friends had had a book about it, and they'd pored over it together, curled up in the friend's bedroom. Their favourites were an Austrian who tripped over his own beard, and a Russian who was hugged to death by a drunk bear.

The thing that had most struck Mab was that if you were famous for the way you died, you'd never know. You might have hoped all your life to be remembered for something, but it would never occur to you that it wouldn't be for any of the things you'd done when you were alive. Sometimes it had made her sad, that thought, but at other times it had seemed like a kind of comfort. However much of a nobody you were, there was always a chance you might make it on to the news in the end. And if it did happen, everyone who'd known you would have to say nice things about you, like a grand version of circle time in primary school. *Mab was always kind*, they'd say. *Mab was good at drawing.*

Later, after Max died, and her mother, she was horrified that she'd been so amused by people dying. For a while, whenever she found anything dead – even a fly – she felt a terrible pang of sorrow for its lost life, and wanted to bury it and mourn it. Granny Jenny indulged this fetish, but Aunt Hazel disapproved of its ghoulishness, and of Mab's lavish obsession with death. Probably, Mab thought now, this was one instance when the effect of one relative's reaction followed by another had been helpful. She'd been allowed to work through her feelings about mortality with the insect funerals, then encouraged to stop at more or less the moment when the rituals were becoming an unhealthy fixation.

Lying in bed beside Danny, Mab smiled to herself. Imagine telling Hazel that, she thought. Here's the one thing I'm grateful for, in the tug of war you fought over us for ten years – a decade that had included regular changes of school and home and domestic politics, as if she and Nessa had been the only citizens of a country that ricocheted between the most liberal of democracies and a kind of atheist theocracy whose mores startled Mab even now. Hazel had outlawed all sweets, except chocolate so dark that no child would eat it, along with a bizarre assortment of foods that she believed to be somehow morally corrupting: fruit yogurts, individually wrapped cheeses, baked beans which came with sausages in the tin. Mab had sometimes tried to come up with a rationale that linked them all, but she had never managed it. Then there had been the rules about their clothes, which were a good deal stricter than any school they'd ever attended, and when they should bathe, and when they could watch television (not often) – and worst of all, the hated piano lessons.

It was a shame, Mab thought now, watching Danny's face twitch with the fleeting emotions of his dream, that the piano lessons had been so awful. She still remembered with an acute and trembling pleasure the nights when she'd lain awake listening to Con playing the piano at Lowlands. Mab had had no idea back then what music it was she was playing, but occasionally, on Radio 3 or Classic FM, she would hear a piece she recognised instantly, which evoked the joy and anguish of that summer so precisely that she was sure it must have been one of Con's. Bach, mainly, she knew now. Had their own piano lessons been unbearable because the memory of Con's playing had been so poignant? Because they couldn't bear the idea of that mystical sound floating up the stairs being reduced to scales and finger exercises and the sarcasm of their teacher? Perhaps it had simply been the association with Hazel that had tainted them, but either way Mab wished she had persisted. It would be a lovely thing to be able to play Bach like Con.

Danny yawned and stretched.

'Morning, sleepyhead,' Mab said.

'How long have you been awake?' he asked. 'Did I take up too much room?'

'Not long,' Mab said. 'And no. Even in sleep you're the model of courtesy. You don't need to keep asking.'

Danny chuckled. Mab stroked his cheek, and then she climbed over him and out of bed.

'Getting up?' he asked.

'It's almost eight,' Mab said. 'I was going to make coffee.'

This was the second morning in a row that Danny had woken up in her bed, and Mab liked it. The day before they'd both had early shifts, and they'd done the classic co-worker romance thing of arriving at the bookshop separately, even though that was just a game, really, because Mab was pretty sure everyone knew they were seeing each other. But it had given the day a kind of sparkle, and she'd liked that too, and Danny coming home with her again and them having the evening together. Almost like old married people, she'd said, and Danny had smiled, and Mab had felt a flash of guilt that she could feel so happy when her father had just died, but she'd told herself it wasn't an accident – that Danny was being extra nice because of the circumstances.

This morning, though, the sparkle didn't feel quite the same. She was still happy to have Danny there, but the magic spell of making her forget about everything else wasn't working so well. She hadn't spoken to Nessa since the Greenwich afternoon, and she knew she ought to. The days until her father's funeral were passing: Mab didn't know when it was, but it couldn't be far off, and they still hadn't decided what to do. She felt a clutch in her stomach, exactly like that dream where you have to do an exam you've forgotten about and haven't done any work for.

So while the kettle was boiling for their coffee, she texted Nessa. Or rather, she started texting her and then deleted the words and called her instead. Nessa picked up straight away.

'Hello?'

'Hello,' Mab said. 'Are you on your way to work?'

'It's Saturday,' Nessa said. 'I don't work on Saturdays.'

'Oh.' Mab pulled a face. 'Did I wake you?'

'No, no.' There was a short pause. 'How are you?'

'I'm OK. Danny's here. We've both got to work today, but not until later.' Mab screwed up her face again, listening to herself. 'I'm sorry I haven't been in touch, Nessa.'

'I haven't either,' Nessa said. 'And I'm sorry too. I've been talking to Inga a bit. It's been helpful.'

Mab's heart did a huge jump. 'Talking about what?' she asked.

'Dad, mainly. And my anger with him.'

'Anger?'

'Aren't you angry too?' Nessa asked.

'As in angry he's died?'

'Well, sort of. I mean, that's what's brought it out.'

Mab nodded, even though Nessa couldn't see her. 'I'm glad you've talked to Inga.' She hesitated. The kettle had boiled, but she didn't want to bang around with cups and coffee jars while Nessa was on the phone. 'Are you feeling a bit better?' she asked.

'I wouldn't put it quite like that. I think there's a lot to talk about, actually.'

'For us to talk about, you mean?' Mab held her breath while she waited for Nessa to reply.

'Well, yes, I suppose so.' Another pause. 'The funeral, for instance.'

'That's why I was ringing, actually,' Mab said. 'We don't even know when it is. I'm worried they'll all wonder why we haven't asked.'

'Who will?' Nessa asked. 'You mean Ursula? Who cares about her?'

That was such an un-Nessa-like thing to say that Mab was silenced for a moment. 'Not just her,' she said. 'Con too. Maybe even...' Aunt Hazel, she'd been going to say, but Hazel definitely wouldn't care. And who else was there, except their father himself, looking down and wondering why his daughters were going about their lives as if nothing had happened?

'I do know when it is, actually,' Nessa said. 'I spoke to Con yesterday.'

'Oh.'

'I was going to ring you this morning. I wanted to think things through before I spoke to you. The funeral is next Saturday, in Wellington. A week today. Con said it's going to be very small and no one expects us to go, but if you want to, I'll pay for the flights. I'll come with you. If that's what you want to do.'

'Is Con going?' Mab asked.

'Yes.'

'And Philip?'

'I didn't ask.'

'OK,' Mab said. 'Why is it my choice, though?'

'Because I don't want to go.'

Mab bit her lip. 'Let's not, then.'

'Don't you want to think about it?' Nessa asked. 'I'm serious about paying for the flights. I don't want to sway you.'

'I don't know.' Mab sighed. This felt like a big decision to be making when she hadn't even had a cup of coffee yet. 'I sort of feel we ought to go. It's his funeral. It's...'

'He won't be there, Mab. We won't get to see him. And you know, I'm not sure he'd have come over if one of us had died.'

Her voice sounded brittle now. Beneath the surface layer of irritation, Mab could hear all the hours Nessa had spent weighing things up.

'No,' she said. 'You're right.'

'And it's not – the funeral will be an hour at most. A couple of hymns, maybe, and someone talking about him who won't know anything about us, or what he did to us. It's not like...' Nessa's voice petered out. Mab heard her sniffing. 'And Con said there'll definitely be something in England if we want there to be. A service or a gathering or whatever.'

It made Mab feel strange to know that Nessa had spoken to Con again. 'OK,' she said. 'You're right, there's no reason to go all that way. It's really nice of you to ask me, to say you'd pay for it, but it's stupid to feel we ought to be there.'

'Good.' Nessa sounded so relieved that Mab felt a sudden press of tears. 'Con suggested – she said she'd record it, if we wanted her to. Video, even.'

And suddenly Mab knew why these casual mentions of Con felt so odd. They hadn't seen Con for nearly twenty years, either – and she hadn't been in New Zealand; she'd been in Somerset all this time. At Lowlands, as far as Mab knew. So why hadn't she bothered with them? Why hadn't she ever got in touch? And why, now, was she chatting to

Nessa on the phone, offering to video their father's funeral for them?

Mab thought she knew the answers to some of these questions, but not all of them. And there were other questions, too. What had Con thought, all these years, about her and Nessa and everything else? And how had their father's death changed things?

Chapter Thirteen

July 2005

On the fourth night that Mab and Nessa were at Lowlands, there was a thunderstorm.

It had been the hottest day yet, and all day the air had felt heavy and hard to breathe. Even in shorts and T-shirts they'd been sweaty and uncomfortable. They'd wanted to go swimming again, but Philip was busy with his schoolwork and Max had been given some odd jobs on the farm, and Con didn't think it was safe for them to go on their own. She would have taken them herself, she said, but she had too much to do. She had some work that she did sometimes, shut up in her little office, and she had washing and ironing and all the other jobs their mother did, too. But Mab hadn't minded too much about the swimming, because she and Nessa had gone to see the kittens again.

They'd seemed a bit bigger and stronger to Mab, even though it had only been a few days since they last saw them, and Lucy had let her take one of them outside to look at the farmyard, but only if she kept it strictly in her arms all the time. Nessa had pretended she wasn't interested in the kittens, probably because she wanted Lucy to think she was more grown-up than Mab, but Mab hadn't cared. They'd stayed quite a long time, and Nessa had been patient and hadn't hurried her away, even though she'd been worried beforehand that Lucy would think they were a nuisance. Lucy was nice, Mab thought, although not as nice as Con, or even Philip. And after lunch they'd played in the garden of Con's house, climbing the apple trees and making a den in the big laurel bush that sprawled across one corner of the lawn and had a network of tunnels and tiny rooms hidden away inside its branches.

It had been a nice day. Even the boring bits of it, the times when they'd just lain in the long grass and listened to the bees and picked daisies, had had a sort of special colour that Mab couldn't describe. Waiting, or expecting. Getting closer to something, and at the same time knowing it might take a long time to arrive. She wasn't sure what the thing was: it could have been seeing their mother, or her getting better, but she didn't think it was that because she was trying not to think about Mummy. Nessa had said the days would go faster if they didn't, and Mab had worked out that if she stopped trying to picture her, then there were moments when it felt almost as if she was there, watching them, and that was a lovely feeling, warm and comforting like a secret she was keeping to herself.

By teatime, though, everyone was tired and grumpy, and the sky looked much darker than it should, and long before the thunder started properly there was a sort of rumbling, growling sound that you couldn't quite hear, as if it was coming from inside you.

'What have you kids been doing today?' Max asked, as he helped himself to seconds of macaroni cheese.

'We're not kids,' Nessa said. 'I'm only a year younger than you.'

Mab looked at her. It was the first time either of them had stood up to Max.

'Oh yeah?' Max's eyes rested on Nessa for a moment. Mab was worried he might say something really terrible now, but he didn't. Maybe he liked people standing up to him. 'What have you kid and you slightly older person been doing today?' he said, nodding his head at Mab and Nessa in turn.

'We've been climbing trees,' Mab said, because she thought he might be impressed by that. Everyone knew boys liked climbing trees.

'Huh.' Max scooped a large forkful of macaroni into his mouth and swallowed it almost without chewing.

'What about you, Max?' Con asked. 'What did Jim have in store for you?'

'Painting one of the little barns,' Max said. 'I don't know why you'd bother painting a barn – the cows won't care.'

'Maybe it helps to preserve the wood,' Con said.

Max shrugged. 'He gave me twenty quid, anyway.'

'Gosh.' Con looked surprised. 'That's a lot.'

'I was there for five hours,' Max said. 'It's less than the minimum wage.'

'Not for a sixteen-year-old,' Philip said. 'It's less for younger people.'

Max looked as though he might argue with him, but instead he sighed and rubbed his forehead with the back of his hand. 'It's bloody hot,' he said. 'Do you think there's going to be a storm?'

'It certainly feels like it.' Con looked around the table. 'Who wants a choc ice? I bought some more this morning. I found the mint ones you like, Philip.'

When they'd finished, Max went outside to see if there was any sign of the storm, while Mab and Nessa helped clear the table.

'Nothing yet,' he reported, banging the back door behind him. He seemed more cheerful than usual, Mab thought. He'd certainly eaten a lot – three helpings of macaroni and two choc ices – which did often make you feel better. 'Anyone fancy Monopoly?' he asked. 'Or is that too hard for Mab?'

Mab was startled: he'd never used her name before. 'I can play Monopoly,' she said. 'We've played it at home.'

But Con shook her head. 'Monopoly takes too long,' she said. 'What about something else? Cluedo? Or a card game?'

'Sorry,' Max said. 'Let's play Sorry.'

'Only four people can play, though,' said Philip, 'and there are five of us.'

'I'll sit out,' said Con. 'I've got my knitting.' Con was making a jumper for Max. Mab hadn't seen anyone knitting before, and she liked watching Con. Max had chosen the colours himself, green and blue stripes. Every evening there was a new stripe, and the jumper was a bit longer.

Mab and Nessa hadn't played Sorry before, but it wasn't hard to learn the rules. You had to move your men around the board, but you were told how many places to move by picking up cards, not rolling a dice. The fun of it was that sometimes you could send other people's men back to the start, or change places with them – and you could choose who to do it to, so you could deliberately set one particular person back if you wanted to. If that person was about to win, say, Max said, when he explained the game, but Mab could tell from the way he narrowed his eyes that that wasn't the only reason you might have.

At first the game was quite boring, with all four of them plodding along and no one either ahead or behind. Then Philip drew a number 11, which meant one of his men could swap places with someone else's, and he sent Max's leading piece back to near his start.

'That's stupid, Philip,' Max said. 'You'd have been better to choose Mab's piece, then you'd be nearly home.'

Philip smiled at him. 'It's my choice,' he said.

Max shook his head. 'It's patronising, giving them special treatment.'

'I'm not,' Philip said. 'I'm giving you special treatment. Don't be a bad loser.'

'I haven't lost yet,' Max said. 'I'll get my revenge.'

But Max didn't have much luck. He kept drawing cards that meant he could only move a couple of spaces, and once he couldn't move at all. Mab was the luckiest: she had a run of high number cards, and twice she got to swap her pieces with Nessa's and get her own men closer to her home zone. She and Philip were in the lead; they both had two pieces safely home and two to go. Then things changed: Max drew a *Sorry* card and sent one of Philip's men, which was two spaces from the end, back to the beginning, and for three goes in a row Philip had to move his third man backwards and couldn't restart the last one. Then Max drew a number 11 and swapped places with one of Mab's men, which was a silly thing to do because it didn't really help Max, but no one said anything.

'This game gets a bit boring after a while,' Philip said.

'Don't be a bad loser,' Max said, imitating Philip's voice. He kept trying to pretend that he didn't really care about the game, and that they were only playing to entertain Mab and Nessa, but it was obvious that he was enjoying himself now he was doing better. After a few more goes, it looked as though he was sure to win. He had two men home and two very close, and he was concentrating very hard on the board.

'Sorry!' Mab held up the card triumphantly. She tried to catch Nessa's eye, but Nessa was looking at Max. And in that instant something occurred to Mab; something she hadn't seen before. Nessa liked Max. Maybe even liked him as in fancying him, although that was stupid, Mab knew, because he was their half-brother. Nessa probably just wanted to be his friend –

wanted him to treat her differently from Mab, because she was closer to Max's age than to Mab's. All of this went through Mab's head very quickly – too quickly for her to work out everything it made her feel – but for a second she wondered if it made any difference to what she was going to do with the *Sorry* card. No: there was only one thing to do.

'Sorry, Max,' she said, and she scooped up his leading man and put it down again on his start square.

'Damn you,' Max said. Con looked up, but she didn't say anything. He said it quietly, and Mab didn't blame him for being annoyed. But he went on looking angry. Angrier than she'd expected. Philip was right, she thought: he wasn't a good sport.

And then on Nessa's next turn she got a *Sorry* card too. Mab was in the lead now, and she was sure Nessa would send one of her pieces home, but she didn't. Without even stopping to think about it she picked up Max's other man, the one that was still close to home.

'What the fuck?' Max said.

'Max!' Con put down her knitting.

'What the actual fuck?' Max said again. 'There's no fucking point playing if you don't understand the rules.'

'I do understand the rules,' Nessa said. She looked him straight in the eye, but Mab could see she was shaken by his reaction. She'd thought she was showing him that she was a match for him, that she dared to stand up to him, but it hadn't had the effect she'd expected. Mab felt a quiver in her belly. The swearing was still ringing in her ears: it was shocking and thrilling all at the same time. Their father swore sometimes, but she'd never heard another child say *fucking* before.

'No you don't,' Max said. 'You just want your baby sister to win.'

'I want you not to win,' Nessa said.

Just then there was an enormous crash of thunder, so loud that it shook the house, and they all jumped.

'Woah!' said Philip. 'That felt close. Did anyone see the lightning?'

The others were looking out of the window, wondering about the thunder, but Nessa didn't take her eyes off Max. 'I want you not to win,' she said again, more quietly.

Max stood up. 'I've had enough of this stupid game,' he said, and he tipped the board up and scattered all the pieces, all the cards, on the floor.

'For goodness' sake, Max,' Con said, and at the same time Philip said, 'Who's the baby now, then?' and Max threw the board at him.

'You can all fuck off,' he said, and he marched over to the door and threw it open, letting in a burst of wind and rain so violent that it could have been a furious ghost.

'I'm sorry, girls,' Con said, coming over to help them pick up the game pieces. 'Max has always been too competitive for his own good.'

'He's always been a monster,' Philip said, and his mother raised her eyebrows at him.

'Nessa is competitive too,' Mab said, wanting to explain things. She knew the row had been half Nessa's fault.

Con smiled. 'It would do Max good to have sisters,' she said.

'He's got me,' Philip said, 'but I know I'm not the sort of brother he'd really like.'

'He's very lucky to have you,' Con said.

'He doesn't think so,' Philip said. Con started to protest, but he said, 'It's all right, I know it's true.'

'I'd like to have you as a brother, Philip,' Mab said. 'You're so kind.'

She wasn't sure quite what she expected then, but probably a cuddle, or at least a smile. She wouldn't have minded Philip cuddling her, she thought, even though he was quite bony and might jab you without meaning to. But Philip hardly reacted at all. He blinked, and looked away from her, and then he got up.

'I think I'm going to go to bed,' he said. 'I expect the storm will keep us awake, but I'm going to try to get some sleep.'

'Maybe you could have a day off schoolwork tomorrow, Philip,' Con said. 'Maybe we could all do something together.'

Philip stopped in the doorway. 'Maybe,' he said. 'But I've got a lot to do still.'

'There's all of August to come,' his mother said. 'You need a holiday.' She smiled. 'I bet everyone else will be taking it easy. It's only a month since you finished your GCSEs.'

'I'll decide tomorrow,' Philip said. 'Good night, Mum. Good night, Mab and Nessa.'

When he'd gone, Con glanced towards the back door and sighed. 'Shall we get you two upstairs?' she asked. 'What about a bath before bed?'

Chapter Fourteen

The storm got noisier and noisier. The curtains in their bedroom were thin, and each flash of lightning lit up the room. Then the thunder would explode in the sky like a bomb going off, and the rumbling and grumbling afterwards sounded like rubble falling, Mab thought. Like great cities in the clouds being demolished. It was no wonder people used to be frightened of storms.

'Philip was right about it keeping us awake,' she whispered, but Nessa didn't reply. She was curled up with her back to Mab, lying very still. She might be asleep, but Mab thought she probably just didn't feel like talking. Sometimes Nessa liked to have time for her own thoughts, and Mab knew to keep quiet when she did.

Nessa was probably thinking about Max, Mab guessed. Mab was thinking about Max too. He had been unkindest to Philip, she thought, and angriest with Nessa, but the only reason he didn't bother being too horrid to Mab was because he thought she didn't matter. But if Nessa had stood up to him because she wanted Max to be her friend, it had had the opposite effect.

Mab would have liked to talk to Nessa about it all, but instead she lay quietly in her bed, looking at Nessa's back and playing the scene in her mind again. Reliving the little thrill when Max said *what the actual fuck*.

And then, through the window, she heard Max's voice, and Con's.

'Come in now, Max,' Con was saying. 'You're soaked.'

Mab noticed the noise of the rain then – a steady, soft battering against the walls and the windows and the ground outside.

'It doesn't matter,' Max said. 'It's not cold.'

'You might get struck by lightning,' Con said, but Max laughed. Perhaps she'd meant to make him laugh, Mab thought. Con knew how to deal with Max, she could tell.

'That's what the lightning rod's for on Jim's barn,' he said.

'A tree might fall on you,' Con said.

'The roof of the house might fall in.'

'True. At least we'd all die together then.'

'Who would you care more about?' Max asked. 'Me or those little girls?'

'That's a ridiculous question, Max. You're my son.'

'The bad son,' Max said.

'Nonsense.'

'The troublesome son.' Max made a sort of laughing sound. 'As opposed to the weirdo son.'

Mab held her breath. They didn't know she could hear them, she told herself. But even so she mustn't make the tiniest sound, because she really shouldn't be listening to this conversation.

'You're both my sons,' Con said. 'Just that. Mothers don't make those distinctions.'

'They say they don't.'

There was another sound from outside, a scuttering sound,

and Mab thought Max must have kicked something, a stone or a piece of wood.

'All that time you've spent with those girls,' he said.

'I thought that might be what this was about.'

'What *what* was about?' Max said. 'I don't care. It's just annoying for you. You've got enough to do. And they're not your responsibility.'

'I don't mind,' Con said. 'They're very sweet children.'

'They're a pain in the arse,' Max said. 'I can't stand them, especially the older one.'

'Don't say that,' Con said. 'Their mother's dying.'

'Is she? I thought she was getting better.'

'It doesn't sound very hopeful.'

There was another thunderclap just then, and when it rolled away the voices outside had stopped.

But Mab could still hear every word they'd said, as though the lightning had written them across the sky and left them hanging there. *Their mother's dying.* Con didn't know, Mab told herself fiercely. She was just saying it to make Max feel sorry for them. Daddy wouldn't have told them Mummy was going to get better if it wasn't true. But in that moment, she understood that Con was more likely to be telling the truth than Daddy. He wouldn't have wanted to tell them until it was certain, she thought. He wouldn't have wanted to tell them before he sent them off to stay with Con.

Nessa must have heard what Con said too, Mab thought then. She lay very very still, not even turning her head to see if Nessa had moved. Perhaps she could get out of her bed and climb in beside Nessa, and they could listen to the echo of Con's voice together, even if they couldn't talk about it. But she didn't move, and nor did Nessa. Perhaps she was asleep after all. Would it make those words go away if Nessa hadn't heard them? Was Nessa thinking the same thing, hoping Mab was asleep?

Mab's heart was beating so loudly and so fast that she was sure Nessa must be able to hear it, but even though she lay there for a long time with the throb of it in her ears, keeping up its rhythm against the noise of the wind and rain outside, Nessa still didn't move. Even when Mab turned her head, and gave a little sigh so that Nessa would know she was definitely awake, there was no response.

And then Mab shut her eyes. Nessa was right, she thought. It was better to pretend they hadn't heard. That way they could forget about it, and they could go back to believing everything would be all right. The shell necklace she'd made when they got back from the beach was in the drawer beside her bed. Behind her closed eyes, she made a picture of her mother wearing it, smiling at her, and for just a second the awful pain inside her faded a bit.

But then her eyes opened again sharply. If their mother was dying – if there was even a tiny chance she was – then Mab didn't want to be here another single day. She didn't want to miss any more of the days she could be with Mummy. In the morning, she would tell Con she wanted to go home. If Daddy still had his meetings, she and Nessa could cope on their own. Nessa was thirteen now, and she was very responsible.

Now she'd had this idea, Mab couldn't understand why she hadn't had it before. She shut her eyes again, and at last she felt her heart starting to slow down. And then, over the noise of the storm, she heard the sound of the piano. Con was back inside. Everything was peaceful. And despite the storm, still howling and crashing outside, Mab went to sleep.

Chapter Fifteen

M ab meant to wake up early the next morning so she could talk to Con as soon as possible about going home, but when she opened her eyes the little clock beside her bed told her it was almost ten o'clock. She didn't think she'd ever slept so late.

Her first thought was that she had let her mother down, and wasted several hours when they could have been making arrangements to leave – and her second was that Nessa wasn't in her bed. Nessa must have woken up and slipped out quietly so she didn't disturb her. Mab felt a bit panicky. She could talk to Con on her own, of course, but it would be much better if she and Nessa did it together, and that meant talking to Nessa first and getting her to agree to the plan.

Mab got out of bed and put her slippers on. It was still raining outside, although not as heavily as last night. She looked at yesterday's clothes, the yellow T-shirt and blue shorts that she'd felt too hot in, and decided to keep her pyjamas on for now.

Con was on her own in the kitchen when Mab came in. She

was sitting at the big table with a cup of coffee and a pile of papers.

'Good morning!' she said. 'I'm so glad you had a long sleep.'

'Where are the others?' Mab asked. 'Where's Nessa?'

'She's gone to the farm. Jean and Lucy were going into town, and they offered to take Nessa with them.'

Mab stared at her. Nessa couldn't have heard anything last night, then. She must have been asleep all the time. And that meant it was just Mab's secret, what Con had said. Mab's heart tumbled again, with fear and surprise and a bit of indignation. What was Nessa doing, going off without her? Had they even asked if Mab wanted to join in?

'Can I go too?' she asked.

Con tidied her papers into a pile. 'I'm afraid they've probably gone by now,' she said. 'But I thought you and I could spend some time together this morning. I thought you might like to learn to knit. You've watched me enough.'

Mab shook her head. 'No, thank you,' she said. She was worried that might be rude, but Con just nodded.

'OK,' she said. 'What about some painting? Or we could watch a film, perhaps. We've got lots of DVDs. We could make some popcorn.'

Mab didn't know you could make popcorn yourself, and the idea of watching a film with Con, in the middle of the day, was quite tempting. But it also sounded like the kind of thing grown-ups offered you when they knew you wanted something else. Could Con know what she wanted? Or was she just being extra nice today because of the row over the Sorry game?

'That's very kind of you,' Mab said, in her most determined voice, 'but what I want, actually, is to go home.'

Con didn't look surprised. 'I know it's been longer than you expected,' she said.

Mab was standing a few feet away from her, holding her

ground, but when Con stretched out her arm, Mab couldn't help going towards her. It felt very good to be hugged by Con. She was soft and warm and strong. For a few moments Mab let Con hold her, and then she pulled back.

'Daddy's meetings must be finished by now,' she said. 'And Mummy must be wanting to see us. I think we should go home.' The expression on Con's face made Mab waver for a moment, but she made herself carry on. 'You've been very kind to us, but we're not your responsibility.'

That was exactly what Max had said last night. The words had come into her head and out of her mouth without her thinking about them. Would Con notice? Would she realise that Mab must have heard them talking?

'Nessa can look after us both if Daddy's not home yet,' she said, in a rush to cover up those other words. 'And there's Karen next door, if we need anything. We'd be fine, we really would. And we could go and see Mummy.'

'I'm sure you'll be able to see Mummy soon,' Con said.

Mab's hands had screwed themselves up into tight fists. 'I want to see her today,' she insisted. And then something occurred to her. 'If Daddy can't come, couldn't you take us? Couldn't we just drive there today with you?'

There were tears in Con's eyes now, tears that looked alarmingly as though they might spill over any moment. Mab had always hated seeing grown-ups cry, and it was worse with Con, because Con didn't seem like a person who cried very often.

'I'm sorry,' Mab said. 'I'm sorry to be ungrateful.'

'No,' Con said. She shut her eyes for a moment, and when she opened them again her lashes were all wet. 'You have absolutely nothing to be sorry about, Mab. This whole situation...' Her voice trailed away. 'I'll ring your father.'

'Thank you,' Mab said.

'You're very welcome.' Con put her arms around her again, very gently this time. 'Listen to me, Mab. None of this is your fault, do you understand that?'

Mab nodded, but she really didn't know what Con meant. And then suddenly she did. She meant that Mummy *was* dying. Mummy was dying, and none of the grown-ups knew what to do.

Chapter Sixteen

March 2024

Some of the things fuelling Nessa's anger with her father were old wounds; things so well understood that she was surprised they still had the power to hurt her. But others were new, or at least newly understood, such as the passing off of her father's absence, during their stay at Lowlands that summer, with a story about important meetings. For a start, his career had been in the doldrums in 2005. It had been years since anyone in the art world had paid any attention to him, and if that had changed suddenly that summer, there would have been some evidence of it later. He would not, for instance, have gone to New Zealand and stayed there if there had been galleries in London taking an interest in his recent work. And for another thing, no meetings could have been important enough, pressing enough, to keep him away from his wife for so long when her devastating prognosis was just becoming clear.

Inga was being very patient about hearing all this. She needed to say things more than once, Nessa had found. She should probably say it all to a therapist, as Inga suggested, but she baulked at doing that. She told Inga it was too soon after her father's death, although she suspected Inga knew that wasn't the only reason. Meanwhile, their evenings had settled into a pattern which involved Nessa coming home to find Inga preparing supper, and Nessa talking while she cooked, and while they ate it, and while Inga washed up.

'You're certain he wasn't with your mother during that time?' Inga asked now.

'Yes,' Nessa said. 'When we got back from Lowlands and we all went to see her, it was clear he hadn't visited for a while. I remember registering that, and reminding myself he'd been in London. Having his meetings.'

She lifted her wine glass to her lips and emptied its contents – not quite half a glass – in one go. She was drinking too much, and she was sure Inga had noticed. But one thing you could say for the Swedes: they were less prudish about alcohol than Brits were. They didn't feel the need to comment.

'I almost can't bear to think about it,' Nessa said. 'About my mother in hospital, realising that she was dying, and my father just absenting himself. Sending us away so he could...'

'But she had her mother,' Inga said. 'And her sister.'

They had definitely covered this ground the night before, or the night before that, but Nessa had no recollection of it. Each time she came back to her material it felt fresh and raw.

'Fat lot of good Hazel would have been,' Nessa said. 'She's the last person I'd want by my sickbed. Not so much offering succour to the dying as pointing out where they'd gone wrong in life.' Sometimes she felt a bit guilty about bad-mouthing Hazel, who had, at least, stuck with the job of bringing them up. But Hazel, she reminded herself, had never had any qualms about bad-mouthing her dead sister when the mood took her.

'What about your grandmother?' Inga asked.

Nessa looked up at her. She looked lovely in an apron, Inga. You weren't supposed to think that – to objectify your partner as a traditional home-maker – but it was true. She had her hair pulled back in a clip and the sleeves of her blouse rolled up, and the apron had a classic Scandinavian pattern of stylised birds and leaves on it. She'd brought it from home: not just from Sweden, but from Clapham, so that she could cook for Nessa in her hour of need.

'Are you sure you don't mind me going on like this?' she asked. 'You must have heard it all already.'

'I haven't heard so much about your grandmother,' Inga said. She bit her lip and grinned. 'No, I don't mind. It's important to talk about it.'

Nessa nodded. 'I hope you know that I appreciate you, Inga. Everything about you.'

'I do.' Inga smiled.

There was a tiny quiver of contrariness, then, inside Nessa's head, but she scolded it away. She wasn't going to do that this time – wasn't going to turn aside just as Inga began to take things for granted. And not just because she needed Inga to play therapist-cook for her: because Inga was worth more than that.

She reached for the wine bottle and poured herself another glass. 'Do you need more?' she asked, but Inga indicated her own glass, which was still two-thirds full. 'I'll slow down,' Nessa said. 'I've had more than my share.'

'Not for my sake. There's more in the fridge.' Inga waited a moment. 'Your grandmother. Tell me about her.'

There were other people she needed more badly to exorcise, Nessa thought, but it would do no harm to stop thinking about her father for a bit. God, she was relieved that Mab hadn't insisted on going to New Zealand. She hoped Mab wouldn't regret it later; wouldn't resent being steered away from it.

'Granny Jenny was a dyed-in-the-wool hippie,' she said. 'She lived in a commune in Devon. She once took us to see the place where it used to be. It had been turned into holiday lets by then. It was an old farm, nothing special, but Granny talked about it as though it was paradise.'

'I expect it was more the people than the place.'

'Yes,' Nessa said. 'Of course. All her friends. All her lovers. I asked her once whether Mum and Hazel had the same father, and she laughed. I didn't think it was such a stupid question: I couldn't see any similarities between them at all. But Granny Jenny insisted they did. He was called Bert, of all things. She was never married to him, of course. It was the late sixties, flower power and psychedelics. After a while he went off somewhere else, and Jenny stayed, and the children, everyone's children, all grew up together.'

'It sounds quite attractive,' Inga said. 'Sharing everything.'

Nessa pulled a face. 'Not my scene at all. Hazel and I agreed on that, at least. She ran away when she was sixteen. Ran away to boarding school, of all things. The same one she sent us to, years later. She'd managed to organise herself a full scholarship, and she never looked back. A-levels, university, the civil service.'

'Repatriated into the establishment,' Inga said.

'Exactly.' Nessa grinned. 'Touché.'

'But your mother stayed?'

'She stayed longer, yes. And then she managed to get herself into art school in London. She lived in a squat run by someone Granny knew. And she met my dad, God help her.'

Nessa paused. She lifted her wine glass again, then thought better of it. Whatever Inga was making smelled delicious, and she wanted to be able to appreciate it. Pea soup, apparently, and there was some meat browning in a pan too. But she'd got back to where she started, and she couldn't resist scratching the itch now.

'Granny Jenny tried to talk to me about my father sometimes,' she said. 'She was – well, she'd embraced the idea that you couldn't possess people. She tried to explain that to me. He was a man who resisted being tied down, she said. An artist; a free spirit. But to go off with some floozy when Mummy was dying...' Nessa despised that word; despised the idea of denigrating women with language like that. The thrill it gave her to use it came with a bite. 'Perhaps it was Ursula,' she said. 'I don't know when he met her, but I think it was in England. I think they went to New Zealand together.'

She'd seen a picture of Ursula once. When had that been? In a birthday card from her father, perhaps? Him and Ursula together on the beach. She looked nothing like a floozy. She was a rather severe-looking German – not unlike a taller version of Angela Merkel, Nessa thought now. She could hardly blame Ursula for marrying her father after her mother had died, but she hated the idea that she'd taken up with him before that. But was it worse if he'd merely been having a fling, then, with someone who meant nothing? *He found it all very difficult,* Granny Jenny had said. *He was frightened of death.* Well, it had come for him now, Nessa thought. Even if he'd got away with an easy exit.

Chapter Seventeen

Nessa had gone quiet again after the phone call on Saturday morning. But she had too, Mab admitted. Neither of them had been in touch with the other. Checking in every day or so would be the normal thing to do, but they often seemed not to do the normal thing, she and Nessa. And perhaps there wasn't that much to talk about, now they'd decided about the funeral. Or rather, they were doing their talking to other people: Mab had Danny, and Nessa had Inga. Which was fine, except that Mab would have liked to know what Nessa was saying. She'd have liked Nessa to want to talk to her. There were things left hanging; left turning and turning in her mind.

The odd thing about not going to New Zealand, she thought, as she walked back from the station on the fifth or sixth evening after their father's death, was that it meant life just carried on as if nothing had happened. Mab understood Nessa's reasoning about the funeral, but part of her was sorry she'd agreed with her, because it wasn't really a thing you could apply reason to. It made it feel as if their father was no different from any other man who'd died on the other side of the world. And even if he hadn't functioned as their father for two decades, saying goodbye to him meant something, surely. It gave you closure. And there was nothing like flying 12,000 miles to mark an occasion.

It was no good dwelling on it, though, because it started to make her feel resentful of Nessa – suspicious, even – and that wasn't fair. Except that maybe it was. Maybe it was time to admit that it was.

Oh God, Mab thought. She'd fought for years to stop herself picking at this scab, but there it was, as red and raw as ever. The scab that covered an impossible fact, an inconceivable idea: a memory it suddenly seemed impossible to ignore any longer.

But she must, Mab told herself. There was nothing to be done about it; nothing to be gained from thinking about it. She walked the last hundred yards to her front door slowly and deliberately, imagining the troubles and pleasures of the people she passed and pushing her own as far out of sight as she could. The old man walking with two sticks, and the mother marshalling three children and a buggy along the pavement: what sad stories did their lives contain?

Danny wasn't supposed to be coming round this evening, but as soon as Mab was inside the house she was overtaken by a feeling of panic. It was partly because of the train of thought that had pursued her home, but it was also, she admitted, a pattern that was becoming familiar. Bereavement had made her incapable of being on her own: it had made her hungry, and sometimes weirdly dizzy and nauseous, but mainly it had made her crave other people's company. She couldn't think how she used to spend her evenings, even last week. Listen, she said to herself, as she climbed the stairs to her bedroom: how about having a bath, and then eating Pot Noodles and streaming a film. How would that be?

But her attempt at consoling herself backfired. Suddenly, there was a memory she hadn't thought of for years: Con, suggesting they watch a film together on that rainy day when Mab had first understood that her mother wasn't going to get better. *We could make some popcorn,* Con had said.

They *had* watched a film that day, she and Con. Con had rung her father and made him promise to come to Lowlands that evening, and then the two of them had watched *The Lion King*, sitting on the sofa in the playroom. Mab could remember the texture of the sofa: the fat ridges of the corduroy, and the exact shade of green. She could remember the rain against the window, not letting up. Nessa had gone out with the family from the farm that day. With Lucy and her mother.

Mab stood very still outside her bedroom door. The house was silent: everyone was either out or in their own rooms. It seemed to her, just then, a strange way to live, among people you hardly knew. People you hardly saw, most days. She most likely wouldn't see anyone all evening, and she couldn't bear that thought, even though she knew it was ridiculous not to be more resilient, and dangerous to let herself get too dependent on Danny. She shouldn't get into the habit of spending every evening with him, she told herself, just because her father had died, when she didn't really know how he felt about her, or she about him.

She took a deep breath, and counted slowly to ten. And then she pulled out her mobile and called Danny.

'I'm coming,' he said, before she even realised he'd picked up.

'So she was your father's first wife?' Danny said. 'She was the one he left for your mother?'

They'd come back to the pizza place, because Mab was hungry and there was no food at home. Because it sort of felt like their place now. Mab wasn't going to tell Danny everything

– she definitely wasn't going to do that – but she'd found herself wanting to tell him about Con.

'Yes.'

'And she took you and Nessa in that summer?'

'She was a nice person,' Mab said. 'And she and my father – they were friends, sort of.'

'OK.' Danny grinned. 'You win. Weirder family than mine. So your mum was in hospital, and your dad took you to stay with his ex-wife.'

'We thought Mummy was getting better,' Mab said, 'but one night I heard Con telling my half-brother Max that she was dying. Con thought we were asleep, but...'

'Hey.'

Danny took her hands and held them tight, because Mab had started crying again. And it was so hard, so hard, to distinguish the Mab who'd lain in bed that stormy night, who'd wanted her mother so badly and known that she was going to lose her, from the one who'd lived through the last week in a sort of trance, and who wasn't going to her father's funeral even though he had come to Lowlands that evening, just as he'd promised. It was hard to distinguish the two Mabs because they were the same. Because the child Mab, who was going to be nine very soon, was still there inside, frightened by the things she knew.

'And then what happened?' Danny asked.

Mab took a deep breath. 'The next morning, after the storm, I told Con I wanted to go home so I could see my mum, and she rang my dad. And he came, that evening. But he made everything worse, not better.'

Danny nodded, as though he understood more than he possibly could.

'And after that,' Mab said, 'something terrible happened. Something really shocking. And everything – nothing...' She swallowed. She tried to stop herself, to make herself think before she said any more, but she couldn't. 'Max died. He fell off a ledge in the barn, at the farm next door. It was a place he used to go – a place to sit, a bit like a tree house but with no railing or anything. It used to have some purpose, the ledge, and there were footholds in the wall, so it wasn't too hard to get up there. But he – that day... And I found him. I went into the barn and I saw him lying there.'

'Oh, Mab.' Danny leaned across the table. 'I'm so sorry. How awful.'

'It was.' Mab brushed at the tears on her face. She felt very strange now: it was as if there was a third Mab, a reckless one, trying to tell the other two what to do. She wasn't going to tell Danny anything else, she reminded it. She really wasn't. But she'd got to the edge of the precipice now, and there was a dreadful temptation to jump off. To let herself go – let all of it go – and see where she landed. Danny was looking at her, a great gentleness in his face.

'I don't know what to do, Danny,' she said.

'About what?'

Mab shook her head.

Danny did a little sniff which was half a chuckle, half a gesture of sympathy.

'I can't help you unless I know what it is,' he said. 'Why don't you tell me?'

When Mab had finished, Danny didn't say anything for a while, just sat there and shook his head very slowly.

'That's quite a thing to have carried with you,' he said eventually.

Mab nodded.

'You must have... I can't quite get my head around it, to be honest. Have you talked to anyone else about it?'

'No,' Mab said. 'You're the first person.' She smiled at him uncertainly, thinking that it felt like too much to have landed him with. And trying, also, to get used to the idea that it wasn't something that lived inside her head any more. That it was something that could be talked about. 'We saw a counsellor after my mother died, but I didn't ... this didn't feel like the kind of thing I could tell her.'

Danny raised his eyebrows. 'I really can't imagine what it must have been like to have something like that preying on your mind all the time.'

'I've done a pretty good job of not thinking about it,' Mab said. 'I couldn't, to start with. And not just to start with, even. There's never been a moment when I could. I had to push it away, because life wouldn't have worked otherwise.'

'But you're sure about it? About what you saw, and...?'

Mab hesitated. Danny was right: however hard she'd tried to keep them out of sight, the events of that day had been playing on repeat at the back of her mind all these years. And when things were constantly circling in your head they could get distorted, she knew that. Especially things that had happened when you were eight, in the middle of other terrible things. Speaking the words aloud had made them seem fanciful and far-fetched.

But as she sat there, looking at Danny, she felt the mist in her mind settle, the swirl of doubt and fear and disbelief, and she knew that what she'd told him was the truth.

'I'm sure,' she said.

Danny breathed in sharply and then let the breath out again slowly, as though he was making time to think.

'I shouldn't have told you,' Mab said. Her heart was beating fast now, the landscape shifting. She'd lose him, she thought.

She should have listened to her cautious self and held back. She'd jeopardised her future by letting the past back in, and it wasn't worth it. It wasn't worth losing anything else because of what had happened that summer.

'I'm sorry,' she said. 'You don't have to say anything. We don't have to talk about it any more. Please, let's just forget it.'

'It's not really the kind of thing you can just forget,' Danny said.

'But it's not fair to drag you into it.' Mab kept her voice as even and as light as she could manage. 'You've got Liam and Aaron and your mum and your granny. You don't need my mess as well.'

Danny shook his head. 'That's not how it works, Mab. You don't just pick and choose which bits of people's lives you're going to deal with and which you're not. Not when you love someone.'

Mab stared at him. Her mouth opened, but it took a while for the words to follow. 'Do you?' she said. 'Love me?'

'Sounds like it.' Danny grinned now, his lovely grin that was like the sun suddenly coming in through a window. 'You're supposed to say something back,' he said.

Mab shook her head wonderingly. Hadn't she tried to tell herself, earlier this evening, that she didn't know how she felt about him? What an idiot she was. 'Of course I love you,' she said. 'I did even before you knew who I was.'

'Oh, I knew,' Danny said. 'I knew you were way out of my league.'

'Well, you know better now.'

Mab leaned back against the wall, looking at him as he laughed at her, and looked at her, and pursed his lips to stop himself smiling for a moment. Life, she thought. Life was so strange. None of that other stuff had changed, but – it was as if she had a raft under her now to help her across those troubled waters. For an improbably long time neither of them said anything, just held each other's hands and let the delicious pleasure of the moment filter through them. And then at last Mab squeezed his hand.

'Thank you,' she said.

'For what?'

'For everything. Saying those things. Listening to me. Being so nice.'

'Well, what can I say? I'm a nice guy.'

Mab smiled again – and then she sighed. She didn't want to spoil things, didn't want to go back to thinking about the past, but that was how they'd got here, after all. With Danny saying *you don't just pick and choose which bits of people's lives you're going to deal with.*

'Oh Danny,' she said, 'what should I do?'

'What do you want to do?' he asked.

'I don't know.' The nine-year-old Mab was shrinking down inside her again now, curling up in fear. 'I don't want to do anything, but I can't – I'm not sure I can go on for the rest of my life with this inside me. Not being sure what it means. Always wondering whether I've put two and two together and made five.'

'Is there anyone you could talk to?' Danny asked. 'Anyone who could help you work out whether – whether it means what you think it means?'

'But if I talk to people about it, I can't shut it away again. There might be – there could be consequences.'

'It was a long time ago,' Danny said, 'and there won't be any actual proof. What you saw; what you think happened. It's circumstantial at best.'

'But if it's true...' Mab fixed her eyes on him. 'If it's true and it all comes out – don't you understand what that would mean?'

Danny smiled. 'But you've told me now, right? They'd have to kill me too.'

'Don't,' Mab said. 'Don't make a joke of it.'

'I'm sorry.' Danny stroked her hand. 'That was stupid. It's what I do, making light of stuff. Coping mechanism.'

'It's OK. It's just – I feel like a dog with an itch, going round and round in circles because I can't reach it. Can't think of the right answer. I can't ignore it now, but once I say something...' She shook her head. 'But I'm thinking ... maybe it's enough that I've told you. Maybe that'll make a difference, being able to talk about it.'

There was a silence. Mab watched Danny's face; watched him putting words together. 'What I think,' he said at last, 'is that you should talk to your stepmother.'

'Con?'

'Yeah. She was there, right? She was in the thick of it.'

'But I haven't spoken to Con for twenty years,' Mab said, 'except when she called to tell me my dad had died. Although...'

She hesitated. This was one of the things that had been niggling at her. One of the pieces demanding to be put together.

'I've been wondering,' she said, 'why Con never saw us again. I mean, apart from the obvious reason. Apart from Max dying.' She hesitated. 'She was so kind to us. I always thought – I always wished she'd taken me and Nessa in, to tell the truth, and brought us up at Lowlands. I hoped we'd go for holidays, at least. But if she knew: if she suspected what I'd seen... That might be a reason to keep us away, mightn't it?'

'It could be,' Danny said. 'If she wasn't sure, and she decided not to say anything, but she...'

'But in that case, I can't just barge in and start asking questions,' Mab said. 'Not after all this time.'

Danny made his frowning face again; his thinking face. 'Isn't there – you said there might be a memorial service, right?

You could start by asking about that, maybe. Use that as a way in.'

'I'm not sure,' Mab said. 'I'm really not sure if it's the right thing to do.'

But she knew it was. It was the only thing to do. And Danny knew it too, because he didn't say anything else, just looked at her and waited.

'OK,' Mab said. 'OK, you're right.' She touched her phone to check the time. 'It's too late to ring now, though.' She frowned. 'Is it Tuesday?'

'Yeah.'

'The funeral's on Saturday. She might have gone to New Zealand by now.'

Danny shrugged. 'I expect she'll have data,' he said. 'Or wifi.'

'I don't have her mobile number,' Mab said. 'Just the one she rang me from the day my dad died. The landline.'

'So try that then.' He smiled at her, and for a moment all Mab could think about was him saying, *when you love someone.* She mustn't screw this up, she thought. She mustn't let all her mess spoil things.

'Ask her if she'll buy some flowers for the funeral for you,' Danny said. 'How's that for an idea?'

'Brilliant.' She wouldn't have thought of sending flowers, but of course that's what she should do. A wreath with a card on it. *With love from Mab.*

'OK then.' Danny yawned. 'Time to go?' he asked.

'Time to go,' Mab agreed.

Chapter Eighteen

Philip was coming to the funeral. Con hadn't counted on that: Philip didn't like travelling, and he had no more reason to mourn Roy than any other man whose father had left when he was four. But duty was something Philip understood, and it was his duty to his mother, to her, that he was thinking of now. Ever since that evening at the King's Head he had been solicitous and attentive.

He'd insisted on making all the arrangements for the trip, too: booking the flights and an Airbnb and hiring a car. If Con had gone on her own she would probably have stayed with Ursula, but she was glad not to be doing that, despite the extra expense. She was, altogether, more delighted than she could admit that Philip would be with her. In the absurd game of being married to Roy – being formerly married to Roy – having a son to bring to his funeral felt like a trump card. That was an unworthy thought, a frivolous thought, but...

Sorry, she thought suddenly, as she flicked her indicator to overtake a people carrier travelling at sightseeing speed along a straight stretch of road. Hadn't the children played Sorry that summer? And Max had lost his temper, predictably enough.

Well, it was Roy who'd been *Sorried* now, removed from the board for good, and there was really no reason on earth for Con to see Ursula as the opposition, but you never knew when a trump card might be helpful. There was something about Roy, despite – or perhaps because of – his resolute rejection of resentment or bad blood, that put you on your mettle. Ursula had kept hold of Roy until the end. The funeral was happening in a church near Ursula's house, and she was organising it, but Ursula had no children. Philip would be the only one of Roy's children at the funeral; possibly the only blood relative, unless Ursula had dug up some long-lost cousins.

Con passed a 30 sign and slowed down. She was on her way to B&Q this afternoon. You never knew how death would affect you, she thought. When Max died she had cleaned the house, over and over again, for weeks: scrubbed every corner, as though there might be some truth hidden beneath the recalcitrant cobwebs. This time it was DIY. Since Roy's death, she'd kept noticing things in the house that didn't work. She'd replaced all the spent lightbulbs with LEDs, changed the loose knobs on the kitchen cupboards, rehung the curtains that sagged down from broken hooks. This was her third trip to B&Q. Stain remover, picture hooks, a new hinge for the garden gate. She flicked on her indicator again and turned into the industrial park, following the signs for PC World and Carpetright.

When she thought about moral issues, Con tried to couch them in the abstract. *If you were a person who... If you found yourself knowing...* She was no wiser than the next person, but she felt wiser when she was advising an imaginary other rather than grappling with her own choices.

If you found yourself protecting a child, say. A child who might have done a terrible thing which no one knew about;

which no one would find out about unless you said something. Not an evil child: not the kind who had killed James Bulger or Brianna Ghey – although even then you were perhaps on sticky ground with the notion of evil. No, a child who probably hadn't meant to do what they'd done, except perhaps in the minuscule fragment of time in which they'd done it, and possibly not even then. Who might just have been there and done nothing to help, or even been unable to do anything, which was a different thing again. You didn't know, because you hadn't asked them. You hadn't let them know that you knew – suspected – what had happened. Because if you had ever spoken to them about it, that would have put things on a different footing, and you might not have been able to stop the ball rolling out of your control after that.

But what you hadn't reckoned with, when you'd decided not to say anything, not to do anything, was that the tiny fragment of time in which this terrible thing had happened, and the not much longer fragment of time in which you'd chosen your course, would expand and expand until they filled your whole life. That they would change everything that happened afterwards: would change who you were, even. That what you could do with the rest of your life would be squeezed and squeezed until there was almost nothing left.

What difference did it make? you'd asked yourself at the time. What good could it do to pursue the whole truth? Things happened sometimes that shouldn't have done, and if they couldn't be undone, perhaps the best thing was to accept the obvious, blameless explanation: the one everyone else accepted. There were lives still to be lived, and if one life had been lost already, why choose to ruin another? To ruin more than one other life, in fact, including your own? But the thing was – the thing was that life didn't work like that. Truth mattered, it turned out. Secrets corroded. Uncertainty corroded even more. You knew that now.

If it had just been your own life that was affected that would have been one thing. That would have been you accepting the burden of guilt, or whatever this was, in return for protecting the child. Securing their future. But you honestly had no idea if that was how it was. You had no idea at all whether it weighed, still, on the mind of the child, who wasn't a child any more. Whether they ever thought about it at all.

Philip was home already when Con got back. He'd taken to leaving work early: he'd accrued so much holiday, he'd told her, that he'd never be able to take it all, so it suited everyone if he reduced his hours for the time being. Con was glad he hadn't decided to take this week off completely, but she liked him coming home at four o'clock rather than six. He'd been helping with the DIY – the things she couldn't reach, or which needed more than two hands.

He must have been listening out for her car, because he opened the front door before she got there.

'They've upgraded us to premium economy,' he said.

'Who have?'

'The airline.' He beamed. 'I rang them up and told them we were going to my father's funeral, and they upgraded us. They said if the flight's not full they'll move us into business class when we check in.'

'Well done,' Con said. 'That'll be nice.'

'It will,' Philip said. 'The seats are wider in premium, and you have more leg room. And the food's better too. On a flight that long it'll make a big difference.'

Con smiled. He might be quoting the British Airways website, she thought, but you couldn't be sure because that was exactly how Philip talked most of the time. He seemed to be looking forward to the trip, though, and Con hadn't expected that. Perhaps, bizarrely, it would do them both good. Getting away from Lowlands for a bit, and signing off on the unfinished business that was Roy Fothergill: yes, she could see how that might be a good thing.

She patted Philip on the shoulder, and hung up her coat, and he picked up the B&Q bags and preceded her into the kitchen. As Con passed the hall table she noticed the light on the answerphone flashing. Ursula, she thought, checking on their plans for the nth time. She picked up the handset and pressed the replay button, and a familiar voice emerged.

'Hello Con, it's Mab. I hope you don't mind me ringing. I just wanted to talk to you about the funeral. About you getting some flowers for me, perhaps.' There was a short pause. 'I don't have your mobile number, and I think you might have gone already – to New Zealand, I mean – in which case never mind. But otherwise, would you call me back?'

Chapter Nineteen

'It's Con,' Mab said. She and Danny were standing behind the till at the back of the shop, discussing an event next week, so when her phone buzzed she held it up for him to see.

'Take it in the office,' he said. 'Go on, it's fine.'

Mab wasn't sure whether he meant that it was fine for her to use the office – a grand name for a glassed-in cubbyhole – or that she'd be fine talking to Con, but she went, sliding her finger across the screen to answer the call.

'Hello, Con.'

'Mab.' There was a tiny pause. 'Is this a good time?'

'Yes,' Mab said. 'I'm at work, but if you can hold on two seconds... OK. Sorry. Hello. Thank you for calling back.'

'Not at all.'

There was something in Con's voice that made Mab wonder whether she'd been expecting Mab to call sooner. Whether, perhaps, Mab could have called any time in the last nineteen years and Con would have been happy to hear from her. But that was a stupid thing to think, because for most of those years Con had been the grown-up and Mab had been the child. And... She stopped herself.

'I just wanted to ask – I'd like to send some flowers for the funeral. A wreath. But I thought it might be easier for you to buy them locally, if you're there in time.'

'Of course,' Con said. 'We're not arriving until Friday, but perhaps I could ask Ursula to order them, if you wouldn't mind that.'

'No, of course,' Mab said. 'I could ask Ursula myself if you... Or actually, you know, I can google florists in Wellington, can't I? How stupid of me. It just seems such a long way away.'

'I'll do it,' Con said. 'I haven't organised anything myself, in fact, so thank you for reminding me.'

'Are you sure? I don't want to put you to extra trouble.'

'You're not. One phone call, two wreaths. Or would Nessa want a separate one?'

'I don't know. I haven't talked to Nessa about it.'

If Con thought that was odd, she didn't say so. 'One wreath from you and Nessa, then, unless you let me know otherwise. Any preference for flowers?'

Mab thought for a moment. Should it be her preference, or her father's? How could she possibly know what flowers he liked? And then something came into her head: that painting, that portrait of Con, with the lilies. Weren't lilies funeral flowers? 'Perhaps lilies,' she said. 'Not white lilies though – maybe those pink ones, you know, with the black spots?'

There was a silence, then, and it felt suddenly as though Mab's insides had dissolved. Had Con guessed that Mab had thought of the picture? If she had, it was the first time either of them had referred to the past, and that felt...

But when Con spoke again, she sounded exactly as she had before. 'Pink lilies,' she said. 'Fine. I'll ask them.'

'Let me know what it costs,' Mab said.

'Don't worry about that.'

'Please do,' Mab insisted. 'Otherwise they won't really be from me. From us.'

'OK. I won't spend too much.'

'I'll leave that to you,' Mab said. 'I don't have any idea what flowers cost. But – we're not coming to New Zealand. I assume you know that? So the least we can do...'

There was a tiny sob then. She did her best to stifle it, but she knew Con had heard.

'Dear Mab,' Con said, 'are you all right?'

And suddenly there she was, the Con who had sat on their bed at night, who had drawn Mab into her arms on the sofa while they watched *The Lion King*. Whose voice and presence and certainty had seemed to offer all the comfort Mab might ever need.

Mab could hardly speak, but she needed to, or Con might ring off. And she might never get up the courage to call her again.

'No,' she said. 'Not really.'

'I'm so sorry. I should have...' There was a longer silence; so long that Mab wondered if the call had failed. But then Con spoke again. 'Listen, Mab, when I'm back from New Zealand, why don't you come and see me? Would you like that?'

'Yes,' Mab said. 'Thank you.' She hesitated. 'Nessa said – we were wondering if there might be something in England for Dad. A memorial service or something. Perhaps we could talk about that.'

'Of course.' After another pause, Con said, 'Are you sure about not coming to the funeral, Mab? It's not too late, if you want to be there. You could probably get on the same flight as me and Philip.'

'No,' Mab said, even though she wasn't sure at all. 'It's – well, it's–' If she said it was too expensive Con might think she was asking her to pay for the ticket. Might think that was a shameful reason to miss your father's funeral. She bit her lip. 'Nessa and I talked about it,' she said, 'and we made a decision. But if we can do something here...'

'We certainly can.'

'I'd better go,' Mab said. 'I'm at work, and I ought to – but thank you. For organising the flowers, I mean.'

'You're very welcome,' Con said.

After she'd ended the call, Mab didn't move straight away. She could see most of the shop from here: the displays she'd reorganised that morning; the scattering of customers browsing the shelves; Danny talking to someone at the till. The office wasn't soundproof, but the voices and footsteps and the clink of china from the café sounded like a track of muffled white noise you might play to soothe your nerves. And then Danny's customer headed for the door, and Danny looked over and caught her eye, and he raised his eyebrows. Mab nodded, did a thumbs up.

'All good?' he asked, when she emerged.

'Yeah,' she said.

'Flowers?'

Mab nodded. 'She suggested I went to visit her when she's back from New Zealand.'

'Good,' Danny said. 'Good.' He put an arm round her, kissed her quickly. 'Do you feel better?'

'A bit, I think.' She leaned into Danny's chest, not caring any more whether anyone saw them.

'How about the cinema tonight?' he asked, his voice in her hair.

'Maybe.' Mab shut her eyes. 'Yes, I mean. Good idea.'

'Do you want to sit down for a bit? I could make you a cup of coffee. Find you some paperwork.'

'No, honestly.' Mab straightened up, managed a smile. 'I'm fine. I'll go and tidy the children's section.'

As she headed across the shop, she wondered if she ought to have consulted Nessa about the flowers. Should she tell her she'd rung Con? And would Con expect – would Nessa expect – that they'd go together to Lowlands next week?

Part Two

Chapter Twenty

July 2005

They were gathered in the kitchen, like an audience waiting for the curtain to rise and the leading man to stride onto the stage. All his children sitting around the table, Con thought. Anyone else would have seen the awkwardness of it, but not Roy. Roy loved spectacle. Loved keeping people guessing, too.

'What time did he say?' Max asked. Even he was onside tonight, the prospect of seeing his father exciting enough to override the chagrin of sharing the occasion with his half-sisters. Perhaps he was confident of being the favourite, Con thought, with a pang of maternal angst, even if the field was wider than it usually was when Roy showed up at Lowlands.

'He'll be here soon, I'm sure,' she said. Passing Max's chair, she put a hand on his shoulder and felt the hard lines of the muscles beneath his T-shirt. Not just the effect of a bit of manual labour at the farm, she thought, but the tension of anticipating his father's arrival.

For her part, she was glad that preparing supper gave her an excuse to be on her feet, even if the truth was that everything was ready. Mab and Nessa had laid the table, picking flowers from the garden to fill a couple of vases. Roses, white and pink and red, and a separate jug of sweet peas. The smell of them lay heavy over the kitchen: the scent of high summer. On the stove an Irish stew was keeping warm. Roy's favourite – but she'd made it for the children's sake, Con told herself. All of this – twelve years of effortful goodwill, of pleasing him – had been for the children's sake. Because she wanted to make the most, for them, of the little Roy offered. To make their memories of their father happy ones.

That wasn't the whole truth, though. It was the noble explanation; the one that made people shake their heads and murmur that she was a saint. The rest of the truth was more complicated. Con had no expectations – no desire, even, to win Roy back – but that didn't mean there was nothing for her to gain from his gratitude and his friendship. From his admiration, which she squirrelled away inside her against a rainy day.

She lifted the lid off the stew, letting out a waft of rich gravy, and just then the front door opened, as though she'd summoned a genie. Roy had a key: he'd always liked to have a key. It meant he could slip in unawares, which he occasionally did – but not tonight. Tonight four sets of ears were on high alert, and three of his children were on their feet, rushing to greet him well before he reached the kitchen. Con watched them go, her heart clenching. Philip had stood up too, but he hadn't moved. Philip wasn't one for exuberant greetings. But Con could hear Mab shrieking, and Nessa's and Max's voices raised too, the puppyish scuffles taking place in the hall, and over all of it Roy's Shakespearean boom.

'Hello! Hello! Max, Nessa, Mab – and where's my Philip? What a welcome for your old dad!'

A moment later they were all in the kitchen, Roy smiling, and the children smiling too. Somehow he had arms enough, embraces enough for all three of them, and a hand free to grasp Philip's, too.

'Philip, my man. How are you? It's good to see you.'

'Sit here, Daddy!' Mab insisted, patting the chair next to hers.

'Steady on, Queen Mab,' Roy said, a hand on her head. 'I have to greet the rest of the company first.' He lifted his eyes across the table and met Con's gaze, his smile shifting a gear.

It was only a few days since he'd dropped the girls off, but he looked different, Con thought. You might think he'd look tired and careworn, but – her heart clenched again, a different kind of clench. She should have guessed. Damn it, she should have guessed. Meetings, my arse. Words came to her lips, a question that would let him know she'd rumbled him, but she bit it back. For the sake of the children, she told herself. It was better for them to have the warm and genial Roy, not to prick his bubble and watch him shift into petulance. And honestly, why should she care what he did any more? Let him breeze in with the glow of sex about him, the bonhomie of a man buoyed up by new love. Nothing should surprise her any more. He was an old devil, and it was good for her to remember it. But those little girls, weeping in their beds: how could he do that to them, and then arrive like the hero of the hour?

'My Lady Constanza,' Roy said, with a theatrical bow. Dropping his eyes from her sightline, Con thought viciously, to avoid her scrutiny. 'I have a gift for you. Now, or later?'

'Later,' Con said, but the children were chanting, 'Now! Now!' as if the gift was for them.

'Now?' Roy swivelled round to take them all in, and then he lifted his hands in surrender. 'Wait here then, all of you. Or – Max, come and give me a hand, there's a good chap. You've been building up those muscles, I can tell.'

Max grinned delightedly. Putty in his father's hands, Con

125

thought. He always had been. 'I wish Dad was here,' he'd snarl, when they had their worst clashes, and it was all Con could do not to remind him that Roy had left of his own free will. It was better that Max idolised his father. Better in the long run. It was hard, taking the blame for Roy's lack of conscience, but the last time it had happened she'd had support from an unexpected quarter. Philip had waited until his brother had stormed off, then said, 'Why don't you tell him it's not your fault Dad's not here? Why don't you say anything?' And Con had shaken her head, and said, 'Because that's not what he needs to hear.'

Philip glanced at her now, as Max and Roy left the room again, and Con felt a little flicker of pleasure. Philip wasn't easy either – she had no idea what went on in his mind, most of the time – but he was growing up, she thought, into a son who would look after his mother. Or perhaps that was wishful thinking.

There was more noise in the hallway now – it sounded like a big present, whatever it was – and Roy called, 'Stay there, everyone. Stay where you are and shut your eyes.'

Con watched the girls squeeze their eyes shut, then Mab peeking through her fingers to check that Con wasn't looking. 'Eyes shut,' Con said, obeying, and there was another bump and scrape, then Roy said, 'OK! Open them!'

There was a painting propped up in the doorway – a huge painting. And one Con recognised.

'Oh!' she said. 'I thought that had been sold, years ago?'

'I got it back.' Roy beamed, delighted with himself. 'I thought you'd like to have it.'

Con stared. He'd painted it that first summer, when he'd finished the one of her father. That had been one of his less successful portraits – he'd been trying too hard to flatter, Con always thought, and he'd given him an air of benign grandeur that was all wrong, although her father had been thrilled with it. Sitters were the worst judges of their own portraits, Roy always said. They compared them with what they saw in a mirror – or worse, what they saw in their heads.

But the picture of her was wonderful. It was softer and looser than his other work from that time – it had an almost Pre-Raphaelite quality, the flow of brushstrokes caressing the outlines of her hair and her face and that green dress she'd loved so much. And the lilies around her, not anchored in a vase but floating free, as if they were part of a tapestry, or perhaps waiting to be assembled into a formal arrangement. She looked young and ravishing: exactly herself, but more than herself. The version of her that Roy saw; that Roy could conjure with his brush. With his touch.

'It's you,' Mab said. 'Is it you?'

'Yes,' Con said.

The boys were staring too, and she realised they'd never seen the painting before either.

'Did Dad paint it?' Max asked.

'It was the summer we met,' Roy said, sliding an arm around Max's shoulders as though they were men sharing a confidence. 'I came here to paint Mum's father. He was the Lord High Sheriff of the county, or something like that. He wore a black coat with a white lacy bib, and a hat with feathers on it.'

Mab giggled.

'He looked very fine,' Roy said, with an inflection of mock-reproach and a lift of his eyebrows that made Mab giggle even more. 'He was delighted with it, wasn't he, Constanza?'

'He was,' Con affirmed. She was still staring at the picture, wondering why Roy had brought it, and how he'd laid his hands on it. She'd hated selling it, but she hadn't allowed herself to show it, or she thought she hadn't. They'd needed the money, and no one wanted to buy anything Roy was painting at the time. Con had asked whether he could paint another version, a copy for them to sell, but he'd growled at her. She could photocopy it if she wanted to, he'd said. If she'd known he'd be gone in a couple of years anyway, she might have said no, she thought. Might have insisted on keeping it. But having it back now was more complicated.

'Are you pleased?' Roy said. 'I thought you'd be pleased.'

'I am.' But she still didn't look at him. They had no money, he and Robin. Anything there was should be kept for the girls, for looking after them when their mother was gone.

'A fortieth birthday present,' Roy said, with a smile that admitted he knew he was a couple of years late, or perhaps that he had no idea at all how old Con was.

The children were watching, perhaps surprised by the coolness of her response. Mab had moved closer to the painting and was reaching her hand tentatively towards it, as though she knew she shouldn't touch it but almost couldn't bear not to.

'Thank you,' Con said. 'But...'

Roy shook his head, a gesture just for her. *Later*, he meant. Or simply *don't*. Con was trying to think where the painting had gone, who had bought it from them. An American, perhaps. Yes, an American living in London. Perhaps they were going home now, and had decided not to take it with them. Roy's star had fallen further since then: even his old work was out of favour these days. Perhaps he hadn't had to pay anything for it. Con hoped so.

She gathered herself then, pushing her hair back from her face.

'Who's hungry?' she asked.

. . .

Things went smoothly for a while. There was plenty of stew, enough to fill those hungry male bellies and to staunch, for a while, the flow of testosterone around the table. Mab wasn't keen on the lumps of meat, Con could see, but she made a pool with her mashed potato and piled them up in the middle of it and then ate from the outside in, mixing the potato with gravy. Nessa ate all the vegetables and then the meat, cutting it into little pieces and adding a smear of potato to each bit. Con kept her eyes on them, because Max was monopolising the conversation and she was watching out for signs of fretfulness from the girls – for the dawning realisation that Max, at least, thought his father had come to see him just as much as them.

There had been no mention of Robin. That must mean the news was bad, Con thought. Even Roy, with his penchant for keeping the limelight to himself, would surely have wanted to pass on any good tidings as soon as he could. But the girls hadn't asked about her, either. It wasn't until Con slipped upstairs to fetch an aspirin that she understood why. They had packed their things, certain that Roy had come to collect them: that they would be going back with him tonight and would see their mother tomorrow. They had left their cases in their room, but just inside the door, so that it would be the work of a moment to collect them. So that there could be no quibble about whether they were ready; whether it might inconvenience him to take them.

Con stood on the landing for a minute or two, looking at the tragic still life: two small, battered cases, not the garish plastic kind you bought for children these days, but cases old-fashioned enough to have belonged to their mother as a child. Perhaps even their grandmother, before her flight to the hippies. Boarding school fare from the early 6os, if that was the kind of family Jennifer had come from. They had been placed carefully on their sides so that the latches wouldn't come undone. For a moment it was almost as if Mab and Nessa themselves were sitting there – and perhaps a part of them was, Con thought. Sitting quiet and forlorn in their borrowed bedroom, while their public selves, the ones they spirited up for their father, smiled and laughed downstairs.

When she came back into the kitchen Con had the sense that the atmosphere had changed, although it was impossible, at first, to know whether it was simply her perception of it that had shifted. Roy had drunk several glasses of wine – certainly more than he ought to have done if he was going to drive back to Buckinghamshire tonight, with or without the girls. Con suspected that Max might have helped himself from his father's glass while she'd been gone (that was exactly the kind of thing Roy would delight in, she knew), but perhaps the colour in his cheeks was simply due to the heat and light that radiated from his father. Philip was quiet, looking down at his plate and occasionally, touchingly, at the portrait of his mother which still sat where Roy had set it down, just inside the kitchen door. The little girls were quiet too. The brightness that Roy's arrival had kindled in their faces had faded; they looked tired and pinched.

Max was still holding court, and the others had stopped interrupting him, except for Mab, who was valiantly keeping her end up.

'They killed more people than the London bombings,' Max was saying. 'More than eighty.'

'Who did?' Mab asked.

'Some terrorists,' Max said loftily, 'in Egypt.'

'Egypt where the Pharaohs come from?' Mab asked.

'Yeah, except this was this week, not 5,000 years ago,' Max said.

'It's not a very nice thing to talk about, Max,' Con said.

'It's happening in the world.' Max looked straight at her, raising one shoulder slightly in a gesture that reminded her suddenly, powerfully, of Roy. 'Aren't we supposed to talk about the world? Are we supposed to stick to rainbows and fairies?'

He glanced at his father, but Roy didn't do more than twitch his mouth.

'There are plenty of things we can talk about,' Con said. Her voice sounded tired and pinched too, she thought. She didn't want to be reminded about bombing, about geopolitical unrest. There was enough going on in this house for her to worry about. 'Pudding, for example. I've made an apple crumble. Max, why don't you go and find the ice cream?'

Max pushed back his chair with a show of reluctance, but he couldn't resist the temptation of ice cream. He was only fourteen, after all, Con thought, with a sudden rush of affection. How much of his belligerence was down to the need to prove himself worthy of his father? She watched him go out towards the garage where the old chest freezer lived, the shorts she'd bought him in the spring already too small. It was startling to think that in another four years he'd be eighteen, and Philip twenty. Those four years would pass in a blink – and would they be grown-up then, her boys? Would she have done a good enough job?

Philip had started collecting the plates, and Nessa got up to help him. Mab took the opportunity to climb off her chair and onto her father's lap.

'When we've had pudding, Daddy, will you take us home?' she asked.

Con reached up to get the bowls out of the cupboard.

'Not tonight, little Mab,' Roy said.

'Why not tonight?' There was an edge to Mab's voice that Con recognised.

'It's late,' Roy said. 'You need to be in bed soon.'

'We can sleep in the car,' Mab insisted. 'We've packed our things. We're all ready to go.'

Nessa had halted, her back to her father and her sister. None of them were watching, Con thought, but they were all listening. Even Philip.

Roy sighed, and Con imagined him adjusting Mab into a more comfortable position on his knee. 'It's better for you to be here for a bit longer,' he said. 'It really is, Mab. Aren't you happy here?'

'It's not because of that,' Mab said. 'It's because we want to see Mummy.' She stopped. '*Is* she getting better, Daddy? Are you telling us the truth about that?'

Con's head whipped round, just for a second, but it was long enough for Roy to register the movement and to catch her eye.

'No one can ever tell what's going to happen, my darling,' Roy said. 'The doctors are doing their best. But Mummy is quite poorly still.'

'I know she's dying,' Mab said, her voice querulous now.

Nessa turned sharply, wide-eyed. 'Don't say that!' she said. 'How dare you say that?'

'Because it's true.' Mab was crying now. 'It's true, isn't it, Daddy?'

It was rare to see Roy confounded, but Con had no sympathy to spare for him. The bit of her mind that wasn't taken up with desperate compassion for the little girls was wondering how Mab had guessed the truth – and then it hit her, as sharply as a tile falling off a roof. The night of the storm, talking to Max outside, right under their window. Damn it, how could she have been so stupid? It had been noisy, the wind and rain and thunder making a great racket, but you could never tell with sound. The eaves projected over the terrace at the back, and none of the windows closed properly.

Not that it mattered how the child knew, of course. And not that any of them could have prevented her knowing it for much longer, either. It was just the agony of this moment, of understanding that Mab had kept the knowledge to herself. Laid her plans so carefully, because she didn't trust the adults to see her side of things.

'I'm afraid the new treatment isn't working very well,' Roy said, 'but we haven't given up hope.'

'Hope?' Nessa said, the word as brittle as a sheet of glass. 'You said they were going to make her better.'

He should reach out his arm to her, Con thought. He should gather her in and hold her and comfort her. Comfort them both. But that was the thing about Roy: he didn't believe in his capacity to make a difference, or didn't care to try. He looked desperate to escape, as he always did when there were emotions in play that he couldn't command.

Con came round the table, scooping up Nessa and sweeping her into an embrace that included Roy and Mab, binding the four of them into a makeshift shelter, enclosing the girls in a consolation that was far, far from what they wanted or needed, but which was the best this evening, this kitchen could afford them. For a moment Con forgot everything else. Forgot Philip; forgot Max.

'What the fuck's going on?'

Max banged the tub of ice cream down on the table, and Nessa started backwards, breaking the knot of arms and bodies that had held her.

'If we're playing fucking Happy Families,' Max said, 'you might remember who actually lives here. Whose mother this is.'

'Mind your filthy language,' Roy roared. 'You selfish little prick: can't you think about anyone else for even a second?'

There was a deathly silence then, except for the soft sound of Mab whimpering, deep in her father's arms. Max's expression broke Con's heart. Oh God, he was so much his father's son. The two of them bellowing at each other like silverbacks, and the room so thick with tragedy you could hardly breathe.

'It's all right, Max,' she said. 'Mab and Nessa are just a bit upset.'

She moved towards him, ready to give him a hug, but he pushed past her, pushed past Philip and tore out of the room, nearly knocking the precious painting over in his haste to get away.

Chapter Twenty-One

March 2024

Philip was home later than Con had expected, but the reason for it was immediately obvious. She was outside – she'd laid the tea things on the little table at the side of the house – and she saw him coming up the garden path with an armful of flowers. She remembered her conversation with Mab the previous day, the discussion of funeral wreaths, and for a moment she wondered whether Philip might have overheard; whether she ought to have mentioned it to him.

These weren't funeral flowers, though. They were cheerful spring blooms, daffodils and tulips and some pretty frothy yellow ones Con didn't know the name of. Philip saw her sitting at the table, and came round the side of the house towards her.

'It's rather late,' he said, 'but I only thought of it today.'

He held the bouquet out to her and Con took it, feeling her heart quicken.

'Thank you,' she said. 'That's very kind of you. Very unexpected.'

'It's because of Dad,' Philip said. There was a trace of anxiety on his face now, as though he was afraid he'd done the wrong thing.

'Yes,' Con said. 'It's very sweet of you. Very thoughtful.'

Too many adjectives, she thought. She often caught herself doing that with Philip. Naming his emotions for him.

'Is it warm enough to have a cup of tea outside?' she asked. 'I thought it probably was.'

Philip nodded, and put his briefcase carefully down on a spare chair. Con laid the flowers on the table, then poured the tea and cut them each a slice of fruit cake. Sometimes it felt ridiculously formal, this daily tea party, but once you started dismantling your rituals there was precious little left to hang life on. Tea at five thirty, supper at eight. Often some television, or Scrabble, or reading. It could have been Roy she spent her evenings with, in her sixties, but instead it was his son. Who was as different from him in every respect as it was possible to be.

'I got the flowers from the florist near the station,' Philip said. 'They had so much choice. I didn't know where to start.'

'You chose well,' Con said. 'They're beautiful. Very springlike.' More adjectives. It was because she was nervous.

'I told them to choose,' Philip said. 'I'm glad you like them. I told them we were going away for a few days and they said they would last until we get back.'

Going away for a few days, Con thought. Travelling 12,000 miles for a four-night stay, then back again. 'Almost as long in the air as on the ground,' Ursula had said. 'You'll hardly begin to get over the jet lag. You're welcome to stay longer, you know.' But Con had demurred. They'd got a good deal on the tickets, she'd told Ursula. She could hardly believe they were doing it, though: that they would be on their way the day after tomorrow. It seemed absurd, suddenly, to be going all that way when Roy was already dead.

The truth was that she hated the thought of seeing where Roy had lived; of putting any flesh on the bones of the life she'd refused to imagine him living for the last two decades. If Roy was capable of doublethink, she thought, then she was too. She kept in her head a whole set of Roys, stacked inside each other like matryoshka dolls. The Roy who wrote those elegant letters, like a pen friend she'd never met. The Roy who had railed against the art establishment with the passion of the great artist he believed himself to be. The Roy she had fallen extortionately, wantonly in love with. The Roy who had failed her, and Robin, and all his children.

'We need to order some flowers for the funeral,' she said, as she poured the tea. 'A wreath.'

She looked at Philip's flowers, their tight buds ready to burst open. And then she hesitated – but the words insisted on being spoken. 'I spoke to Mab today. She wants me to buy flowers from her as well. From her and Nessa.'

'Mab,' Philip said. 'I remember her.'

Con's heart accelerated again. 'It's a long time since we've seen them,' she said. 'She's grown up now. She must be twenty-seven.'

'Yes,' Philip said. 'She was eight when we last saw her.'

Con nodded. For a moment she couldn't speak. She waited for Philip to say something else. *That was the summer Max died.* Or – but there was nothing else, really: everything led back to that. And he didn't say it. Relief flowed through her. Shameful relief, but there it was. It was too late for anything else, she told herself. She and Philip could weather this hiccup and go back to the status quo they'd honed so carefully together. But then she remembered what she'd said to Mab: *When I'm back from New Zealand, why don't you come and see me?* She remembered why she'd said it – the muffled sob at the other end of the line – and something twisted tight inside her.

'She was a dear little girl, Mab, wasn't she?' she said. 'You were very kind to them, Philip.' And then there was another response hanging in the air between them: *And Max wasn't.*

But that one went unsaid too. Con breathed out slowly, gently. She wouldn't tell him that Mab was coming to visit. That could wait until they were back from New Zealand.

'I've had a few letters of condolence,' she said instead. 'People must have seen the announcement. Ursula put it in *The Times*.'

'Who from?' Philip asked.

'A couple from old friends,' Con said. 'People we knew a long time ago. And one from Lucy.' She raised an eyebrow. 'Lucy Fidler, from the farm. I thought that was very sweet of her.'

'Lucy,' Philip said.

'You must remember her?'

'Of course. But she went away. She went abroad, didn't she?'

'I think she did, for a bit.' The children had played together when they were little, Max and Philip and Lucy, but the friendship hadn't survived into their teens, and Con had been sorry about that. She'd imagined, at one stage, that Lucy might mediate between them. That they might work better as a trio than Max and Philip had ever done as a pair.

'What did Lucy say?' Philip asked.

'Not much. Just that she was sorry to hear the news, and she remembered your father well. She's done well for herself – she's working in London now, at an auction house. You can read the letters: there's a nice one from our best man, too. I don't think I've seen him since the wedding. Roy used to meet him in London, when we were...'

She stopped. Nostalgia wasn't a good idea. Philip nodded, as though he understood, or wanted her to think he did, and she smiled.

'I've bought sausages for supper,' she said. 'Pork and leek. From the butcher in Maltock.'

'Delicious,' Philip said. 'Do you mind if I have a shower first?'

'Not at all. There's ages.'

He hesitated before getting up, though. 'I'd like to see the letters,' he said. 'Lucy's, and the others.'

'Of course.' Con smiled again, quickly. 'I'll get them out for you.'

When Philip had gone inside, she sat for a while longer; poured herself another cup of tea. She couldn't remember now why she'd put the table in this position in the garden. It was a heavy iron thing, difficult to move, and it had been in the same place since they came here from the big house all that time ago. It caught the evening sun, but for that purpose a spot further round would have been better: the sloping shadows from the roof had already reached the chair Philip had just vacated. It must have been to avoid the view of the house, she thought. The old house; the house she'd grown up in, and her boys too. The trees along the fence were taller now, but when they'd first moved here you could see the chimneys and the gables quite clearly. The attic windows.

Had she imagined, back then, that as time went on she'd make her peace with the past? She must have done, or else she'd have moved further away, surely. They could have gone anywhere, she and Philip, once she'd sold the house and paid off the debts. Had it been because of Max? Because she'd felt she should stay close to her dead son?

And if so, was that a noble explanation or a cowardly one?

139

Chapter Twenty-Two

Mab had forgotten it was a Granny Jenny weekend. They went once a month, she and Nessa, on the first Saturday of the month. That didn't feel often enough when they were there, but in between visits the month rolled by more quickly than Mab expected, and as each one approached she always began to dread going. It was partly the fact that Aunt Hazel usually came with them: Hazel had a car, which made it quicker to get there, and also meant they didn't have to see her at other times, but it was a lot to deal with in one go. And this month it felt worse. It was the day of their father's funeral – that's what Nessa was talking about, on the other end of the phone.

'It'll mean we're together today, at least,' she was saying.

'With Hazel,' Mab said.

'She'll be nice,' Nessa said. 'Bereavement decorum, you know.'

'Is that a thing?'

'Being kind to people who've lost their father?' Nessa said. 'I think even Hazel might recognise that as a thing. Even when she didn't approve of the father. Anyway, Mab, if you can get to Wanstead station by ten, she'll pick us up.'

'Sure,' Mab said. 'I'll be there.'

It was nine o'clock now: that meant leaving in fifteen minutes. But Mab was up already, luckily. She'd woken early, and found Yvonne in the kitchen, just back from buying pastries. They'd split an almond croissant from the new bakery round the corner. Mab knew what the prices were there, and she'd been thinking, when Nessa rang, that Yvonne might not be staying in Littlemore Road much longer if her disposable income could stretch to four-pound croissants on a Saturday morning. Although wasn't that what the media kept saying about their generation: they couldn't afford to buy houses, so they consoled themselves with almond croissants?

'Where are you off to?' Yvonne asked, when Mab ended the call.

'To visit my granny,' Mab said. 'She's in a home in Epping. We go and see her once a month.'

'Epping Forest?' Yvonne said. 'That sounds nice.'

'It's not really. It's on a main road; it could be anywhere. But the staff are nice, and it doesn't make much difference to her. She's got dementia.'

'I'm sorry.'

Mab shook her head. 'She's had it for years.' Her whole life, Hazel said sometimes: a gentle slide from psychedelics towards the brain's own version of oblivion. Hazel didn't have many nice things to say about anyone except her husband, Alan. The most boring man in the world, Nessa called him, doing her own inadvertent imitation of Hazel. Like a human Sims character you'd specially configured to have no distinguishing features. Mab thought Hazel had probably picked him precisely because there was nothing to object to.

141

Mab got up, sweeping the crumbs of pastry into her hand and tipping them into the sink.

'I'd better get going,' she said. 'But thanks for the croissant. It was delicious.'

'Pleasure.' Yvonne had her running gear on; no doubt her plans for the day were more energetic than Mab's. 'I'm sorry about your dad too. Is it his mum you're going to see?'

'My mum's mum. But it's his funeral today, in New Zealand. It feels a bit weird not to be going.'

If Yvonne thought it was weird too, she was too polite to say anything. Mab rinsed her coffee mug and headed for the stairs.

As she pulled on her boots, she tried to still the turbulence that Nessa's phone call had stirred up in her head. She wasn't used to having things she didn't talk to Nessa about. Actually, that wasn't true, because those things had always been there, but since the conversation with Danny she couldn't put them away again in the way she used to. And there was also, now, the fear that the consequences of what she remembered might be more serious than she'd admitted to herself. That talking to Danny had set something in motion which she might not be able to stop.

The home was called Forest View, which was probably a violation of the Trade Descriptions Act, Mab thought, unless you counted the flimsy saplings along the fence at the front as a forest.

Granny Jenny was in the lounge, settled in a chair by the window. The back garden was small, but there was a flowerbed in which daffodils were blooming at the moment.

'Hello, Granny!' Mab squatted down in front of her and took her hands, and she beamed. She was past recognising any of them reliably, but she was always delighted to see Mab. She looked enough like Robin to fool her, Hazel said. 'It's Mab,' Mab said, 'and Nessa and Hazel.'

'Hazel?' Granny Jenny looked surprised. 'What's Hazel doing here?'

'She always comes with us,' Mab said.

'Is she still alive?'

Mab bit her lip, glad the others couldn't hear. 'Definitely. She drove us here.'

Nessa had dragged some chairs over, and Mab stood up and helped arrange them. They'd brought Turkish Delight, Granny's favourite, and once they'd opened those and handed them round Hazel reached into her bag.

'Look what I've got, Mum,' she said. 'Some photos.'

They hadn't talked, on the way here, about their father, but Hazel raised her voice again to old-people volume and said, 'Roy's dead, Mum. Do you remember Roy? Robin's husband?'

'Roy was an artist,' Jenny said.

'That's right. He went on being an artist, even though no one ever liked his paintings. And now he's dead, and it's his funeral today.'

'Is Robin at the funeral?' Jenny asked. She glanced at the group around her.

Hazel smiled tightly. She didn't like having to explain things. 'Shall we look at the pictures, Mum?'

They must have seen this album before, Mab thought, but not for a long time. It was nice of Hazel to have brought it. Occasionally she would do something like this that made Mab feel guilty about being so critical of her. Mab couldn't imagine anything she'd have liked more today than looking at photographs of her parents, and of her and Nessa as little girls.

'Look!' Nessa said, 'I remember that dress! And your pigtails, Mab!'

'Was that our house?' Mab asked.

Nessa nodded. She held the album out for her grandmother to look at. 'Do you recognise us?' she asked. 'Do you think we've changed?'

The photographs were in colour, but the colour had altered over the years. Printed cheaply, Mab thought. Her hair looked greenish in some of the photos. The album carried on after their mother's death – there were shots of the two of them in Granny Jenny's garden, and in the uniforms of the hated boarding school – and it gave Mab a shiver to think of Hazel taking on the album and continuing to add to it. But it was lovely to see their mother before she was ill. To see their parents together. Their father had been handsome, Mab thought: it was easy to see why women had fallen for him. He wore his charm casually, threw his children in the air with an effortless grace, almost as if he had imagined them studying him, decades later, and reaching a judgement about him.

But the other thing that struck Mab was how diligently Nessa had looked after her. Before Robin's death they often appeared on their own: Nessa on a bike, pedalling in front of the house; Mab wearing nothing but a nappy, standing at the sink and pouring water from one plastic cup into another. But after that, they were together in almost every shot, as if Nessa had made sure they were never separated. Her hand would be on Mab's shoulder, or around Mab's waist, and if they weren't standing next to each other, Nessa's eyes were often caught darting between the camera and her sister. Mab remembered Nessa's care, of course, just as she remembered her mother's beauty and her father's roguish smile, but the photographs brought those things back into focus. They made her wonder whether it had been a sacrifice, or whether cleaving so closely to Mab had meant as much to Nessa as it had to her. They made her feel that she hadn't noticed, at the time, the unwavering intent in Nessa's gaze. That she'd underestimated her sister's vigilance. And that left a strange taste in her mouth.

'Look at me,' Hazel said, pointing herself out in a group shot taken outside a theatre. 'What a fright I was in that dress.'

Granny Jenny was in that picture too. 'I remember that day,' she said suddenly, leaning forwards to look more closely. 'We had tea at Fortnum's.'

'So we did,' said Hazel. 'It was Nessa's birthday. The girls had ice-cream sundaes.'

She looked delighted: not just because her mother had emerged from the mist and produced such a clear recollection, but because it proved something, Mab thought. Proved that she had given them the right kind of childhood: the theatre, and ice cream.

Mab smiled at herself then, imagining that a photograph album could tell you the truth about anything. Except that Hazel *had* given them all those things, of course. She'd probably done her best, in fact, to provide what she thought they needed. Perhaps it was mean of them to remember her terrible cooking, and the lists of chores; the rules and the scolding. At least you'd known where you were with Hazel. Granny Jenny had been the kind of grandmother who loved to promise things that never came to pass, not with the wrong intentions but with hopelessly good ones. A dog, for instance. Although there had been a dog in the end: one winter Granny Jenny had acquired a vicious Jack Russell from somewhere. Ripper, he'd been called. Nominative determinism at its finest. What had become of him? He hadn't lasted very long, as Mab recalled. There were certainly no pictures of him in the album.

When they'd finished with the photographs there was a lull in which none of them knew what to say. They ought always to have props for these visits, Mab thought. Show and tell.

'How's your boyfriend, Granny?' she asked, and the old lady

perked up again. This was a running joke: she mentioned a different man every time they asked her. No one was sure which of them lived at Forest View, and which had drifted through the commune all those decades ago. She loved being asked, though.

'Ooh, he's in my bad books,' she said.

'Who is?' Nessa asked.

'Eric, of course. Hasn't been to see me for ages. I don't know why I give him the time of day.' Mab and Nessa laughed and she grinned at them delightedly. 'Oh, I could tell you a thing or two about men,' she said. 'I really could.'

The rest of the visit passed cheerfully enough, indulging Granny Jenny's colourful reminiscences about her romantic history, but as they were leaving, Mab caught her grandmother looking at them with a knowingness, a wistfulness, that took her by surprise.

'Is everything OK, Granny?' she asked.

Her grandmother frowned. She'd been tall and straight-backed as a young woman, and even into her fifties, when the photos in Hazel's album had been taken, but she'd crumpled in on herself as the dementia took hold. You wouldn't know her, Mab thought, from those pictures, and most of the time she didn't seem to know herself, either. But there were glimpses of lucidity occasionally, like the moment when she'd remembered the theatre. And perhaps...

'Did you want to say something?' Mab asked. 'Did you want to ask something?'

'Where's Michael?' Granny Jenny's voice was anxious. 'I haven't seen him all day. Do you know where he is?'

'Michael's gone, Mum,' Hazel said. 'Years ago. I'm sorry.'

'Gone?' the old woman said. 'Oh dear. I'll have to tell Robin. She's so fond of him.'

Mab gave her a kiss. 'It's lovely to see you, Granny. We'll come again soon.'

The residents' lunches were being wheeled along the corridor when they emerged from the lounge, and the smell of institutional food, mingling with the smell of old people and disinfectant, made Mab feel nauseous. She'd felt a bit weird, though, ever since that expensive almond croissant. So much, she thought, for chic bakeries.

'Who's Michael?' she asked Hazel, as they signed out in the visitors book.

'Her brother,' Hazel said crisply. 'He was much older than her. He hardly spoke to her after she went off with the hippies. He never forgave her for breaking their parents' hearts.'

And there it was again, Mab thought: the chain of sadness, of broken hearts and broken promises and broken bonds, that you could follow back through the generations of their family. What hope was there for you, if that was your heritage? Was it still possible to find someone nice, someone kind, and live blamelessly with them? Or would life insist on tugging at the chains, forcing you to pay attention to the past?

Chapter Twenty-Three

The three of them sat in silence in Hazel's car on the way home. Nessa wondered what the others were thinking: whether the visit to Forest View had felt better or worse than usual to them, or like a particularly odd thing to do on this particular day. She was always conscious of entering an alternative reality when they visited Granny Jenny – not just the alternative reality of her mind, but the half-world in which she and her fellow residents lived, populated by the very old and their uniformed carers. A science fiction world, almost, which made life outside seem stranger and more surprising than it had before, as if you saw for a moment, when you emerged into the daylight, some disconcerting truth that slipped away before you could grasp it.

The photo album had been a good idea, Nessa thought – and it had made her think. Looking at the pictures of her and Mab as children, she'd been struck by how much things had changed; how far they'd drifted away from each other. She felt a sudden desire to hold Mab's hand or put an arm round her shoulders, as the younger Nessa had done so often. But she was in the front seat and Mab was in the back, and it was impossible to talk with Hazel there. In the rear-view mirror, she could see Mab staring out of the window, watching the outskirts of London gathering them back in.

Nessa felt a sudden pressure in her chest; a disconcerting awareness that not knowing what Mab was thinking made her anxious. A muscle memory, perhaps, called up by loss and nostalgia. After their mother died, she'd done so much thinking for Mab – explaining her feelings to her and helping her make sense of life. It had got to the point when she'd almost been able to see inside Mab's head: when she could almost reach in and rearrange things so that Mab would feel better. Mab was twenty-seven now, and this latest trauma wasn't on the same scale as their mother's death. But even so, Nessa felt a flash of fear at the idea that she'd lost sight of her sister's thoughts. There was something inside her, something she couldn't quite admit to, that was afraid to let Mab go.

They were turning onto the North Circular now: they'd be back at Wanstead station in a few minutes.

'You decided not to go to the funeral, then,' Hazel said.

Nessa didn't turn her head. 'Evidently,' she said. And then she relented: it was too easy to be brusque with Hazel. 'It's such a long way to go, and there's going to be something here. A memorial service.' She turned her head now to catch Mab's eye.

'That's sensible,' Hazel said. And then, without moving her face at all, she said, 'I'm sorry he's dead. I should have said so. It's no secret that I disliked him. He ruined my sister's life. But he was your father, and it's hard to lose a father.'

That was a rather surprising statement from someone who had never known their own father, Nessa thought. But before she could reply, Mab was speaking.

'He didn't ruin her life. He gave her us. Don't you think that was a good thing?'

'Yes.' Hazel's voice sounded pinched, but there was a flush

149

of emotion on her cheekbones that Nessa couldn't remember seeing before. 'That was the best thing that ever happened to her.'

The silence in the car felt very different now. Nessa waited – and she could tell Mab was waiting too – for Hazel to carry on, to say more about their mother or them or their childhood, but she didn't. What was wrong with this bloody family? No one ever said anything; no one ever talked about even the most important things. And now she and Mab had caught the habit too.

Five minutes later Hazel had dropped them in the station car park, and they were watching her drive away.

'Mab,' Nessa said, seizing what felt like a moment of conviction, 'why don't you come back for lunch? We haven't seen much of each other since – and it's – today's – well, it would be nice to be together for a bit longer. Without Hazel.' She hesitated. Mab wasn't looking at her. 'We could talk about the memorial service, if you like. We could think about what we'd like.'

'We can't just decide on our own,' Mab said. 'There's Con and Philip too.'

'Of course. But we can still talk about it.' Nessa hesitated. 'So is that a yes, then? For lunch?'

'OK,' Mab said. 'I can't stay long, though. I'm helping Danny with an event this evening. A book launch.'

'Good.' Nessa smiled. 'I'll text Inga and let her know we'll be home soon. She's making something Swedish, I think. A special treat.'

Mab was just being Mab, she told herself. A bit distracted. A bit vague. And it was good that work was keeping her busy. But when she looked up from her phone, Mab was looking straight at her, and the expression on her face wasn't what

Nessa was expecting at all. It was gone in a second, but she was sure she hadn't been mistaken.

She looked down for a moment, pretending she hadn't seen. Inga would tell her she ought to say something, but Inga didn't know everything. That look might not have been directed at her: Mab could have been thinking about Hazel still, or their father.

'OK,' she said. 'Shall we go?'

'Actually,' Mab said, 'I'm sorry, but I think I'd better not. I have to be at the shop by four thirty, and by the time...' She smiled quickly. 'Say hello to Inga for me, though.'

She disappeared into the station before Nessa had a chance to reply. Nessa stared after her. What was going on? she wondered. Was it really just the timing, and Mab not wanting to be in a rush? Or had Nessa's voice given away her discombobulation, and made Mab realise she'd seen that look? And if so...

Nessa shut her eyes. The mention of Con and Philip... Of course Mab would be thinking about them today, but could that be – was she was thinking about that other death? The one they never talked about?

Chapter Twenty-Four

July 2005

M ax's abrupt exit from the kitchen released some of the tension in the room, but only in the same way as popping the cork out of an over-shaken bottle of champagne. The emotions that had been drowned out briefly by the shouting match between Max and Roy bubbled over now in a hysterical outburst from Mab.

'I want my Mummy!' she shouted, with a violence Con had never suspected her capable of. 'I don't want to be here any more! I want to go and see Mummy *now*!'

Nessa was silent, but she was very pale, and Con could feel her trembling.

'I'm sorry about Max,' Philip said, when Mab's wails abated briefly. 'He shouldn't have said those things. We're very happy to have you here, we really are.'

'Shut the fuck up, Philip,' Roy said. 'Stop being so bloody sanctimonious.'

Con pulled back sharply. 'Roy!' she said. 'How dare you? What's got into you?'

'What's got into *me*?' Roy shouted. 'What's got into me is

that someone has told my daughters their mother's dying, and both my sons are behaving like morons.'

'No one's told us,' Nessa said quietly. 'We've just guessed. We guessed that you weren't telling us the truth, Daddy.'

'Philip's been so nice to the girls,' Con said. She was trembling now, too. She was desperate not to cry, but she could hear the wobble in her voice. 'Don't lump him together with Max.'

Roy snorted. 'No chance you could mistake him for Max,' he said.

Con felt the words as another stinging blow. Perhaps you couldn't tell, she told herself, that the disdain in Roy's voice was directed at Philip, not Max. Perhaps Philip couldn't tell, at least. Mab had continued to howl, and Nessa was murmuring to her now, trying to calm her. Con glanced at Philip, whose expression was blank. She wanted to go to him, to reassure him, but Mab was gripping her too tightly – and Philip wouldn't want it, she thought. Not in front of all these people.

In the middle of the huddle of bodies Roy sat like a stranger. That was an absurd word, but it was the one that came to her, that stuck. Roy, who was the cause of so much of the upset, was behaving as though he was the one being imposed on. The one whose rights and expectations weren't being satisfied. God damn him, Con thought furiously. Why did she go on letting him ask things of her? She should never have agreed to have those little girls here. No one else would have done, even with Roy's special pleading. But the strangest thing was that she couldn't regret it. Despite everything, she was glad she'd taken them in.

'Daddy,' Nessa said now, her voice striving desperately for calmness and authority, 'why don't I go and get our cases? All you have to do is drive us home. I can look after Mab if you have things to do. Con has been very kind, and Philip has too, but we really want to be at home, near Mummy, so we can go and see her.'

'Not tonight, my chuck,' Roy said, apparently oblivious to the effort it had cost his daughter to speak with such self-control. 'In a day or two, perhaps. Let me see what I can do.'

'But why?' Nessa asked. 'Aren't you going home? Are you staying here?'

Roy laughed. 'So many questions! You're quite the little interrogator, aren't you?' He took Mab into his arms properly then, but only so that he could stand up, holding her above her sister and looking straight into her face. 'Queen Mab,' he said, 'my best and bravest Queen Mab. I can rely on you, can't I? You know I'm doing my best. I'll come back and get you very soon.'

And then he set her on the ground, ruffling her hair as he did so, and patted Nessa perfunctorily on the shoulder.

'Chin up, Philip,' he said. 'I'll see you soon too. Say goodbye to your wretch of a brother from me.'

'Is that it?' Con managed to say. 'You're just going to walk out and leave me with all four of your children, having upset the whole lot of them?'

'You'll be glad to see the back of me, Constanza,' Roy said, with barely a trace of apology. 'I'm sure you'll have everything calm and ship-shape by bedtime.'

'No, Roy.' Con stood in front of him. 'This isn't the time for that.'

'For what?' He laughed. 'For self-knowledge? A dash of irony? What the hell's left to us, then, Con?'

And then he was gone, banging out of the front door as noisily as he'd arrived.

Con didn't expect to sleep that night. Fury and indignation roiled inside her, making her head throb and her heart race, and although she'd checked every room and found every child asleep, she couldn't help fearing that they might wake again, any of them, and want her. Want things from her, some of them – maybe all of them – that she simply couldn't give them.

Mab and Nessa had succumbed meekly in the end, taking their nighties and toothbrushes out of their cases but insisting on leaving everything else packed. Con had made them hot chocolate, read them a story, suggested they made cards for their mother in the morning. 'So we can take them to her,' Mab had said, and Con had nodded, and not said that the post might be quicker.

Philip had been in bed by the time she looked in on him, reading his A-level Physics textbook by the light of the bedside lamp he'd had since he was five.

'You know your father loves you,' Con had said, knowing it wasn't the right thing to say, but not being able to think of anything else. 'It's a difficult time for him.'

Philip hadn't replied. Con had smiled at him and touched his hand, and then he'd put his book on his bedside table, and she'd bent to kiss him.

'Good night,' she'd said. 'Sleep well, my darling.'

'He likes Max better,' Philip had said, when she'd almost reached the door.

'That's not true.' But Con hadn't been able to turn and face him. Roy's preferences were all too easy to spot. All too painful, as she knew from bitter experience.

'He does,' Philip said. 'I behave better than Max, but he likes him better.'

Con did turn round then; she went back to his bedside and perched on the edge of the mattress. 'Your father has always been capricious,' she said. 'He says what's in his mind, which isn't always what he really thinks. And I think he knows...' She took Philip's hand, which he yielded up to her less unwillingly

155

than she'd feared. 'I think he understands that Max needs his encouragement more than you do. He can see how grown-up you are these days.'

'He didn't exactly encourage Max today,' Philip said.

'No.' Con put a hand to his face, and felt him stiffen. Too much, she thought. 'No, he lost his temper. He's never been very good at dealing with emotional stress.'

Philip didn't say anything more, and after a minute or two Con got up.

'Try to sleep,' she'd said. And then she'd made her way down the landing to Max's room.

Max had been the most angry and the most truculent, as she'd expected.

'So he went without even saying goodbye to me, the fucking coward?'

'He's in a state,' Con had said. 'It'll be better next time. He'll make amends.'

'It wouldn't have happened if we hadn't had those kids here.'

'Maybe not,' Con had said. But then Roy might not have come at all, she'd thought. Maybe not all summer. 'Don't blame them,' she'd said. 'None of this is their fault.'

'Hnh.'

Con had tried to hug him, but Max had pushed her away.

'It's not my fault either, Max,' she'd said.

'You could have not married him.'

'And then I wouldn't have had you.' She'd tried again, putting a hand on his arm, but he'd wriggled out of her reach.

'You'd have been better off.'

'I would not, Max. Don't say that.'

'He called me a selfish little prick.' Max's voice had cracked.

'I know.' Con had stayed very still. 'He shouldn't have said that. I told him so.'

'But you both think it's true.'

'No.'

'You do. You think I should have been nicer to the kids.'

'Maybe,' Con had admitted, 'but I understand how you feel. It's an awful lot to ask of you. Your home. Your mother. Your summer holidays.' She'd hesitated. 'The fact that they're your father's daughters.'

Max had kicked the chair beside his desk. 'I fucking hate him.'

'Your father?'

'I hate everyone. I hate my life. Why the fuck should I be nice?'

Con had sighed; a loud, what-the-hell-do-I-know sigh.

'It's not so bad, Max,' she'd said. 'The girls won't be here much longer, I promise. And your father will be sweetness and light next time he comes. You'll see.'

'I don't care if I never see him again,' Max had said. 'He's the selfish prick, if you ask me.'

Con couldn't disagree with that statement, but she could hardly agree with it either, out loud, to Roy's son, so she pursed her lips in what she hoped Max would perceive as an ironic gesture.

'Time for bed,' she'd said. 'It's after midnight.'

She'd felt wretched when she left him, but when she put her head round the door half an hour later he'd been in bed and snoring gently, and she'd felt such a sense of relief that tears had risen in her eyes. She'd stood for a few moments looking at him, remembering how sweetly he'd slept as a baby, even when he'd screamed for most of the day, and she'd felt that strange, desperate, unnameable love you feel for your children when things are at their most difficult. Everything will be all right, she told herself, as she came back along the landing. Everything will settle down again.

And now here she was, lying awake in the darkness, full of love and anguish. Would Roy come back in a couple of days, as he'd promised? She didn't mind having the girls, but it wasn't the right place for them. Perhaps she should get in touch with Jennifer or Hazel?

She turned over restlessly. She'd left her curtains open, as she often did when she thought she wouldn't be able to sleep. Outside, the sky was very clear and still, the moon visible over the distant trees. But in the corner of the window, where the skyline dipped down lowest, the first seep of dawn had just appeared.

Chapter Twenty-Five

This was another morning when Mab had meant to wake up sooner. She'd made a new plan, lying in bed last night: she would wake up extra *extra* early, and she'd wake Nessa too, and they would get dressed very quietly and sneak out of the house and walk to the village, and then they'd find someone who could tell them how to get to the station. If they got home by themselves, surely no one would send them back to Lowlands. Con might not even want them, after they'd run away. They'd be like the children in the pony books, taking things into their own hands. The only thing that could make the plan better, she'd thought, as she'd drifted towards sleep, was if they had actual ponies to ride home on.

But here she was now, just awake, and it was ten past eight already, and she knew it was already too late for them to leave without anyone noticing. And she could see now that her plan wouldn't have worked, anyway. They didn't have any money, and she didn't know, although Nessa might, which station was nearest to their home. And they didn't have a key to the house, if Daddy wasn't there. And everyone would be really cross with them.

She clenched her face up to try to stop the tears that were already trickling out of her eyes. Yesterday, when she'd woken up late, Nessa had already gone out. At least this morning Nessa was still in her bed. At first Mab thought she was asleep, but then Nessa moved her arm and rolled towards her.

'Morning,' she said. 'Did you sleep well?'

'I slept longer than I thought.' Mab hesitated, wondering if she should tell Nessa about the running-away plan, then decided not to. 'Did you?'

'I woke up a long time ago,' Nessa said.

'Oh.'

Mab wanted to ask what she'd been thinking about all this time, but she didn't do that either. She thought Nessa might be remembering yesterday morning, when she'd gone out with Jean and Lucy. Nessa hadn't told her anything about it, except that the shops were exactly the same as the ones near home, but Mab had felt jealous and she didn't want Nessa to talk about it again. She hugged her knees up to her tummy.

'Do you think Daddy will come back for us today?' she asked.

'I don't know.'

'I think today or tomorrow,' Mab said. 'He said very soon.'

'Mab,' Nessa said. She sat up in her bed. 'I've been thinking.'

'What about?'

'Well – I don't think Daddy likes telling us things he knows we won't want to hear. He didn't tell us that Mummy's treatment might not make her better, and he didn't tell us we'd be here so long.'

'No.'

'And last night he told us he'd come back for us soon, and that we could see Mummy then. But I think it might not be as soon as you hope.'

'But why?' Mab could feel herself starting to cry properly now. 'Why can't we see her?'

'That's the other thing I've been thinking about,' Nessa said. 'I think the treatment is making Mummy feel poorly.'

'Why would they give her treatment that makes her poorly?'

'Because that's the way it works sometimes,' Nessa said. 'Some treatment can make you feel worse for a bit, but that's all part of it making you better.'

'Oh.' Mab thought for a bit. 'So there's still a chance they can make her better?'

'That's what I think. I don't think they'd give her the treatment if they didn't think it might work.'

'So if we're patient,' Mab said, 'she might get better? Properly better?'

'Maybe,' Nessa said.

Mab bit her lip. 'I heard Con saying she was dying. The night there was that storm. She was outside the window. I thought you might have heard too.'

'Are you sure?' Nessa frowned. 'Do you think you might have been dreaming?'

'I don't think so.' But Mab wasn't completely sure now. And anyway... 'Con might not know,' she said.

'Exactly.'

'I wish they'd tell us the truth,' Mab said. 'I wish Daddy would.'

'I do too,' Nessa said. 'But let's—' She smiled at Mab. 'Let's try to have a nice day today. I think that's the best thing we can do. The sun's shining. Maybe we could go swimming again.'

Chapter Twenty-Six

Con had slept a little in the short hours around dawn, but she'd woken at her usual time, and she'd hauled herself out of bed, conscious of the need to be on her toes this morning. A cup of tea before anything, she thought, as she glanced down into the dark hall. That had been her mother's mantra, and without her noticing it had become hers too. No day could begin without that totem of English life.

The kitchen was blessedly empty, the house blissfully quiet. Con filled the kettle, then opened the back door. Outside, there was that breathless, limpid stillness that promised a day of sunshine and heat; that encouraged you to fill your lungs while the last vestige of dawn remained in the air, the pale scent of dew on morning petals.

Con stood for a few minutes on the back doorstep, looking out at the garden: the strip of terrace, and beyond it the lawn, the shrubberies, the orchard. In her parents' day they'd had a gardener, but there was no money for that now, and everything was unkempt. The house too: the rooms they didn't use hadn't been cleaned for months, and the neglect was beginning to show in the patches of damp that crept across some of the ceilings, the peeling paint on the windows. Con didn't dare face this fact yet, but there might not be enough money to stay here much longer. She dreaded the thought of leaving Lowlands, but perhaps, for the boys, a move wouldn't be such a bad thing. A move into a town – a city, even – where there would be more on offer for them. A fresh start, she told herself. For Max, especially, even though he was barely old enough to remember the time his father had lived here with them.

The memory of last night's ugly scene rose up in her mind now, and she felt her face twitch as she recoiled from it. Roy should never have been allowed to have children, she thought viciously. But then she heard Max saying, *you could have not married him*, and her reply – *then I wouldn't have had you* – and her stomach lurched at the idea of a life without her sons: her wonderful, imperfect, irreplaceable sons. All would be well, she told herself. Wherever they were, whatever life did to them, she would stick to her boys like a lioness. She'd be their fierce defender, the provider of everything they needed. She would haul them through all this – through their embroilment in Robin's illness, through every act of thoughtlessness and selfishness by their father. She'd be enough of a parent for both of them, and she'd keep Roy's image as wholesome and as benign as she could in his sons' minds, too – for their sake, not for his.

She took a deep breath and turned back into the kitchen. A pot of tea this morning, she thought, rather than a bag in a cup. And perhaps she should make pancakes. Would that be too much? She could make the batter, let the girls flip them. Max too, perhaps, if his pride would allow it.

It was tempting, she thought, as she broke eggs into a bowl, to blame Roy for everything that went wrong in their lives, but perhaps that wasn't entirely fair. Max had always been difficult, but he'd been worse for the last few months, and there was nothing to tie Roy to that timescale – nor his daughters. Roy had been gone for twelve years, and Nessa and Mab had been with them for barely a week. But the shadow cast by a father's desertion lasted a long time, and its effects could ebb and flow. Certainly the girls' arrival had stirred things up. They were living proof that Roy had a new life and new responsibilities that put his sons a poor second – and now his daughters were here, needing attention from Con, too. And fourteen was a difficult age; anyone could tell you that. You wanted to be grown-up and independent, but you needed to feel secure in order to spread your wings. You needed a protective parent to struggle free of. You certainly didn't want to find yourself jealous of half-sisters who had no biological claim on your mother. To resent them occupying her time; occupying your space.

Con smiled then, feeling the little release that came with finding her way to the root of a problem. Smiled, too, at the thought of poor Max – who hadn't had his teenage growth spurt yet; whose voice hadn't broken – doing battle with the furious sense that he shouldn't need his mother enough any more to be jealous of her paying attention to other people.

Chapter Twenty-Seven

Nessa suggested that they put on their summer dresses, the ones Daddy had bought them the day before they came to Lowlands. They were nice and cool and very colourful: a flowery pattern of pinks and turquoises with dashes of yellow. They wouldn't be much good for climbing trees, Mab thought, but Nessa was right that wearing them made it look as though they'd decided to have a nice day. It would make Con happy, Nessa said, and Con had been so kind to them.

And Con's reaction when they came into the kitchen showed they'd done the right thing.

'Well, look at you two!' She beamed. 'Aren't you the picture of summer?'

'Daddy bought them for us,' Mab said.

'What a nice thing to do.' Con turned back to the bowl she was mixing something in. 'And how nice of you to put them on today.'

For a moment Mab wondered whether something was wrong, but when Con turned round again, she was still smiling.

'I'm making pancakes,' she said. 'I'm counting on you to help me toss them.'

.   .   .

Flipping the pancakes was harder than it looked, but it didn't take Mab long to get the hang of it. Her first two goes ended with a crumpled mess, but the third one turned over exactly like it was supposed to.

'That one's yours,' Con said. 'I'll eat the others.'

'That's not fair,' Mab said, but Con grinned and shook her head.

'They all taste the same,' she said – though that wasn't quite true, Mab knew. She'd eaten a piece that had flown out of the pan and it had tasted like Play-Doh.

Nessa managed to flip one too, and they were all sitting down to eat them when Max appeared in the doorway.

'Good morning!' Con stood up straight away, and held out her arms to Max. Mab looked down at her plate. Max had been horrible last night, but she knew what it felt like the morning after a row.

'Do you want to make your own pancake?' Con asked. 'Or shall I do it?'

'Don't bother,' Max said.

'There's plenty of batter.'

Con kept smiling at him, but Max wouldn't go near her. Perhaps they should finish their pancakes and get down from the table, Mab thought. She caught Nessa's eye, but Nessa just shrugged her shoulders.

'I'll have toast,' Max said. 'I'd prefer toast.'

'OK.' Con looked at him for a moment longer, then she sat down again. Max put some bread in the toaster and poured himself a glass of milk. He was humming something under his breath – or at least Mab thought that's what he was doing. It sounded almost like a growl, like an animal deciding whether to pounce.

'Where's the Nutella?' he asked, when the toast popped up.

'On the table,' Con said. 'I'm afraid we've almost finished it.' She smiled at the girls, to show it was OK, even though it was them who'd finished the Nutella. Mab had smeared it on so thickly you could hardly taste the pancake.

'Oh, great,' Max said. 'Thanks a lot. You bought that jar for me.'

'I'll get more today,' Con said.

'You shouldn't be feeding them Nutella anyway,' Max said. 'They're fat enough as it is.'

'Max!' Con frowned.

'It's true,' Max said. 'They're like fat little piglets.'

'That's complete rubbish,' Con said. 'You're just annoyed that the Nutella's gone.' Her voice sounded very firm, but she didn't say anything else; didn't punish him. Maybe she thought that would make things worse, Mab thought. They'd seen what happened when Max lost his temper. Nessa was staring straight ahead, trying to look as though she hadn't heard. It wasn't true, Mab wanted to tell her – *she* might be a bit plump, but Nessa certainly wasn't.

Max seemed pleased with the effect he'd had, though. 'It's not rubbish,' he said. 'Their mother must be a gorgon.'

And then Mab snapped. 'She's NOT!' she said, her voice coming out louder and more squeaky than she meant. 'She's absolutely beautiful!'

Max grinned. 'Oh yeah? How did she produce two hideous trolls like you, then?'

'That's enough, Max.'

Con sounded properly angry now, but sad as well. She'd wanted this morning to be nice, Mab thought. She'd tried really hard, with the pancakes and everything. How dare Max be so horrid? But you could see he didn't care. He was scraping out the Nutella pot and smiling to himself.

'But then genetics isn't very reliable, is it?' he said. 'I mean, how do you explain me and Philip having the same parents? I'm normal and he's...' He laughed.

'He's what?' said Philip. No one had noticed him coming through the door.

'Philip,' Con began, but he held up a hand.

'No, I want to hear what Max thinks I am. Apart from not being cruel and immature like him.'

'You haven't got enough brain to be cruel,' Max said.

'I've got enough brain to pass my GCSEs,' Philip said. 'You wait and see what happens on results day.'

'Oh my God, just in case we'd forgotten for a second about your GCSEs.' Max laughed loudly. 'Maybe you can pass exams, Phil, but that doesn't stop you being fucking mental.'

'Stop it, Max,' Con said. 'I don't know what's got into you. You'd better go up to your room.'

'Nah,' Max said. 'I'm not doing what you tell me until you remember whose mother you are. I'm going over to the farm. Have fun with the two little pigs and Nutcase Boy.' He grabbed the toast from his plate, folded the two pieces together and shoved them in his mouth, and then he was gone.

'Good riddance.' Philip looked a bit pale, but he managed to smile at Mab and Nessa. 'Don't take any notice, he's just trying to be as unkind as he can. He's...' Philip shook his head. 'He'll calm down. Won't he, Mum?'

'Let's hope so.' Con sighed. 'I'm sorry, girls. But Philip's right, Max is just being vile. I'll deal with him later. I'll make sure he apologises.'

'Don't bother,' Nessa said. The blank look had gone and she looked the opposite now, over-bright and over-cheerful. If you didn't know her, Mab thought, you might think she didn't care about what Max had said. 'I know what boys are like. There are some really mean ones at school.'

'I'm sure there are.' Con couldn't quite manage a smile, but the corner of her mouth twitched as though she was trying. 'Well, all the more pancakes for us, eh? Philip, do you want a go at tossing one?'

The rest of breakfast felt a bit strange – almost as though they were on a ship that was going to sink, Mab thought. Like the people on the Titanic eating their dinner as if everything was OK. Max would be pleased to know that he'd managed to upset every one of them, she knew. Perhaps that's why they were all doing their best to pretend they were fine.

'Maybe you could take the girls swimming later, Philip?' Con asked.

'We were hoping we could go swimming today,' Nessa said. 'Weren't we, Mab?'

Mab looked at Philip. He hadn't spent much time with them since that first day, but he nodded now. 'Could it be in the afternoon?' he asked. 'Then I could get some work done this morning.'

'Of course,' Con said. 'Maybe we might have a little go at knitting this morning, Mab?'

Mab wasn't really sure she wanted to learn to knit, but she didn't want to disappoint Con. This was the second time she'd asked. 'Yes please,' she said.

'What about you, Nessa?' Con asked. 'Will you join us?'

Nessa's face hadn't quite settled back to normal, between the extremes of blankness and brightness, and you could see both in her expression now. 'Would you mind if I went for a little walk?' she said. 'I promise I won't go too far.'

'You could pick some more flowers if you like,' Con said. 'There are lots in the garden at the moment. It's a shame not to enjoy them.'

Their mother always said it was a shame to pick flowers, but maybe, Mab thought, it was different for garden flowers. Or maybe Con was just trying to think of something nice for Nessa to do.

'OK,' Nessa said. 'Does it matter which ones I pick?'

'Not really,' Con said. 'I don't do much to look after them, I'm afraid. They're a gift from nature every year. I could give you a basket, if you like.'

'OK,' Nessa said again. 'I'll just... I'm just going upstairs quickly first.'

When she'd gone, Con found a shallow basket with a tall handle and left it on the kitchen table for Nessa, and then she took Mab into a little room she hadn't seen before. There were cupboards along one wall, a table by the window and a couple of comfy-looking chairs. 'This was my mother's sewing room,' Con said. She nodded at the old sewing machine on a shelf behind the door. 'That needs mending, like most things around here.'

Mab thought that must be a joke, but she wasn't sure enough to laugh. Con opened a cupboard which turned out to be full of wool.

'What colour do you fancy?' she asked, taking out a bag and opening the drawstring. 'This is nice fat wool to start learning with.'

Just then Mab heard the back door opening, and when she looked out of the window a moment later she saw Nessa heading off down the garden. She'd changed back into shorts and T-shirt, and she hadn't taken Con's basket. Mab itched to be with her, to be able to talk to her. To crawl into their den under the laurel bushes and make models of Max out of twigs which they could break into pieces like voodoo dolls. But Con was smiling at her, holding out the wool.

'I'd like the blue, please,' Mab said.

Chapter Twenty-Eight

Mab seemed to like the knitting at first, and it gave Con huge pleasure to sit with her and show her the stitches, to watch her beginning to get the feel of it. For a little while she felt as though everything else had lifted, like the morning mist, leaving only the quiet intimacy of this scene which reminded her so powerfully of her own childhood: two heads bent over a scrap of material, and the gentle clack of needles.

A thought occurred to her then – barely a wisp, a vapour trail, but it was unmistakably there: if Robin died, perhaps the girls could come to her. Could live at Lowlands. There was something so precious about this child, in particular. No: about them both. There was an innocence in Mab, and a wonderful braveness in Nessa, that made her fear for them dreadfully. And to have daughters... If Roy had stayed, she thought, she'd have had more children. Girls, perhaps, the same ages as Mab and Nessa.

The idea was desperately alluring, despite the moral quagmire: the fact that they were someone else's daughters; the fact that she had her own children, her boys. She couldn't admit to it. She could never suggest it. But if she was asked... Philip wouldn't mind, she told herself, and Max would surely come round eventually. It would mean Roy was here more often, if all his children were under one roof.

She looked down at the child beside her, the head of tangled, tabby-coloured curls, and she felt a great wave of love. How strange life was. Her supplanter's daughters; the children she should hate most in the world. But she had never really blamed Robin. She knew Roy too well for that. When it had happened, part of her had been pleased to be rid of him, and for the uncertainty to be over. And Robin was an innocent, not a temptress: Con had almost pitied her, and she hadn't been wrong. Please God, she thought, may Robin never find out about this new woman, whoever she is. Please God, may his daughters never know – and may she, Con, have the protecting of them. May this gentle, tranquil morning last forever.

But after a while Mab's head started to turn towards the window, quick glances a less observant person might have missed. Not exactly wanting to escape, Con thought, but wondering about her sister. And then she felt a tug of guilt: Max had run off in a foul mood, and she'd hardly thought about him while she'd been sitting here with Mab, let alone about Nessa. Should she have gone after him? Or was her instinct right, that it was better to let him cool off? She would make sure she had some time alone with him later, she thought. Perhaps she could take him into town with her; take him out for tea. Buy him something.

'Are you worrying about Nessa?' she asked.

'A bit.'

'Shall we go and look for her?'

Mab shrugged. Her knitting had faltered: there were two dropped stitches in the last row. Con held out her hand, and Mab yielded it up.

'I'll sort this out,' Con said, 'and then we'll go and find Nessa.'

'I'll find her,' Mab said. 'She's only in the garden.' She hesitated. 'We made a den. I expect she's waiting for me there.'

'OK.' Con smiled. 'Let me know if you can't find her. You could take a picnic lunch out there, if you like.'

Mab was already on her feet. 'Thank you for the knitting,' she said. 'I liked it.'

'Good.' Con allowed herself to take Mab's hand for a moment. 'I liked it too.'

A minute later, she saw Mab running down the garden towards the orchard, her dress billowing around her. Like a petal blown on the breeze, she thought. A gaudy peony. The two of them had looked so charming this morning in their matching frocks. They'd smiled so delightfully when they'd managed to toss their pancakes. But Max's spiteful words echoed in Con's head again, and she sighed. She had to put him first – she would, without question, even if that meant relinquishing her greedy desire to look after the little girls. But she could let the fantasy linger in her heart, even so. No one needed to know it was there.

She put Mab's knitting in a muslin bag, then went back to the kitchen to wash up the breakfast things. They could have sandwiches for lunch, she thought, as she dried the frying pan. And this afternoon, while Philip took the girls swimming, she'd go shopping. See if Max would come with her. She felt calm now, confident of her ability to make things better. A fragment of tune came into her head as she went upstairs to check the bedrooms and gather up dirty clothes for the wash. A lullaby she used to sing to the boys: *Hush little baby, don't you cry...* Silly: they were too old for that now. But perhaps they would never be entirely too old to need their mother.

As she came down the stairs with her arms full of clothes she heard a sound below, and looked over the banister to see Philip in the hall.

'Everything all right?' she started to say – but then there was something else, a noise from outside the house. It was hard to place at first: an almost inhuman sound. Before Con's mind had identified it, her body had responded. Dropping the laundry around her, she ran. Ran towards it, as it resolved into Mab's voice, uttering a wail of curdling desolation.

'What is it?' Con grabbed her by the shoulders as they almost collided in the kitchen doorway. 'Mab! What's happened? Is it Nessa?'

'Max,' Mab sobbed. 'It's Max. In the barn.'

Chapter Twenty-Nine

March 2024

The thought came to Mab at exactly the moment when Nessa took out her phone, outside Wanstead station, to text Inga and let her know they'd be home soon. At exactly the moment when the thought of what Inga might have made for lunch came into her head. Herring. Horseradish. Black bread. There was a wave of nausea, more powerful than any she'd felt this past week or two – and then, riding on its coat tails, a sudden, stupefying insight: perhaps I'm pregnant.

It wasn't very likely, she told herself. Or was it? She'd run out of pills a little while ago, but only for a few days. Yes, she'd felt strange lately, tired and hungry and emotional, but her father had just died, and the worst bits of her past had been raked up, which was enough to throw anyone off their mettle. And it didn't seem like the way things worked, finding out you were pregnant just after you'd lost a parent. The world ought to give you space to deal with one big thing before another happened, surely?

But it was possible. It was possible enough that Mab couldn't sit through lunch with Nessa and her girlfriend not knowing whether it was true or not.

'Actually,' she said, 'I'm sorry, but I think I'd better not.'

Nessa looked up, frowning. Ach, Mab thought, Nessa would hate her sudden change of mind. She'd be offended. Mab smiled, doing her best to convey apology.

'I have to be at the shop by four thirty,' she said, 'and by the time...'

It wasn't even two o'clock yet, she realised. But if she stood here much longer, she might be sick. 'Say hello to Inga for me, though,' she said. And then she ducked into the station, leaving Nessa standing in the car park looking after her.

All the way into London along the Central Line, and out again down the DLR, Mab's head fizzed. The nausea had ebbed again, but she could feel it there still, waiting for her. It was mad, she thought, but she had the strangest, strongest sense that she was right. Almost that it was meant to be: at the moment when her father died, leaving her an orphan, his grandchild was coming into being in her belly. A grandchild the size of a pea, or a bean, or whatever it was by now. It was a terrible idea, terrible timing, but there was a part of her that really badly wanted it to be true. Danny's baby, with half her mad genes and half his. Another link in the chain that went back through her beautiful dead mother and her feckless dead father, through Granny Jenny and her brother Michael and their parents whose hearts had been broken, sixty years ago, when their daughter ran off to be a hippie. Through Danny's redoubtable grandmother, too, and the long line of his family.

But that thought caught her off beat, sent her grasping for a handhold as the train jolted to a stop. What would Danny think? Danny had said he loved her, but they'd only been together for a few months. Less than six months, even if you counted right back to that first drink at the pub after work. That was too early for a baby. The nausea surfaced again then, fuelled by a surge of terror. She couldn't bear to spoil things with Danny; couldn't bear to overface him. She'd already made him the only living person to know that for nearly twenty years she'd kept a secret that might have devastating implications. How could she tell him she was pregnant, with all that other stuff still hanging in the balance?

Keep calm, said the little voice inside her that did its best to sound like Nessa, when she needed Nessa's reassurance. It's not a done deal yet. Let's wait and see, and then we can make a plan.

There was a chemist she passed every day on the way home. When she got off the train, she stopped first at Greggs (a sausage roll probably wasn't the best thing for the baby, or indeed for morning sickness, but it was what she felt like, and it helped pep her up) and then at the chemist. It was only a small shop, but it had a bewildering selection of pregnancy tests. Mab stared at them for a few seconds, then chose one she recognised from an ad on the Tube. It promised an accurate answer on the day her period was due, which set Mab's mind racing again. When *had* she last had a period? They'd always been wildly irregular, so the answer might not be much help, but she really couldn't remember. She laughed to herself as she tapped her phone to pay. Think of all the things mothers have to remember, and she couldn't even keep track of her own body. The woman behind the till smiled at her, presumably imagining the suppressed laugh was one of excitement and anticipation. Mab was too ashamed to put her right.

'Thank you,' she said, as the woman slipped the box into a paper bag. Not to disguise it, Mab thought, but to make a bit more of a ceremony out of it. Requiring her to unwrap it when she got it home.

.   .   .

The test was positive, of course. She'd known it would be. She'd known it was part of the unravelling and reravelling of her life, the upheaval she seemed to have so little control over.

But she did have control over this, she told herself, as she curled up on her bed, hugging her knees to her chest. She had time, and she had choices. She could spend the rest of the afternoon, the rest of the evening, thinking it through. That thought made her feel calmer. But it didn't last long. She had to be at the bookshop by four thirty, didn't she? She had to help Danny with the event this evening. She closed her eyes, shutting out the world for a minute while she rested her head on her pillow. Well, she could think it through tomorrow. She wasn't working; she had no plans.

She'd have liked to sleep a little before going out again, but she didn't dare. She let herself lie down for a few minutes, then got up and went down to the kitchen. Aster was there, making another of his stir fries. Piles of vegetables sat in neat heaps on his chopping board. When he saw Mab, he started.

'Oh, Mab!'

'Hello.'

Mab really didn't want to have a conversation, and usually that wasn't a problem with Aster, but today he seemed oddly agitated, shifting from one foot to another and then saying, 'Can you wait here for a moment?'

'Sure. Do you want me to watch the pan?'

He shook his head. The ring wasn't on yet, Mab saw. Aster darted out of the room, and Mab filled the kettle: she didn't feel like tea, but she had to do something with the time before she left for the bookshop. The time that was shorter than she wanted, but longer than she could skip over. Before the kettle had boiled, Aster was back, clutching an enormous bouquet of flowers.

'They're for you,' he said.

'For me?'

'For your father,' Aster said. 'Because of your father. I haven't seen you to give them to you.' He blushed. The flowers dripped on Mab's shoes when she took them from him. He'd clearly been keeping them in a jug of water in his room.

'Thank you,' she said. 'That's really kind, Aster. I'm really touched.'

What she was actually thinking, looking at him and seeing the way he was looking at her, was that this was the last thing she needed. That the flowers weren't really anything to do with her father, except that it had given Aster an excuse. She'd seen that look in men's eyes a hundred times before: Aster had wanted to give her something, and he'd seized his opportunity. She should be flattered. She should be kind. But her feet were wet now, and she had no idea what to do with so many flowers. She stared wildly round the room, and spotted, like a miracle, a bucket by the back door.

'I'll put them in here for now,' she said, 'and find something better later. When I'm back from work.'

Aster nodded, and blinked a little, and Mab was filled with remorse, even though she definitely hadn't been unkind. 'It was my father's funeral today,' she said, 'so this was good timing.'

Aster nodded again. He seemed to have used up his conversation for the day: that was something, at least. The flowers, now she looked at them more closely, were hideous. They were so exotic that they looked almost fake; like blooms that had been cast in glass and then turned back into something organic and weirdly sinister.

'Thank you,' she said again, in case her distaste had shown on her face, and then she turned away as quickly as she dared.

But as she carried the flowers up to her room, Mab realised that she'd made a decision. She hadn't needed an evening to think about it, after all. She'd just needed to be distracted from it for a moment, then catch sight of it again – to feel that flutter of excitement at being dealt a new card, an unexpected card with the power to tell her fortune.

She would keep the baby. She would do her best to be a good mother. There had been too many broken links in her family: she'd lost her mother when she was very small, and she couldn't give up her child. Whatever else happened, she was going to do her best to change the story of her family from this point onwards.

Chapter Thirty

'No Mab?' Inga said, when Nessa came in through the front door. Nessa shook her head, conscious of a tinge of irritation: it wasn't as if she'd lost her sister on the way home, she thought.

'She's got a work event later,' she said. 'She decided the timing was too tight. She sends her love.'

'How was she?' Inga asked, wiping her hands on her apron. 'How was the visit?'

'Exactly as it always is,' Nessa said. 'She's in the pink of health, Granny Jenny.'

She took off her coat and hung it up in the lobby, then paused for a moment, opposite the mirror, to collect herself. It wasn't Granny Jenny she was irritated by, and it wasn't Mab, either, although she couldn't shift the sense that something was going on with her sister. But it certainly shouldn't be Inga: Inga had been an angel this past fortnight. She'd cooked and she'd listened, and she'd held Nessa in the middle of the night when sadness and confusion had threatened to overwhelm her. If she was a bit too opinionated sometimes, a bit too New Age for Nessa's taste, those were small things. But even so...

It was almost, Nessa thought, as she stared at the worry lines that had gathered around her eyes, that Inga had become too indispensable lately. She'd have floundered without her, and that was a scary thought. Nessa had held things together her whole life: she'd never needed to rely on anyone else. But her father's death – it was the last thing she'd expected, but her father's death had unbuckled her. That's what it felt like. As though the armour she'd been wearing all these years had come undone, and the loss of its support was making it hard for her to go on being the person she'd always been.

Her reflection gazed back at her, processing that thought – that this loss had hit her harder than she'd expected. Or not so much the loss itself, perhaps, but the forays into the past, encouraged by Inga, and the visit today, the photo album, and Mab... Nessa badly wished that Mab had come home with her today. She'd wanted to be with Mab for a bit and for it to be as easy and natural as it had been when they were little. Before their mother died, even – when they both had pigtails, and Mab still had her baby teeth. Before Nessa had had to take charge and make decisions.

She remembered, then, the thought she'd had as her sister had disappeared into the Tube station ten minutes ago. Had she been right? Could that really be what was on Mab's mind: all those things they'd never talked about, and which Nessa had done her best to forget? Was this the moment when they had to address them, because the past was breaking through the surface of their lives now, insisting on being seen? But could they – how could they...? They'd hardly managed to talk about their father, even. And this... There was a lot at stake, she thought. Questions of honesty, and of trust, and of guilt. Did they really have to dig all that up? Hadn't they managed fine all this time without thinking about it?

Nessa looked at herself for a moment longer: she adjusted

her hair, settled her breathing, prepared her smile. None of this, she thought, was for sharing with Inga. She needed to think about it, to work out what to do. And for the moment she needed to put on a cheerful face.

Coming back into the kitchen, she wrapped her arms around Inga, inhaling the smell of fried fish and soused onions.

'You're too good to me,' she said. 'My little hausfrau.'

If Inga had noticed that she'd taken a long time to hang up her coat, she didn't mention it. 'You don't mind another Swedish meal?' she asked.

'I like Swedish meals,' Nessa said. 'But you don't have to cook all the time, you know.'

'I don't.' Inga took Nessa's elbows in her hands and planted a kiss on her lips. 'It's only because of your visit to your grandmother today. To have something ready when you got back.'

Inga had cooked at least five times this week, but Nessa didn't point that out. She liked cooking, Inga kept insisting, and it was something you could do, when people were grieving. And Nessa was grateful. She liked the food Inga made – but what she liked best was watching her at work in the kitchen. She'd never been much of a cook herself, but she loved the alchemy of it, and the deft, performative way Inga chopped and sliced and stirred. It was like silent music, she thought. Like food ballet. It soothed her nerves, and it filled her head with nice things; easy things.

It was half past two by the time they sat down. Inga had put flowers on the table, and a couple of candles in white holders.

'You always make it feel like a special occasion,' Nessa said.

Inga shrugged, but she looked pleased. 'It's just our way. Having nice surroundings makes the food taste better.' She watched Nessa take her first bite, then smiled in satisfaction at her reaction. 'Do you want to tell me about your granny, or about Mab?' she asked. 'Or shall we talk about something else?'

'Something else,' Nessa said. 'Please.'

'OK.' Inga took a bite too, and when she'd finished chewing, she said, 'Tell me about your first love.'

'My first love?' Nessa laughed. 'Well, I've told you about Josephine...'

Inga shook her head. 'You were already in your twenties when you met, weren't you? Wasn't there someone before?'

'There were a few people at university, but none of them was important. I was just – finding my feet.'

Inga nodded. 'Tell me about the first one,' she said. 'The first time you fell in love.' She cocked her head, pursed her lips playfully. 'A teenage crush, perhaps?'

There was a sudden buzz of noise in Nessa's head. 'A teenage crush isn't love,' she said. But that was the exact opposite of what she meant. It was the most perfect expression of love, she thought, before cynicism and fear and preconceptions could taint it. She could still taste it, the agony and delight – the feelings she'd had no name for.

Inga smiled. 'You don't have to tell me if you don't want to. I can see I've stepped on a sensitive nerve. I'll tell you about mine, if you like. It couldn't be more embarrassing, I promise you. Mine was a teacher, and I sent her an anonymous Valentine card. I forgot that she knew my handwriting. I wanted to fall through the floor in her class the next day.'

Nessa barely heard her; not after *I can see I've stepped on a sensitive nerve*. Inga was right about that. The memory was exquisitely tender. Nessa had never talked about it, even to Mab. Especially not to Mab, although she'd always wondered whether Mab had guessed. Ach – and there it was again, that territory she so dreaded exploring: not just those secret feelings of hers, but everything that had happened that summer. All the awful mess of it. Mab had been so young; it was hard to know what she'd noticed, or what she might have thought. What might be in her head now.

'Was it a girl or a boy?' Inga asked, cocking her head again. 'You can tell me that.'

'I really don't feel like talking about it,' Nessa said. 'But it's not very interesting, I'm afraid. Nothing like a teacher.'

'OK.'

Inga looked displeased. Openness was one of her watchwords; she didn't like them to have secrets from each other. That was ridiculous, Nessa told herself, when they'd only been together for a few months. Who bared their whole soul, the tiny details of their past, after so short a time? But it wasn't anything to do with time, she knew that. It wasn't anything to do with whether she loved Inga, or Inga loved her. It couldn't be opened so easily, this particular door. She'd locked it tight years ago and never spoken of it again.

Chapter Thirty-One

Danny was already at the bookshop when Mab arrived, making a pyramid of this evening's author's books in the window. He grinned when he saw her, and climbed out from behind the books to come and greet her.

'How was it?' he asked.

'I haven't heard,' Mab said.

'Not the funeral,' Danny said. 'I was thinking of your visit today. Your grandmother.'

'Oh. Yes, that was fine.'

'Any drama with Nessa?'

Mab shook her head.

Danny looked at her carefully. 'And you're OK?'

She hadn't thought this through, Mab realised. She hadn't put two and two together and deduced that she'd have to work out what to say to Danny, how to be with Danny this evening, with those two pink lines on the pregnancy test front and centre in her head.

'I'm a bit tired,' she said. Here was one thing she could do: try not to lie to him. Try to tell him the truth, even if it wasn't the whole truth.

'We can manage without you, if you want to bunk off.'

'No.' Mab mustered a smile. 'No, I'm fine. What shall I do? Glasses? Chairs?'

'Check how many we've got coming,' Danny said. 'Then yes, either of those would be great.'

The launch was for a local author who'd written a collection of ghost stories set in the area, and it had attracted quite a crowd. She'd been a teacher at St Bernard's primary, and her ex-pupils clearly remembered her fondly. Mab kept overhearing women in their thirties and forties referring to her as Mrs McCrae, then giggling at their mistake. The story she read aloud was good, Mab thought. And they almost sold out of their stock during the book-signing, which was always a win for the shop.

But even though the event had started at five thirty, the last stragglers didn't leave until after nine o'clock.

'You should have kicked them out,' Mab said, as they shut the door on the final guest.

Danny shrugged. 'They were having a good time,' he said. 'And we rely on local custom. Maybe they'll come back and buy more books.'

Mab looked at him for a moment – at his kind, busy face – and she felt something shift inside her which was surely not the baby, the tiny embryo, but which felt connected to it, somehow.

'You're a good person, Danny,' she said. 'I'm lucky to know you.'

Danny looked a bit surprised, but pleased, too. 'Thank you,' he said. 'You're a good person too. You did a great job tonight.'

Mab laughed, and then, without her meaning it to, it turned into a yawn.

'Tired?' Danny said. 'More tired than before, I'm sure. All

that running around. Let's close up quickly and go and grab something to eat.'

'I don't...' Mab began, and he turned back to look at her. 'I might just need to go home,' she said. 'It's been a long day. And the funeral, you know. It's been on my mind all day.'

That was a good example of the truth, but not the whole truth.

'We could get a takeaway,' Danny said. 'I could come home with you, stay for a bit.'

Yes, Mab wanted to say. Yes please. But instead she shook her head. She wouldn't be able to not tell him about the baby if he came back with her. She'd only ever managed to keep one secret in her whole life, and now she'd told that to Danny it felt even harder to keep anything from him. And she really wasn't ready to tell him. She needed to get used to the idea herself, and try to prepare herself for his reaction. Whenever the thought of it crept into her head, the idea of how his face might look when he found out, she felt faint.

'You're so kind,' she said, 'but I sort of feel as though I need to be on my own tonight.' She tried to smile again, but everything felt twisted and complicated inside her now and she could tell the smile wasn't convincing. 'Do you mind?'

'Of course not,' he said. But Mab could tell that he did, a bit. That he couldn't understand – or perhaps that it had changed his idea of where they'd got to, the two of them. He'd thought they were at the stage when if one of them was ill or sad they'd want the other one around, and the other one would want to look after them. She could see that thought process playing out in his face, the whisper of disappointment and the realigning that followed it. The slight withdrawal.

Oh God, she thought. Could the stakes really be that high? But perhaps this was about more than tonight. Perhaps Danny wanted to come home with her so they could pick up the conversation about Lowlands. Did he, possibly, want to say that on reflection, he thought she ought to tell someone what she'd seen? Talk to the police, even? Was that flicker in his face not about him feeling rejected, but recoiling from her a little? Perhaps he'd decided that he would stick with her if she did the right thing now, followed his advice, but otherwise...

So maybe she should change her mind, Mab thought in a panic. Maybe she should let Danny come home with her, and listen to him, and... But then either she'd have to be on her guard all evening, maybe even lie to him, or she'd have to let the news about the pregnancy spill out – and if he was already having doubts because of what she'd told him about that long-ago summer, he'd hardly be delighted about being landed with her baby. And also, what if she didn't want to do what he suggested? What if she wasn't ready to do anything?

Damn it – why had she confided in him? Why had she let her guard down after all these years? Hadn't she learned her lesson: that love is too complicated and too precarious to risk encumbering it with anything more than the slightest of burdens?

And then there was another thought. Perhaps she wasn't cut out for a nice, wholesome relationship. Perhaps Danny was right to pull back. Fothergills had a habit of making people unhappy.

'I'm sorry,' she said. There were tears behind her eyes now, but she couldn't let him see them. 'I just need to crash. I'll see you on Monday.'

'OK.'

But that was another blow: skipping over Sunday, not suggesting they meet up tomorrow. There was no mistaking his disappointment now. Mab tried another smile, and then she reached up to kiss him at exactly the moment he turned away towards the office, so that the kiss missed his cheek and grazed his ear. That made her feel foolish and clumsy, but Danny turned back, put his arms around her and hugged her tight. And that felt so good, so very good, that Mab almost cracked. For a moment she couldn't work out why she was sticking to her guns – whether it was for the greater good of their relationship, or because it was better to scupper it now before anyone's heart got properly broken – but she was too tired to think any more. That bit was true, at least: she was completely shattered.

'Good night,' she said, when Danny released her at last, and before he could say anything she pushed open the door and stepped out into the night.

'It's you and me now, baby,' she said, as she headed off up the street. Listen to her, talking to a bunch of cells. But it felt good. It felt comforting to have a confidante hidden away inside her. She was definitely keeping the baby, that was for sure. Everything else – well, just at the moment everything else felt like a mess. She'd upset Nessa and Danny, and there basically wasn't anyone else. Perhaps she'd end up marrying Aster, eating stir fry and living in a house full of horrible flowers. She tried to laugh at herself, but this time the laughter turned into tears, and she walked on up the road seeing the world – the Saturday evening pub-goers, and the ghostly blossom on the trees in the park – through a blurry veil of misery and exhaustion.

Chapter Thirty-Two

Con and Philip arrived back at Lowlands on Tuesday afternoon, and Con was in bed by seven o'clock that night, hoping to kill off the jet lag. But sleep proved elusive.

She couldn't tell whether it felt as though they'd been away for a long time, or no time at all, but as Ursula had predicted, she'd hardly managed to get the days the right way up while they were in Wellington. It had felt as though she'd turned nocturnal – or perhaps the sun had, shining all night and hiding away during the day. Philip had managed better, addressing himself scientifically to the problem of jet lag, but it had seemed to Con rather apt to drift through the weekend so topsy-turvy, never quite sure whether she was awake or dreaming. You had never known where you were with Roy, either. Never known whether he was coming or going, preparing for a grand entrance or a sudden, stealthy exit.

Ursula had insisted that Con and Philip sat next to her at the front of St Hugh's, a stone-built Gothic revival church that looked disconcertingly as though it had been transplanted from Somerset. Sitting beside Ursula had been disconcerting too, and

Con had been glad of Philip on her other side. Just the three of them in the family pew, which seemed peculiar for a man who had gone through wives and lovers with such gusto. But the church had been moderately full, even if Con hadn't known a single face. She hadn't recognised anything of her one-time husband in the eulogy delivered by the young priest, either – and she hadn't much liked Ursula, although perhaps that shouldn't have been a surprise.

She was glad to be home, anyway, even if the inversion of night and day had caught her out again on the return leg. Was she pleased to have gone? she wondered, lying awake as the night crept tauntingly past. Probably. She was pleased to have done the right thing, although there wasn't a soul who would have noticed if she hadn't, except for Ursula. It had cost a small fortune, and she had no expectation of being left anything – even enough for the plane tickets – in Roy's will. Ursula had told her, with characteristic candour, that the house was in her name. Con had waited to hear more – whether there was anything for Philip, or for Mab and Nessa – but there had been no more disclosures, and she certainly wasn't going to ask.

Seeing the house and the neighbourhood, glimpses of the city and the coastline, Con had found it hard to imagine Roy living there. The people who came to the funeral must have been friends, but they could have been hired extras for all the connection Con could discern to the man she'd known. Ursula's friends, she'd felt sure, not his. The house – an angular, white-painted, large-windowed villa just outside the city – was filled with Roy's recent paintings, and the sight of them had made Con sad. They looked to her like knock-offs of Klee or Kandinsky, painted for people who wouldn't know the difference. Had he changed so much? Con wondered. Had the modest success they'd brought him made Roy happy? He, who had so hated mediocrity and compromise?

Lying in her midnight bed at Lowlands Cottage, Con thought about his letters – those strange, formal epistles on thick vellum that had punctuated the last two decades. They had been intended, she felt sure, to persuade her that his life was just as he wanted it, and she'd seen through that. But she had succumbed to another layer of deception, she realised now. They had lulled her into a false sense of amity, those letters. They had presupposed a friendship she had never meant to grant him again after that terrible summer; after that cataclysmic evening when he'd brought her portrait back to Lowlands like a get-out-of-jail-free card.

Except, she reminded herself, that that evening hadn't been the final act of their drama. Roy's grief for Max had been genuine and profound, and she'd been grateful to have him beside her during those terrible days when the house was crawling with police and they'd had to organise a funeral for their fourteen-year-old son. She'd been sufficiently grateful – and sufficiently numbed by the loss of her child – that when he went back to his daughters and his dying wife, the rage she had felt towards him had faded. She hadn't had the capacity for it, she thought now. She hadn't had the capacity for anything except looking after Philip, and when Roy had started writing to her she had been gratified, somehow, that he had wanted to. That he had felt there was something between them that was still worth cherishing.

Was it odd, she wondered, that what had been rekindled by Roy's death wasn't her love for him, but her hatred?

The next thing Con knew it was eight o'clock, and the sun was shining. March was almost over, and the English weather had settled, for the moment, into a steady warmth. It was a day to be outside: to enjoy the solace of the burgeoning spring. The magnolia and cherry and buckthorn she'd known since she was a child were blooming, full of the bright promise that never failed to lift her spirits.

But Con didn't get up straight away. She had the feeling, this morning, that she'd been given a chance to reset her life, and she needed to start out on the right path. On a new path, that is, because who could ever tell whether a path was the right one until you'd followed it a little way? Wasn't it, indeed, one of the many ironies of life that all too often you only realised you were on the wrong path when it was too late to turn round? But she mustn't think like that. She must hold on to this idea that life could be different. That she could be different. Roy was dead, and she had woken up to a new day. Didn't that count for something?

Her bedroom door opened silently, and a cat appeared, its head and then its body and the curl of its tail. Not her cat: it belonged at the farm, but it had taken to visiting her recently. She'd come upon it in the garden at first, then once or twice in the kitchen when she'd left the door open. It had never ventured so far into the house before. Perhaps, Con thought fancifully, it had noticed their absence, and had come to see what was what, now they were back.

'Hello,' Con said. 'How did you get in?'

The cat leapt onto her bed and approached her lap, purring. It was a skinny tabby, its coat almost entirely grey and black. Like all the farm cats at Lowlands, Con thought. How many generations of them had she seen? She remembered Mab, aged eight, sitting cross-legged on the floor with a kitten in her arms, begging to be allowed to keep it. It couldn't possibly be the same cat, Con told herself. More likely a great-grandchild of one of those wriggling babies Mab had met. But even so, she was prepared to accept it as a sign. A suggestion, rather: that this new life, this new path, should include Mab. And she'd already invited her to visit, hadn't she?

Well then, Con said to herself, as she stroked the tabby's head and it arched its back in pleasure: that was where she would start. She would ring Mab today, and make an arrangement with her.

Chapter Thirty-Three

The last few days hadn't gone well for Mab. Saturday evening felt like a long time ago now: she'd been in the infancy of this muddle then, oblivious to its sharper edges. When she'd got back to her house after the book launch, she'd run a deep bath and lain in it until there was no more hot water to top it up with, and by the time she'd got out she'd half-persuaded herself that the situation might turn out to be less fearsome than it first seemed. She'd heard Hazel's voice, that exasperated tone of hers saying *You worry too much, Mab*, and although it had never seemed true before, it had felt almost comforting.

On Sunday she'd slept late, so late that when she woke up her mind had been wiped clean, and for a full minute, maybe two, she'd thought it was an ordinary day. The sun had been shining and there was blue sky between the slanted rooftops opposite, and even a bird singing somewhere. She'd remembered Yvonne's almond croissants and thought maybe she could buy something like that for herself this morning – splash out, because she'd done all that overtime last night. And then last night had crept back into her mind, and a cloud had passed over the blue sky.

Oh yes. She was pregnant. She'd missed her father's funeral. She'd offended Nessa and upset Danny. For good reason, but even so. It wouldn't have been such a good reason if she hadn't talked to him about Max and Lowlands: about what she knew, or thought she knew. Was pretty sure she knew, actually, and was also sure, now, that she should have told someone a long time ago. But now she'd told Danny about it, it meant she couldn't tell him about the baby. Not that it was a baby yet, more a sort of tiny seed inside her – but even so, Mab could feel its presence already. She could tell it was going to hang in there. And if she needed any proof of its power, she got it the moment she tried to sit up: a crippling wave of nausea.

So Sunday had passed in a bit of a blur. She'd hardly got out of bed, except to totter to the bathroom and throw up. She'd told her housemates she'd got food poisoning: told Yvonne, at least, when she met her on the landing, and word had got round. Charley had brought her a bottle of tonic water and a packet of Ryvita, which they assured Mab was the best cure, and Mab had managed to eat a couple of the crackers, washed down with tonic water, and had felt a bit better – but also guilty, because Charley's sympathy wasn't for the right thing. But you weren't supposed to tell people you were pregnant straight away, she knew that. People who weren't the father, that is. And then that had made her think of Danny again, and the disappointment on his face when she'd left the shop last night, and her stomach had clenched and another surge of nausea had overtaken her.

She couldn't, she mustn't tell Danny the truth, and she mustn't lie to him either, but she needed to say something. She couldn't leave him hanging all day. She reached for her phone and typed a message. *Feeling really ill today. Staying in bed* :(

A reply had come back within seconds, causing another

lurch in Mab's stomach, another spasm of nausea. *Shall I come and look after you?*

She'd hesitated. Of course she wanted Danny to come. She'd never had a boyfriend before who would have offered to look after her when she was ill. Why was she keeping him away, exactly? What nonsense had she told herself? But it wasn't nonsense. Or at least it was possible it wasn't, and that meant she needed some time with a clear head to think it through, and her head was anything but clear today. And meanwhile her past and her future were a lot to take on, even for Danny. *So so kind but better not,* she'd texted back. *See you when I'm feeling better.*

That had dealt with Sunday. That and a lot of sleep and watching *Love, Actually* on her phone under the duvet, and consuming the rest of the tonic water and Ryvita. But then there had been Monday, when she got up and went to work and only lasted an hour before Danny sent her home again.

'You weren't making it up about being ill,' he'd said. 'You shouldn't come in until you've had twenty-four hours without symptoms.'

That might take quite a long time, Mab had thought, but she'd been close to tears at that point so she'd just nodded and put on her coat.

'I want to give you a big hug,' Danny had said, 'but I don't want to catch your bug. The shop'll be up shit creek without both of us.'

'It's OK,' Mab had said. The rational part of her was fighting hard to see it as a good thing that there was this cover story, because it gave her some time. No one needed to know she'd even suspected she was pregnant yet, let alone done a test. But another part hated the idea of any more deception. That part wanted to throw up its hands at the chaos Mab had created around her and bully her into telling the truth – all of it – to Danny, so that she'd know where she was.

But for the moment the rational part won. She'd managed a sort of smile, and blown Danny a kiss and taken herself home, stopping on the way to buy more tonic water and Ryvita, because they really were the best things.

And then she'd spent quite a lot of Monday on the internet, and that had made her really scared. She'd read about the chances of miscarrying (much higher than she'd thought – which made her realise how attached she'd already got to the idea of having a baby), and about all the things she shouldn't do and shouldn't eat (a bewildering number) and the things she should do, like taking vitamins. She'd read about the side effects of pregnancy and how long they could go on, and she'd realised things would almost certainly get worse before they got better. That was if she was actually pregnant in the normal way, because there were also any number of stories about ectopic pregnancies and hydatidiform moles out there to make you feel the chances of that were pretty small.

And then she'd been gripped by an overwhelming terror about what she'd got herself into, and an overwhelming need to speak to someone about it. She'd battled for quite a long time with the idea of ringing Danny, or perhaps Nessa, but then it had occurred to her that there was another option, so she'd rung her GP instead, blessing Nessa for making sure she'd registered with one and marvelling at the fact that she'd put their number in her phone. As the line rang, and she sat in a queue to be answered, she'd remembered the accounts on the internet about how underfunded the health service was, and the scare stories about appalling maternity care, so that when the receptionist picked up at last, her expectations were so low that she burst into tears before she could explain why she was ringing.

And perhaps it was because of the tears, or because she had no idea how far on she might be, or perhaps she was just lucky –

but somehow, by the time she put the phone down, she had an appointment with a midwife for the next morning.

And so here she was, on Tuesday morning, having texted Danny to say that she wasn't ready to come back to work yet, sitting in a waiting room with a lot of other women who were a lot more pregnant than her. Several of them smiled at her in a way that was probably meant to be sympathetic and encouraging, but made Mab feel like a fraud because she had no belly at all yet, and had only, now she came to think of it, done one pregnancy test. Should she have done another one, to be sure? There'd been two in the packet. Would they send her away again and tell her to–

'Madeleine Fothergill?'

That name again, Mab thought, as she put up her hand. If this was another role for her alter ego, though – the one in charge of passports and bank accounts and tenancy agreements – things might go a bit better.

'That's me,' she said. And then the woman smiled at her, and before she knew it Mab was in tears again, and the other women in the waiting room were probably looking at her, but she didn't care any more. She'd only just started out and she was already crying at the least thing, but it was hardly a surprise, she told herself, that she wasn't much good at being pregnant.

There were two of them, a midwife and a student midwife, whose name was Cheryl. Mab hadn't heard the name of the other one, because of the weeping. She kept trying to see her badge, but it was hidden in a fold of her dress. They were both very nice. Mab felt like a fraud again, having all this scarce resource lavished on her, but they both kept telling her not to worry. They seemed to be happy with the one test and the nausea and the fact that she hadn't had a period for a longish time, although it surprised them a bit that Mab had no idea exactly how long.

'I think we'll book you in for an early scan,' the older one said. She was fiftyish, Mab reckoned; a comfortable, smiling person. 'Then we'll know where we are.'

'OK,' Mab said. 'I'm sorry. I've never really bothered about keeping count.'

'It's difficult to be sure of dates anyway if you have an irregular cycle,' the midwife said. 'It's better to be sure. I'll book the scan for you now, and then we can talk about everything else.'

Everything else turned out to be quite a lot. A lot of questions, and a lot of information, some of it accompanied by leaflets, and at the end of it all a cardboard folder with her name on that she was to take home.

'Are you sure?' Mab said, when they handed it to her. 'What if it turns out I'm not pregnant?'

Cheryl laughed then, but the older midwife squeezed her hand. 'I'm going to be a bit surprised if that's the case,' she said, 'but no one will mind.' They'd asked Mab about the father and Mab had said yes, she had a boyfriend, and no, she hadn't told him yet, and they'd nodded and not said anything else. But now the midwife said, 'Is there someone who can come with you to the scan?'

'Yes,' Mab said. The scan was on Friday, which was three days away still. Possibly she'd have told Danny by then, although the rational part of her wanted to wait until she was sure there actually was a baby, and the other part was running even more scared than before, because this had all got much more serious much faster than she'd expected. Otherwise – maybe she could ask Nessa, although she knew before the thought had even formed itself properly that she didn't want to do that.

'It doesn't matter if there isn't,' the midwife said. 'But it can be quite an emotional moment.'

Mab nodded. And they've already seen me weep because someone called my name, she thought. Her lip trembled again.

'Yes,' she said. 'I'll bring someone.'

'Good.' The midwife leaned forwards to type something into her computer, and suddenly Mab could see her name badge clearly. Robin, it said. She was speaking again now, giving some final instructions or encouragement, but Mab couldn't hear her. She had never, since her mother died, met another woman called Robin. She knew she shouldn't read anything into it, but it was impossible to ignore the coincidence.

Was it a good omen or a bad one? Would she ever meet this Robin again, or would it be a different midwife each time? It was all she could do to hold her tears in now, as she nodded and stood up and said thank you. For a moment she thought Robin was going to give her a hug, and she thought how nice that would be, but all she did was hold Mab's arm for a moment and tell her that it was perfectly normal to have big emotional swings, and that she should look after herself. Get lots of rest.

And then that was it, and Mab was walking back across the waiting room, and back out into the street, with the brown folder stuffed into her bag.

Chapter Thirty-Four

Con pushed open the door to the garden and stepped outside. She didn't have to leave for the station for another hour. Everything was ready for lunch, for Mab, and she didn't know quite what to do with herself. She was more nervous, she realised, than she'd been before Roy's funeral. Was that absurd?

She tried to calm herself by remembering the girls' first arrival at Lowlands. They'd got out of the car with a heart-rending mixture of curiosity and reluctance: Nessa tall for just-thirteen, a girlish version of Roy with some of her mother's elfin charm, and Mab a slight, undergrown eight. Con remembered her so well, that little girl, but she hadn't the least idea what to expect from Mab today. What kind of person would she have become? Had she hardened? Would any of that sweetness and innocence have survived?

For a few moments Con stared at the roses on the fence, thick with buds and new crimson foliage, and then she turned away. Remembering that visit was unbearable; the tension of anticipating Mab's return even worse. She needed to walk: to walk briskly and get out of breath, so that the beat of blood in her head had some purpose.

She went back through the house and out of the front door, then turned along the road towards the big house. She didn't often walk that way any more, but she forced herself to do it sometimes. To revisit the farm; come close to the barn. Jim and Jean had sold up and moved away a few years ago, and Con had felt both relief and a tearing, visceral regret at the severing of another link to the past.

As she walked along the lane now, between hedgerows splodged with blossom, she thought about that letter of condolence from Lucy. A kind letter, and an unexpected one. That letter and then the cat, visiting her in bed the day before yesterday: what had they meant? What had they made her feel? Con wasn't used to asking herself questions like that, but perhaps she should, before Mab arrived. Perhaps she should think about the questions that had bubbled up the day Roy died – two weeks ago today – after she'd rung Mab and Nessa to tell them the news. Had they ever thought of her, those girls? Had they wondered why she'd never been in touch? Had she meant anything to them?

And now, as she waited for Mab, there was another question. Could either of them have guessed how eager she was to see them again?

Surely not, she told herself. She had rung them both to tell them Roy had died, but after that it had been them who'd phoned her. Nessa first, to talk about the funeral, then Mab, to ask about a wreath. There'd been that catch in her voice, then, that had released a trigger in Con's mind: there'd been the eager acceptance of her invitation that had made her heart soar.

As to the rest – surely they must have thought, if they ever thought about it at all, that it was grief that had stopped Con from staying in touch. Her grief and theirs, too much to bear in one room. They'd have thought, perhaps, as they got older, that Con had done her bit, taking them in that summer – done more than anyone could have expected – and been rewarded for it in such a horrifying way that it would be too painful for her to see them again.

And that was a plausible explanation, Con thought. Perhaps it was part of the truth, in fact, but it wasn't all of it. There'd been her guilt, too: guilt about her desire to take them in, which had required her to punish herself, to make certain the temptation would never be renewed, by cutting all ties with them. And there'd been something else, of course. Something she could hardly name, but which had begun to nudge at her again these past two weeks. Something she might have to face up to, after all this time.

There was the farm gate now, and the familiar shapes of the roofs. The big house was beyond it, but there wasn't time to go any further, even if she'd been able to persuade herself to do it. Con turned, and walked briskly back towards the cottage. And then she took the car keys off their hook and picked up her handbag, and two minutes later she was driving away towards the station.

Only a handful of people got off the train at Yeovil, and only one of them was a young woman, but even so Con wasn't sure it was Mab. Might she have missed the train, perhaps, or... But she was coming towards Con now, and venturing a smile, and suddenly there was a glimpse of the child Con had known.

She was beautiful; that was the first thing you noticed. Beautiful enough, Con felt sure, to shape, and perhaps even to disrupt, her life. But she had none of the aloofness that so often accompanies beauty: her face was eager and gentle. Her hair, acorn-brown and falling below her shoulders, looked unkempt –

not artistically dishevelled but unbrushed – and she was wearing jeans and a baggy sweatshirt, carrying a backpack over her shoulder.

'Con,' she said. 'You haven't changed.'

Con laughed. 'That's not true,' she said, 'but I'm glad I'm still recognisable. You...' She hesitated. 'You look – grown-up, Mab.'

'I don't feel it.' Mab laughed a little self-consciously, then opened her arms to offer Con a hug. 'It's lovely to see you.'

'It's been much too long,' Con said. 'That's my fault.'

Mab shook her head, and her hair brushed Con's face as they drew apart. 'We knew where to find you,' she said. 'You probably didn't have any idea where we were.'

That wasn't true, but Con didn't rebut it. She couldn't tell yet whether Mab was watching her words, or perhaps testing for a response. In any case there was too much to say, too much to explain – and she still had no idea what Mab might want from her.

'Shall we go?' she said instead.

When they were in the car, silence fell. Con negotiated her way out of the car park, then turned north. They'd take the scenic route, she thought.

'So how are you?' Mab asked. 'How was New Zealand? The funeral?'

'It all went well. It felt oddly...' Con looked at Mab. 'The church could have been lifted from an English village. I'm not sure whether your father had ever been inside it, to be honest. Ursula chose it. She chose everything. As you'd expect, of course.'

'What's she like?' Mab asked.

'Businesslike.' Con smiled. 'I've got a copy of the service sheet for you, and the eulogy. And lots of photos.'

'Oh, thank you!' Mab's face lit up. 'That's so kind. I've been feeling a bit odd about it. About not going.'

Con glanced at her again. 'There wasn't much sense of him in the service. And there was no one there I knew except Philip and Ursula. I was glad you hadn't come, actually.'

'But if we had, there'd have been four of us,' Mab said.

Tears welled in Con's eyes. 'That would have been nice,' she said.

But the silence grew awkward again after that. They were emerging from the town now, fields opening up on both sides. They'd be home in twenty minutes. Back at Lowlands.

'Philip sends his love, by the way,' Con said. 'He's at work today, I'm afraid.' She hesitated. 'He lives at home still, which is very nice for me. He works for the council.'

'Oh!'

Mab's response was invested with as much interest as a monosyllable could hold, but it still didn't give Con many clues.

'What do you do, Mab?' she asked.

'I work in a bookshop. Not very high-flying, I'm afraid, but I like it.'

'That's what matters,' Con said.

'Nessa works in finance,' Mab said. 'She's the successful one.'

'It feels strange knowing so little about you,' Con said, before she could stop herself. She held her breath, waiting for Mab to say that that was, after all, Con's fault, but she didn't. She smiled – a sweet, spontaneous smile that reminded Con so much of the child Mab that she felt winded. All this, she thought, she had denied herself. For nineteen years she had done without the comfort of Mab's presence; without her friendship.

'There's not much to know, really,' Mab said. 'I work in a bookshop. I live in a shared house in the wrong bit of Lewisham.

Nessa thinks I ought to do something a bit more ambitious, but...'

'But you're happy?'

'Yes,' Mab said. 'Or at least...'

Con waited. There it was again, the same shift, the same tremble that she'd heard on the phone. Was it just Roy, or was there something else? The why-have-we-never-seen-you-again question, after all?

'Actually,' Mab said, with a sudden acceleration, 'I didn't mean to say this so soon, but if I don't I might not dare.'

'Go on,' Con said.

Mab glanced at her. 'It's just ... there's something I wanted to talk to you about.' She sighed. More than a sigh: a deep wrench, as though she was tearing something out of her chest. 'I'm really not sure whether I should, though. I've been thinking and thinking about it.'

Con's heart dropped and caught itself again. It hadn't occurred to her that Mab might know – might suspect... But if she did, if that's what this was, then it was better for it to come out, she told herself. It would be worse – much, much worse – to let her leave without voicing it. Mab's face was full of distress now: Con reached a hand across and touched her knee.

Mab swallowed. 'I really don't know what to do. But the thing is, I don't actually have anyone else I can talk to about it, Con.'

Con was surprised by how calm she felt. It was almost a relief to have the decision taken out of her hands. And it meant she could do the right thing now.

'You can talk to me,' she said. 'Whatever it is, you can tell me.'

That much she could do, she thought. That much she could give Mab, after all this time.

Chapter Thirty-Five

Con was just the same as Mab remembered. Her hair was still cut short, greyer now but still with streaks of dark brown, and her clothes were familiar, a well-worn dress and cardigan. Mab recognised the countryside too, and the approach to Lowlands. But as they got close Con drove straight past the house, straight past the farm.

'Oh!' Mab said. 'I thought you still lived at Lowlands?'

'We live in the cottage now,' Con said. 'Lowlands Cottage. Maybe you remember it from last time?'

They pulled up in front of a house that looked like a smaller version of the real Lowlands; the old Lowlands. It was made of the same sand-coloured stone and had the same tiled roof, and primroses swarmed along the grass verge in front of it.

'It's pretty,' Mab said.

'It's more practical for two. And – well, we had no choice, really. I couldn't...' She smiled quickly. 'The big house ate money, and there wasn't enough.'

'I'm sorry,' Mab said.

'Don't be. It was years ago, anyway.'

Mab didn't reply. Her mind was still reeling from what she'd said in the car – the expectation she'd set up. Con had seemed nervous afterwards, although she'd tried to hide it. That made Mab nervous, too – but she still had a get-out, she told herself. There was the baby: she could tell Con she was pregnant, and say nothing about the past. But then...

She'd thought and thought about it on the train – about whether confiding in Con was the right thing to do. And then when she'd seen her at the station, she'd felt a surge of relief that was almost like – no, it wasn't the same, she mustn't think that – but it was the next best thing, perhaps. The closest thing left to finding her mother waiting for her on a railway platform. And she'd wanted to tell her everything: to let everything that was troubling her and tangling up her life spill out. But if Con had guessed what was on her mind – if they both suspected the same thing – if that meant it was true... Oh, what was she to do?

Con was opening the front door now, and there was – blessedly – something else to command Mab's attention. This house was nothing like Lowlands on the inside. It wasn't just that it was smaller: the ceilings were low, and it felt dark and claustrophobic. Mab couldn't help the flash of disappointment – for Con and Philip rather than herself, of course, except that whenever she'd imagined this moment, returning to Lowlands at last, it had always taken place in the old house. She'd pictured herself so many times back in that lofty kitchen, with its chaos of cupboards and discarded clothes and piles of books, then climbing the stairs to find the little room where she and Nessa had slept.

'Come in,' Con was saying. 'There are hooks there for your jacket.'

'This is sweet,' Mab said. 'Oh, I recognise that picture.'

She was looking for the painting of Con – the one Roy had brought that night – but she couldn't see it.

'I couldn't bring much with me,' Con said, noticing her exploring glances. 'The new people bought a lot of the furniture, and the things they didn't want were sold.'

Mab blushed, and turned away to hide it. It must have been terrible for Con, all that.

'You've made this very nice,' she said, although she couldn't really bring herself to like this house. Couldn't really imagine Con living here. She followed her through to the kitchen, where she could smell lunch in the oven. At least that was something that hadn't changed: the comfort of Con's cooking. Mab had felt sick on the train, but hunger was on the prowl now. She hoped they'd eat soon.

'Tea?' Con asked. 'Or coffee?'

'No thanks,' Mab said. 'Just a glass of water would be lovely.'

Con poured herself a cup of coffee and put it on a tray with a glass of water for Mab.

'Let's go outside,' she said. 'It's so nice to see the sun.'

They went through the little sitting room and out into a bit of garden that gave the same impression of getting along on its own as the garden at the big house had done. Con put the tray down on a wrought-iron table and pulled out two chairs. They weren't in the sun, but the table looked too heavy to move.

'Here,' Con said, when they were sitting. She passed an envelope across the table.

It was a shock to see her father's face on the front of the order of service. He looked older than Mab had expected, and for a moment pity filled her mind. All that moving around, she thought, and the quest for professional success, and losing touch with his children. But the thought was gone as soon as it appeared. He'd made those choices himself, hadn't he? Certainly no one had made him settle on the other side of the world and leave his children behind.

She'd never looked at her father through an adult lens before, Mab realised. As a child she'd always wanted to think well of him, to excuse him, to hope for better things ahead: she'd wanted him to be a good man, deep down. Sitting here opposite Con, it occurred to her that he really hadn't been. And it occurred to her, too, that her baby would have no grandparents – not on her side, at least. She stared at the service booklet for a moment, at the dates on the front that measured out the span of her father's life, and then she put it down on the table.

'You can take it home,' Con said. 'I put a copy in there for Nessa, too. And the text of the vicar's eulogy. You can read it now, if you like, or...'

'Not now,' Mab said. But she hesitated. 'What did the vicar say? Did he mention us?'

'Yes.' There was a half-smile. 'And me, and Philip. Ursula is nothing if not principled.'

Mab liked the implication that they were on the same side. She'd always felt that with Con, despite the fact that back in the day, her mother had been the equivalent of Ursula.

'It was very nice of you to be so kind to us that summer,' she said.

'It wasn't hard.' Con pursed her lips. 'It wasn't your fault. None of it was your fault.'

And then, to Mab's dismay, her face crumpled. Her kind, familiar face. 'The thing you wanted to talk about, Mab,' she said. 'I think I know what it is, and I'd rather not wait any longer, if you don't mind.'

'OK.' Mab's heart throbbed.

'I can't account for myself,' Con said. 'I should have done things differently, I know that.'

'*You* should have done things differently?' Mab stared at her. Perhaps, if she'd known, Con ought to have said something – but she surely couldn't think Mab would blame her for that?

212

Oh, but she wasn't sure she could bear to have this conversation now. Not right now: she hadn't eaten anything since eight o'clock, and she felt empty and exhausted, the nausea worrying at the corners of her.

'Con,' she said, 'I'm so sorry, but could we – do you mind if I eat something first? I'm... the thing is, you see, that I'm pregnant, and...'

Con's face changed again: changed completely. 'You're pregnant?' she said. 'Oh, dear Mab, that's such wonderful news.'

'I'm not sure that it is,' Mab said, 'but actually I can't think at all just now. I don't know if you remember what it's like – I just need some food.'

'Of course,' Con said. 'Of course. Do you eat quiche? I hope you do. It has bacon in it; I should have asked if that was OK.'

'I eat anything,' Mab said. 'Except the things I can't any more because of – but I think quiche is fine. I'm sure it is. Let me help you.'

She started to get up, but Con put a hand on her shoulder. 'Stay here. I'll bring it out. As quick as I can, I promise.'

When Con had gone inside, Mab shut her eyes, fighting down the nausea and trying to calm her racing heart. Con would assume now that what she'd wanted to talk about was the baby, and perhaps that would mean they could leave everything else alone. What Con had said, about knowing what Mab was going to say – it must mean that she knew what Mab knew; suspected what Mab suspected. That's what Mab had wanted to find out, and now that she was sure of it, she felt a desperate urge to put the lid back on the past. She could let Con mother her and make a pleasant fuss about the baby, and pretend there was nothing else to talk about.

Because it wasn't only hunger that had overtaken her just now: it was the look on Con's face, too. The crack in her voice when she'd said *I should have done things differently*. It was the sickening realisation of what opening this Pandora's box might mean.

Chapter Thirty-Six

It was ridiculous, Con thought as she lifted the quiche out of the oven, to set so much store by a baby. To let it change the whole landscape of her mind. But there was something so welcome, and so timely, about the news. There had been no births in the family, after all, since those two deaths so close together, nineteen years ago. She'd almost been expecting another death after Roy's, but instead there was this. A new life. A child entirely unrelated to her, just as Mab was, but...

Con sighed, and shook her head. Ah, she was a foolish old woman. But for today, just for today she could play the role of the surrogate grandmother, couldn't she? She heard Mab's voice again, saying, *I don't actually have anyone else I can talk to about it.* That couldn't be true, not really: she knew how young people spoke sometimes. But today she could do her part, listen to Mab's worries. She could wave her off with a smile on her face. That would be something – a small, serendipitous something – to set against the list of her failures.

While she uncovered the salad bowl and took cutlery out of the drawer, she let herself remember the summer when she'd been pregnant for the first time. She and Roy hadn't been married, not even engaged, and she'd been terrified that he'd run a mile when she told him, but instead he'd been thrilled. Overjoyed. It still made her smile, remembering his reaction, even though she knew, now, that his delight had been partly about Lowlands: about her being an only child, her parents already approaching seventy. He'd imagined more money than there was. But that hadn't been the whole truth either. The most infuriating thing about Roy was that he'd never been all bad. 'I'll be a father,' he'd said. 'I'll have a son, and he'll have the most beautiful mother in the world.' And then he'd painted her portrait. *Madonna of the Lilies*, he'd called it.

Mab was looking at the rose bushes when she went back outside. The sun had moved round a little further, and the fence was bathed in golden light.

'I planted those the year we moved here,' Con said. 'I've hardly done anything to them since, but they're more prolific every year.'

'What colour are the flowers?' Mab asked, reaching a hand to one of the tightly-clenched buds.

'Pink,' Con said. 'It's a beautiful rose, but I don't remember its name. Isn't that awful?'

Mab shook her head, as though the obligations of gardening were well beyond her comprehension. 'The quiche looks delicious,' she said.

Con had brought out some bread too: she wasn't sure how much Mab would eat. She remembered the pregnancy sickness well, and how a little and often was what was needed.

She let Mab eat in peace until she put her fork down.

'Good?' she asked, and Mab nodded.

'Thank you.'

'My pleasure.' Con smiled. 'So, the baby...'

'I only found out at the weekend,' Mab said.

'New news, then.'

'Yes. But I've got a scan tomorrow morning. I'm not very good on dates and things, so they want to check.'

Con nodded. 'And your ... boyfriend?'

'I haven't known him very long,' Mab said. 'He's called Danny. He's lovely, really lovely, but I–' She sniffed. 'I haven't told him yet. You're the first person I've told, actually, apart from the midwife.'

'I'm flattered.'

'Guess what her name is,' Mab said. 'The midwife I saw. She's called Robin. I couldn't... I didn't...'

And then she was crying – crying volubly, copiously, just as she had as a child – and Con was out of her seat and rushing to comfort her.

'I'm not unhappy about it,' Mab said, between convulsions of weeping. 'It's not that. I'm really happy, actually. But I shouldn't be happy, I should be cross with myself for letting it happen. I know I don't deserve it. I'll just make a mess of things.'

'Why?' Con asked. 'Why on earth do you not deserve to be a mother?' Did this happen to young women who had lost their mothers? she wondered. She could imagine them feeling anxious and overwhelmed, but not undeserving.

'I'm no good at things,' Mab said. 'At life.'

Con shook her head. 'I don't know much about you, Mab, but you've got a job, a partner. You're warm and thoughtful and honest. I'm sure you'll be a wonderful mother.'

'I'm not,' Mab said. 'And I don't know if Danny will stay.'

'You think he might take fright?'

'Maybe.' Con had put paper napkins on the tray, and Mab grabbed one now and blew her nose. 'It's all a bit complicated.'

'Tell me. I'm used to complicated, believe me.'

Mab made a sound that was half laugh, half sob. 'The thing is, I told Danny – I told him things I shouldn't – and that's why I...'

The tears started again then, tracing rivulets down her cheeks until she mopped at them with the damp napkin. Con handed her another, and Mab tried to smile but just made herself cry more helplessly.

This was no good, Con thought. Maybe whatever was on Mab's mind had nothing to do with what had happened here at Lowlands two decades ago, but if it did, it had to be faced. She'd prepared herself for that, hadn't she? And if it was something else entirely – well, that wouldn't advance things on Con's side, but it should make it easier for Mab to confide in her.

'Dear Mab,' she said, 'dearest Mab, it sounds to me as though there are things you can't carry any longer. It sounds as though it's high time you let them out.'

'I'm not sure I can,' Mab said. 'I should never have told Danny. I wish I hadn't.'

Con took a deep breath. 'Maybe,' she said, 'it's not just you who knows these things.'

Mab lifted her face then, and looked straight at Con. For a moment she said nothing, but when she spoke her voice sounded different. Almost lyrical, Con thought, as though what they were sharing was an ancient saga, not a sorry piece of family history.

'I wondered,' she said. 'All this time I thought that might be why you didn't want to see us.'

And then there was a spasm of anguish. 'It was, partly,' Con said. There was a choke in her voice now, the calm exterior fracturing. 'I wanted to so badly, Mab. All these years I've wanted to be part of your life. I've kept in touch with Hazel, made sure I've known how you were, but now – I wish I'd done things differently. I should have told the truth, and then–'

'But you couldn't have done that,' Mab said fiercely. 'I'd never have forgiven you. Nessa has been – I couldn't have survived without her.'

'Nessa?' A strange buzzing started in Con's head, as if a bluebottle had got inside it. 'What about Nessa?'

'But you know,' Mab said. 'You said so. You said it wasn't just me who knew about it.'

There was a tiny silence then, a punctuation mark you couldn't have defined, in which so many things turned and paused and doubled back that Con almost lost sight of where she was, and with whom. Of what was being said.

'I thought I did,' she said. 'But perhaps... Will you tell me, Mab? Please will you tell me?'

Part Three

Chapter Thirty-Seven

July 2005

It was much hotter in the garden than it was in the house, even in the little room where she and Con had been knitting. Mab liked the feel of the sun on her shoulders, and the way her dress floated a little bit away from her body because the material was still new. She crossed the garden to the corner where the laurel bushes were, the dark green leaves hiding a skeleton of bare branches that criss-crossed and twisted around each other. They were brilliant for climbing, and for sitting on, and for spying on the house from, and the gaps between them made secret places on the ground where you could have picnics and read books, or just sit and talk. She and Nessa had built a den in the furthest away place, right up against the main trunk. They'd brought blankets and cushions that they'd found in the garage and laid them on the ground, and hung a pair of old curtains over some of the branches to make it more private.

'Nessa?' she called, as she ducked into the bushes. She might not be able to see her straight away, because of the curtains, but she was sure this was where Nessa would be. Nessa didn't answer, but that was probably because she was annoyed that Mab had stayed inside for so long and not come to find her. Mab guessed that she was still upset about the things Max had said at breakfast, even though it was just Max being stupid.

Mab was actually a bit worried about Nessa. She'd been thinking about her while she was knitting with Con. She'd noticed Nessa looking at herself in the bathroom mirror earlier on, before they came downstairs. She'd been brushing her hair more carefully than usual, frowning at herself as she judged the effect. Mab had thought it was because they were wearing Daddy's dresses and Nessa wanted them to look nice for Con, but she wondered now if she'd been making an effort for Max. She'd remembered other things too, like Nessa whispering into her pillow at night as if she was imagining a conversation with someone, and times when she'd looked as though she was listening to what Mab was saying but it turned out she hadn't heard any of it. Maybe that was all to do with Max too, Mab thought. Maybe Nessa had been thinking about him a lot, and hoping he'd come round to liking her more.

It all seemed a bit strange to Mab, not just because Max was so horrible but because he was their half-brother. But perhaps it wasn't that kind of liking, just wanting to be friends. Mab was sure Nessa understood things better than her, anyway, and that she had good reasons. Perhaps it was something to do with their father – with getting them all on the same side so Max didn't feel jealous any more. But whatever it was, if Nessa was trying so hard to get into Max's good books, she must be really upset about him being so nasty to her in front of other people.

'I'm sorry I was so long,' she said, as she clambered over the branches towards the den. 'Please don't be cross, Nessa. I expected you'd come back inside when you'd finished picking flowers, and then we could both...'

And then she stopped, because she'd reached the den and pulled back the curtain and Nessa wasn't inside. Mab stood still for a moment, thinking. Where else could Nessa be? Might she have gone to the stream? Or what if she'd gone to the farm to look for Max so she could challenge him – not to a duel, people only did that in stories, but to answer him back? Perhaps she'd gone to say the things she wished she'd thought of at breakfast, or hadn't wanted to say in front of other people.

Mab had got out of the tangle of laurel branches now, and she stood for a minute at the edge of the garden looking at the house in one direction and the orchard and the stream in the other, and the farm path straight ahead across the lawn. If Nessa had gone to the farm to look for Max, maybe it would be a good idea to go and see what was happening. She could go quietly, Mab thought, not calling for Nessa, and then if Nessa and Max had made up and they were having a nice time together she could creep away again. And if they were arguing, maybe she could make them stop. And in any case, there were the kittens. Lucy had said they could come any time to see the kittens, and no one had said Mab couldn't go on her own. That wasn't why she was going to the farm, she told herself. It was just that if she didn't find Nessa she could go and see the kittens while she was there.

It didn't take very long to cut across the garden and follow the path Con had shown them through the big field. Mab couldn't exactly creep secretly, because you could see her coming a mile off in her colourful dress, but even so she pretended she was a spy going on a mission. There were a couple of trees in the field, and she hid behind each one for a little bit and peered round it to make sure no one was coming before she went on. There were some buzzing flies around that distracted her a bit, but she did her best to ignore them and keep concentrating on her mission. When she got to the gate she climbed over it so that no one would hear it squeak, even though it took her much longer to do that than to open it and slip through. She couldn't see or hear anything from there, because most of the farm buildings were hidden from view behind the big metal milking shed. She crossed the first bit of yard and made her way stealthily towards the main courtyard, staying close to the metal walls all the way.

She wasn't really expecting to see anything, of course. It was just a game she was playing. But when she got to the corner she stopped very suddenly. Nessa was running out of the yard towards the other path, the one that went round a couple of fields towards the stream, then led back to Con's garden from the far end. Mab could only see Nessa's back, and she was quite a long way away, but if she'd had to guess she would have said that Nessa looked upset. Maybe she was just imagining that, like she'd imagined Nessa coming here to find Max – but why else would she have come to the farm?

Before Mab had decided whether to call out to her, Nessa reached the gate and disappeared through it. She was certainly running fast, Mab thought. Maybe, whatever had happened, it was best if she didn't know Mab was there. She might want to be on her own for a bit, if she was upset. Mab bit her lip. It would be OK for her to go and see the kittens now, wouldn't it? And if she saw Max and he was in a bad mood still, that might be a clue about what had happened to Nessa. Yes, she'd do that, she decided. She'd knock on the door of the farmhouse and see if anyone was there.

She didn't need to stay hidden any more, though. If people saw her, they might think it was strange if she was creeping around. So she came out from behind the milking shed and walked towards the old barn, and when she got to it the door was open and she could see sunlight coming through from the other side, and she thought she might as well go through it. She liked the old machinery, and the big wooden rafters in the roof, and the stacks of hay bales. She thought she might climb on them a bit if no one was around.

But she'd hardly stepped inside the barn before she realised something was wrong. Someone was lying on the floor, not moving, and it only took a second for her to see that it was Max. He wasn't just lying down to have a rest, because his legs and arms were all spread out in the wrong way.

Mab knew straight away that he was dead.

And scattered around him, on the floor of the barn, there were flowers. Flowers that Mab was sure had come from Con's garden.

Chapter Thirty-Eight

March 2024

C on didn't say anything at first when Mab came to the end of her story, and when she did speak what she said wasn't at all what Mab was expecting.

'There weren't any flowers,' Con said.

'What?'

'I went straight over to the farm, do you remember? I ran to the barn, and I saw Max, but there were no flowers on the floor anywhere.'

Mab took a deep breath. Had she thought she could avoid this part of the story? Or had she forgotten to include it, caught in the heat of recollection?

'I took them,' she said. 'I know I shouldn't have done. It was destroying evidence. But I knew Nessa must have brought them. I knew it meant she'd been there, and that you'd guess that.'

She ought to be crying again now, but she wasn't. Something inside her had dried up, and her tears had dried up with it.

'I'm so sorry, Con. I should have told you the truth straight away. I know it wouldn't have brought Max back, but it would have meant you... But I was too frightened. I needed Nessa too much. I'd heard you telling Max that our mother was dying, and I knew you wouldn't have told him unless it was certain. And I couldn't have managed without Nessa after she died.'

'What did you do with them?' Con asked.

'With what?'

'The flowers,' Con said. 'The police searched the farm. They searched every inch of the barn, too. They didn't find any flowers.'

Mab stared at her. 'I'm telling the truth,' she said. 'Why would I lie about it? I saw Nessa running away, and I saw flowers on the floor around Max's body, and I picked them all up before I ran back to the house to find you. I threw the flowers over a fence. I don't remember where, but it's not hard to get rid of things on a farm. No one was looking for flowers.'

She felt panicky now. The one thing she hadn't expected was that Con wouldn't believe her.

'I suppose not.' Con's face looked strange: very heavy and grey, as though all the blood had drained out of it, and all the momentum that had kept her going all this time had ebbed away too.

'I know this doesn't make any difference,' Mab said, 'but it has tormented me. Growing up knowing that the person I loved most, the person who loved me most, had done something like that.' *Probably* was what she usually said to herself, or *might have* or *could possibly have*. But telling the story out loud to Con had solidified it in her mind.

'What do you think she did, exactly?' Con asked.

Mab swallowed. Making her spell it out wasn't like Con, but she deserved to hear it if she wanted to. 'I think she pushed him off the ledge,' she said. 'They thought he'd fallen from there, didn't they? They knew he used to climb up and sit on that ledge?'

Con nodded.

'I don't know whether Nessa meant to push him or whether it was an accident,' Mab said, 'but I thought and thought about it afterwards, and I reckoned if it had been an accident she'd have said something. She'd have been the one to raise the alarm.'

'So you think she went over to the farm to look for him, taking the flowers with her, and climbed up to the ledge after him, and then – what, he laughed at her, or said something unkind, so she pushed him off?'

'Something like that.' Mab's head was ringing now, an alarm bell set off by the fact that she'd betrayed Nessa, but also by the fact that Con wasn't reacting as she'd expected.

'It's a difficult climb,' Con said. 'It was, rather. They cut away the ledge after Max died. I can't imagine Nessa managing to climb up there with an armful of flowers.'

'She was good at climbing,' Mab said. But she realised as the words came out that it was her eight-year-old self speaking, defending her sister's prowess. It had never occurred to her, that day or afterwards, to consider the logistics. That wasn't the point, though. The point was that Nessa had been at the farm when Max fell, and she'd run away, and she'd never said a word about it. And Mab had been terrified ever since of what that meant.

Mab waited for Con to speak again, but she didn't, and that was infinitely more painful than the recriminations she'd expected.

'What are you thinking?' Mab said eventually. 'Please tell me, Con. I know you must be angry.' She swallowed hard. 'The thing is, I think I always believed that you knew. That you'd guessed, but you'd decided not to say anything out of kindness to us. I thought that was why you didn't see us again – because you couldn't bear to, after what Nessa had done.'

'No,' Con said. 'That wasn't it.'

Mab waited, but once again Con went in a different direction from the one she expected.

'How did she seem when you next saw her?' Con asked.

'Nessa?'

'Yes. When you saw her again, back at the house, how did she seem?'

'We were all in turmoil by then,' Mab said. 'Nessa was crying, and so was I, and...'

'But if you thought she'd killed Max, surely you'd have been looking for signs – in how she behaved, and what she said. You'd have been trying to work out if she looked guilty.'

'No,' Mab said. 'I wasn't thinking like that at all.' The mist had cleared in her mind now, leaving the whole day clear and sharp. The day that had changed the course of their lives. 'I was desperate for Nessa not to realise I'd seen her. I thought if she knew I had, then she'd think she had to tell me the truth, and that would be the end. I couldn't let that happen.'

As she finished speaking, they heard the sound of a car coming up the lane and stopping in front of the house.

'Philip,' Con said. 'Philip's home.'

She looked at Mab then, her face full of anguish. 'Dear Mab, we need to stop talking about this now. But we'll carry on. We... I'm so sorry. Perhaps I can come to London. Or you can come back. But not now, all right?'

'All right,' Mab said – although she hardly knew what she was agreeing to, or why. The world seemed to have turned inside out: she'd just told Con that Nessa had killed Max, and Con was apologising to her. Perhaps it wasn't the world, though; perhaps Con had gone mad. Perhaps that's what losing a son did to you. Mab shut her eyes for a second, in case that might help her understand, but all it did was make her feel dizzy. And when she opened them again a man was coming out of the house. A man who looked much older than thirty-five, but who couldn't be anyone but Philip.

Chapter Thirty-Nine

July 2005

Philip came out through the back door just after Mab reached the house, while she was still trying to explain things to Con, out of breath from running and crying and the pain in her knee. Con was holding her shoulders and shaking her and asking questions faster than Mab could answer them, and Mab was feeling even more scared than she'd done a few minutes ago in the barn, because she'd never seen a grown-up so shocked and upset before. She'd thought Con would be able to sort everything out. She'd thought all she had to do was get to Con, and then everything would be OK.

'What is it?' Philip asked. 'What's happened?'

'It's Max,' Con said. 'He's fallen. I think he might be dead.'

'Have you seen him?' Philip asked. Mab glimpsed his face, which was very pale but very calm, the way Philip always was.

'I'm going now.'

Con let go of Mab and started running across the garden. The shaking and shouting had only lasted a few seconds, probably, but it seemed to have taken ages and ages. Con should have started running as soon as she'd seen her, Mab thought, because maybe Max wasn't dead – maybe he hadn't been when she left. Maybe Con could have saved him if she'd got there quicker.

But she knew that wasn't true. Max hadn't moved or made a sound while Mab stood there, with her heart crashing and her brain thinking how much he looked like a poor dead bird. He'd gone on lying perfectly still while she picked up all the flowers. Mab knew she shouldn't have done that, because you weren't supposed to touch anything when people were dead, and because it had slowed her down, but she'd been so frightened that she'd moved faster than she'd ever moved before, and–

'Are you OK, Mab?' Philip was asking. 'Did you find Max? Did you see him?'

Mab opened her mouth to answer him, but all that came out was a great sob.

'Stay with Mab,' Con shouted over her shoulder. She was already at the gate, running faster than Mab would have thought she could. 'You stay with her, Philip. And ring 999.'

Later, Mab wondered why Philip hadn't gone with his mother. That would have been the natural thing to do, but maybe he'd thought of staying with her before Con had suggested it. Mab was glad, anyway. She didn't want to go back to the barn, to see Max again, but she really really didn't want to be on her own either. She was starting to shiver, even though the sun was still shining. Even though it was still a hot summer day. It was funny, she thought, that it made no difference to anything else when someone died, just as it didn't when a bird or a beetle or a mouse died.

'Come inside,' Philip said. He grabbed her hand, not roughly but firmly, and took her with him into the hall, and then he rang the police and the ambulance. When they asked him what had happened, he looked at Mab and she whispered a few words and he repeated them into the phone. 'My sister found him,' he said. 'My little sister. She thinks he fell from a ledge high up in the barn. She said he wasn't moving.'

My little sister. If Mab hadn't already been crying, those words would have made her start. But she didn't say anything – didn't let Philip know that she'd noticed, even. She understood that she wasn't supposed to be pleased about anything just now, because Max was dead.

Max was dead.

She'd been the first one to know, the one to tell Con, but even so Mab hadn't really understood what had happened until now. Or at least, she kept feeling that she was understanding it just at that moment. It kept coming into her head like something new. This morning he'd been alive and rude and unkind, and now he was dead and he'd never be any of those things again, and however horrid he'd been she was very very sorry that he was dead, and she could see Philip was too. He was trying hard to sound calm and sensible on the phone and to look after Mab, but he looked so pale that Mab thought he couldn't have enough blood in him, and then she thought maybe when your brother dies – your real brother, who you've always known – it makes it hard for your body to keep going. He was still holding the telephone, even though there was no one on the other end any more. Mab put her hand on his arm, very gently.

'I'm sorry,' she said.

'Why are you sorry?' Philip asked.

'I'm sorry about Max,' Mab said. 'I'm sorry I had to tell you and Con about it.' She should have said *your mother*, but she forgot.

'I haven't taken it in,' Philip said. 'It's the shock. It makes things not feel real at first.' He frowned, and shook his head slightly as if that might clear the shock. 'It must have been a shock for you too, Mab. A terrible shock. Did you hear something, or did you just happen to go into the barn?'

'I just happened to,' Mab said. 'I was looking for Nessa, and the door was open. I didn't hear anything, and I didn't see anyone. Except Max.'

She expected to feel funny now, because she'd told a lie. A big lie. But she didn't. It sounded like the truth, she thought. Certainly Philip seemed to think so, because he was nodding, as though he was trying to picture the scene. And now she'd told it once, she thought it would be easier the next time. She wanted to say it again, to practise the words – *I didn't see anyone* – but she didn't. She didn't know how she knew this, but she did: if you said things too many times, they sounded less true. She would only say it again if someone asked her. But she got a chance to practise lying again sooner than she expected, because of what Philip said next.

'Did you find Nessa?'

'No.' Mab shook her head. 'She said she was going for a walk, and Con said she could pick some flowers, but she wasn't in the garden and she wasn't at the farm.'

'We'd better find her,' Philip said. He was good at being a grown-up, Mab thought, with the bit of her brain that wasn't thinking about telling lies, or about Nessa. Quite a lot of her brain was thinking about Nessa, though, especially since Philip had asked about her.

As it turned out they didn't need to go and look for Nessa, because when they got to the back door there she was, coming down the garden from the direction of the orchard and the stream. Mab knew why she was coming that way, and knew that she'd taken longer than she needed to coming back, but she pushed those thoughts away because she knew how much depended on saying the right things now. She could feel her heart beating very fast and very hard, not like her heart at all but like someone else's that had been put in her chest by mistake and was trying to get out again.

'Nessa!' she shouted, before Nessa was close enough to say anything. 'Oh, Nessa, it's Max! Max has fallen off the ledge in the barn and I found him lying on the ground and he's dead.'

And then she ran towards Nessa and threw herself at her and put her arms tight around her, so that Nessa couldn't say anything and Philip couldn't see her face. And Nessa wrapped her arms around Mab as well, and the two of them clung together for dear life in the middle of Con's garden as the first sound of the sirens floated over the fields.

And very soon after that it stopped being their little tragedy, a terrible thing that had happened to Mab and Con and Philip and Nessa, and started being something that other people were in charge of. The house and the farm filled with people in uniforms who spoke kindly to Mab but still frightened her, and who asked her the same questions so many times that by the end she had almost forgotten about the flowers and seeing Nessa, and her story sounded perfectly true without them. They asked Nessa questions too, and she spoke very calmly and quietly and told them exactly where she'd been on her walk, and how she'd paddled in the stream and thrown sticks into it and watched them disappearing on the current. And listening to her, Mab felt a great gushing wave of relief, as warm as the sun had been on her back that morning, because she knew that Nessa was strong enough for both of them, and if they could get through this danger Nessa would always be there with her. Nessa would always look after her.

After that there were no more days at Lowlands, because their father arrived that afternoon, and it was arranged that he would take them home the next morning, and that Aunt Hazel would look after them while he came back to be with Con and Philip. And the funny thing was that although she had longed to go

237

home, Mab felt a terrible pain when she thought about leaving Con, and about not knowing what was happening to her and Philip. But there was also another wave of relief, because once they were away from Lowlands she and Nessa would be safe. No one would ask them any more questions. And they would see Mummy, of course. That mattered much more than not seeing Con any more, Mab told herself, and she felt the blood rush to her cheeks at the thought that even for a moment she had wanted to stay with Con instead of going home. She must never, ever tell anyone that. But she was getting good at not telling people things. She was an expert at it already.

She and Nessa didn't see much of Con or their father that last evening. They were given boiled eggs and toast and put to bed early, and Mab fell asleep much faster than she'd expected. The next morning, the house felt very quiet. The relief was still there inside Mab, but there was a little ache of worry, too, that grew and grew as they ate their bowls of cereal and packed their cases. A worry she knew would never quite go away, however good she got at keeping secrets.

It was actually several worries mixed up together, Mab thought, as she stood for the last time in the hall at Lowlands, waiting for the goodbyes to be over and the journey home to begin. There was the main worry, that someone would find out about her finding the flowers and seeing Nessa running away, and that once they knew she'd lied about those things they would suspect Nessa of killing Max. Then there was the worry that she wouldn't manage not ever to talk about it to Nessa, because she very badly wanted to know what had happened. She wanted it to be a secret they shared rather than one they had to keep separately.

But she knew that wasn't possible. She knew because Nessa hadn't said a single word to her about where she'd been. She hadn't asked Mab a single question about finding Max, either, or about why she'd gone to the farm, although she'd listened carefully when Mab answered the police lady's questions. She hadn't said anything like, *What do you think happened to him?* or even, *Can you believe Max is dead?* There hadn't been much time when they'd been alone together, but there'd been enough to ask those questions. There'd been the time in bed last night, and the time after they woke up this morning, and all Nessa had said then was, 'Let's go down and have breakfast, Mab, and then we can pack our things and be ready to leave.' So Mab knew Nessa didn't want them to talk about Max, and Nessa was always right.

And as well as the worries about never telling anyone she'd seen Nessa, and about having this big thing sitting between her and Nessa and pretending it wasn't there, another worry had started up this morning. One that wove its way between the other worries so quietly and stealthily that she didn't see it coming until it was right there, staring at her.

If Nessa had killed Max, even by accident, and Mab was the only one who knew, did that mean she was in danger?

Nessa loved her, Mab knew that. Nessa was fierce and brave, but she used those things to protect Mab, not to hurt her. Until yesterday, though, it would have been impossible to imagine Nessa killing anyone, even an animal, and that meant nothing Mab thought she knew about Nessa was certain any more.

It had probably been an accident, Mab told herself, as their father came downstairs at last and the front door opened and sunshine came flooding into the house. That was the most likely thing. The ledge wasn't very big and if Nessa had climbed up after Max and they'd been arguing, he could easily have fallen off. In fact Nessa could have fallen off instead, Mab realised, and that made her feel so cold and numb that she decided she wouldn't think about the ledge or the falling any more.

. . .

As the car pulled away from Lowlands Nessa took her hand, and relief came trickling back through Mab's body. She rested her head against Nessa's shoulder, and slowly, slowly, things started to settle, and the worries began to fade, until the main thing left in her mind was how glad she was to have Nessa beside her, to be able to lean on her, and everything else had begun to seem strange and unreal. Max being dead instead of thinking up more ways to tease them. Their father being so quiet, because of course Max had been his son, and the last time he'd seen him he had shouted at him. Con and Philip being left on their own, just the two of them, in that big house. It was as though none of that had anything to do with them any more. As though it was something that had happened once upon a time, not yesterday.

Mab felt guilty now about letting herself think terrible things about Nessa, but the further away they got from Lowlands, the more that didn't matter either. It was just part of the strangeness and unreality. Part of what she wasn't going to think about any more. What she needed to concentrate on instead was that they were going home. That they could see Mummy at last.

But even though it was what Mab had hoped for ever since they got to Lowlands, there was a bit of her that dreaded going home now. Dreaded seeing their mother. Because Mab knew now what it felt like when someone died. She knew people *could* die, even the most unlikely ones, and that it changed the lives of their families completely. And she knew that the next person to die would almost certainly be Mummy.

When she shut her eyes and imagined the future, all she was sure of was her and Nessa, holding hands so tightly that neither of them needed to say anything at all.

Chapter Forty

March 2024

M ab stood up as Philip came across the garden towards her.

'Mab,' he said. 'I'm very glad you're still here. I left work early so I could get home before you left.'

'Hello, Philip,' she said. 'What a lovely surprise!'

He stopped a couple of feet away from her and held out his hand. Mab took it, grinning. He had grown a few inches since she last saw him, but his hair was cut in exactly the same way, a bit longer on top than was fashionable, and his glasses could have been the same ones he'd had nineteen years ago. But his face had aged, acquiring the gaunt look that thin men sometimes develop. He looked somehow uncared for, Mab thought, although she knew that was a ridiculous thing to think about someone who lived with Con. His clothes were immaculate – a suit and tie, which seemed surprisingly formal for a council employee – but even so there was something about him that suggested he might recently have been picked up after floating for months on a life raft, then given a bath and new clothes before being paraded for the media.

'You look well,' she said, in case any of this train of thought had showed up in her face. 'Your mother's been telling me about New Zealand.'

Philip glanced at Con, then nodded. 'It was a nice funeral,' he said.

'Have you had lunch, Philip?' Con asked. 'There's some quiche left.'

'I had my sandwich,' he said. 'Shall I make coffee?'

'Not for me,' Mab said, but Con was accepting, thanking him, and so Philip turned and went back inside.

'Mab,' Con said. Her voice was quiet, calm, but deadly serious. This was why she'd accepted the coffee, Mab thought; so that they could talk for a few more minutes. 'Since you've been so candid with me, I feel I ought to tell you why I was surprised by what you said just now. I feel I should explain what I was expecting you to say.' She hesitated, and Mab recognised the strange impatience and reluctance of someone who has kept secrets for too long: who can hardly imagine what it will feel like to share them. 'The thing is,' Con went on, 'that I have – like you, I've spent the years since Max died keeping something to myself. A suspicion. But not about Nessa.'

'About me?' Mab asked.

This had never once occurred to her, but in that instant she could see it was the obvious thing for Con to believe. It was she who'd found Max's body; she who'd come running back to the house in a state of such distress.

'No!' Con almost laughed. 'No, that never even crossed my mind. No.' She stopped. Mab's heart was racing again, in the wake of the sudden jolt when she'd imagined herself as the focus of Con's suspicions.

'You were so brave,' Con said, 'telling me about Nessa. I'm not as brave as you. But you must have guessed by now who I mean.'

'Not Philip?'

Con nodded, very slightly, and Mab frowned.

'But Philip was here,' Mab said. 'He was in the house when I arrived. He came out from the kitchen.'

'He'd only just got back. I heard him come in a few minutes before you, through the front door. He wouldn't have come that way unless he'd been to the farm. And he was flustered. Very unlike himself. I'd just come downstairs with the laundry, and I was starting to ask him if he was all right when I heard you screaming. I ran towards you then, and ... well, you know the rest.'

'Goodness,' Mab said. 'But surely...?'

'Max tormented him,' Con said simply. 'I can see that it could have become intolerable. That morning – you won't remember, but Max said something deeply unkind to Philip.'

'And to us,' Mab said. 'To me and Nessa.'

'Yes.' Con sighed. 'I should have... I've blamed myself very much. I didn't reprimand him properly – and I didn't go after him that morning, either. I left him to himself, knowing how angry he was. And how badly he'd upset his brother.'

Mab didn't remember Philip being badly upset. She remembered them all eating pancakes, and the kitchen being rather quiet. But she'd been a child, and Con knew Philip better than anyone. 'You had too many things to think about,' she said. 'You were looking after me that morning. It's my fault, really.'

Con did her half laugh again, then she leaned across and touched Mab's arm for a moment. 'None of it was your fault,' she said. 'You were caught in the eye of the storm.'

'But do you really think Philip could have–'

'You've believed it of Nessa,' Con said. 'She was a lot smaller than Max. Philip might not have looked very strong, but...' She shook her head, as though there were some things she couldn't bring herself to say out loud. 'And you'd been here less than a week. Philip had had years of it, and during those last few

243

days there was an audience for Max's taunts. An additional torment.'

Mab's head was buzzing again. How could Con be so calm? Had she sounded so matter-of-fact when she was telling Con about Nessa? She was sure she hadn't. Con's words rang in her ears: *Philip had had years of it... An additional torment...* There was something weighty about Con's tone, as though she had allowed herself – forced herself – to imagine a deliberate act; the extreme that Mab had always shied away from. Not a rush of blood, a fatal misjudgement, but something planned.

'Philip–' Con began, but then she stopped. Philip was coming out of the house, bringing coffee and a plate of chocolate biscuits. She caught Mab's eye, and Mab nodded.

'Have you been talking about the memorial service?' Philip asked, as he set the tray down.

'The funeral, you mean?' Mab asked.

'I thought you were coming to talk about organising a memorial service?' Philip said.

'Oh!' Mab smiled. 'Yes, I was. I am. We seem to have spent a long time talking about New Zealand, though, and – well, I've been talking about myself, actually.' She sounded falsely bright; she hoped Philip wouldn't notice. It was hard to turn her mind away from the conversation with Con. To adjust herself to what had been said. 'You're right, though. We must talk about that.'

Philip had taken the chair next to his mother, and was pouring coffee carefully into two cups. 'Would it be just for us?' he asked. 'Or for other people as well?'

'I should think other people,' Mab said. 'Don't you?'

When she'd thought about the service she'd imagined there being quite a crowd, although their identities had been hazy. The idea of the four of them in an empty church was awful: the four people Roy had hurt most in the world, gathered together in his honour. No, there needed to be enough people there to make it feel like a different sort of occasion. To cushion them from themselves. But who else might there be to ask? 'Old colleagues, maybe?' she said. 'Old friends?'

'Yes.' Philip frowned slightly, and Mab wondered if he'd been thinking the same thing as her. 'When did you last see him, Mab?'

'Not for years,' Mab said. 'Not since I was fourteen. He had that exhibition in London, and we saw him a couple of times while he was over. I thought after that we'd see him more often, but...'

Had Philip spent time with him on that visit too? she wondered. Or since then? His next statement didn't answer that question, and Mab was glad of it. The details were best left vague. She could imagine the dead Roy enjoying the spectacle of his children competing over who had met him last.

'I hadn't seen him for years either,' Philip said. 'I thought about going to visit him a few times, but I never did.'

'He could have come here,' Con said, with more edge to her voice than she usually allowed herself.

'It was interesting to see New Zealand, though,' Philip said, making a leap which Mab recognised, from some recess of her memory, as characteristic. 'It's very beautiful. What we saw, that is. We didn't have much time for sightseeing.'

'I'm sorry not to have come,' Mab said. She wasn't sure she meant it any more, but Philip nodded. For a moment she met his gaze, and she was struck by the fact that they gave the impression of understanding each other, but that she had no idea whether they really did. It felt – it was almost as if some invisible hand was guiding them, drawing out a string of words into a safe, coherent dialogue, like a tug boat steering them through perilous waters. She reached for the water jug and refilled her glass.

'So would the service be in the church here?' she asked.

'I can ask the vicar,' Con said, 'but I'm sure she'd agree. The church isn't exactly overused these days.'

'And we'd choose readings and music, I suppose, and – I don't know – maybe speak about him?' Mab twisted her hands together in her lap, concealing the dismay that filled her suddenly. But she needed the end to be marked, she thought. Even if her father's death didn't mean the end of anything, really. 'Perhaps you can't see the point, though. You've already been to the funeral.'

'But you haven't,' Philip said. 'We should do it for your sake. For you and Nessa. He was your father too.'

'Thank you,' Mab said. 'Thank you, Philip.'

Except that she barely managed to say it, because she'd remembered Philip, nineteen years ago, speaking to the emergency services and saying *my little sister*, and how touched she'd been. How in those few seconds she'd imagined herself growing up at Lowlands with Philip and Con, if her mother was really going to die.

Because everything in their family was so complicated.

What Con had said to her a few minutes ago swirled in the space between them all now, a ghost threatening to rise up and devour them, but also a source of astonishment. Gentle Philip, kind Philip: could he really have killed his brother? Could Con truly believe that? But Con was right; Mab had suspected Nessa all these years. She had learned to accommodate it, and her life had grown around it, just as it had grown around the death of her mother and the desertion of her father. She had clung to Nessa despite it – clung to her more strongly, perhaps, because of it – and she could see that the same was true of Con and Philip. She looked at them both, noticing the way Philip's face contained anxiety and remoteness and a touching eagerness all at the same time, and Con's was agonisingly raw, watching her son. Weighing, no doubt, the terrible things she had just spoken aloud.

Con stood up, suddenly brisk. 'Who feels like stretching their legs?' she said. 'We could walk down to the church, if you like. I don't think you saw it last time, Mab.'

She made it sound as though last time had been, perhaps, a few months ago; an occasion similar to this.

'Good idea,' Philip said.

Con's eyes were still on Mab. 'It's not far,' she said. 'Ten minutes. But perhaps you don't have enough time?'

'I'm sure I do,' Mab said.

'Good.' Con hesitated, as if trying something for size and then discarding it. 'Let's leave everything. We can clear up later.'

The church was larger than you might imagine, given the size of the village. It was built from the same stone as all the buildings at Lowlands: built at the same time, Mab imagined, presumably to service the family in the big house. It lay in the opposite direction from the farm, and on the way they passed a string of houses Mab hadn't known existed. They, too, had presumably serviced the big house once upon a time, although they boasted sizeable extensions these days, and had people-carriers parked outside.

They were almost at the lychgate before it occurred to Mab that Max must be buried here, among his ancestors. She and Nessa hadn't come to his funeral: had that been Hazel's doing, or Con's? She wondered for an awful minute if they were going to visit Max's grave now, but Con led them purposefully up the path to the main door.

'It's beautiful,' Mab said, when Con had found the light switch. There was some elegant carving on the ends of the

247

pews, and a large stone font that looked very old. Mab didn't feel at home in churches, but she liked the stillness of them, the way even the air felt tranquil.

'You were married here, weren't you?' Philip asked, and Con nodded.

'And...' Philip hesitated, and for a moment Mab's breath stopped. But Con intervened.

'And there are my parents, on the wall.'

She indicated a plaque, gold-edged, that testified to the lives and deaths of Thomas Hanson, Esq., and Elizabeth, his wife, in a style that would have been perfectly at home in the eighteenth century. Mab had forgotten that Con's father had been High Sheriff of Somerset; had perhaps never known that her parents had already been dead for fifteen years by the time she and Nessa had first come to Lowlands. She stared at the plaque for a moment, calculating. They must have been elderly parents. And both dead within eighteen months of each other.

In the silence Mab felt danger looming again, each in-breath an opportunity for a question she dreaded.

'The stonemason was left instructions,' Con said, rescuing them again. 'I'm not sure my father trusted me to rise to the occasion.' She smiled.

Oh, that familiar smile, Mab thought. It struck her, as they walked slowly down the aisle, just how much Con had had to bear, as the matriarch of this fatally fractured clan. Not just her husband's desertion and the death of her younger son, but the fact that he'd died still furious at the intrusion of his half-sisters. Not just the need to sell her family's house and make a new life with Philip, but believing all along that she was keeping a terrible secret for him. It made Mab's own troubles dwindle in comparison.

But that thought brought the present reality of her life back into focus, and as her mind shifted she felt, in the semi-darkness of the church, a sudden sense of oppression. She couldn't take on Con's sorrow. Not just now. Because what had happened nineteen years ago was important, of course it was, but there were things that were more pressing. Things Mab needed to pay attention to more immediately.

Con was looking at her, noticing the change in her demeanour. 'What time's your train, Mab?'

'I was thinking I'd catch the three fifty.' She hesitated, worried about seeming ungracious. 'Perhaps I could get a taxi, if you have a number?'

'I'll take you,' Philip said. 'It would be a pleasure.'

For a fraction of a second Mab held Con's eye, and Con nodded.

'Thank you, Philip,' Mab said. 'That would be very kind.'

'Let's head back, then,' Con said. 'It's almost three now.'

Chapter Forty-One

Mab and Philip didn't talk much in the car. It was as if they were both too shy without Con's enabling presence. As if the slightness and strangeness of their connection was suddenly evident to them both: half-siblings who had spent a week together nineteen years ago and hadn't seen each other since. Whose previous encounter had ended in a tragedy so appalling that it had sundered their family completely, and who were meeting again now because the father they had shared, but hardly known, had died on the other side of the world.

Mab toyed with the idea of saying some of this, but it felt too risky.

'What do you do for the council?' she asked instead, when they'd driven in silence for a while.

'I'm an accountant,' he said. 'I work in the audit department. We oversee financial performance and the use of public funds.' He glanced at her. 'Basically, I make sure the council spends its money efficiently, and help prevent fraud.'

'That sounds interesting,' Mab said, although in truth it

sounded like the most boring job she'd ever heard of. But Philip looked pleased.

'Most people don't think so, but it is. It's very varied. No two days are exactly the same, but it doesn't take you too much by surprise either.' He smiled, then asked, 'What about you?'

'I work in a bookshop. People don't think that's very interesting either.'

'I expect it is if you like reading.'

Mab laughed, although she wasn't sure whether he'd meant it as a joke.

'It's been nice to see you,' Philip said. 'I hope you'll come again.'

'I will,' Mab said. 'We'll have to meet up to plan the memorial service.'

'Yes, of course.'

Philip sighed then – but not, Mab thought, with sorrow or misgiving. More because they'd said, for now, all that needed to be said. She smiled at him, and they didn't say any more until he dropped her at the station.

'You should be in plenty of time,' he said, and Mab leaned over and kissed him on the cheek before she got out of the car. The sun was bright still, and she squinted as she watched him drive away. His little car – dark grey and modest-looking – seemed so much in his image that she couldn't help smiling again as it disappeared into the stream of traffic.

Perhaps she ought to feel differently about Philip, given what Con had told her this afternoon. She definitely shouldn't be allowing herself such a surge of pleasure at finding him so unchanged; at having him and Con back in her life, like two more tent poles to help hold up the flimsy structure of her family. But the truth was, she thought, as she swiped her ticket to pass through the barrier, that it was harder to imagine Philip being implicated in Max's death than Nessa. He'd always been so measured: you couldn't by any stretch call him volatile or violent. Whereas Nessa was an unstoppable force – especially back then she had been. And she'd wanted Max to be her friend, or at least to recognise her as an equal. Mab had always been sure of that: she'd imagined Nessa fired up, that day, with the rage of a woman scorned.

What was certainly true, Mab thought, as she made her way down the platform, was that she and Con couldn't both be right, which meant – well, Mab needed to think about that. To ponder the possibility that she'd carried a false suspicion, a false interpretation of the facts, in her heart all these years, and to adjust to the idea that Nessa's innocence would – might – mean that Con was right about Philip. It crossed her mind that she might never know the answer; that there might be no simple truth to uncover. Logic said there must be, but it seemed to Mab that it might be unrecognisable after all this time. That it might be as corroded and distorted as the Roman artefacts you saw in museums, reduced to fragments an expert had to piece together.

As the train pulled in, she pushed the feverish chain of premise and rebuttal away. The point was that the secret she'd kept so carefully all this time was less certain now, and the most urgent consequence of that was that her reason for avoiding Danny this week was less convincing, too. Although she could hardly untangle her thinking about all that now. It felt like a classic Mab muddle, impossible to explain. But that's what she had to do, she realised. She had to see Danny tonight. She had to explain, and to apologise, and to ask him to come with her to the scan tomorrow. Because Danny and the baby mattered more than any of the rest of it, didn't they? They were her future: her chance to set things back on the right track.

Outside the train window, the clouds over the Somerset

Levels were spectacular. Before she got back to London, this wide slab of sky would be filled with sunset colours, its pinks and purples and peaches reflected in the silvery channels of water that criss-crossed the landscape. The world was beautiful, Mab thought. Surely there was happiness to be found, if you looked hard enough. Surely it was waiting for her, just around the corner.

She shut her eyes for a moment and let hope wash through her. She'd been an idiot, but it wasn't too late. She could imagine Danny's smile now, his arms around her. His pleasure at the news. And then she took out her phone and clicked on Danny's name in her contacts list.

She had half hoped that Danny would offer to come and meet her at Paddington, but that had been too much to expect, she told herself, as she changed from the Elizabeth Line to the overground at Whitechapel. It was enough that he had agreed to come at all.

They were going to the pizza place again – the scene of their happy memories. The place where Danny had said, *You don't just pick and choose which bits of people's lives you're going to deal with.* Mab had felt horribly nervous all the way to Paddington, but as she crossed London she talked sense into herself. Everything would be fine. Danny loved her. It was a bit soon to be having a baby together, but timing wasn't everything. She just needed to say things in the right way, so that he understood.

It was bang on seven fifteen when she arrived, but Danny was there already, sitting at a table in the window. He smiled when he saw her, but it was a more guarded smile than usual. That was hardly surprising, Mab thought, but her nerves flared up again as she took off her coat and sat down.

'So you've been to see Con,' Danny said.

'Yes. Just as you suggested.' Mab was conscious of injecting a shade too much sugar into that sentence, to appease him, but it was true. He had suggested it.

'I thought you were still ill,' he said. 'People have been covering for you at work.'

'Oh, Danny,' she said, 'please don't – I mean, I have been ill, but it's...'

He held up his hands. 'OK. My bad. Tell me.'

'Tell you?' Mab frowned. His tone of voice wasn't exactly aggressive, but it wasn't his familiar gentle voice; the one that made her feel safe and wanted. For a moment she thought she might start crying, just like that, before they'd even started talking properly, but she took a deep breath, steadied herself.

'Tell me what this is all about,' Danny said, taking her question at face value. 'Your illness. Your silence.' He shrugged. 'Your conversation with Con.'

Mab bit her lip. Whichever tug was in charge of this conversation wasn't doing a very good job, she thought. She'd been planning to lead into the baby news gradually, to make sure they were on a good footing first, but Danny's snippiness irritated her. Why was he being like this? Didn't she deserve the benefit of the doubt? And then something inside her was swelling up, pushing words to the surface before she could stop them.

'Well,' she said, 'what it's mainly about is that I'm pregnant.'

It only took a millisecond for her to realise that Danny wasn't going to react in the way she'd hoped. That she'd completely failed to make it sound OK.

'Pregnant?' he said. 'Since when?'

'I'm going to find out tomorrow. I'm having a scan.' *Do you want to come?* she was supposed to ask next, but those words felt wrong now.

'OK.' He sat back, stared at her for a moment, then leaned forwards again and put his head in his hands. 'OK.'

'So that's why I've been ill. That's why I've been off work.'

Danny had a glass of Coke in front of him: he took a slug from it, then set it back carefully in exactly the same place.

'How long have you known?' he asked.

'I did the test on Saturday,' Mab said.

'Saturday after the book launch?'

'Just before.'

'And you didn't tell me then?'

'God, Danny, given how you've reacted I wish I hadn't told you now.' Mab was trembling, whether with anger or distress she couldn't have said. With both, actually. 'It's taken me this long to get my head around it. I couldn't...'

His expression was impossible to read. Was he really upset that she hadn't told him sooner, or just shocked by the news and finding an excuse to be angry? Or some strange misogynistic muddle of the two?

It just went to show, said a knowing voice in her head, that you were never really on safe ground with men. They could seem soft and loving and grateful to have you, but only on their terms. Only if it didn't get too real. Part of her knew that wasn't fair on Danny, but he wasn't making any progress in digging himself out of the hole he'd got into, and Mab wasn't going to be able to hold back her tears for much longer. And she was damned if she was going to weep while he sat there stony-faced, blaming her for something that really wasn't her fault. The couple at the next table were pretending they hadn't noticed the beginnings of a row, looking deliberately away.

'OK,' Mab said, pushing her chair back, 'I think I'd better go.'

'Don't do that,' Danny said.

'Why not?' Mab was on her feet, the rush of outrage driving

her still. She knew it wouldn't last further than the door of the restaurant, but she'd take that.

'Aren't you going to let me say anything?' He sounded plaintive – no, pitiful.

No, said the voice in Mab's head. *Don't be taken in by self-pity.*

'I think you've said enough, honestly,' Mab said. 'I know it's a bit of a surprise, but it's pretty clear that it's not a good one, and that's all I needed to know.'

She made it further than the door, as it turned out. She made it as far as the corner of the street before her emotions got the better of her. She stopped there for a few moments, bent double to brace herself against the upsurge of nausea and misery and pain. And then she forced herself to stumble on, in case Danny followed her out of the restaurant. She couldn't bear him to see her in this state. She couldn't bear to see him ever again, for that matter. Oh God, she thought, that meant she couldn't go back to the bookshop. She'd have to find another job, and who was going to employ someone who spent half their time vomiting? What on earth was she going to do?

She made it halfway home before the inevitable happened. There was no resisting it, really. For as long as she could remember she'd only had one person to call when bad things happened – and although one day, maybe, she'd be the kind of person who could figure things out on her own, that day hadn't come yet. She pulled out her phone and dialled.

Chapter Forty-Two

'I sometimes think,' Nessa said, 'that Mab got all our mother's genes, and I got Hazel's.'

Nessa had cooked this evening – or rather, she'd collected a ready meal for two on the way home. She hadn't been entirely sure whether Inga would be around tonight: she'd stayed over almost every night lately, but they hadn't talked about moving in together, so Inga's presence wasn't something Nessa could count on. She wasn't sure she wanted a formal acknowledgement, just yet, that things had moved on, but she'd been happy when Inga had appeared at the door ten minutes after she got home this evening. That she hadn't looked quizzically at Nessa, doubting her welcome. And although the ready meal wasn't exactly home cooking, it signalled that Inga wouldn't have to look after her forever. That things would return to normal. And that that normal might include assuming Inga would be there; buying enough Thai curry for two.

And these conversations – they were part of this new normal they were travelling towards, too. There was so much to say once you started, Nessa had discovered. Although sometimes she set off on trails that led nowhere.

'In what ways are you like Hazel?' Inga asked her now. 'What parallels do you see?'

Nessa shook her head. 'Mab is so like our mother. Or at least–' All she really remembered about her mother, she realised, were the things she'd been determined not to forget; the things she'd set in resin in her memory to preserve them.

'You described Hazel as a misanthrope,' Inga said. 'You're certainly not that.'

Nessa laughed, despite herself. 'You're right. I'm being ridiculous. Maybe we've talked enough about me for a while. Let's talk about you this evening.'

'I like talking about you,' Inga said. 'I don't have so much to say.'

'Tell me about your day,' Nessa said. 'Your colleagues. Your meetings.'

'They're not as interesting as you, or your sister. I've been wondering about her.' Inga took a sip of her wine.

'I think Mab's in love,' Nessa said.

Inga cocked her head. She waited a moment, then said, 'What sort of question would that be an answer to?'

'What do you mean?'

'Well...' Inga picked up a stick of satay, looked at it for a moment, then set it down on her plate. 'The thing I've heard most often about you and Mab is how close you are. How you looked after her when your mother died. How she depends on you. So when your father died, I imagined she would need lots of support. I've been wondering whether she hasn't asked, or you haven't felt so able to give it.'

'OK.' Nessa frowned. She and Mab hadn't spoken – hadn't even texted – since the visit to Granny Jenny last weekend, but Inga didn't know that. 'I agree that Mab being in love might well be the answer to that question,' she said, as evenly as she could manage. 'That's what I've assumed, anyway.'

'Did I offend you?' Inga asked. 'I didn't mean to.'

'No,' Nessa said. 'No, I'm not offended.'

'But you don't want to talk about yourself any more, as you already said.'

Inga dipped the satay stick into the bowl of peanut sauce, then offered it to Nessa, who shook her head. The truth was that Nessa had thought quite a lot about Mab's silence, and it unnerved her to realise that Inga had guessed that. Perhaps even guessed that she was worried about it.

'I suppose I just feel...' she began – but she was saved from formulating whatever thought she might have been working towards because her phone rang just then, pealing out its personalised Mab alert. She looked at Inga; a quick, ironic, what-a-coincidence glance. 'Mab,' she said, picking up the phone from the table.

Inga smiled at her. She had a good smile, Nessa thought. In that moment it occurred to her that she loved Inga; that she hoped Inga loved her too.

'Take it,' Inga said. 'I'm going to go and buy us some ice cream.'

She kissed Nessa's head on her way to the door, as Nessa clicked to answer the call.

'Hello, sweet Mab,' she said. 'How are you doing?'

'Not so good.'

They weren't on FaceTime, but Nessa could see Mab's face even so, tear-stained and crumpled. The warm feeling that Inga's smile had left her with swelled to fill her whole body. Not because Mab was upset, of course not, but because she'd called Nessa.

'I'm so sorry,' she said. 'What's happened? Or is it just...?'

'Could I come round?' Mab asked. 'I don't want to go home. I need to talk to you.'

'Of course you can.' Nessa glanced towards the front door. 'Inga's here, but I can ask her to leave.'

'I don't mind,' Mab said. 'I'm going to call an Uber.'

'Shall I save you some food?'

'Yes please. I haven't eaten anything for hours. Thank you, Nessa.'

She rang off before Nessa could say anything else. Nessa stared at the blank face of the phone, feeling the pressure of tears behind her eyes, and something lifting from her shoulders while something else – something old and familiar – settled back on to them. Whatever was going on, she thought, it was no good them being apart. Life just didn't work without Mab in it. For a moment longer she sat where she was, uttering what might even have been a silent prayer, and then she got up to clear away the dirty plates and set a new place for her sister.

'This is so good,' Mab said. 'Thank you.'

'It was better when it was hot,' Nessa said. Inga was in the kitchen, spooning ice cream into bowls.

'It's fine,' Mab said. 'I was so hungry.'

'Feeling better?'

'A bit.' Mab's face was still blotchy, her hair tangled. 'But it's not what you think. It's not just Dad.'

'I guessed as much.'

Mab attempted a grin, but it was almost immediately blurred by tears. 'I'm sorry. Honestly, I...'

'What is it?' Nessa asked. 'What's upset you? Is it Danny?'

'Partly,' Mab said. 'It's – I'm pregnant.'

'Pregnant?' Nessa sat back, her mouth open in pantomime astonishment.

Mab grinned again, through her tears. 'Yeah, I know. Total fuck-up, eh? It ought to be harder, making a whole new person.

It shouldn't be able to happen just because you run out of pills for a few days.'

'Is it a fuck-up, though?' An image of Mab with a baby in her arms floated into Nessa's mind. A Raphael Madonna. Would it be the worst thing, her and Danny settling down?

'Pretty much a fuck-up,' Mab said. Her face trembled then, her mouth turning itself upside down.

'Does Danny...?'

'I told him this evening. I didn't expect him to be overjoyed, but horrified would be closer to the mark.'

'Oh, Mab.' Nessa leaned forwards and gripped Mab's hand. 'And do you want... have you thought about–'

'I've been to see the midwife and everything,' Mab said. Her voice sounded, now, like the five-year-old Mab's – or perhaps the on-the-cusp-of-nine-year-old's, that evening when they'd eaten birthday cake and listened to the grown-ups arguing about who was going to look after them. 'I'm having a scan tomorrow.'

'I'll help you,' Nessa said. 'I'll come with you to the scan.'

'Would you?'

'Of course. Of course I will. But... Maybe you need to give Danny a bit of time.'

Mab shook her head. 'I don't think so. I've blown it. Or he has. I can't...' She clamped her mouth shut to stop the trembling.

'What happened?' Nessa asked.

'We had an argument. Or at least – he was cross with me already. But I thought – I thought when I told him about the baby it would sweep all that away.' A convulsive sob stopped her speaking again, and Nessa waited. 'He'd been so nice before that. So kind to me.'

'About Dad?' Nessa asked.

Mab nodded. 'And... oh, it's complicated. But I thought – I thought we'd be OK.' She sobbed again, burying her face in her hands.

261

'Tell me,' Nessa said, stroking her shoulder. 'We can untangle things, I'm sure we can.'

'You don't understand,' Mab said. 'It's not … it's–'

Inga came back into the room, bringing two bowls of ice cream with her. She'd eaten hers in the kitchen, Nessa thought, to be tactful.

'I can go,' Inga said. 'I think that would be better. I'll leave you two alone so you can talk.'

But Mab sat up then, not in a hurry but as though she'd made a decision, or perhaps realised something. Remembered something. 'No.' She rubbed at her eyes; dried her tears. 'There's no need. It's nothing. It's not – oh, you know.'

Nessa looked at her carefully. *It's complicated*, Mab had said a moment ago. *You don't understand*. 'Tell me anyway,' she said. 'Maybe I can help.'

'Ice cream will help,' Mab said, picking up the bowl Inga had put in front of her. 'I'm sorry to be so dramatic. I'm just a bit all over the place at the moment. I think it must be the hormones.'

'OK.' That sounded plausible, Nessa thought, but she wasn't totally convinced. 'What about Danny? Why don't you text him?'

Mab pulled a face; a comedy effect with a mouth full of Ben and Jerry's. 'I'm not going to do that.'

'He might just have been shocked,' Nessa said. 'He might come round to the idea.'

Mab shrugged.

'Seriously, Mab, you can't play games over this.'

'What?' Mab looked furious now. She put her spoon down. 'Is that what you think I'm doing?'

'No,' Nessa said. 'I'm sorry, I didn't mean that. I just–'

'I didn't come here for a pep talk,' Mab said. 'Believe me, I'm taking this seriously. I've got a pregnancy folder and a million leaflets.'

Nessa grinned. She'd always thought she didn't want children, but she felt a sudden pang of jealousy: a sudden longing to see Mab's baby. 'What time's your scan?' she asked. 'Which hospital?'

But Mab shook her head. 'Don't worry. It might turn out to be nothing, and then I'd feel like an idiot if you'd taken the morning off.'

Nessa started to protest, but it was clear that Mab had made up her mind. Perhaps she wanted to prove something, Nessa thought. Perhaps that wasn't such a bad thing.

'If you're sure,' she said, and then, 'Do you want to stay? There's no need to traipse back across London. We can make up the sofa bed.'

Mab tipped her head to one side, as if she was considering it, although Nessa had the feeling she wasn't really.

'I'd better not.' She didn't give any more explanation, but Nessa nodded, smiled. 'I can't face the Tube, though. I might call another Uber.'

'There's no rush,' Nessa said. 'Have some tea. Tell me more about what you've been up to.'

'There's really nothing else to tell,' Mab said. 'I think – I should probably get home. Get to bed. I'm sorry to crash in and then...'

Five minutes later she was gone.

'Well?' Inga asked, when Nessa had shut the door behind her. 'Do you feel better about her now, or worse?'

Nessa laughed. 'Good question. We'll see.'

Inga looked at her. She could tell there'd been holes in their conversation, Nessa thought. Anyone could tell that. Anyone would find it surprising that Mab had arrived in such a rush and left again just as precipitately. Mab never used to be so flighty, but maybe finding out you were pregnant would do that to you. Losing your father, finding out you were pregnant and arguing with your boyfriend. She sighed.

'Bedtime, I think,' she said. 'Thank you for the ice cream. And the clearing up.'

'My pleasure.'

Nessa waited, hoping for more, for some words of wisdom, but Inga turned away, back to the kitchen to turn off the lights.

Chapter Forty-Three

Mab shut her eyes as the Uber wound its way through the outskirts of London, the city landscape bathed in the dull glow that hung over it from dusk until dawn. For a while she thought she might sleep, but when the driver lurched away clumsily from a red light, nausea clutched at her, and with it a sudden alertness, a sudden awareness of the enormity of her situation. She was pregnant, orphaned, probably jobless. She suspected the sister she'd always relied on of something that wasn't quite murder, although it might possibly stretch that far. She'd lost her baby's father, the nicest man she'd ever gone out with. It was as if she'd played a truly disastrous round of Jenga, pulling out one block and then another as the edifice of her life crumbled around her. Thank God she'd stopped short of dislodging the final piece tonight. She'd gone to Wanstead thinking she might do that. She'd told Danny her story; she'd told Con. The words were there, ready.

Ach, she thought: perhaps she should have played that last move and been done with it. Seen what happened if she told Nessa she'd spotted her at the farm that day. Caught her off guard when her mind was filled with Danny and the baby. Things could hardly be worse, could they?

She knew that wasn't true, though. Just because she'd peered behind the curtain that had shrouded that dark piece of their past from view, it didn't mean she had to tear it down. It didn't mean she and Nessa couldn't go on exactly as they always had. Look at this evening: Nessa had fed her and comforted her, offered her a bed, volunteered to come with her to the scan in the morning. There was Inga too, now, provider of ice cream and assistant mother-carer. But no, that wasn't Inga's role, Mab thought. Inga's purpose – Inga's agenda – was to protect Nessa, not her. Wasn't that what had stopped Mab tonight? That moment when Inga had suggested she should leave: hadn't that been a signal that she understood there was something serious to be said? A warning, even? Or was that paranoia, a wild flaring of Mab's imagination?

In any case, she told herself, she'd been wise to hold her tongue. For one thing, she had no one else to turn to if she jeopardised her relationship with Nessa: no one except Con, whom she'd seen today for the first time in nineteen years. Con liked her, Mab thought. Con cared about her, or had done back in the day. But Con, for all her kindness, had made her call back in 2005. She'd chosen Philip.

Chapter Forty-Four

Con slept soundly that night, despite the turbulence that Mab's visit had stirred up. But she woke to cold and rain, a surprise after the warmth of the last few days. The rain was the heavy kind that seems likely to keep going all day, and she lay in bed for a while listening to it, and watching the patterns it made on the window. Philip had already left for work, so the house was empty and quiet.

Sometimes, when she first woke, she imagined herself back in the big house. She would follow, in her mind, the route from her bedroom, along the landing and down the wide staircase to the hall below, then through the passage to the kitchen with its old range, its cluttered table, its wide windows onto the garden. It wasn't so much that she missed the house, she thought, as that she missed the life she'd had there. The presence of children, and the feeling that life was still barely half run. The sense of space all around her, which was both a worry and a comfort.

This house – which had been called the gardener's cottage when she was growing up, although a live-in gardener was already a distant memory by then – was, as she'd said to Mab, much more sensible for two people, and she despised herself for disliking it so much. It was tainted by association, she thought now. She'd brought with her a burden of secrets and guilt and sadness that no house could cope with.

Philip had left a cup of tea for her on the kitchen table – a daily kindness – but it was cold by the time she got downstairs. She put it in the microwave and pressed the button. No point wasting it, and she was past pretending that she cared very much what tea tasted like. The hum of the microwave merged with the steady drum of the rain, a gentle percussion that sounded somehow anticipatory, as if she might be waiting for something. For a phone call, or for someone to arrive – or maybe just for the unfurling of the strands of thought which she'd bound up so tightly the night before.

The microwave pinged, and she retrieved the teacup and took a tentative sip. Perfectly good, she told herself. She had some work to finish this week – the copy edits on a non-fiction book for children about Pompeii – and she really ought to get on with that rather than maundering in the past. Three hours at her desk, she bargained, and then, if the rain had cleared, she'd go for a walk and allow herself to think.

The rain didn't stop, but it was lighter by noon, reduced to a springlike drizzle, and Con donned her waterproofs and set off across the fields. She found herself taking the path that looped round towards the farm, following the far bank of the stream and circling the big house at a safe distance. Everything was swathed in mist and water today in any case, the landscape a greenish blur dotted by trees still waiting for their new leaves.

So, she thought, as she swished through the wet grass. What was she to make of Mab's visit? The day had been a heady mixture of pleasure and pain, so finely balanced that it was hard to tease the two apart. She had loved seeing Mab, getting a sense of the young woman she'd become, but the thought of the two decades she had missed tormented her. And the news of Mab's baby had filled her with hope and joy – a sense of life opening up again, of new beginnings – but it had also brought her own babies powerfully to mind, and sharpened the awareness of loss to a point she almost couldn't bear.

It had never been possible, she thought, to map her life in any conventional way: to see it tidily laid out, or to survey it calmly. Demons and dragons leapt out from it; chasms opened up, ready to swallow her. The life she had now, with Philip and her work and the cottage, was like a walkway around the edge of a volcano: a path you could just about manage without holding your breath, as long as you didn't look down.

But she'd done that yesterday. She'd looked down – looked back. She and Mab had talked about Max's death. Afterwards, when Philip appeared, she'd pushed it all out of sight again, smothering the great bonfire of emotions that had taken hold of her briefly. But she was conscious, this morning, that the mantle of suspicion and guilt she'd worn for so long had shifted: that its familiar weight felt less certain. Perhaps Mab was right, and Philip hadn't killed Max. He'd come home last night, after dropping Mab at the station, so cheerful and buoyant, and Con had seen him for a moment through Mab's eyes and wondered how she could have suspected, all this time, that he was capable of killing, or of keeping silent about so calamitous an accident.

Was it possible, she wondered, as she opened the kissing gate onto the bank of the stream, that she had transferred her own guilt to Philip: the guilt she'd felt about failing to manage Max; about failing to look after him properly, or to love him enough? It felt simple enough to acknowledge that she'd always blamed herself, deep down, for Max's death – so had Philip been a convenient proxy? Had her silence, the sacrifice of her life to protecting her older son, been a penance for her own sins, rather than his?

She wanted to think that it had made no difference: that Philip had never wanted any more from life, and that she had loved him no less fiercely. She had certainly felt ready, even that day, to excuse him if he'd lost his temper, lost his grip for a moment. Max had that effect on people. And for her...

Ah, here was the rub. It had been easier, she admitted, to bear the idea that Philip had pushed Max than that Max had jumped. A moment of fury from a brother who'd been teased and taunted every day – a confluence of circumstances that tipped over into tragedy – that was comprehensible. The universe threw up such things. Dark holes devoured teenage boys every day: those who tempted fate on motorbikes, or with drugs, or by pushing people beyond their limits. But the idea that Max had been driven to such despair that he'd thrown himself off that ledge – that Con had failed to notice the desperation inside him – was intolerable. Forgiving Philip was easy compared to forgiving herself for such neglect.

The rain gathered force again, and Con stopped under an oak tree whose roots ran down to the banks of the stream, exposed and knotted like the veins on an old man's hand. For a few minutes she half sat, half stood, resting against its broad trunk and watching the water flowing past.

There had been, she admitted, a certain bitter consolation in cleaving to an answer. But if it wasn't the right answer, where did that leave her? What had happened to the truth?

The coroner had decreed that Max's death was an accident. He hadn't mentioned the possibility that someone else had been involved because no one had told him that anyone else had been nearby. The inquest had been straightforward. Mab's account of discovering Max's body had been read out; the Fidlers had confirmed that they had gone out that morning, and had left

Max clearing out one of the stables on the other side of the yard. Lucy had been in the farmhouse, but had heard and seen nothing. Con had attested to the fact that there had been an argument over breakfast that morning, but that it had been nothing exceptional. The coroner hadn't pressed her, and she'd been grateful for that.

But she had never believed the explanation he'd given: that Max had simply slipped. That he'd attempted a climb he'd made many times, to a perch he was in the habit of visiting, and on this occasion he had missed his footing and fallen. Even now, Con couldn't accept that: Max had been strong and confident. He'd upset everyone else that morning, but he hadn't been particularly distressed himself, and he'd settled to the job Jim Fidler had given him. There was surely more to it than a loose piece of masonry, an uncharacteristic loss of concentration. Philip had been nearby, and had returned flustered; Mab had seen Nessa running from the scene. Neither of them had admitted to being at the farm that morning. Those couldn't both be coincidences, could they? And what about the flowers Mab claimed to have seen, to have gathered up and taken away?

Perhaps, she thought, what Nessa had been hiding all this time was the fact that she'd seen Philip. Could it, even, have been a three-way scuffle that had resulted in Max falling? Had Nessa and Philip been protecting each other all this time?

Con sighed. The rain was falling faster and faster: she was going to get wet on the way home. But she'd made a decision. She couldn't go on any longer not knowing what happened to Max. It had eaten away too much of her already. Seeking the truth might be painful – it might be catastrophic – but she needed to ask those unthinkable questions now. And she had the perfect opportunity to bring Mab and Nessa and Philip together: a meeting to discuss a memorial service. The thought made her insides quiver, but she knew it was the right thing to do. When she got back to the house, she would ring the vicar and ask whether they could use the church. She'd see if they could pencil in some possible dates, and start writing a list of people they might invite, and then she'd contact Mab and Nessa and suggest they all came to Lowlands next weekend.

Chapter Forty-Five

Mab had forgotten to set an alarm, so it was lucky that she was woken by a crash from the kitchen. She grabbed her phone. Nine thirty: OK, she had plenty of time. The phone needed charging, though. She needed a shower. She needed to get her act together.

When she got downstairs, Yvonne was in the kitchen.

'Morning,' she said. No expensive pastries this morning, Mab saw. Yvonne was holding a bowl of yogurt. She was still in her pyjamas.

'No work today?' Mab asked.

Yvonne pulled a face. 'I was in the office until two,' she said. 'I'm going in late today. What about you?'

'I've got a hospital appointment,' Mab said.

'Oh.' Yvonne made a different kind of face, appraising this information.

'Nothing serious.' Mab smiled, and averted her eyes from the yogurt as nausea crept up on her again.

There'd been a missed call from Danny this morning, presumably wondering whether she was coming into work today. Fuck him, Mab thought – although even as a thought the sentiment felt too strong. She could see things from his point of view. She'd told him something undeniably disturbing about her family, her past, and he'd taken it on the chin. He'd found out that she'd gone to Somerset when she was supposed to be ill, and he'd been covering for her. She'd summoned him to meet her for dinner, dropped her bombshell about being pregnant, then flounced out of the restaurant before he'd had a chance to compose his thoughts.

That didn't mean he hadn't behaved badly, of course. He'd had the easy part: all he'd needed to do was be nice to her, step up to the mark, and he'd blown it. And now he was getting off scot-free, walking away without any ties to Mab's freaky family. He might feel a bit miffed, but he'd get over it. He wasn't, as Hazel would say, the injured party. He'd shown his true colours last night, Mab told herself. But part of her didn't believe that. Part of her feared it was her, not Danny, who'd messed everything up. She shouldn't let him slip through her fingers so easily, said the voice of reason in her head.

That voice wasn't getting a hearing today, though. Mab was almost a mother now, and mothers needed to stand their ground. They needed to be right about things. So the first thing was to find out if there really was a baby inside her, rather than one of those weird tumours she'd read about on the internet. It was hard to believe, Mab thought, as she poured herself a glass of water and attempted to drink it without retching, that anything as benign as a baby could make you feel so unwell.

Her appointment wasn't at a hospital, but at a place called a diagnostic centre, very new and sleek. Mab didn't have to wait long for her scan, or for her answer.

Ten weeks, the woman told her, pointing at the smudges on the ultrasound screen that were apparently bits of her baby. The ten weeks dated back to the start of her last period, she said, or two weeks beyond the date of conception. That seemed a pretty confusing way to reckon things, but by that point Mab's head didn't really have room in it for maths.

She was going to have a baby, then. For the last few days she'd had a sneaking suspicion that she was making it up, and that there would turn out to be a more logical – or a more outlandish – explanation. But no: the explanation was the one that had dawned on women for thousands of years. Millions, in fact. She was going to produce another human being who would grow up into a child, a teenager, an adult like her. In seven months, or whatever the scanner's calculations meant, that person would exist. They would have a name – a name she would have chosen for them. It was mind-blowing. And it made her feel, somehow, effortlessly competent. Look what she could do without even thinking about it. Look what she was capable of.

It was all over in a few minutes, and then Mab was walking out of the building, clutching the little picture the radiographer had given her as if it was a lucky charm. Her nausea had lifted, and in its place was hunger – the sudden, grasping hunger she was beginning to get used to. There was a café on the corner – the greasy spoon kind rather than the hipster kind, but a cheerful-looking place with a few other people sitting inside having coffee – and Mab went in and ordered an omelette and a bowl of chips and then, as an afterthought, a milkshake. If she was having a baby, she was surely grown-up enough to go into a café on her own and order whatever she felt like eating. It was a good feeling. She'd relied on other people all her life, and now someone was going to rely on her, and she was ready for it.

There was another missed call from Danny, but he hadn't left a message, hadn't sent a text, so he couldn't really have wanted to get hold of her. He wasn't exactly putting himself on the line. Mab felt a spasm of distress at that thought, but it didn't last long. She was OK. She was going to be fine.

Mab's sense of conviction wavered a little when she'd finished her chips and her milkshake and realised it was still only eleven thirty. What was she going to do now, she wondered, if she had no work to go to? What was she going to do all weekend, and for all the days after that?

She paid her bill, smiled at the waiter (who couldn't have been more than eighteen, but grinned back at her in a way that made her fear he was about to ask for her number) and took herself out onto the street. It was a grey day, threatening rain, but it wasn't cold. She could walk, she thought. She could take herself to a park. London had plenty of things to offer, didn't it? But the thought of tourist attractions reminded her of the afternoon in Greenwich, and that led straight back to the second part of last night's drama and the question of whether she'd done the right thing, chickening out of asking Nessa about the day Max died.

She wasn't going to dwell on all that any more, she told herself firmly as she walked to the bus stop. She was going to put it away and let the back of her mind deal with it. Because the trouble was that it wasn't the kind of thing you could just have a little think about: it was more like being the prime minister and realising you had the nuclear codes in your head, or your desk, or wherever they kept them. You couldn't just idly wonder what would happen if for some reason you activated them. You had to keep the consequences in sharp focus all the time, and remember that you'd need a very good reason to turn the world inside out.

That analogy was probably a bit over the top, Mab thought, as she spotted a bus approaching, but it was good to remember that some bits of her life were still intact, and that they were precious. Most of her happy memories involved Nessa, and that wasn't something she could risk destroying on a whim.

This aimless day reminded her, in fact, of the school holidays which she and Nessa had spent with Hazel. At first Granny Jenny had always had them for the holidays, because Hazel would be working, but as they got older – as Hazel got more worried about the hippies being a bad influence – they'd spent more time in London. Hazel would give them a list of museums and art galleries, Mab remembered, and money for the bus. They'd resented it, but generally they'd done what Hazel suggested, because she would quiz them about it in the evening. She'd want to know which room, or which picture, they'd liked best, her expression so eager and intent that they couldn't lie. Perhaps it was those outings Nessa had been channelling when she'd suggested they went to Greenwich the day their father died. They'd never been to Greenwich back then, but they'd visited the Tower and the London Eye as well as every museum going. Mab had loved the Eye, but her favourite place had been the zoo.

She'd got onto the bus just now without really considering where she was going, then climbed up to the top deck and made her way to the front without thinking about that either, but as she slid into the empty seat on the left an idea settled in her mind. If this was a day to be filled, like those long-ago London holidays, and she was free to choose her favourite thing, then she would go to the zoo. She'd take her baby to meet the penguins and the meerkats. She was already on her way, in fact: this bus would take her all the way to the middle of town, and then she just had to walk across Regent's Park.

The other front seat was occupied by a woman in her late thirties and a little boy of three or four, presumably her son. The boy seemed to Mab preternaturally quiet, as though he was making a huge effort to suppress his excitement, but maybe that was just Mab projecting her own feelings. The woman caught her eye and moved her face a little, perhaps suspicious of Mab's broad grin but offering, even so, the suggestion of a smile in response. People needed practice, Mab thought. She needed practice too. It was ages since she'd sat at the top of a bus like this: the streets looked different from up here, the map of South London laid out in road junctions and traffic lights. You could picture all the possible paths ahead, like a board game you hadn't played yet.

Mab liked the feeling of riding through the city, being borne through its tangle of streets and lives and people towards a future she had no certain idea of. For a moment she imagined herself as the protagonist of a film; imagined familiar faces watching her embark on its opening scene. Her mother, and her father, and Nessa. Hazel and Granny Jenny. Danny. Con. Philip. Even Yvonne and Aster and Charley from Littlemore Road, and all the people she'd known and forgotten about. Lucy from the farm, and her old Year 6 teacher, and the girl at the horrible boarding school who'd helped her catch up with the maths the others had already done. People talked about how your life flashed through your head before you died, but it seemed to Mab that you ought to look back over your life before you gave birth, too. You ought to play the memorable scenes in your head – all the kindnesses and happinesses and excitements – so your baby could understand the world it was coming into.

It wasn't until the bus was carrying her across the river that Mab remembered what had happened the first time she went to the zoo. A detail of that visit, long forgotten, that rose up now in vivid colour in her mind.

Chapter Forty-Six

September 2006

Despite Nessa's promise that no birthday would ever be as bad as her ninth, Mab had been sure she would dread every single one of them, because they would always make her think of her mother's funeral. However far away she got from that awful day, each year her birthday would remind her about it.

But Nessa had tried hard to stop that happening. Especially the first time Mab's birthday came round again – her tenth – Nessa tried so hard that it almost worked. Hazel must have done some of the arranging, but it was Nessa who'd had all the ideas. She'd planned every bit of the day to make sure it was so busy and lovely and surprising that Mab wouldn't have time to think about the year before. So that for ever afterwards, it would be this birthday she'd remember, not the last one.

It had started with them going out for breakfast, a treat so extravagant that Mab couldn't imagine how Nessa had persuaded Hazel to let them do it – but Granny Jenny was there too, so maybe that bit had been agreed with her. Maybe she had paid for the waffles and ice cream and hot chocolate that had almost made Mab sick. Then there'd been presents, beautifully wrapped and stacked in a pile on the coffee table in Hazel's sitting room: some books from Hazel and a bottle of Matey bubble bath from Nessa, and – most thrillingly – an iPod. It wasn't one of the new ones, but Mab hadn't cared about that.

'I feel like Dudley Dursley!' she'd said, and Nessa had laughed because she'd known what was coming next.

'Ready for the zoo, then?' she'd said, and even Hazel had smiled broadly at Mab's excitement.

In some ways it was lucky this birthday fell on a Saturday, because it meant they weren't at school and Hazel wasn't at work, but in other ways it wasn't, because no one else was either, and the zoo was very busy. It was full of families, groups of teenagers, older couples – almost every kind of person you could imagine.

'Perhaps we could visit some of the less popular animals,' Hazel suggested. 'You might get a better view if we can avoid the crowds.'

But Mab had been entranced by the big signs near the entrance showing photos of the giraffes and the giant tortoises, the gorillas and the lions and the snakes, and she wanted to see everything – the popular animals as well as the unpopular ones.

'Can we stay all day?' she asked. 'I don't want to miss anything.'

Because even though Hazel lived quite near the zoo, Mab knew this was a treat that might not come round again very soon. And more importantly, she knew everyone wanted this day to be special for her, and she wanted to stretch out that feeling – the happy feeling that came with everyone being nice, and her being at the centre of it – for as long as she could. She might be ten now, but she didn't care if people thought she was seven or eight, skipping from one excitement to another with

Nessa close behind, and Hazel and Granny Jenny following more sedately, as adults did.

Some of the people they passed, or stood next to while they peered through glass or wire mesh, grumbled a bit about the zoo. Mab heard them saying that it wasn't as good as some other zoo they'd been to: that the animals were boring, or that it was badly laid out. But it seemed to Mab the most magical place she'd ever seen, and every new exhibit they discovered was instantly her favourite. There were the penguins in their funny white pool with big curving slides, the butterfly house, the aquarium, the outback area where the kangaroos lived – and there were more kinds of monkeys than she could remember the names of.

'I like these the best,' she said, as they watched the gibbons swinging from arm to arm between tree branches. 'Look how clever they are! They're like acrobats in a circus. And their sweet little white faces!'

'If we go and see the squirrel monkeys you can walk right through their enclosure,' Granny Jenny said. 'Wouldn't that be fun?'

'Really?' Mab asked. 'You can touch them?'

'I don't expect they come that close,' Hazel said. She looked at the map she'd folded into her pocket. 'It's a bit of a walk. Would you like to have some lunch first?'

They'd passed several places that sold food, and Mab would normally have been dying to try a hot dog or a toastie, but she was still full of waffles and ice cream, and she didn't want to waste time eating when there was so much more to see.

'I'm not really hungry,' she said. 'Maybe a bit later.'

'All right.' Hazel looked at the map again, then pointed. 'It's this way, I think.'

The sky had been very grey earlier, but the sun had come out now and it felt almost hot as they followed the path towards the squirrel monkeys. When they passed a kiosk with seating outside it, Granny Jenny stopped.

'I'm gasping for a cup of tea,' she said. 'I might wait here for you. You can tell me all about the monkeys afterwards.'

Hazel looked at the kiosk sign, then at the girls. 'I'll stay with you, Mum,' she said. 'I'm sure Nessa and Mab will be fine on their own. It's only just round that corner. Come straight back, though, Nessa.'

Nessa nodded, grinned, then grabbed Mab's hand. This was going to be the best bit of the day, Mab thought. Just the two of them, and no grown-ups. Perhaps the monkeys *would* come close if they saw two children on their own?

When they got to the entrance, there was a banner outside warning them to take care. *Meet Norman Nine Fingers*, it said. *He tried to feed the monkeys*. There was a picture of a cartoon boy holding up a hand with a dripping stump where his fourth finger had been, and a monkey with blood dripping from its mouth, waving its arm triumphantly. Mab giggled.

'Hazel wouldn't've let us go in if she'd seen that,' she said.

'How could they eat a whole finger?' Nessa scoffed. But Mab hurried on into the enclosure, just in case she had second thoughts.

The squirrel monkeys were even more adorable than the gibbons. They had black heads that looked as though they were wearing little caps, and yellowish arms. And the enclosure was much bigger than Mab had expected, with lots of big trees and ropes strung between their branches. It had only opened last year, they read, and had been designed to look like the forests of Bolivia.

'Those must be young ones,' Mab said, pointing at a group that looked smaller and livelier than the others, playing in a tree above their heads. They were leaping about as though they were playing chase, but a kind of chase that involved jumping from branch to branch, dropping down and scrambling back up, and sometimes wrestling with each other.

'There's a mother with a tiny baby on her back,' Nessa said, and Mab swung round to watch as the monkey carried her baby along the full length of a branch, then settled herself against the trunk to feed it.

For a moment Mab was silent. 'Did Mummy do that?' she asked.

'Yes. I remember her feeding you.'

'Really?'

Nessa nodded. 'You were almost as cute as that baby monkey.'

Mab laughed. 'No tail, though.'

'No tail,' Nessa agreed.

There was a pause, and in it Mab sensed an agreement that they wouldn't mention their mother again today.

'Look,' Nessa said, 'those young ones are coming back.'

Sure enough the little group they'd seen before – or perhaps another group, four or five of them – was racing along a rope towards a fork in one of the big trees, where several criss-crossing branches made a sort of treehouse for them to play in. There was a lot of loud chattering and squealing and jittering, limbs and tails flying around, monkeys swooping and grabbing – and then suddenly a louder shriek, and one of them was falling, and the others were stilled for a moment, watching, until it landed in a bush below. In the gap before that happened Mab screamed, and several people turned to look at her.

'Is it OK?' she managed to say. 'Why aren't they coming to check?'

'There it is,' Nessa said. 'Look, you can see its head. It's fine.'

Sure enough, the little monkey's face poked out through the thick leaves of the bush for a moment, then withdrew again. Mab and Nessa kept watching, but it didn't appear again.

'Why isn't it coming out?' Mab asked. 'Do you think it's hurt? Should we tell someone it fell?'

'It's probably embarrassed,' Nessa said. 'Monkeys aren't supposed to fall out of trees.'

'Why did it, then?' Mab asked. 'Did one of the others push it? Do you think they were squabbling, or...'

And then she stopped suddenly. She could feel Nessa standing very still beside her, as though a shockwave had run between them. What had she said? What would happen now?

While they stood there, not looking at each other, the little monkey sidled out from the bush and climbed back up the tree trunk towards its friends. It turned its head to glance at Mab and Nessa as it passed, as if it was thanking them for their concern, but neither of them reacted.

'Maybe it lost its balance,' Nessa said after a minute or two. Her voice sounded very strange. It was as if they'd just witnessed something really terrible, Mab thought, but she knew it wasn't the monkey either of them was really thinking about.

'Do you think they do that?' she asked. 'Even when they're so used to climbing?'

'I don't know.'

'Maybe they do sometimes,' Mab said. She hesitated, holding her breath. 'And maybe they squabble sometimes, too, and then...'

'There you are!' said Hazel's voice behind them.

Mab held on a moment longer, and then she turned round to see Hazel and Granny Jenny coming towards them.

'Have you both got all your fingers still?' Granny Jenny asked. She laughed, waggling her hands at them. 'There's a terrible poem I remember. *The Lion and Albert*. "Mother! Yon Lion's 'et Albert!"'

There was a sort of glaze in the air around them: Mab could almost see it. Like when it's very hot, she thought, or the camera's a bit out of focus. She glanced at Nessa, who had lifted her eyes to watch the monkey disappearing back into the trees.

'This is rather fun, isn't it?' said Hazel. 'How many of them are there?'

'Lots,' Mab said. 'We've seen lots.'

Granny Jenny smiled at her. 'Has it been a nice birthday, Mab?'

'Yes.' Mab smiled too. She smiled at Granny Jenny and Hazel, and then she reached for Nessa's hand, and felt it squeeze hers. Another key had turned in another lock, she thought, keeping all that dangerous stuff out of sight. She breathed out.

'It's been a lovely birthday,' she said. 'But I think maybe I've seen enough of the monkeys now. What shall we do next?'

Chapter Forty-Seven

March 2024

The zoo had changed quite a lot. The penguins had moved into a new pool, and the old one sat sad and deserted. It was listed, someone told Mab as she stood looking at it, but no one could work out what to use it for, so it was being left empty for now. And one group of monkeys had been moved into the old aviary, but not the ones Mab and Nessa had seen – or so Mab assumed, because the walk-through enclosure was still there. Mab wasn't sure whether she wanted to go back to that or not. In fact she wasn't sure, now, whether it had been a good idea to come here or a really terrible one. But it had cost a lot to get in, so she was definitely going to make the most of it.

The woman on the gate had told her that the penguins were being fed in half an hour, and although there were already quite a few people gathered at the new penguin beach when she found her way there, she got a seat near the front. And there was something utterly beguiling about the penguins; something you couldn't fail to be cheered up by. Although Mab didn't need cheering up, she reminded herself: she was doing fine, doing great. And she was going to be a good mother. Look at her, bringing her baby to the zoo when it wasn't even due to be born for months yet.

But somehow, as she watched the penguins diving for their food, and waddling along their artificial beach, and crowding around their keeper like a bunch of primary school children, Mab suddenly felt not fine at all. She felt desperately, inexplicably sad, overcome by a flood of loneliness and fear and hopelessness that she could do nothing to resist or to reason away. Before she knew what was happening, tears were rolling down her cheeks. Worse, she must have been making a noise, because people nearby were looking at her, starting to murmur and shift in their seats. Mab swallowed, and buried her face in her hands, but there was no disguising her misery now, either from herself or from other people.

'Are you OK?' said a voice, and Mab felt someone's hand on her shoulder. She turned, and recognised, with a shock, the woman from the bus. Her son was sitting beside her, gazing at the penguins with a rapt expression that made Mab's tears well up again.

'I'm sorry,' she said. 'I'm fine, really.'

She mustn't cry in front of the child, she told herself. She mustn't spoil the penguins for him. But she remembered the way she'd grinned at this pair on the bus, and she felt ridiculous. The whole feel-good film script she'd conjured up had vanished: it was as if her life had collapsed into a black hole inside her.

The woman hadn't moved; her hand was still resting on Mab's shoulder. The hand of a practised mother, Mab thought. The kind of woman she'd never be.

'It's just that I'm pregnant,' she found herself saying, 'and I've split up with my boyfriend. And I don't...' She gulped, struggling for self-control.

'Bobby's dad's not around either,' the woman said. The

pressure of her hand on Mab's shoulder increased for a moment. 'It's not easy.'

But here she was, bringing him to the zoo. There he was, turning his head now with a flicker of curiosity, a dark-haired angel with long lashes and big brown eyes.

'He's adorable,' Mab said.

'Sometimes.' The woman half smiled. She looked tired, at close quarters, but she had a nice smile. For a moment Mab thought she might suggest exchanging numbers; that this chance encounter might lead to a friendship. But the little boy was tugging at her sleeve now, wanting her to pay attention to the penguins. To him. And this was London, where strangers rarely even spoke to each other.

'I'm sorry,' Mab said again, and then, 'thank you.'

She stayed where she was for a couple more minutes, and then she got to her feet, catching the woman's eye again and attempting a smile. Perhaps that would be her in a few years, sitting here with her little boy, offering wisdom and comfort to a stranger. Managing parenthood on her own, even if it wasn't easy. After all, she and Nessa had grown up with no parents at all.

But perhaps, she thought, that proved the point.

The squirrel monkeys seemed less animated than Mab remembered. There was plenty of swinging and perching and chattering among the trees, and even a little girl – younger than the ten-year-old Mab whose shadow still lingered here – calling out to them delightedly. But none of it seemed to carry any meaning. There was no flash of recognition; no sudden moment of clarity.

Mab shook her head, and smiled at herself. What was she about today? Imagining herself as the protagonist of a movie;

looking for a connection with a kind stranger – and now hoping that a troupe of monkeys might offer an insight that would make everything fall into place? That a fragment of conversation from eighteen years ago might show her the way forward?

But that bit wasn't as mad as the rest, was it? That scene from her birthday had come back to her this morning because it had been charged with as much static electricity as a lightning bolt. Mab had known at the time what it meant: she'd recognised guilt in Nessa's face. That was why it had nestled in her subconscious, fuelling the corrosive suspicions that had eaten away at her childhood.

She gazed up into a tree that might or might not be the same one she and Nessa had stood under eighteen years ago. Two monkeys were sitting listlessly on a branch, as if waiting for the humans to entertain them for a change. One of them blinked at her, but neither of them moved. So where were the answers, then? Mab asked herself. And what exactly were the questions?

Part of the trouble was that everything was so tangled up. There was all the recent turmoil – her father's death, being pregnant, messing things up with Danny – and there was the agonising question of what Nessa might have done to Max. Those were separate things, but it wasn't possible to push the second one aside and hope that everything else would settle out somehow. Mab had got by on that strategy for nearly two decades, but it wouldn't hold up any more. And it was almost impossible to think straight about anything, especially if she was just the old Mab, not some supercharged maternal version, or the unexpected heroine of a rom com.

There ought to have been another thought after that – a thought that began 'but' or 'and so' – but Mab wasn't sure it was coming. The monkeys still hadn't moved, and their expressions looked baleful now, as though she'd failed to live up to their expectations. Mab remembered the sign from last time –

Norman Nine Fingers – and how it had given her a little thrill. This time the threat felt more credible. It was a relief when her phone pinged.

Danny, she thought, with a lurch of joy. If it was, she'd reply this time, because...

But the text wasn't from Danny. It was from Con, inviting her and Nessa for lunch at Lowlands on Sunday so that they could discuss the memorial service.

Joy was followed swiftly by disappointment – and then a creep of apprehension. Seeing Con and Philip again would be nice, of course, but... The four of them being together again after all this time – that was a big deal. Had Con thought of that? It meant the two suspecters and the two suspected in the room together, and the truth in the room with them. What were the chances of getting through the day without it finding its way out?

But that was the final spur Mab needed to move on to the 'and so' thought. To action. She couldn't leave things to chance; couldn't risk Nessa being exposed without giving her the opportunity to tell her side of the story first. She turned abruptly, and headed out of the monkey enclosure. And then she stopped to compose a message to Nessa.

Can I come round again tonight? Need to talk more. I'll bring food.

The answer came back in less than a minute.

Of course. I'll be home by six. No need to bring anything – Inga's cooking.

Chapter Forty-Eight

Philip was home from work early again, and Con was conscious that it took a little more effort than usual to muster her habitual welcome. It wasn't that she'd counted on having more time alone, or even that she particularly wanted it, but as she heard his car pulling up, she couldn't suppress a flutter of – what? Simply the feeling you get when a taxi arrives before you need to leave, she thought.

She was sitting at the desk in the sitting room, replying to a couple of letters from old friends who'd heard about Roy's death. The farm cat, which had taken to visiting her regularly, was curled in a chair beside her, but when the front door opened it lifted its head, and a moment later it was gone.

'Hello?' Philip called.

'In here,' Con said.

She could hear excitement in his voice, and the flutter of emotion in her chest turned towards curiosity and misgiving. He came into the room smiling.

'How was your day?' Con asked.

'Good,' he said. 'It was good.' He stopped, looking at her, the smile still in place. 'I've got a surprise for you.'

'Oh?'

He was almost jumping from one foot to the other with suppressed excitement. He looked years younger, Con thought, and rather comical. She smiled back at him, reproving herself for that fleeting desire to be left alone a little longer.

'How exciting!' she said. 'Can I see?'

'Not yet. It's coming on Sunday.'

'And you won't tell me what it is?'

He shook his head. 'That would spoil the surprise. But you'll like it.'

'I'm sure I will,' Con said, although the misgiving hadn't quite disappeared. 'How nice of you.'

'Shall I put the tea on?' Philip asked.

'Yes please. I was just finishing something off, but I'll be through in a moment.'

When he'd gone, she thought about the messages she'd sent earlier, inviting Nessa and Mab for lunch. She hoped the surprise wasn't going to make that difficult. Could it be a dog, she wondered, or a new car? Would Philip buy either of those things without consulting her? Or a piano, possibly? There'd been no room in the cottage for her grand piano, and she'd never got round to finding the cheap upright she'd promised herself. Never quite felt able to sanction the expense. That had been a loss – but her fingers would surely be too stiff to play after all this time.

'I spoke to the vicar,' she said, when he'd poured the tea. 'She's happy for us to have a service in the church.'

'Good,' Philip said.

Con was conscious of being alert for clues in his face, as though any conversation that touched on the past might lead him to reveal something. It made her feel a little ashamed – but she was committed now, she told herself.

'I've asked Mab and Nessa to come for lunch on Sunday so we can discuss it,' she said. 'That won't interfere with your surprise, will it?'

'No.' Philip smiled again, as though he'd forgotten briefly what he'd got up his sleeve. 'No, it'll make it better.'

Chapter Forty-Nine

Mab timed her arrival at Nessa's flat for six thirty, hoping to avoid being alone with Inga. There was something a bit scary about Inga, she thought, although her apron softened the effect. The smell in the kitchen was delicious too. Mab was hungry again. Hunger occupied her evenings now, as well as any other bits of the day nausea was prepared to give up to it.

'So how was it?' Nessa asked, when she'd kissed her.

'How was what?'

Nessa raised an eyebrow. 'The scan. Did you go?'

'Of course I did.' Mab took out her phone and unfolded the piece of paper she'd stowed under the cover. 'It looks like one of those blob tests.'

'Rorschach,' said Inga. Mab turned to look at her. 'The blob tests,' Inga said.

'It doesn't, though.' Nessa was staring at the scan picture as though it was a sacred icon. 'You know, Mab, the last time there was a baby in the family, it was you.'

'I suppose it was.' Mab felt a quiver of unease, knowing what she'd come for. She didn't want to talk about the baby: it felt wrong to use it for small talk while she steeled herself to accuse its aunt of killing someone.

'Did Danny come?' Nessa asked.

'To the scan? No.'

'Have you spoken to him?'

'No.'

'Oh, Mab...'

Mab couldn't tell whether that was an exclamation of pity or what-are-we-going-to-do-with-you dismay. Either way, Danny was another avenue she wanted to avoid tonight. Nessa knew her well enough to read the signals, at any rate. An orange light, this time. Not ready for this.

'Let me get you a drink,' Nessa said. 'Soft, I assume? We've got some nice apple juice.'

'Thanks,' Mab said.

'And Inga's made spag bol.'

'Lovely.' Mab smiled at Inga.

So they'd eat, she thought, and then she'd ask Nessa about Max. It would be fine. At least, it might not be fine, but by the end of the evening she'd know.

Inga's bolognese was delicious. Mab had two helpings, and Nessa and Inga filled the time by talking about their plans to redecorate the flat. Mab could tell there was a subtext, a message about their relationship moving up a gear, but she didn't respond to it. She wasn't going to think about the stakes; about what Nessa had to lose. Instead she watched them smiling at each other as they discussed different shades of blue, and felt dread and anticipation pooling inside her.

There was some ice cream left over from last night, and Mab waited until it had been fetched from the freezer before she signalled her intent. She took a deep breath and held it for a moment before she let it out again. Now. Ready.

'There's something I need to talk to you about, Nessa,' she said. 'Something we probably should have talked about years ago.'

It was like taking a knife to the conversation. Silence, and adrenaline, and two faces turned towards her. Mab couldn't quite believe what she'd just done: the work of a second, changing everything.

For a moment she considered retreating from it, perhaps inventing a question about their father, but the look on Nessa's face told her it was too late for that. Nessa knew what was coming, Mab was sure. That struck such a depth of cold through her that the air left her chest, and with it the wild hope that she might be mistaken. Why else would Nessa look like a wildcat on guard?

Sensing the sudden curdling of the air, Inga looked from Mab to Nessa.

'Do you want me to leave?' she asked.

'No,' Nessa said. 'Why should you leave?' Her voice was as light as a cloud, but Mab wasn't deceived.

Inga kept looking at her for a moment, and then she tilted her head slightly. 'You should eat your ice cream,' she said. 'Whatever there is to say, it's a shame to waste it.' But Mab was feeling sick again now, and Nessa's appetite had clearly gone too.

Mab had never got as far as practising the next bit; never imagined herself framing her suspicions in actual words. What she could feel from Nessa wasn't hostility or anger or fear, but a sort of desperate expectancy. *I went to see Con yesterday*, she thought, almost aloud. But no; that wasn't the way in. The reason for her argument with Danny, perhaps? Or the simplest, straightest line to the truth.

'Since Dad died,' she said, 'I've thought a lot about Mummy. About the summer she died, and especially the time we were at Lowlands.' She caught Nessa's eye again, and swallowed. 'About Max's death, and...'

Nessa was sitting perfectly still. Nausea rose up through Mab's belly, into her chest and her throat. But she couldn't stop now.

'I saw you, Nessa. I saw you at the farm that morning. You know I went there to look for you, and that's how I found Max's body. But before I got to the barn, I saw you running away. Taking the path to the stream.'

'Yes,' Nessa said.

'You didn't say anything,' Mab said. 'Not a word, ever. I never knew whether you'd seen me. Whether you knew that I'd seen you.'

'I saw you,' Nessa said. 'But I hoped... I didn't think you'd seen me. I thought if you had, you'd say something.'

Mab shook her head. She could feel her lips trembling, and she fought to keep control of them. 'I couldn't think about it,' she said. 'When I was little, I just couldn't think about it.'

Nessa nodded. She was very calm, and that made Mab angry.

'I knew you'd lied about where you'd been for my sake,' Mab said. 'I knew we'd both decided to keep it secret because if anyone knew, it would... And I needed you too much.' She stopped, choking back tears again. 'I was grateful to you. Of course I was. I've always been grateful, Nessa. I couldn't have survived without you. But I can't–'

Nessa's face hardly moved. Did she not understand how much she'd guessed? Mab wondered.

'Don't think I haven't felt guilty,' Nessa said. 'That I haven't wished things had happened differently that day. But how would it have helped if I'd told the truth?'

'It wouldn't have made things better for us,' Mab said. 'But...' She swallowed again, but the lump in her throat was too big to shift. Con didn't believe Nessa was guilty, couldn't believe she'd had anything to do with Max's death. But she had, hadn't she? 'I went to see Con yesterday,' she said. 'Do you know what she's suspected, all this time? That Philip killed Max. That he pushed him off that ledge.'

'Goodness,' Nessa said.

'Goodness?' Mab couldn't describe the feeling inside her now, the hot broil of anger and disbelief as the idea she'd had of her sister all this time started to crumble. 'Is that all you can say? Con lost one of her sons and has lived ever since believing such a terrible thing about the other one, and it's all your fault.'

'My fault?' Nessa's forehead folded into a puzzled frown. Not a genuine one, Mab was sure. There must be nothing in the centre of her. Had all her care and kindness been a front? A shell?

'Of course it's your fault,' Mab said. Shouted, actually, because she couldn't contain her rage any longer. 'Both bits of it are your fault. Philip couldn't have killed Max, because you did.'

'No.' Nessa shook her head. 'No, Mab, I didn't kill him.'

'Maybe it was an accident,' Mab said. 'Maybe you didn't mean him to fall. But he did, and he died, and – and Con...'

'You've got it wrong,' Nessa said. 'That isn't what happened.'

'Don't deny it now,' Mab insisted. 'You've already admitted it. You said you felt guilty. That you wished things had happened differently. That you didn't tell the truth.'

'Yes,' said Nessa, 'I said all those things, and I meant them. But I didn't push him – God, did you really imagine that I had? That I'd climbed up to that bloody ledge?' She laughed, looking at Mab with the same sort of disbelief Mab had been feeling towards her. 'Did you really think I was capable of murder, little Mab?'

The atmosphere in the room had sharpened to fracture point, as if the things both of them had said were hanging in the air between them like shards of ice.

'Tell me what happened, then,' Mab said. 'Tell me the truth. What were you doing at the farm, anyway?'

'I didn't see what happened,' Nessa said. 'I wasn't in the barn. I was nearby, and I heard a cry – a shout – and I went to look. When I got there, Max was lying on the floor. I felt – I was terrified. I was sure he was dead, but I touched him, felt for breathing, for any sign of life. And then I ran.'

'You didn't go for help,' Mab said.

'No. And I didn't stop you going into the farmyard. I didn't stop you finding him.'

'Why didn't you?'

Nessa shook her head. 'I can't tell you. I was frightened. I wasn't thinking straight. You ... you did the right thing. You were marvellous, Mab. But I'm so sorry I let you find him.'

Mab could hear the tinkle of the ice crystals, a sinister chime in her ears for every word Nessa spoke.

'That's what I've felt guilty about all this time,' Nessa said. 'That and the fact that I never admitted I'd seen him – seen his body – before you got there. But it wouldn't have made any difference, Mab. He was dead. He fell a long way, and the floor was very hard.'

There was a little noise now that didn't come from either of them. Mab had forgotten Inga was there.

'This has been harrowing for me to hear,' she said, 'so I can only imagine how it has felt for you both. Not just this evening, but your whole lives, holding these secrets. Things you have never spoken to each other about.'

Mab felt her blood rising again. Did Inga think that was the end of the matter? That she could round off the conversation in that couples-therapist way, and draw a line under the whole thing?

Inga tilted her head, like a bird gauging the direction of the wind. 'But it's very good to bring things out in the open. It's very brave. It means you can begin to process it. And it's a good time, after your father's death.'

'Yes,' said Nessa. Her voice was shaky, but she sounded relieved.

She'd been thrown a life belt, Mab thought. She was going to make it safely to shore now. Mab couldn't bear to look at her, or at Inga. Had Inga guessed that Nessa was lying? Was she deliberately gaslighting Mab? What was next: a small smile, and more platitudes? *You were so young. It was so long ago.*

Despite herself, Mab reached for the wine bottle and poured a slug into an empty glass. She was angrier than she could ever remember being. Here, in front of her, was the person who was the closest thing she'd had to a mother for most of her life. But all this time, that person had been deceiving her. Except that Mab hadn't been deceived: she'd known the truth all along, hadn't she? She'd known, and she'd pushed the knowledge away as best she could.

But the worst of it wasn't that she'd been complicit in concealing Nessa's guilt. It wasn't even that she knew, now, that she'd been right to suspect her. The worst thing was that Nessa still hadn't told her the truth. Mab knew her sister well enough to be certain of that. Her tone of voice was guarded, her expression cagey. Her words sounded rehearsed: a story she'd had ready all this time. And that meant nothing had been resolved at all. It meant Mab was in a worse position than ever, because there was a chasm between the two of them now that she couldn't imagine crossing.

Inga and Nessa were looking at her, waiting to see what she was going to say next.

'I think I'd better go,' she said.

'Mab,' Nessa said. She made a move forwards – half-rose from her chair – but she froze when Mab flinched.

That was a mistake, Mab thought. Amid the anger and confusion there was a tiny curl of fear now. Nessa would never hurt her, she told herself, but she didn't believe it unequivocally, and that was a terrible thing too.

'I'm very tired,' she said. 'It's been a long day.'

Nessa didn't reply. Mab gathered herself and tried again, forcing herself to meet Nessa's gaze. 'We can talk tomorrow,' she said.

And then there was a shift in Nessa's face. 'Did you get a message from Con? About Sunday?'

Mab nodded.

'Are you planning to go?'

'Yeah.' Mab was trembling again, but she attempted a smile, and hated herself for it. But she'd shot her bolt, for tonight at least. She didn't have another plan. She needed time to think, and it was better for now that Nessa thought she'd accepted her story.

Nessa folded the napkin that had been sitting crumpled beside her bowl. They'd each had one – grey and white linen napkins laid out by Inga. They reminded Mab of the beginning of the evening, the spaghetti bolognese and the posh apple juice, and she was filled with sadness. The best bit of her life had been Nessa, and that was over now. It was like finding out all over again that their mother was dying.

'Let me call you an Uber,' Nessa said.

It was only eight thirty, and she could perfectly well get the Tube, but Mab nodded again. Let Nessa take care of her, she

301

thought. Let her think that nothing had changed. And let herself have this final comfort.

On her way out of the flat she noticed a vase of tulips in the kitchen, red tulips that had gone past their best and started dropping petals. That wasn't like Nessa. She was a thrower-out; a tidier-up. And then, as the front door closed behind her, another chill swept through Mab. Flowers, she thought. Nessa hadn't mentioned the flowers around Max's body. Surely she'd have included that detail if she'd been telling the truth? She'd have wanted to explain how they'd got there – to say she'd dropped them out of shock, perhaps. That sealed it, surely. That was more than an expression, or a tone of voice. That would convince even Con.

Mab had reached the street now, and she looked around for the Uber. Christ, what if Nessa hadn't ever ordered it? What might that mean? She was on the point of running when she spotted a silver car at the corner. Heart throbbing, she waited for it to approach.

'Mab?' the driver said. 'Going to Littlemore Road?'

'Yup.'

Mab slid gratefully into the back seat. Stupid, she told herself. There was no need to be melodramatic: things were bad enough without that. But she could forgive herself for a touch of hysteria. Her head was still fizzing with the omissions and evasions in Nessa's account.

The other thing, apart from the flowers, was that Nessa hadn't explained why she'd gone to the farm that morning. Mab had asked a straight question, and she hadn't answered it. But what other reason could she have had except to look for Max? Nessa had promised to take Mab to see the kittens again, but she wouldn't have done that on her own. And she wouldn't have wandered that way randomly, because she'd known Max was there, and there'd just been that row – so it must have been a deliberate decision.

Mab remembered puzzling over this as a child, though, and looking at it as an adult it felt even more odd. If Nessa had fancied Max and he'd rejected her then that would all fit neatly, but Max had been their half-brother. Mab had read something, once, about people inadvertently falling for their half-siblings when they met them in adulthood, not knowing who they were. But if you did know... Surely Nessa had been old enough to understand the taboos? And if Nessa had simply wanted to be friends with Max, to get on his side after the argument at breakfast, the flowers would have been a bit much. Perhaps that was exactly the point, though. Perhaps she'd taken them because she happened to have them in her arms, because she'd done as Con suggested and picked some from the garden, and while she was doing that she'd had the idea of going to talk to Max? And then he'd laughed at her, accused her of having an incestuous crush on him. Mab could well imagine Nessa losing her temper then. The surge of anger, and the misjudgement of their positions. The shove that was only half intended.

Mab shut her eyes. Her head was pounding, and nausea swirled through her. She could hardly keep hold of the threads of inference in her head. But one thing was clear now. After this evening the suspicions she'd nurtured and feared and shrunk from for so long had coalesced into a single hard fact: she felt certain that Nessa had been capable of killing Max.

Chapter Fifty

M ab's visit had left Nessa troubled and on edge. She'd always hated seeing Mab upset, and she was dismayed by the news that Mab had seen her leaving the farm on the day Max died and had kept it secret. That she'd grown up with it lodged in her mind, and Nessa had never known.

While Inga cleared the table, Nessa poured the last of the wine into her glass, and then, after a moment's hesitation, added what was left of Mab's. She'd drunk more than she should already, but there was a kind of recklessness in her tonight. A thread of devil-may-care that she knew was dangerous.

She'd wondered at the time, of course, whether Mab had seen her that morning, but when Mab had said nothing, that day or afterwards, Nessa had assumed that she hadn't. She'd thought she could forget about it; put it behind her. It hadn't occurred to her that Mab might have kept such a secret, because she'd thought Mab had no secrets from her. She'd been wrong about that, clearly. Wrong about what had been going on in Mab's head this past fortnight, and these past two decades. Although there'd been moments since their father died when she'd wondered whether Mab had been thinking about Max, hadn't there? And before that, too, occasionally. The day at the zoo, for example; Mab's tenth birthday.

A clatter of plates in the sink brought her back to the present.

'I ought to be doing that,' she said. 'You cooked.'

'No, you sit,' Inga said. 'It's five minutes, anyway.'

Nessa watched her for a moment, her competent back and the swift movements of her elbows. She loved Inga because no one else had ever looked after her like this, she thought. Was that a good reason to love someone? She felt suddenly doubtful. Not just about her feelings, but Inga's too. This evening had had the effect of making everything less certain.

'Shall I make tea?' she asked.

'The kettle's already on.'

'You're a wonder.'

Inga smiled over her shoulder. What was she thinking? Nessa wondered. Sometimes it was hard to tell with Inga. Perhaps she'd written things off, now and then, to some Scandinavian quirk, when she should have paid more attention to them? Or was she being paranoid? She probably was. She mustn't let herself spiral into panic; into vandalising her carefully assembled life.

But it was certainly true that Inga had behaved strangely this evening, intervening in the conversation like that. At the time Nessa had been grateful: it had headed Mab off, calmed things down. But Mab had hated it, and Nessa wasn't sure, now, whether it had been a good idea. Wasn't sure what Inga's motivation had been, either.

The clattering of crockery stopped, and Inga brought two mugs over to the table.

'So,' she said. 'Two visits in two nights.'

Nessa didn't answer. She put her hands around the mug,

inhaling the soothing smell of fennel. It was probably a good thing there was no more wine, but she wished there was.

'I should think Mab must feel relieved to have got all that off her chest,' Inga said.

'I hope so.'

She waited for Inga to continue, but she didn't. Inga was waiting for her to speak now, Nessa realised. Waiting for her to fill in the gaps. Her heart twitched.

When Inga had cut across the conversation with Mab, Nessa had assumed that she believed her story – that she was protecting her from Mab's accusations because she thought they were crazy. But what if Inga had guessed that Nessa was keeping something back? What if she'd just wanted to hear the whole truth herself first? Perhaps she liked the idea of having a hold over Nessa. That didn't sound like Inga, Nessa tried to tell herself, but what did she know?

So now there were two people for her to deal with: two people wanting explanations. Inga had cut Mab off before she could say any more, but Nessa was pretty sure Mab knew that she'd left things out too. Surely Mab had enough on her plate, though, without getting bogged down in the past? She had the baby to worry about, and Danny. Surely, once she'd calmed down, she'd accept Nessa's account of that day? She'd want to put it out of her mind and focus on sorting out her life.

But maybe she wouldn't. And Inga was still here. Inga was looking straight at her.

'If you don't want to talk about it, that's fine,' Inga said. 'You've talked a lot this evening already.'

But Nessa knew that wasn't what she meant. She meant more or less the opposite, in fact.

'I don't, honestly,' she said. 'You heard what I told Mab. I had nothing to do with Max's fall.'

Inga nodded slowly. 'OK.'

Damn it, Nessa thought. She bit her lip. 'Look, Inga, this involves ... someone else. I can't – it's all so long ago. I really can't see why it matters. But...' No, she thought. She wasn't going to be drawn into saying more than she wanted to. 'If you don't believe me, that's fine. You can go now, if you like. I don't want you to stay if you don't trust me.'

'Good heavens.' Inga sat back in her chair. 'That seems quite defensive to me.'

For the first time Nessa could feel herself trembling. 'You'd be defensive if your sister had just accused you of murder.'

'I'm not sure she did,' Inga said. 'In fact, she clearly didn't. She said she was sure it must have been an accident. It was you who mentioned murder.'

'Oh, so it's my fault, is it? Is that why you shut Mab down – because I leapt to the conclusion that I was being accused of killing Max, and that means I must have done it?'

'No, I–'

'So what: you think I need you to help manage the situation? Maybe you think it would be fun to make me into some kind of moral case study, like your fucking charity?'

'My charity works in schools,' Inga said. 'You know that. I work with children.'

'I was a child when Max died,' Nessa said. 'Doesn't that count?'

'Nessa,' Inga said. 'I understand that you're upset. I understand that I'm here, and I'm an easy target. But don't question my motives, OK? I'm your partner, and I love you, and I don't believe you've killed anyone. I don't need you to tell me anything more, either – I just said so a moment ago. But it would be nice to feel that we were both on the same side. It would be nice if you didn't shout at me.'

Nessa stared at her. She could feel the rush of heat inside her, throwing out phrases she might hurl at Inga, and for a few moments its energy was too much for her. But as she sat there, dizzied by the whirl of thoughts and emotions, Inga reached across and took her hand.

'You look exhausted,' she said. 'Why don't we go to bed? Or if you want to be alone, I'll leave now and you can go to bed.'

'No,' said Nessa. 'I don't want you to leave.'

She hadn't known that was true until she said it, but it was. She didn't want to be left alone. She didn't want not to be believed, either, but that was a different thing.

'OK. Good. So I won't. I'll stay with you.'

'Thank you.'

Inga lifted Nessa's hand to her mouth and kissed it. 'Do you want the fennel tea, or would you rather have cardamom milk? That's very calming. It should help you sleep.'

'All right,' Nessa said. 'Thank you.'

The whirlwind had gone now, fizzling out like a sparkler reaching the end of its stick, and Nessa felt very strange; very small. Like a child, she thought. Like a little girl whose mother has died, leaving her with a younger sister to look after and more problems, more worries, than a thirteen-year-old should ever have to cope with. Everything had changed after her mother's death, she thought, as tears rose in her eyes. No: before that. On the day they left Lowlands. That's when it had happened. The loss of innocence. The end of her childhood.

Chapter Fifty One

Perhaps it shouldn't have been the last thing Mab expected, but it was.

The house was quiet when she came in, but there was a light on in the kitchen. She hesitated for a moment outside the door, and then she pushed it open, and there was Danny. Just Danny, and all the lights on, like a stage set.

'Oh!'

That was a hopeless greeting, she knew that, but it was all she could manage. She was too surprised; too bamboozled by this latest twist to the evening.

'Charley let me in,' he said. He was sitting at the table with a copy of *Vogue* which had been lying around for weeks. Yvonne must have bought it, Mab thought, pointlessly. No one else would have done. She swallowed.

'I'm glad you're here,' she said.

He hadn't got up yet, let alone come towards her, but Mab felt pretty sure he meant to be nice. There wouldn't be much point in coming, otherwise, would there? Not unless he wanted to make her have an abortion, and that didn't seem like something Danny would do.

'Do you want some tea or anything?' she asked.

'I made myself one.' He held up a mug. 'I found your teabags, I think.'

'OK.'

Mab couldn't take her eyes off him. It wasn't much more than twenty-four hours since she'd last seen him, but it felt like an age. It felt as though she'd been fending for herself, standing on her own two feet, for weeks. But she thought about how she'd walked out of the restaurant last night, how she hadn't answered his calls, and her stomach turned over.

'I called you a few times,' he said. 'And I tried to come this morning, to the scan. I came here, but you'd already left. Then I went to Lewisham Hospital and told them my girlfriend had a scan booked, but you weren't on the list.'

'Oh, Danny.'

She'd been an idiot, Mab thought. Wasn't that the truth? She hadn't given him a moment to breathe last night before she'd stormed off.

'I'm sorry,' she said. 'I really am. I'm so glad you're here.'

He still didn't get up. Mab longed to have his arms around her, to hear him telling her that everything was OK, but it was clear that wasn't going to happen just yet.

'Did you have the scan?' he asked.

'Yes.' Mab thought about digging out her phone so she could show him the picture, but she wasn't sure this was the right moment. 'I had it at this diagnostic centre place.'

'And...?'

'The baby's fine,' Mab said. 'I saw its heartbeat.'

She was crying again now. She'd cried more this past fortnight than she could ever remember crying before, except when her mother died. More different kinds of tears, too. She wasn't sure what kind these ones were.

'And you're keeping it?' Danny asked.

Mab was startled. Hurt, almost, although he had a right to ask, of course. 'Yes,' she said. 'But you don't...' She swallowed. When she'd walked in and seen Danny she'd imagined a happy ending, but she could see now that she'd been too hasty. He'd come to find her, he'd asked about the scan and heard her apologies, but he looked totally unmoved. Unyielding. The unexpectedness of that was enough to dry up her tears again.

'Tell me what you're thinking,' she said. 'I can't bear you just sitting there. If you're breaking up with me, at least say it.'

Danny's lips tightened. Mab was still standing, but she pulled out a chair now, not quite opposite him, and sat down on it.

'The thing is...' he began. And then he sighed, screwed up his face, tried again. 'It's shaken me up, all this. The baby, and the way you've behaved, and–'

Mab had meant to hear him out in silence, but she couldn't help herself. 'It's not just me,' she said. 'You were horrible last night.'

'You didn't give me much of a chance,' he said.

That was true; she'd said the same thing to herself only five minutes ago. But even so she felt aggrieved. 'I'm all over the place, Danny. Don't you get that? I'm pregnant, and my dad has died, and I'm throwing up every five minutes.'

He nodded, just once. 'I understand all that. That's why I'm here. But this isn't just about you, Mab. I'm... It was a shock, coming out of the blue like that.'

'I'm sorry,' Mab said.

He shook his head. 'You didn't get pregnant on your own, I know that. And I know there's all this stuff with your family. But...' There was another pause while he struggled for words. 'Fatherhood is complicated for me. My dad died in prison.'

'What?' Mab was aghast. 'How did—'

Danny held up his hand. 'Let me say this, Mab. Let me just say it. He wasn't a bad man, but he got dragged into something he shouldn't have, and he got caught, and then – they told us it was suicide, but who knows. He was involved with bad people.' Danny looked away. 'He was younger than I am now when he died. And after that there was only my mum and my granny. So I don't have anything to go on, in terms of fatherhood. It scares me, if I'm honest. Having it landed on me like that...'

'How could you not tell me?' Mab asked. 'How could you let me go on about my family and not tell me that?'

'Maybe I was afraid it would make you feel differently about me,' Danny said. 'I'm ashamed to have thought that, but – I know your family's no picnic, and your dad let you down pretty badly too, but there's no one in our family with a big house in the country. And no one in yours has been to prison.'

'They might yet,' Mab said. The words sounded full of bravado, but she felt deeply shaken. Not by what Danny had said about his father, but by the implication that there was a gulf between them he wasn't sure they could bridge. By the realisation that the worries that had so preoccupied her might seem trivial to someone else. 'I understand you thinking I'm spoilt and self-absorbed,' she said, her voice wobbling. 'But—'

'I don't think that,' Danny said. His face had changed, but there was still a barrier there, like a sheet of glass they were trying to communicate through. 'I didn't mean to judge you. And I didn't mean to tell you about my dad like some kind of cheap trump card. It's just...'

'I understand,' Mab said. 'You're saying I'm not the only one with secrets. With horrible stuff in the past.' She hesitated. She wanted to say that she needed Danny to be better than her father, that Roy's indifference made her desperately fearful for her own child, but this wasn't the time for that. It was his father

Danny was weighing himself against, and he was fearful too. 'I understand I'm not the only one who needs looking after.'

Danny put his face in his hands, and Mab felt a flood of warmth and pity that almost gave her the courage to lean across the table and touch him. But she couldn't move yet; she didn't dare. Instead she said, 'You told me you loved me.'

There was a hesitation, but only a short one. 'Yes.'

'Then doesn't that...' Mab began. 'I mean, isn't that...' She stopped, trying to grasp the thing she wanted to say. The thing that would offer a way out of this muddle. 'Fuck our families,' she said. 'Fuck all of that. I mean not literally, but... Can't we try, Danny? Couldn't we at least try again?'

There was a millisecond when she was afraid that had been exactly the wrong thing to say, but then, at last, Danny's mouth twitched. 'No more blocking my calls?' he said.

'I didn't block them,' Mab said, greatly daring. 'I just didn't answer them. And there were only two.'

'No more not answering my calls, then.'

'I promise.'

He pursed his lips again. For a moment Mab was afraid that stony look would come back, that he'd think better of relenting, but then he lifted an eyebrow. 'Can I see this scan picture, then?'

Mab pulled out her phone and passed the print out over the table.

'Wow,' Danny said. He peered at the tiny image. 'It's got my nose.'

Mab giggled. And once she'd started, she couldn't stop: relief and exhaustion and remorse were a potent brew. But mostly relief, she thought. God, how much relief.

'I really am sorry,' she said, when she'd got herself back under control. 'I thought you were angry about the baby. I went a bit mental, honestly.'

'Me too.' Danny gazed at the picture for a bit longer and then handed it back to her. 'Can I come with you next time?'

'Yes please,' Mab said. And then she sighed, a great shuddering sigh, thinking about what it had been like to imagine life without him. About how close she'd come to losing him. 'I've had the strangest day. I went to the zoo and wept in the penguin pool.'

'Poor Mab.' He smiled again, and at last he took her hand across the table.

'And–' Mab bit her lip. 'I confronted Nessa.'

'About Max?'

'Yes.'

Danny's grip tightened. Ach, this was a mistake, Mab thought.

'And?'

Mab shook her head. 'We don't have to do this. Fuck our families, remember?'

'Yeah, but...'

She looked at him. 'I don't want you to feel–'

'Hey.' He squeezed her hand. 'I appreciate the sentiment, but we can't really pretend they don't exist. Not all the time.'

'If you're sure.'

'I am.'

But there was such a weight of tiredness now. It felt like not just the backwash from the last couple of weeks, but the anticipation of what was to come: her body taking a deep breath and digging in for the long haul of pregnancy. It had held on, Mab realised, until this moment, until she had made amends with Danny, and now it was demanding rest. She sighed, and it turned into a yawn, and back into a sigh.

'I'm so tired,' she said. 'It's been such a day. Could we...'

'Of course.' He was on his feet now, coming round the table and offering his hand. 'It can all keep. Let's get you to bed.'

· · ·

If she'd been on her own, Mab thought later, she might not have made it upstairs: she might have lain her head on her hands at the kitchen table and slept there. But she was so glad to be in her bed; so grateful for the gentleness with which Danny helped her undress. So happy – so very happy – when he climbed in beside her and wrapped his arms around her, and rested his head in the crook of her neck and murmured things she couldn't hear.

She could hardly tell, by then, whether she was awake or asleep. She could hardly tell where her body ended and Danny's began, and it was blissful to imagine that it didn't matter: that they were part of the same being, joined not just by the touch of skin to skin, the new understanding of mind and mind, but also by the tiny being inside her that would link them together inextricably. The child they had made together without meaning to, which had taken root now and was growing faster than she could imagine, doubling and doubling, powered by the minuscule heart that had pulsed on the ultrasound screen this morning, a whale sound from deep inside her.

But even in this state of half slumber, half dreaming, Mab was aware of something else. It wouldn't be forever, this togetherness. Neither of them, nor even their baby, would last forever. Just like her mother and her father and Max, they'd be dead one day: a distant day or a closer one, but it would come, and however hard she clung to Danny now, she couldn't stop that happening. She couldn't hold on to him. Perhaps they could be buried together, she thought, and it would feel like this, curling up in the warm earth, but she knew it wouldn't.

And now there were more tears: silent, uncontrollable tears, plumbing a depth she hadn't known existed until this moment. Because she'd always thought, like any child reared on fairy tales, on rom coms, that love was the end, the answer to everything – but she realised now that all it did was open up a greater darkness. That love was jeopardy: love was the certainty of heartbreak. And although the miraculous creature inside her might feel like an amulet against the perils of the future, it was an even greater jeopardy. Its journey had hardly begun; its hold on her heart was all to come; and she might lose it too, or it would surely lose her. Mab thought, then, of her mother, lying in her bed in the hospice, knowing that she was going to leave her children and that she would never know what became of them, and she understood that however painful betrayal and suspicion might be, this great fierceness of love and fear was more painful still. Love, she thought, as the night held her tight in its embrace, is what opens up the possibility of pain.

But, said a voice in her head that might have come from a dream, or perhaps from her long-dead mother – but that isn't the way to see it. Love is the thing. Love *is* the answer, the end, and pain is the price we pay for it. Mab couldn't tell whether that was a profound thought or a glib one; whether it was something most people realised much earlier in their lives, or that many might never know. But she understood one more thing now.

She understood that her father, for all his selfish grasping at pleasure and all his capacity to make other people love him, had never really dared to love. He had never dared to live on the precipice of loss, to open himself up to all that exquisite potency of need and risk. And that seemed to Mab a far greater tragedy than her mother had suffered, or even Con. It seemed to her that after this one night with Danny, understanding what he meant to her and what they might have together for as long as they lived, she could survive her father's abandonment and her mother's death, and all the other calamities and cataclysms that might come to her. She could be a grown-up, a mother, a person who has lived a full life.

And then she wept again, more tears than she could have believed she had left, which soaked into her pillow and streaked her hair and made her eyes and her face and her head ache with grief and sorrow. She wept, properly, for her father. For his death, and for his life. For the mistakes she would never repeat. She wept, finally, for hope.

Chapter Fifty-Two

Mab and Danny slept late, and woke tangled in each other's arms in a way that would have settled, if it had not been settled already, the way things were between them. Their bodies knew what they wanted, Mab thought, as Danny ran his finger over her shoulder and she trembled with gratitude for the fact that they were alive, and that they had found their way back to each other.

'Did you sleep well?' he asked.

'Mmm.'

The sequence of thoughts that had lulled her to sleep – or perhaps kept her from it a while – filled Mab's head again as she floated up to wakefulness. She'd have liked to share it with Danny, but she felt a little shy, and a little uncertain of her ability to explain; and it was the morning now, and the mystery and the darkness felt a long way away. And apart from the pleasure of being with Danny, what commanded her attention now was the familiar tug of war between nausea and hunger.

'Tea?' Danny asked.

'Not tea.' Mab shuddered. Tea had been all right yesterday.

Today was going to be worse, apparently. 'I'll come down. Tonic water and Ryvita is what I need.'

Danny made himself a cup of coffee and filled a bowl with muesli, and Mab tried not to smell the coffee as she sat opposite him and nibbled at a Ryvita.

'So,' he said. 'Do you want to tell me about Nessa?'

'There's Con too,' Mab said. 'It's all – I hardly know what to think any more.' She did, of course. She knew exactly what she thought, even if it made her head swim to remember it. But she should tell Danny the facts; that was the thing to do. See what he thought.

'That is a lot to process,' Danny said, when she'd finished.

It was lucky neither of them was rostered to work this morning, Mab thought. Lucky, or inspired planning by Danny. They'd come back up to bed halfway through the story, partly so that Mab could lie down again and partly so that no one could walk in and overhear the conversation.

'So Con has always suspected Philip,' Danny said, 'just like you've always suspected Nessa. And Nessa insists she got there after Max fell, but you don't believe her.'

'Yeah,' Mab said. 'That's about it.'

'And it can't be both of them, but it could be neither.'

Mab shook her head. 'Whatever you thought of Max, he wasn't the type to kill himself. And an accident feels too convenient, if Nessa and Philip were both nearby. It's too many coincidences.'

'OK.'

'Maybe it doesn't matter any more what happened to Max,' Mab said, 'but it matters to me whether Nessa has been lying all this time.' She hesitated. 'I don't know if this makes sense, but it matters more because of the baby. I don't want to go on any longer not knowing what Nessa did. What she's capable of.'

'I understand.'

Mab reached out a hand to touch Danny's leg. She needed to check that he was real, she told herself. Everything else felt so much like a dream. Like a recurring nightmare that had shadowed her whole life, and had now spilled over into the daytime.

'I think Inga might know,' she said. 'The way she cut into the conversation last night – she didn't want me to press Nessa any more. Either Nessa's confessed to her or she suspects, and she's protecting her.' She looked at him. 'Would you do that for me? If you knew I'd done something really bad, would you cover up for me?'

Danny raised an eyebrow. 'It would depend on what it was, I think. Whether it was the deliberate shove or the scuffle that went wrong.'

'Inga might,' Mab said. 'I think she definitely might.'

'Do you think she'll be there tomorrow?' Danny asked. 'Is that why you mentioned it?'

But Mab had forgotten, briefly, about the invitation to Lowlands. 'I don't think so,' she said. 'Con's message said "the four of us".'

'I could come, if you're worried.'

Mab sighed. 'Maybe. I don't know.'

'I'm supposed to be working, but...' He pulled out his phone to check the time. 'Speaking of which, I'm due at the shop at two. Do you fancy coming? Seeing how it feels?'

'Am I supposed to be there?'

'Yes, but we can manage without you.'

'No,' Mab said, 'I'll come. That would be good, actually. I could do with spending some time with books.'

'And with me?'

'And with you.' Mab leaned forwards to kiss him, then rolled the other way and levered herself out of bed. Later on, she thought, they could think about tomorrow. About whether she should say anything to Nessa with the others there. Probably not, she reckoned. But maybe she could talk to Con. She could tell Con about last night, about what Nessa had said. After all, it was more Con's business than anyone's. And she was wiser than Mab. Wiser than everyone, pretty much.

And meanwhile, it was back to normal life: to being a person with a job and a boyfriend. That was a nice thought, even if it was only the calm before the storm.

Chapter Fifty-Three

C on had decided to roast a chicken for the girls' visit. Family Sunday lunch: roast chicken with vegetables and gravy, and apple crumble. She still hadn't got used to the idea of cooking for two, even though it had been almost twenty years now, and there had only been three of them for years before that. In her mind, she was still cooking for that summer when there were four children at Lowlands. Maybe for the night when Roy had been there too, and a casserole had simmered on the stove all day.

There weren't quite enough of them to justify a large chicken, but she bought one anyway, a carefully-nurtured rare breed from the butcher in Maltock, and chipolatas to go with it. Because it was a celebration, or because she wanted to feed them well before inciting a showdown? She wasn't sure. Both, probably. Her mind was stacked with contradictions: she felt a surge of pleasure every time she thought about reassembling what was left of the family – gathering in her stepdaughters, reuniting Philip with his half-sisters – but also a settled determination to get to the bottom of what had happened that July day when Max fell to his death, whatever the cost. Then there was the fact that they were supposedly meeting to discuss Roy's memorial service – an event that was pencilled into the vicar's diary, and which Con had already given some thought to – but if things fell out as she expected they would, it was unlikely it would ever take place. Not that Con cared much about that, but she cared about Mab, and Mab wanted an opportunity to say goodbye to her father.

But that in itself was a contradiction, Con thought. An anomaly, at least. Con doubted whether Mab had been to church for years, and she certainly hadn't heard from her father for over a decade, but something in her needed hymns and an organ and a eulogy full of well-meaning lies before she could let him go. Perhaps this was what she and Mab shared: perhaps two decades of cleaving fast to a person they believed to have done something unthinkable had schooled them both so deeply in contradiction that it was impossible for them to see anything straight-on any more.

For her part, she was continuing to hold tight to Philip until the last moment. If she hadn't lived with the possibility of his guilt for so long, she thought, as she watched her gentle son helping with the preparations, it would be impossible to believe it now. She hated the idea of breaking open the safe shell she had constructed around him, but nineteen years of suspicion and denial, of the desperate need to know the truth and the equally desperate fear of hearing it, was long enough. She couldn't take her uncertainty to the grave. Maybe that was a failing in her, but she couldn't help it. She had had these two decades, and so had Philip. Perhaps for him they had felt like real life, but she understood now that for her they had simply been a kind of limbo.

On Saturday, Philip mowed the lawn and cleaned the garden furniture while Con peeled potatoes and rubbed in the crumble mix with terror burning in her chest. On Sunday morning she did something she hadn't done for years: got up early and walked down to the church for the eight o'clock prayer service. Strangely, it made her think not of Max, nor even of Roy, but of her parents. It was a little space, that half an hour, in which they still existed, or she felt as if they did. God only knew what they would think of the mess she had made of her life, she thought, as she walked back up the lane, but at least she was spared their opinions.

The girls were arriving on the eleven thirty train. Philip had offered to go and collect them, and she'd agreed. The table was laid, the food all prepared, but a roast lunch required some last-minute clock-watching and co-ordination to ensure that the various elements were ready on time. Con waved him off, and turned her attention to the gravy.

'Let me come with you,' Inga said again, as they lay in bed on Sunday morning, but Nessa shook her head.

'It's just the four of us,' she said. 'It would look odd if I turned up with you.'

'Are you sure Mab's not bringing Danny?'

Nessa wasn't sure, but that wasn't the point. Taking Inga would skew things, not just for the others, but for her. Besides, Mab had texted her the night before, suggesting they get the nine twenty from Waterloo, and Nessa had taken that as a sign of truce.

'It'll be fine,' she said. 'Don't worry.' She leaned over and kissed Inga. 'Shall I bring you breakfast?'

'No.' Inga laughed, as though that was an absurd idea, and Nessa felt a twinge of pique. But she had to leave in ten minutes, anyway. There certainly wasn't time to produce the kind of breakfast tray Inga might make.

'Just tea, then,' she said, and she smiled.

As she went through to the kitchen, she felt a little swell of optimism. Planning a memorial service for their wretched father was a good thing to be doing, she thought. It was like building a bonfire on which they could burn all the broken pieces of their past; all the messy memories that were better left behind.

Mab was waiting by the barrier when Nessa got to Waterloo. She looked a little washed out, but otherwise normal. Otherwise exactly like the familiar Mab Nessa knew so well – and she was alone.

Nessa kissed her on the cheek, and Mab let her do it, even if she didn't lean in as warmly as she might have done.

'I'm feeling so sick today,' she said, perhaps by way of explanation. 'I don't know how I'm going to cope with the train.'

'Oh dear.' Nessa stepped back, surveying her. 'Can you take anything? Can I get you anything?'

Mab shook her head. 'I've got Ryvita and tonic water,' she said. 'I hope you can't overdose on either of them, because I'm living on them at the moment.'

And perhaps it was convenient for Mab to have an excuse to be so quiet on the train, but Nessa found that she wasn't all that sorry. Mab spent most of the journey with her eyes closed, leaning against the window, sipping tonic water from time to time, while Nessa gazed out at the changing landscape as the train carried them through the south-east suburbs of London, through Surrey and Hampshire, Wiltshire and Dorset and on into Somerset. It took an age, and she hadn't thought to bring a book, but at least they didn't have to change. When they pulled out of Sherborne, and the train manager announced that Yeovil was the next stop, Mab opened her eyes.

'Feeling better?' Nessa asked.

'A bit.'

'Good.'

'I'm hungry now, though. We might have to buy something at the station to keep me going.' Mab caught Nessa's eye, and smiled. 'I won't spoil my appetite, I promise.'

A few minutes later they were climbing off the train, and Mab headed straight for a vending machine on the concourse and bought a packet of crisps and a flapjack.

'Shall I find a taxi?' Nessa asked.

'Philip's picking us up,' Mab said.

'Is he?'

Mab nodded, her mouth full of crisps.

So that was it, Nessa thought: there'd be no chance to talk while they were still alone. Well, so be it.

Philip could hardly contain his excitement as he set off down the road. Just beyond the big house he pulled over onto the verge to make a phone call. He hadn't dared to do it from home: the risk of being overheard was too great, and he was absolutely determined that his surprise should be a proper one. His mother would never guess what it was, he was sure of that. She'd made jokes about a dog, but he thought she might be expecting a piece of jewellery. That was something sons bought for their mothers, and made a bit of a fanfare about, wasn't it? Or perhaps she thought he'd booked her a holiday, although how that could be arriving on a Sunday, he wasn't sure.

What he'd got for her was better than any of those things, anyway. The way he'd come across it was so serendipitous that it had felt as though the universe meant it to happen, and that was part of the pleasure. It meant he didn't have any doubts about it. And everything was on course, the phone call told him. He'd known it would be, but he'd wanted to check. He didn't like to leave anything to chance.

He'd checked that Mab and Nessa's train was on time, too, and he judged his arrival perfectly, pulling up in the short stay area just as they emerged from the station.

He'd seen Mab a few days ago, of course, and he was glad of that, because he might not have recognised either of them otherwise. They'd looked quite similar as little girls, but they were much less alike than he expected now. Nessa was shorter than Mab, and her hair was cut differently, and her face was different, too. She was two years younger than him, he remembered, but she looked older than that. That probably wasn't a very kind assessment, but he wasn't going to share it with anyone else. He certainly wasn't going to say anything like that to Nessa. To tell the truth, he'd always been a little bit in awe of Nessa, and of the way she spoke her mind. He wondered if she still did that. People usually became more confident as they grew up, but not everyone.

Sometimes Philip wondered what Max would have been like if he'd lived, and what he would have done with his life. He didn't often think about Max, but perhaps it was natural that he should today. This would be the first time they'd all been together since the day Max died. Perhaps they'd all be thinking about Max, even if it was their father they were supposed to be remembering? That thought made Philip feel a bit uncomfortable, but not very. Max had been dead for a long time now. It had all happened long in the past.

He put all these thoughts out of his head, anyway, as he climbed out of the car to welcome Mab and Nessa. They were crossing the car park towards him, and Nessa was holding a bunch of flowers. That was a nice gesture, Philip thought. His mother had always liked flowers.

Chapter Fifty-Four

The sun shone down on Lowlands as they approached: on the big house and the little house and the farm, their mellow stones glowing in its warmth. It filtered through the small kitchen window where Con was putting the last of the vegetables into the oven to keep warm; it glanced off the roof of Philip's little grey car, so that an aeroplane flying overhead would see it as a streak of silver snaking up the lane between hedgerows awash with blackthorn blossom. And further afield, it found another car making its way towards them all, towards Lowlands, though still a long way off. Still a couple of hours away.

It had been forecast, this sun, but none of them had paid much attention to that. Their thoughts, this Sunday morning, had been focused on one another, and on the other people, the dead people, who had once been part of their family circle: on Roy and Robin and Max.

Further away still, some of those dead people, and the living people who were congregating at Lowlands, were in the minds of others, too.

Of Hazel, who was walking on Hampstead Heath, thinking about her nieces, and about her sister, and feeling, in the sunshine, a slight softening of remorse. She had done her best, she told herself; but she knew that she could have done better, and as she walked she considered the possibility that it might not be too late to try.

Of Jenny, whose mind was softening day by day without the help of the sunlight, but who felt the presence of her family quite clearly that morning, even though none of them were visiting her today, and some of them had been dead for years. She had the advantage of blurring the distinction between the living and the dead: of not being aware that the dead were lost to her.

And they were in the minds, too, of Inga and of Danny, who had never met any of the dead people but were both aware, as Hazel and Jenny were not, of the gathering of the living that was taking place at Lowlands today, and who knew what was at stake. Who would be thinking for most of today about Nessa and Mab, and about Philip and Con, whom they'd never met either, but had heard a good deal about. They were both, as it happened, at work as the little grey car came up the lane towards Lowlands Cottage, Danny presiding over a surprisingly busy Sunday at the bookshop, and Inga alone in her office, turning things over in her mind.

Could all those thoughts affect, in any way, the group who were now getting out of the car, and the woman coming down the garden path to greet them? Could the heat of the sun pouring down on them from the cloudless sky change the way the afternoon might unfold? Who could say. Certainly the car heading towards them – just now negotiating the Hammersmith flyover and descending to join the Great West Road as it swept out of London – had a part to play in the day's proceedings. But none of them were aware of that yet. None of them except Philip, and even he was blithely innocent of the implications of its impending arrival.

Chapter Fifty-Five

Con wasn't sure you could really tell the difference between this expensive hand-reared fowl and a supermarket chicken. The truth was, though, that she could hardly taste anything at all. She'd filled her plate with meat and vegetables and doused the whole lot in gravy (the gravy smelled good; she had to give herself that) but when she lifted a bite to her mouth, it could have been anything. Porridge, or blancmange, or soil.

She remembered a similar feeling, sometimes, when the children were little. The sense that it had taken so much effort to produce a meal that when it was ready, she had no energy left to consume it. But this was different. This was down to those massed armies of contradiction, facing each other off in her mind. In her stomach, too: in every part of her. Clogging her airways, her blood vessels, her muscles, so that she felt like a fish washed up on the river bank, gasping for breath.

With a great effort, she made herself smile. She should smile, she told herself, because here they all were, Philip and Nessa and Mab, all grown up. All safe and happy, after a fashion. She wished, for a moment, that there was a photograph of them from 2005, but there wasn't, and perhaps that was a good thing.

'This is delicious,' Mab said, summoning Con out of herself. 'It's ages since I've had roast chicken.'

'Yes, it's all excellent,' Philip said, and Nessa was nodding too, murmuring her appreciation.

'Good.' Con smiled again. She mustn't let herself sink into torpor, she thought. She needed her wits about her. But she was going to bide her time. She should feed them first; give them time to talk. It seemed to her important that they should bind themselves together again before she launched her missile, although she couldn't explain why. Perhaps that was cruel, to let them rediscover each other, and get a sense of what they might mean to each other, but Con felt it was necessary. A phrase floated into her head, the voice of her science teacher from forty years ago: to obtain a true reading, the system must be in equilibrium before the start of the experiment. My God, she thought, staring down at her plate, she sounded like a monster. Is that what these past two decades had done to her? And how could she possibly hope that a roast chicken would be enough to settle these three damaged children into any kind of equilibrium?

Even so, they ate. Ate heartily, and talked, and even laughed. If Mab was a shade subdued, Con could think of two good reasons for that. Nessa gave an impression of slight reserve too, but Con had no way of knowing whether that was unusual: she had much less sense of what kind of person Nessa had grown up to be. Mab had the advantage of her visit a few days ago, of course; of having met Philip then. And Philip himself was more animated than Con had seen him for years. She remembered, suddenly, the surprise he'd mentioned the other day: was that still on the cards? Anguish pierced her then. A caravan, she'd thought: they'd talked about taking a caravan holiday, and it was possible that Philip had decided to take the initiative, flushed with the success of his management of the New Zealand trip. Could she really bear to spoil his pleasure? Because whatever the outcome, whichever way the chips fell, he would know, once she spoke, what his mother had suspected him of.

It came down to this, Con thought, as the children gathered up the dirty plates and carried them across to the sink: it was her peace of mind or Philip's. Her need to know the truth, or his freedom to live the quiet life he had made for himself. If she did what she had planned to do today, nothing would ever be the same again.

Mab had eaten too much already, but she couldn't resist Con's pudding. Con had made proper custard with eggs, not the bright yellow powdered stuff Hazel used to produce occasionally, and it was delicious. And the crumble was apple and plum. No one, Mab thought, made crumble like Con.

There was, though, something deeply surreal about this gathering. Con had produced the kind of Sunday lunch that anyone looking in from outside might imagine they'd all shared hundreds of times, when in fact this was the first time they'd been together for almost nineteen years. Con was pink-cheeked and slightly dusty, like the perfect domestic matriarch, but there was an edginess, a restlessness about her that told Mab very clearly what was on her mind. Nessa might have guessed too, although she'd given no sign of it. Nessa was talking to Philip, just now, about their respective jobs, but Mab knew that Nessa knew that Con suspected Philip of the same thing Mab suspected Nessa of. The whole convoluted circle of suspicion and deceit was only just below the surface. Nessa must surely be expecting either Mab or Con to blow a whistle at any moment. Perhaps they all knew that was coming. The conversation had been bright and superficial, full of small detail and empty of anything more. None of them had mentioned the memorial service. Did they all know, then, that that wasn't what they were really here for?

'Thank you, Con,' Nessa said, as she laid down her spoon. 'That was a splendid lunch.'

Con began to smile and demur, but Nessa hadn't finished.

'There are things to talk about, though,' she said. Mab's head whipped round. 'There's Dad's memorial service, of course, but I think–' she glanced at Mab, and then at Con '–I think there are other things to say first.'

No one spoke. Only Philip looked puzzled. Mab could feel her heart pushing up through her chest, making it difficult to breathe. She tried to catch Nessa's eye, but Nessa's gaze was fixed on the vase of flowers in the middle of the table. Whatever she was doing, there was no stopping her.

'There's an elephant in the room,' Nessa went on. 'Or rather – there's someone who's not in the room, isn't there? Apart from our father, that is.' She waited a moment, but none of them were prepared – or perhaps able – to speak Max's name. A ghoulish fascination had taken hold of Mab now. This was absolutely Nessa, this forthright assault, but it was also the last thing she had expected. Was this going to be a confession? Had Nessa planned a dramatic exit afterwards? It was hard to see how.

Nessa raised her eyebrows, as though she was faced with a recalcitrant primary school class.

'The last time we ate together, Max was with us,' she said. 'Con had made pancakes for breakfast. And a couple of hours later, Max was dead.'

Philip moved in his chair. Mab thought he was going to interrupt, but he didn't.

'I don't mean to make a grand melodrama of this,' Nessa

said. 'Or to upset anyone. But there isn't any other way in. Because the point is that things happened that morning that have never been discussed.' She hesitated, just for a second. 'Things that haven't been confessed, but that other people have had an inkling of. And it turns out that those things won't stay quiet any longer.' She looked straight at Mab then. 'And – well, now we're all together, it seems to me that it's time to clear the air.'

Mab waited, again, for someone else to speak – her, or Con – just to say Nessa's name, even, to acknowledge what she was doing, but again there was silence. This was Nessa's show, she thought.

'Mab saw me at the farm that morning,' Nessa said then. 'She saw me leaving just as she arrived, and when she found Max dead, a few minutes later, she was terrified. Isn't that right, Mab?'

Mab nodded.

'She was terrified that I'd pushed him,' Nessa said. 'We all know there'd been an ugly scene at breakfast, and Mab thought – correct me if I'm wrong, Mab – Mab thought I'd gone to the farm to find Max. That I followed him up to that ledge and pushed him off, or–' There was a noise, then, that Mab recognised as coming from her own throat. Nessa glanced at her again, a little more gently. 'No, that isn't what you said, is it? I'm sorry. You thought I argued with Max, that there was a struggle, and he lost his footing.'

'No,' said Philip, but at the same time Mab said, 'You took him some flowers.'

Nessa stared. 'What?'

'There were flowers around his body,' Mab said. 'You'd been picking flowers that morning, so I knew they were yours. I gathered them up and threw them away, so that no one would suspect you.'

335

'No,' Philip said again, and this time they all heard him.

'Philip—' said Con. Her face was full of panic.

'That isn't what happened,' Philip said. 'I was at the farm too that morning, and that's not what happened.'

'Oh, Philip...' Con said.

But Philip shook his head. 'There were three of us there,' he said. 'There was me, and there was Nessa, and there was Lucy.'

'Lucy?' said Con.

'Her parents had gone out, but Lucy stayed behind,' Philip said. 'She was there too.'

If someone had been directing the scene, Mab thought afterwards, they couldn't have managed things more slickly, although they would have had to get the timing so precise to pull off the juxtaposition of events that everyone watching backstage would have been on tenterhooks to see whether it would come off. But no one was watching except the four of them, and there was no script, no director. No one in the wings whispering, 'Now!'

Even so, it happened like a piece of stage magic. Before Philip had finished speaking, the doorbell rang, and he leapt up.

'This is my surprise!' he said. 'I promised my mother a surprise this afternoon, and here it is.'

And then there was nothing for it but to follow him to the door, and when Philip opened it, there was Lucy. A different Lucy from the one Mab remembered, her hair cut very short and her clothes strikingly elegant, but undoubtedly the same Lucy whose name had just been mentioned.

'Hello!' Philip said. 'Hello! How was your journey? Have you brought it?'

It was hard to believe that less than a minute ago they had been discussing the death of his brother, Mab thought. Was this a brilliantly contrived diversion, or was there, after all, something not quite right with Philip, so that he thought his surprise for his mother was really more important than that?

But the next moment Mab's mind, too, was yanked away from the conversation that had just been interrupted. What Lucy had brought with her was a painting – a large painting which was propped up, now, against the door frame. It was covered in bubble wrap, but even so Mab knew immediately what it was.

'That's Con,' she said. 'That's Dad's painting of Con, isn't it?'

'Yes,' said Philip. He was beaming at his mother. 'Isn't that a good surprise?'

But Mab's attention had been caught by something else. Nessa had been the last to leave the kitchen, but as she joined the others in the narrow hallway – as she recognised the painting, and Lucy – the expression on her face changed.

If Philip had been telling the truth, then there were two witnesses here now to the story Nessa had been about to embark on. Two witnesses, according to Philip, who would back up Nessa's innocence. So why, then, did she look so spooked?

Chapter Fifty-Six

July 2005

It was very hot in the garden: it was probably the hottest day they'd had. But Nessa was glad to be outside. Things had worked out perfectly: Mab was going to do knitting with Con, and that meant she could be on her own, without Mab to look after.

'Would you mind if I went for a walk?' she'd said, and Con had suggested she could pick some flowers, and had even found her a basket to put them in, like someone from a Jane Austen film. But before she left the house, Nessa had slipped upstairs to change out of that stupid dress. She'd liked wearing it at first, because their father had bought them for her and Mab, but Max was right that it made her look ridiculous. She was too old for matching dresses. Lately she'd begun to think she was too old for dresses altogether.

She was halfway down the garden before she realised she'd forgotten Con's basket. But it didn't matter: she could pick flowers without it. She could pick flowers while she tried to think things through. She needed to do that, because there were lots of things jumbled up in her head. There was her mother being so ill, maybe dying. Probably dying. That was a big thing:

the biggest thing Nessa could imagine. And there was always Mab to think about – Mab who was so upset about their mother, and at the same time clinging to Con, which made Nessa feel a bit complicated and a bit worried. And there was their father's behaviour last night, which had come as a shock.

But there was more than that. There was something that felt just as big as all those things, and which no one else knew about. Well, one person, maybe. Something that Nessa didn't know what to think about, that felt scary and uncertain and worrying, but also exciting. Something that filled up so much of her mind that it squeezed out most of those other worries a lot of the time, which she knew was a shameful thing.

There were lots of flowers near the house, including the sweet peas she and Mab had picked for the kitchen table, but Nessa wanted to get further away this morning. She walked down the steps from the terrace and across the grass towards the orchard. She didn't know much about gardens, but she guessed that this garden had once been much neater – that it had had proper flowerbeds and tidy lawns. Nessa could imagine people having tea under the trees, and children chasing dogs. Maybe that's what Con's childhood had been like. Now the lawn was more like a meadow. Under the trees it was still damp from the night, and the grass brushed against her legs in a swishy, clammy sort of way as Nessa made her way towards the overgrown flowerbeds.

There were lots of flowers here, many of them hidden from view. Nessa lifted the big soft heads of pink roses, wishing she'd brought the secateurs Con had put out with the basket. The rose stems were tough and spiny, and by the time she'd managed to break one off, its petals had all scattered. After that she settled for flowers that were easier to pick. Most of them she didn't know the names of, but there was something pleasing about choosing a selection that looked pretty together. It was just absorbing enough to leave the rest of her mind free to turn things over.

She was quite sure there had been an invitation – or perhaps suggestion was a better word. What she wasn't sure of was what it meant: what was intended by it. What would happen if she went. And she wasn't sure, either, whether she wanted to. In one way of course she did, she wanted it more than she'd ever wanted anything – but she was worried it might turn out to be something she'd regret, or be ashamed of, or feel foolish about. But if all she did was go...? The words echoed in her ears: *You could come and meet me at the farm, if you want to.*

What she was most afraid of, Nessa realised, were her own feelings. The way this hope and curiosity and dread – it was each of those things, one after another – travelled all the way through her body, swelling up in her chest and lying heavy and squirming in her belly, making her arms and legs ache with anticipation and filling her head like a swarm of bees. She was afraid of what those feelings might do to her if she let them loose. They felt like something which had arrived too soon. At the wrong time, and for the wrong person. She wished her mother was here. She wished she could talk to her. And that made the ache and the heaviness and the buzzing even worse, because she knew that quite soon she would never have her mother to talk to again. She would have to rely on herself, and find the answers to every difficult question without anyone else's help.

Well then, let her start here. Let her go to the farm. Let her trust herself to manage the situation, whatever it turned out to be. She could take the flowers with her, she decided, and explain that it had been Con's idea to pick them.

She had enough flowers now: as many as she could carry. She waded back out of the flowerbed and into the warm damp grass. She stopped for a moment to straighten her hair with her free hand, and then she set off towards the gate.

Now that she'd made a decision she felt better. She was sure it was the right one. She would be careful; she wouldn't say anything or do anything that she might regret. But she needed to find out what the feelings inside her meant, because she couldn't think about anything else until she did.

Chapter Fifty-Seven

March 2024

When Con had thought about this gathering, there had been a veil of uncertainty over it. More than a veil, in fact; and more than uncertainty. It had been like peering into a cave, knowing that once you ventured into it, anything might happen. But one thing had held her steady: she'd imagined herself making the decisions. She had chosen the date; she'd decided what to cook, and what kind of occasion it would be. She'd decided to wait until lunch was finished before embarking on her inquisition – and then she'd wondered whether it was, after all, what she wanted to do. She'd given herself the freedom to defer, or even abandon, her plan.

But then things had been taken out of her hands. Mab must have spoken to Nessa, and Nessa must have decided to ... but Nessa's plans, too, had been thrown off course, first by Philip's interruption and then – startlingly – by that ring on the doorbell. By the arrival of Lucy Fidler, of all people. And by the reappearance of that painting. If they had started with melodrama, they had descended into farce now; into black comedy.

Dear Philip, Con thought, with a sudden sharp stab of

affection. How pleased he was with his surprise. How certain that she would be thrilled by it. How unlike him the whole thing seemed – but also how very characteristic.

They were all in the narrow hall now, five of them and the painting, saying awkward hellos. The girls had met Lucy, of course, that summer. Con heard the kittens mentioned; the ones whose descendant had taken to visiting her.

'Shall we take the painting into the sitting room?' Philip was saying. 'There's more room there.' He couldn't wait to tell her how this had all happened, Con thought. 'You remember you showed me Lucy's letter?' he said, as the picture was set down against the fireplace. 'The one she wrote after Dad died? It had her address on it, and I wrote back to her, and after that we started emailing.'

Lucy was standing beside the painting, her back against the light from the window so that Con couldn't see her expression. But her silhouette was surprising enough. The cut of her jacket, like something out of *Vogue*.

'You told me she worked at an auction house, do you remember? And she does. She works at Sotheby's. And she told me that one of Dad's paintings was coming up for auction. I couldn't believe it when she told me which one. I remember Dad bringing it back to you. I knew it had been sold again, of course, but I'd almost forgotten about it. And I decided straight away that I would buy it for you. Lucy arranged everything.'

Philip looked at Lucy, and Con did too, and Lucy smiled.

'It was no trouble,' she said.

It wasn't quite the first thing she'd said, but it was the first Con had paid attention to. Her smile, her voice, were the same. Deceptively unchanged. Con felt almost numb, but at the edge of her mind a new worry began to form. She'd always suspected that Philip held a candle for Lucy, and she could see that it was in danger of being reignited. Perhaps it already had been, in the

343

course of their emailing and secret planning. But this creature, with her expensive clothes and her expensive haircut, was so far out of Philip's league that Con could hardly begin to compute it.

And what about the question of Lucy having been at the farm that morning? Surely, if Lucy was in a position to incriminate him, Philip wouldn't be jumping about so excitedly now, fetching a knife to cut away the bubble wrap and reveal the wretched painting? But you couldn't be sure of that, with Philip. You couldn't be sure which dots he would connect. Lucy looked relaxed enough, despite the fact that she'd walked into an atmosphere so thick with suspense that she could hardly mistake it.

'Can I get you a drink, Lucy?' Con asked, recovering, at last, a feel for the conventions of hospitality. 'Or something to eat? You must have had a long drive.'

'I'll wait until the unwrapping's done,' Lucy said. 'The drive didn't take long today, actually. But nothing to eat, thanks. I'm on my way to see my parents: I expect you know they're near Bristol now?'

Con didn't, but she nodded all the same.

'There!' Philip stood back, and there, indeed, was the painting. There was the twenty-three-year-old Con, framed by lilies. The very best of Roy's work, Con thought, despite herself. What a shame that it was the last picture on earth she ever wanted to see again.

'I remember it so well,' Mab said.

She remembered too, as they all must, the evening when Roy had brought the painting to Lowlands. The night before Max's death: an occasion of such anger and distress that only a death the next day could have trumped it. Mab wondered again when, and why, Con had sold it. Looking at her face now, she wasn't entirely sure that Con was pleased to have it back. She was making an effort to smile, but it was the effort Mab noticed. More things not being said.

'Mum looks so beautiful,' Philip said. He, at least, was happy. He imagined himself in his father's shoes, Mab thought, bringing Con's portrait home for the second time.

'It's a wonderful picture,' Lucy said. 'I'm so glad it's been returned to you.'

'Thank you,' Con said. She embraced Philip, and then Lucy. 'I'm very touched. We'll have to find a place for it: there's not much wall space here.'

Lucy looked as though she was about to make a suggestion, but if so she thought better of it. Instead her eyes moved from Con and Philip to Mab, and then, after a flicker of hesitation, to Nessa.

Nessa was standing in the corner of the room: not quite out of sight, but as close to it as she could manage. A deliberate choice, Mab was sure. Nessa was deeply disconcerted by Lucy's arrival, that much was clear. Her plan to manage the way the story emerged had been scuppered by this turn of events. In the moment when Lucy's eyes settled on her sister's face Mab waited for something to be said, but it was Con who picked up the thread of the conversation again.

'How about some coffee?' she asked. 'Are you sure you couldn't manage a bowl of crumble, Lucy?'

'Well, if you're going to twist my arm.' Lucy grinned. She made a point of studying the painting again on her way out of the room – wanting it to be paid proper attention, Mab thought, not for itself but, she suspected, for Philip. Lucy knew what he had paid for it, of course. Knew how much thought and excitement had gone into the negotiations. Did she recognise Con's ambivalence? Did she feel sorry for Philip? Or was there something more to it than that?

Perhaps, Mab thought, there had been something between the two of them that summer. They were the same age, of course. Mab half-remembered Con saying that Philip had been frightened of Lucy, but... So had Philip gone to the farm to meet Lucy that morning? Had the two of them witnessed whatever happened between Nessa and Max? And was Philip telling the truth when he said Nessa had had nothing to do with Max's fall, or had he and Lucy agreed to protect Nessa? That might be part of the reason that Nessa was so reluctant to talk about it: because Philip and Lucy were complicit, and the truth would hurt them, too.

'I'm not sure I'd have recognised you, Mab,' Lucy said, as they all went through to the kitchen again. 'How are you?'

'A bit iffy just at the moment, actually,' Mab said. She sat down, and Lucy took the seat next to her. 'I'm pregnant, actually.'

'Oh, congratulations! That's wonderful news.' Lucy put a hand on her arm, and Mab felt ridiculously moved by the warmth in her voice. She remembered the sixteen-year-old who had knelt on the floor with them among the kittens: she'd had a gentleness about her that had been unexpected then, and still was.

'How many weeks are you?' Lucy asked.

'Only ten,' Mab said. 'Hardly at all.'

'That's not hardly at all. That's a quarter of the way through. The most important quarter.'

'I guess.' Mab laughed. 'I've only just found out, actually, so I've missed most of the first quarter.'

Con was bringing the coffee to the table now, and Mab realised suddenly that Nessa hadn't followed them back into the kitchen.

'Does anyone know where Nessa is?' she asked – so that when Nessa came through the door a moment later, everyone's eyes turned towards her. She looked as though she'd been crying: looked, at least, as though the strain of sustaining whatever pretence she'd been keeping up had got the better of her. Mab felt a rush of compassion that almost undid her. This was her sister, the person she loved more than anyone. What had she done, opening this can of worms? Was it too late to stop it?

'Nessa,' she said, her voice high and anxious. 'You remember Lucy, don't you?'

'Yes,' Nessa said, 'I certainly do.'

'Of course you do,' Lucy said, her voice very soft.

'You arrived in the middle of a spell of reminiscence,' Nessa said. 'Just before we got to the bit of the story that involves you, in fact.' She hesitated. 'I'd hoped to avoid sharing it, but I think I have to. I'm sorry.'

Lucy shook her head. 'Don't be sorry,' she said. 'Don't be sorry on my account.'

Chapter Fifty-Eight

July 2005

As she was crossing the field, Nessa remembered that Max was at the farm this morning – or at least he probably was, although he'd left in such a rage that he could have gone anywhere. It didn't matter, though. If she saw him she'd say that she'd come to see the kittens. She didn't care about Max: he was just a stupid boy, like the ones at school. Boys would say anything they could think of to make themselves look funny or clever, and Nessa took no notice of them.

But she didn't see Max as she approached the farm. She didn't see anyone, or hear anything. She circled the barn and crossed the yard and went round to the side door of the house, just as Lucy had suggested. By the time she got there her heart was beating so fast that she could feel it bumping against her ribcage. She told herself it was because of the heat, but she knew it wasn't. She knocked on the door, waited a moment, then tried the handle. As she pushed the door open, a dog barked somewhere inside.

'Hello?' she called. Her voice came out very faint. Stupid, she thought. She took a step inside and tried again. 'Hello? Lucy?'

'Boo!'

Nessa leapt round, a shriek escaping before she could stop it.

'I'm sorry.' Lucy was laughing, reaching out her hands to Nessa's shoulders. 'That was silly of me.'

'Where were you?' Nessa asked.

'In the garden,' Lucy said. 'I heard you knocking.' She looked down at the flowers in Nessa's arms. 'Are those for me?'

'Yes.' Nessa wasn't sure whether that was the right answer to give or not. 'Con suggested I should pick some,' she said. 'I thought you'd like them.'

'That's very sweet of you.' Lucy bit her lip, looking at Nessa. Everything inside Nessa's body had melted, turning itself into a hot weight that pressed down towards the bottom of her tummy. She shouldn't have come. Lucy couldn't possibly know what she was feeling, and she mustn't find out. She'd laugh, and Nessa couldn't bear that.

'Shall we go and sit in the garden?' Lucy asked. 'I've brought out a rug and some lemonade.' She raised her eyebrows. 'Or there's wine in the fridge, if you fancy that?'

'No,' said Nessa. 'Lemonade's fine, thank you.'

'I'll find a vase for those,' Lucy said, and Nessa nodded. The flowers looked a bit wilted now. She'd held them too tightly, she thought. They'd have been better in Con's basket.

In the kitchen, Lucy found a big jug and filled it with water.

'Pretty,' she said. 'Thank you. I'll put them in my room later.'

But she carried the jug back outside, and found a flat place for it to stand near the rug. The garden was much smaller than Con's, but it was better looked after. There were walls around two sides – three if you counted the house – which had plants growing up them, and there were flowerbeds and a little terrace and the lawn where Lucy had spread the rug.

'My parents are out,' Lucy said, as she poured them each some lemonade. 'We'll have peace and quiet this morning.'

'OK.' The thumping of Nessa's heart was louder than ever, and the feeling in her tummy was like an ache and an itch and a worry all muddled up. Lucy was wearing a sundress, a bright blue one that showed up her suntan and was gathered in little pleats across her chest. She was smiling at Nessa, shaking her head gently so that her hair moved sleekly over her shoulders.

'You don't need to look so frightened,' she said. 'I'm not going to jump you.'

'OK,' Nessa said again. She didn't really know what that meant, but she thought she could guess – and she thought it meant that she hadn't been wrong about the feelings, and that Lucy might have them too. That thought was so overwhelming that she almost couldn't speak. 'It's nice being here,' she managed to say. 'It's a nice garden.'

'My mum does it,' Lucy said. 'All the flowerbeds and things. It's not really a farm thing, but she likes it.'

Nessa thought about the garden at home, which no one did anything with, and wondered what it would be like to have a mother who knew about plants. To have a mother who wasn't ill. She starting wondering again what she was doing here, sitting in Lucy's mother's garden, and then Lucy smiled at her again and leaned forwards a bit and touched her hand. The effect of it was so much like an electric shock that Nessa jerked her hand away, but the look on Lucy's face then filled her with dismay.

'Sorry,' she said. 'I'm sorry. I didn't mean...'

'It's OK.' Lucy sat back too. 'It's really OK. It's my fault.'

'No, it's not,' Nessa said. 'There isn't any fault. I was just...' She swallowed. 'I didn't really mean it was the garden that was nice, I meant you. I meant it's nice being here with you.'

'Good,' Lucy said. 'That's good.'

Nessa could feel the heat coming off Lucy's body, a separate heat from the warmth of the sun. She could smell Lucy's skin, a flowery scent that might be soap or shampoo. She could see her breathing, and a little pulse beating in the triangle below her neck. She wanted very badly for Lucy to touch her again, even if it meant another electric shock. She'd be prepared for it this time; she'd know what it meant, and how delicious the feeling was that it left her with. But she also wanted, part of her, to keep things exactly as they were at this moment for ever and ever, before anything could be spoiled.

She moved her hand a little way across the rug, just edging it towards Lucy, but before it had got very far Lucy had lifted one finger to Nessa's cheek, almost as if she was brushing an eyelash off it.

'I'm glad I've met you,' she said. 'I'm glad you like me.'

'I'm glad too,' Nessa said.

If she shut her eyes, she thought, Lucy might kiss her – and then she did shut her eyes, she couldn't help it, and there was a second or two of the most exquisite waiting, when the whole space between them felt hot and thick and smelled like the roses that had fallen apart when Nessa touched them. When she could almost feel, could almost taste...

But she never knew what might have happened, because the breathless suspense was broken by a shout.

'What the fuck is this?'

Nessa jolted backwards. Max was coming towards them across the garden. She'd never seen him looking more angry, or more horrified.

'What are you, a pair of lezzers?' he said. 'Fucking paedo more like, Lucy. Fucking hell. She's only twelve.'

'I'm thirteen,' Nessa managed to say, but neither of them took any notice.

Lucy was on her feet now, facing him. 'It's none of your business, Max. Just piss off and leave us alone.'

'Call the police, more like,' Max said. 'Fucking hell, wait 'til I tell my mum.'

'Try not to be more of a moron than you can help,' Lucy said. 'Bet you'd think it was OK if it was you, don't you?'

'You reckon I fancy you?' Max sneered, but Nessa could tell he did. He absolutely did. That's why he'd been working at the farm, she guessed. 'Chance'd be a fine thing,' he said. 'Snooty fucking bitch like you. Nah, you're more in Philip's league.'

'Leave Philip out of this,' Lucy said. She had her hands on her hips: she looked like a figure from an action movie, Nessa thought, ready for battle. Ready to fight for her. But mostly what Nessa thought was that she really, really wished she hadn't come. Max would tell Con, and then she'd have to lie, and Lucy would too, and Nessa hated the thought of that. This morning was the nicest thing that had happened to her for months and months – for ever – and she couldn't bear to pretend that it hadn't meant anything. She couldn't bear other people to talk about it and ask questions and wonder about it.

'Yeah, that was a joke,' Max said. 'Philip doesn't have a league, does he? Philip's going to live and die a virgin. No one in their right mind could fancy him.'

And then, horrifyingly, there was Philip, coming round the corner of the farmhouse just in time to hear Max's last words.

'What's going on?' he asked.

'The man himself,' Max said. 'If you've come to moon over Lucy, you'll have to get in line. Peppa Pig here's stolen a march on you.' He gestured at Nessa, who was still sitting on the rug and wishing it was a magic carpet that could carry her off over the trees. Carry her all the way home, away from all this.

'Stop it, Max,' Lucy said. 'You're making a fool of yourself.'

'As usual,' Philip said.

'As usual,' Max parroted, mocking Philip's voice. 'Yeah, well, for once someone else is making more of a fool of themselves than me. Bet you didn't know Lucy was a lezzer, did you? Or that Nessa here was a baby lezzer.'

'We weren't doing anything,' Nessa said, betrayal screaming in her chest.

'Only because I got here in time to stop it,' Max said. 'Otherwise it would have been full-on lezzer porn.'

'Go away, Max,' Philip said. 'Leave them alone. Get on with your work, why don't you?'

'Or we could ask them to carry on,' Max said. 'Even you might be turned on by the show, Phil.'

'You're pitiful,' Lucy said. 'You think you're such a big boy with your threats and your insults, but you're just a tiresome little twerp. If I wasn't a lezzer, I'd take Philip any day over you. You can tell anyone you want: I'm not ashamed.'

And then, just like that, Max's bravado evaporated. His voice cracked, and with it his composure. It was hard to tell whether he was crying or shouting; impossible to make out what he was saying. He stood his ground for a moment longer, and then he kicked over the jug of flowers and ran out of the garden, shoving Philip out of the way as he went.

Chapter Fifty-Nine

March 2024

There was a long silence when Nessa stopped speaking. Her account had stumbled a bit, and she hadn't attempted to do more than sketch in the story, but she'd said enough for those who hadn't been there to be able to picture it, and for those who had to conjure it clearly again in their heads. To hear Max's voice, and the others standing up to him. To feel the heat of the sun, and the passionate emotions of the four teenagers in the garden. It all seemed so obvious to Mab now that she couldn't understand how she'd never guessed.

'I'm sorry,' Nessa said, eventually.

'Sorry for what?' Lucy asked. 'Sorry to whom?'

Nessa shrugged. 'I don't know. I don't know any more.'

'I don't think you need to be sorry,' Lucy said.

'I do, though. Mab saw me running away from the farm afterwards. She's known all this time that there was something I hadn't told her, and she thought it was that I'd killed Max.'

'What?' Lucy's mouth fell open. 'Oh, Mab!'

Mab shook her head, trying to control herself.

'I didn't know what to think,' she said. 'I...' She swallowed, gripping the seat of her chair. 'Nessa brought me up, more or less. I'd never have survived without her. But I thought keeping quiet about what she'd done was the price I had to pay. I thought she'd gone to find Max, maybe to confront him about how horrible he'd been, and they argued, and...'

'It was me who was going to confront him,' Philip said. 'That's why I went to the farm. I could stand him being vile to me, but there was no excuse for making you and Nessa so unhappy. I thought I could talk sense into him. But when I got there, I could hear him shouting in the garden, and Lucy answering.'

'So what happened next?' Con asked. The coffee pot was still sitting in front of her, but she hadn't poured it out. They were all absorbed by the past; by the drama that had played out half a mile away, half a lifetime ago. 'You were all arguing in the garden, and then Max ran away?'

'Yes,' said Lucy. 'He ran off, and we all stayed where we were for a minute or two. Nessa was upset, and–' She glanced at Philip. 'Philip was very kind, and very sensible. He said Max would calm down. He said he'd go and talk to him in a bit, and we shouldn't worry.'

'And did he?' Con asked. 'Did he go and talk to him?'

Mab could see the anxiety etched in her face.

'He didn't get the chance,' Lucy said. 'The three of us went out into the yard, and – I can't remember exactly, but I think we were talking about someone walking home with Nessa, or – anyway, we were close to the barn by then. We didn't know Max had gone in there. I thought he'd either gone home, or back to the job he was supposed to be doing for my dad. But then we heard a shout, and...' She shook her head. 'You can imagine the next bit. We ran into the barn, and Max was lying on the ground. We'd all been so angry with him, but–'

'He didn't deserve to die,' said Philip, 'but he did.'

There was a pause then. Philip looked different, Mab

355

thought. He looked exactly as he had when he'd phoned the emergency services later that morning and called Mab *my little sister*. He looked like a person you could rely on: a person capable of greater loyalty and wisdom than you could expect of a sixteen-year-old.

'It was a terrible shock,' Philip went on. 'Max had just been with us, making a scene, and then there he was, suddenly, dead on the floor of the barn. It was very hard to take it in. We all – I suppose we were still thinking about what to do, and... We agreed there was no need to tell the whole story. No one knew we'd been there. It would just mean a lot of questions, a lot of distress, and it wouldn't make any difference. So we decided that Nessa and I would go back home, and Lucy would call 999.'

'I see,' Con said.

'I know we did the wrong thing,' Philip said. 'But we did it for good reasons. For what seemed like good reasons. There wasn't much time, and we were all upset. And after we'd parted, there was no chance to talk about it again. If one of us changed our story, it would have exposed the others. The fact that they'd lied to the police.'

Mab cleared her throat. 'What about the flowers?' she asked. This might seem like a small point to the others, but it was the last piece of the jigsaw. The piece that would confirm that they were all telling the truth. 'There were flowers around Max's body. Did he take them from the garden?'

'No,' Lucy said. 'No. He'd knocked over the jug I'd put Nessa's flowers in and they'd spilled out onto the grass. I gathered them up, so I had them in my hands when we went through to the yard. When we heard Max's scream. After the others left...' She shook her head. 'It was stupid, I know, but I felt so bad about the things I'd said to him. They weren't as awful as the things he'd said, but he was younger than me, and he was in a state. Enough of a state that he'd slipped off the ledge, or lost his footing while he was climbing up. I felt very guilty. And I felt so sorry about it all.'

She couldn't meet Con's eyes, Mab realised. Even though none of them had deliberately stoked Max's rage – and even though inciting rage wasn't the same as the tussle, the shove, that Mab had imagined all these years – Lucy had been the eldest of the three, and she felt responsible.

'So after Philip and Nessa left,' Lucy continued, 'I went back into the barn and scattered the flowers around him. I wanted to check again, too – growing up on a farm, you learn about death – but I wanted to be totally sure before I called the police.'

'But you didn't,' Con said. 'You didn't call the police.'

'No,' Lucy said. 'As I was going back to the house, I saw Mab coming. Before I could do anything about it, she'd gone in through the door at the back, and a moment later I heard her shriek.' Lucy shut her eyes for a moment. 'I panicked then. I should have gone to join Mab, but instead I went into the house. I thought Mab would come there, but she didn't. I waited and waited, but she didn't come. I knew she'd raise the alarm, though. She'd tell Con. I thought it would complicate things if I rang the police too.'

She was still sitting next to Mab, and she took her hand. 'I'm so sorry, Mab,' she said. 'And Con: I don't know what to say. We should have been braver. We should have told the truth.'

'You were very young,' Con said. 'All of you. I can imagine exactly how it was.'

Nessa was crying now. Properly crying, as though she'd gone back to being thirteen and feeling all that pain again. All that confusion. But also, Mab knew, because Con's kindness, her magnanimity, had always felt like an undeserved blessing, and that had never been more true than it was now. Because

Nessa knew what their silence had cost Con: she knew she'd believed Philip was involved in Max's death. She knew that had overshadowed her life.

'All this time,' Nessa said, 'I don't think I've ever thought properly about that day. I've kept it shut away.'

'We all have,' Philip said. 'We've had to. But you were the youngest, Nessa. It was me and Lucy who decided what to do. And he was my brother: if anyone should take responsibility, it's me.'

He was sitting close to his mother, but she didn't turn to look at him. Would she tell him what she'd suspected? Mab desperately hoped not. But she held her breath when Con opened her mouth to speak.

'I don't blame any of you,' she said. 'I don't hold any of you responsible.' She sighed, a shuddering sigh with tears close behind it. 'I'm glad to know the truth. I've always wondered how it happened. How he came to fall.'

'It was our fault,' Nessa said, her voice very small. 'We made him angry.'

'No.' Con shook her head. 'Max had been angry for a very long time. Long before that day; long before that summer. I've blamed myself for that – for not managing him better – but the truth is that it was an impossible task.'

'Because of Dad,' Philip said.

Con didn't reply, but she tilted her head in a gesture of assent.

'Because he left you for our mother,' Mab said. That seemed to her to be where all this had started. Their tragedy – she and Nessa losing their mother – was enclosed inside another one. If they had never been born – if their father had never met their mother – perhaps Max would still be alive.

'No,' Con said again. 'Not just because of that. Because of the way he behaved. The promises that weren't kept, or that were never even made. The belligerence and bad temper. Playing one son off against another; saying unforgivable things and then making light of them.' She took a deep breath. 'I've tried so hard not to speak ill of him, but he was a monstrous father. If anyone's to blame for what happened to Max, it's him.'

'Max took after him,' Philip said. Mab looked at him in surprise: it seemed a daring thing for Philip to say. 'They both had bad tempers, and they didn't think very much about other people.'

'I never let Max see him for what he was,' Con said. 'I made excuses and promised that things would be better next time. I regret that very much. I thought that Max – that you both – deserved a better father, so I tried to make him into one. But all that meant was more disappointment. More fruitless hope. More heartbreak.'

'You did your best,' Philip said. 'You always did. For us both.'

Con reached her hand across the table and he grasped it. She was struggling to hold on to her composure, Mab could see. But she was magnificent. She was like Mother Earth, ravaged but indestructible. After a moment, she said: 'You saw the truth about your father, Philip. That was your superpower. But I know he hurt you too. He hurt all of you: Mab and Nessa as well. But he hurt Max the most.' Her face crumpled, but when she spoke again her voice was still steady. 'I've sometimes thought that Max – that he was walking a tightrope. That if it hadn't been that day, it would have been another. A car accident; a knife. What I've feared most–' She glanced at Mab. 'What I've feared most is that he was so unhappy that he threw himself off that ledge deliberately. I'm glad it wasn't that. I'm glad it all happened so quickly that he could only have known for a second what was coming.'

There was a long silence after that. A silence, Mab thought, full of things settling. Full of understanding and sympathy, as they acknowledged each other's suffering at last. Looking around the table, Mab felt a tremendous warmth. This was the darkness and the light, just as she'd understood them the other night, lying in bed with Danny. This was the pain and the consolation of love – and of truth. None of them had come out of this unscathed – not even Lucy, who was crying quietly beside her – but the story had been told now. The truth had been revealed. If there were still things each of them needed to say, they didn't need to be said just yet. For now they could simply sit, and feel the weight of secrets and guilt and uncertainty lifting from their minds. It was an astonishing feeling, almost as if an angel was passing overhead.

It was Con who broke the silence at last.

'I'd like to walk up to the church now,' she said. 'No one else needs to come.'

But when she stood up, the rest of them pushed their chairs back too.

Chapter Sixty

Max was buried in a shaded corner of the graveyard, next to his grandparents and great-grandparents. Someone looked after this churchyard well, mowing the grass and keeping the hedges trimmed, and there was a profusion of primroses over the Fothergill graves whose pale beauty was hard to resist. Max's headstone was plain, a little smaller than those of his longer-lived ancestors, but elegantly carved in handsome grey granite. It carried his name, the dates of his birth and death, and the words *Beloved son*: no more.

If you had been looking down from above, you might have imagined that the little group converging on the grave had been drawn here by some supernatural force. You might have thought of ley lines, or gravitational pull; of iron filings flocking to a magnet. And that would not, perhaps, have been so far from the truth. The death of this child had set off powerful waves of repercussion that were only now, at last, breaking on the shores of his family's consciousness. Of their souls, you might say, if you were inclined towards the spiritual – and why would you not be, in the lee of this ancient church, which had seen more death and anguish in its time, and more love and hope too, than any of the people gathered here today could reckon?

Certainly you could observe all those emotions in the circle around Max's grave this quiet afternoon. You could see hands reaching for other hands; you could hear tears and heaving sobs and a silence in which minds strove for peace. You would notice, perhaps, the irresistible way Mab's fingers strayed to her belly, and glances exchanged between Nessa and Lucy, and a new confidence in Philip's stance as he supported his mother with a hand in the small of her back, in the immemorial manner of sons at gravesides.

You might even, if you had the right sensitivity, hear the strains of a Bach prelude in Mab's head – a melody leaching out from her memory, where it had lived for almost two decades as a signifier of a lost landscape: of a moment in time when hope and despair were evenly balanced, and Lowlands House held her in safety despite the raging of the storm outside and the fears that filled her mind. Of the ineffable consolation that one human being can offer another in even the darkest of times.

And perhaps you might hear a resonance of the numinous in Bach's exquisite counterpoint: the effort of the human mind to reach for the divine, and to express it, and to diffuse it through the world. Or you might, like Con, claim agnosticism, but still be touched by Bach, and by primroses and old stone, and families reunited around graves. By the rambling roses whose exuberant flowering might, this year, feel less painful.

But what of that portrait, leaning up against the fireplace at the cottage? You might spare a mite of pity for it, that blameless canvas whose return to Lowlands had been the occasion for two such dramatic scenes. No doubt you could understand Con's antipathy for it: for the way Roy had tried to use it all those years ago as a magic charm to mitigate his failures. You could comprehend the pain of seeing, in its skilful brushstrokes, the hopes and expectations of that girl among the lilies. You could acknowledge the irony of its reappearance on this particular day, when the implications of Roy's irresponsibility were being weighed so intimately.

Might you wonder, though, whether it could offer something else now? A bridge to the past, which could transcend all that had gone so bitterly wrong? A rekindling of that sweetly-rendered hope and expectation for the future?

Might you seek to persuade Con that it had been part of a different kind of scene today: a grand catharsis that could, perhaps, bring things full circle – or at least allow the pain of the past to be laid to rest in the earth here with Max?

Might you point out that Philip's motives in returning it to her were utterly different from his father's, and that they represented a kindness, a thoughtfulness, and a resourcefulness in her older son that she had underestimated?

Perhaps you might. Perhaps you might. It would be hard, certainly, for you not to feel the spring breeze blowing across the churchyard just now, as the mourners stood around the grave, and to identify in it the freshness and surprise of optimism.

Epilogue

December 2024

It was one of those fine winter days in the middle of December when you could look up at the sky and almost imagine it was summer. Until your eyes were caught by the bare branches of a tree, that is. Until dusk began to creep out of the shadows at three o'clock. But it wasn't close to three o'clock yet, and the eyes of the two women were absorbed by something nearer at hand than the trees around the house.

Mab's baby lay in Con's lap, fast asleep. Oblivious, as was entirely natural, to the time of year, or the time of day, or the high emotions that surrounded him. He was six weeks old, a bonny boy with black hair curled like tiny leaves over his scalp. *My little miracle*, Mab called him, and although there was really nothing more miraculous about this baby than any other, Con couldn't help agreeing. Here he was, the happy ever after at the end of their story. Not that there was ever an end, really – but this story needed one. It needed a moment when you could close the book and take a deep breath.

'We didn't have any boys' names,' Mab said now. 'I thought of Robin, but that would have felt strange.'

Con nodded, but her eyes didn't lift from the baby's face.

'You don't mind that I didn't call him Max?' Mab asked.

'Of course not.' Con looked up then, and smiled.

'Samuel was Danny's grandfather's name. It felt safer, somehow, going back that far.'

'It's a lovely name,' Con said. 'And he's a lovely baby. You both look so well.'

Mab grinned. 'I thought I'd be terrible at it. But I suppose everyone's got to be good at something.'

'You're good at plenty of things,' Con said. 'But I'm so glad you're enjoying him. Both of you.'

'Danny's been great,' Mab said. 'I couldn't have done it without him. I'm sorry he couldn't come today, but he's used up all his days off. He sent his love.'

Con shook her head. *There'll be plenty more times*, she wanted to say, but she didn't. She wanted to savour this time, this moment, rather than wishing it away in pursuit of the future.

'He's well, though?' she asked.

Mab nodded. 'His family are mad about the baby. His brothers, and his granny. Even his mum, who's...' She shrugged, leaving the sentence hanging. Danny's mum wasn't around much, Con remembered. There'd been heartbreak in his family too.

'And Nessa?'

'Nessa's well,' Mab said. 'She's enjoying being an auntie. She gave Sam this outfit.'

Con had been admiring the little romper suit, which had a puffin on the front and a pattern of waves and fishes in the background. Baby clothes had come on a long way in thirty years, she thought.

'Inga went back to Sweden,' Mab said. 'I don't know if you heard.'

'A new job?'

'Yeah. It was... I don't know. Nessa seems fine about it, though.' She glanced at Con. 'She's seen Lucy a few times, I think.'

'I'm pleased about that,' Con said. There was a whisper of something – an echo of pain – but it was gone in a moment.

'And Hazel's been very kind,' Mab said. 'I shouldn't sound so surprised, I know. Poor Hazel: we were never going to like her, were we? She was never going to be our mother, and she had to... I expect she hated every minute.'

'She didn't,' Con said. 'She didn't hate it. She just worried a lot.'

Mab cocked her head. 'Have you spoken to her?'

'We kept in touch,' Con said. And there it was, the past bubbling up again. But she'd wanted to talk about this. She'd wanted to explain. The baby stirred, scrunched up his eyes for a moment, then relaxed again, falling back into his deep infant sleep with a tiny shuddering sigh.

'You said once that you wished you could have lived here after your mother died,' Con said. 'I wanted that too, I confess. It was ... a fantasy, almost. The two of you growing up at Lowlands with me.' She smiled, partly in self-mockery. 'I couldn't do it, though. It wouldn't have been right. But I kept in touch with Hazel, and with Jennifer. I made sure...'

That last sentence ended in a croak, a clearing of her throat.

'You do understand, Mab? I had to put Philip first, and — I couldn't replace Max. I couldn't allow myself to do that. And it was right that you were with your mother's family.'

'But you didn't–' Mab stopped.

'What?'

Mab shook her head.

'Please tell me,' Con said.

'I thought you might ask us here one holiday,' Mab said. 'I was sure it was because you suspected Nessa.'

'Oh, my love.' Con bent her head again to the child in her lap, then lifted her eyes to his mother. 'I knew you weren't entirely happy. I read between the lines. I kept asking myself if I should suggest–' She hesitated. 'I told myself it was better for you not to come back here. And that it was more than I deserved.'

'It wasn't that,' Mab said. 'Heavens, it certainly wasn't that. But I understand. I do.' She reached a hand to her baby's face, an involuntary gesture of maternal need.

'Do you want him back?' Con asked.

'No.' Mab smiled quickly. Con thought she might say more, but she didn't. It was enough: they'd both said enough. And perhaps that little gesture, that touch, had meant something else. Perhaps it was to acknowledge that they were the same now: that Mab understood what it was to be a mother. But her next words changed the subject.

'I saw you'd bought a piano,' she said.

'A little upright,' Con said. 'I've had to move things around to fit it in, but... I don't know why I didn't buy one years ago.' She did, though. Of course she knew. 'Philip encouraged me. He said he remembered me playing.'

'How is Philip?' Mab asked.

'Very well,' Con said. 'Very well indeed. Enjoying his flat in Yeovil.'

'Good,' Mab said.

'I miss him, of course, but it was high time. And the money from your father...'

Con raised her eyebrows. It was Roy's money that had taken Philip from her in the end. She couldn't escape the irony of that: one of many ironies about those unexpected legacies. Roy doing more than was expected of him, for instance, as he never had in life. Con understanding how much Philip's presence meant to her just as the means arrived for him to leave, and the lawyer's emails arriving just after they'd abandoned the idea of a memorial service. And there was more: there was the fact that Roy had been more successful in his last two decades than any of them had guessed, having done the unthinkable and submitted himself to painting things that would sell – and that he'd left them each some money without trumpeting it in advance; without being praised for it. Although that, of course, was a twist he probably never imagined.

It was too little, of course, to make amends for his neglect, and it came too late for him to ask his children's forgiveness. But the timing could hardly have been better. For Philip; for Mab. For her, even. Although in part, Con thought, the timing had been right because Roy had died. Because his death had allowed them to spread out the map of the past and examine its wrinkles. To understand everything that had happened to them.

'He's got a girlfriend,' she said, when the silence had stretched out for long enough.

'Philip?'

Con nodded. 'Someone from work. I've met her. She's nice. A bit younger than him.'

'That's great.' Mab didn't look surprised. She'd always admired Philip, Con thought. She would never forget the way Mab had smiled at him on that day she'd come for lunch, back in the spring.

The baby's eyes fluttered again just then, and it occurred to Con that he might not sleep all that much longer. If they were going to go out, they should do it now.

'I've arranged something for you,' she said. 'A surprise.'

The wind had got up a little. Mab wrapped the baby's shawl more tightly around his head as they emerged from the front door. He fussed for a moment as she tucked it in, screwing up his face as if to howl, then settled back against her chest. *He's a mini-you*, Mab kept saying to Danny, but sometimes she could see herself in him too, and she liked those moments. Liked glancing down and surprising herself with the sight of him.

She thought at first that they might be going to the church: that Con might have had a plaque put up for their father. But it wasn't that. They turned the other way out of the gate.

'I thought you might like to see the old house,' Con said. 'I asked if I could take you to look round.'

'Oh!' Mab swung towards her, beaming. 'I'd love that.'

The house had changed, of course. Mab could see that it had been renovated quite sensitively, but even so her heart squeezed a little tighter in each room they came to. Some of the furniture she thought she recognised, but there were no curtains, no wallpaper left from the old days. Even the little knitting room was transformed, its packed shelves and cupboards stripped back to plain white walls. Through the windows they could see the garden, which retained no vestige of the rambling wilderness where Mab and Nessa had played: there were paths and hedges, an elegant summerhouse, rose arches and immaculate borders.

How could Con bear it? Mab wondered. Had she been back before – known what to expect?

But as she followed Con down the passage to the kitchen, something changed. Strange, she thought: if you stood still, all you could see was newness and alteration, but when you moved around the house it stirred too, as if it remembered your footsteps. As if your version of it was still here, somewhere.

And the kitchen, of all the rooms they'd been in, was achingly recognisable. The cupboards had been rebuilt in pale oak, the old stove replaced with a gleaming black Aga. But this was surely the same table they had sat around. Those were undoubtedly the same quarry tiles on the floor, the same doors to the garden and the pantry. This bright winter day, even the pattern of the light was familiar, the way the sun didn't quite reach the corners of the room.

And in those shadowy places, Mab was sure, the echoes of their voices lingered. She could hear Max standing up to the world, and Con soothing, placating. The high-pitched voices of the two little girls who shouldn't have been there, and Philip's just-broken tenor. She could hear the faint whisper of the rain on the night of the storm; the sizzle of pancakes, tossed into the air on that final morning.

Mab couldn't say what she felt. She reached her hand for the soft head of the child Mab who had sat just here, just here, in her bright summer dress. She looked out of the window in the direction of the laurel bush den, the stream, the gate that led to the farm. She waited for a rush of emotion, but it didn't come. It was the past, she thought: it was just the past. And it was behind her now.

Also by Rachel Crowther

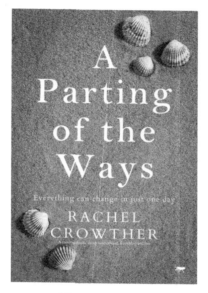

A Parting of the Ways

The truth about two women and an abandoned baby threatens to come to light, revealing buried trauma that will force them to confront the past...

(This book was originally published under the title The Partridge and The Pelican.)

BUY NOW

Acknowledgements

Producing a book with Bloodhound is such a pleasure, and my first and warmest thanks are to the team – especially Betsy, Fred, Tara, Abbie, Rachel, Hannah, Lexi and Trish – many of them authors themselves, and all of them dedicated and delightful and brilliant at their jobs. Hurrah, too, for the wonderful Bloodhound author community, who are such a source of support, enlightenment, entertainment and camaraderie: a rare and precious thing in the world of publishing.

None of my books could have been written without Richard, and this one is no exception. To him (and to Henry James, who has accompanied us on this particular ride) my dearest thanks for his inexhaustible and unstinting support. I'm deeply grateful, too, to Cordelia and Sarah for their generous and invaluable feedback on my work-in-progress, and to Angus and Lucy, my companions on a memorable week in Cumbria, for many engrossing conversations about writing and creativity and much more.

For more than twenty years our doors have been open to our children's friends – a steady stream of teenagers and young adults who have enriched and enlivened our lives. This book was written during the run-up to our last ever set of A-levels, in the company of Louie, Izzy, Tabs and others. It is dedicated to them, and to their many predecessors who have played such a big part in our lives.

About the Author

Rachel Crowther wanted to be a writer from the moment she realised that words could be strung together to make stories, but she fell under the spell of science A-levels, became a doctor and worked in the NHS for twenty years before her first book was published in 2011. After that fiction triumphed over medicine, though, and she hasn't stopped writing since, both as Rachel Crowther and Rachel Hancox.

Rachel has five children and a beautiful new granddaughter, and lives in Oxford with her husband, two youngest children, three scruffy dogs and a grey cat. When she's not writing, she can generally be found singing in choirs, knitting Fair Isle colourwork or making bread. *The House of Echoes* is her sixth novel.

A note from the publisher

Thank you for reading this book. If you enjoyed it please do consider leaving a review on Amazon to help others find it too.

We hate typos. All of our books have been rigorously edited and proofread, but sometimes mistakes do slip through. If you have spotted a typo, please do let us know and we can get it amended within hours.

info@bloodhoundbooks.com

Printed in Great Britain
by Amazon

58252469R00219